I0636816

Unwinding Secrets

-The Elements Book I-

S. Elizabeth Dover

This is a work of fiction. Names, characters, places and incidents are either the product of the author's imagination or, if real, used fictitiously. All statements, activities, stunts, descriptions, information and material of any other kind contained herein are included for entertainment purposes only and should not be relied on for accuracy or replicated as they may result in injury.

Copyright © 2016 Sophia Elizabeth Dover Schweizer

All rights reserved. This publication may not be reproduced, stored in a retrieval system or transmitted, in any form or by any means, electronic, mechanical, photocopying, recording, taping or otherwise, without prior permission of the author.

ISBN:978-987-33-9644-1

DEDICATION

Lala
Betty
Paz

ACKNOWLEDGMENTS

First and foremost, I'd like to thank my parents for all their love and support. Without you backing me up, I would have never finished this process.

To Jenny Busboom for your guidance through my first steps in the editing world and your kind, yet ruthless, critique. My book wouldn't be what it is today if it hadn't gone through you first.

To Christine Hood, for facing the second draft with bravery.

To Flor Tedesco for being my pillar throughout these four long years. Thank you for listening to me for countless hours, helping me perfection my plot and digging up any contradictions. Thank you for your patience and for cheering me on.

To those in high school that made me seek shelter in fiction and helped me discover one of my greatest passions.

Part 1

He stopped and placed his bag on the floor. Making sure that no one had seen him, he closed the door. All the lights were off except for the eerie glow that came from the glass box. The dim source of light created a halo around the body, illuminating her features and allowing him to appreciate her peaceful expression.

He placed his hands over the cool material that separated the young girl from the world. Her long, silvery hair, floated in the liquid that kept her body slightly afloat. Her pail complexion was tinted blue from the glow giving her an ethereal appearance.

The monitor that marked her heart beat drummed along to the ventilator's steady hum. Time stopped for a fraction of a second as she breathed in, her chest slowly rising. This is what I was trained for, he spoke to himself. Quickly brandishing the knife from his pocket, he laid it over the glass.

He fell to his knees and lowered his head; an act of respect that she deserved. He felt pity for her ignorance and the suffering that it would bring her but he promised himself that he would protect her from all harm.

When he raised his eyes he could see the liquid that bathed her body rippled around her figure. Quickly, he rose to his feet and observed her. She had been a prisoner of a peaceful slumber for over seventeen years, forced to live in an unmoving trance. Her body could sense the approach of consciousness and was resisting against the mental restrains. Her eyes darted beneath the seals that they had placed over them and her index finger fidgeted.

Unwinding Secrets

It's time.

Chapter 1

"Everyone off!" The bus driver yelled at all of the sleepy students who must not have noticed that they had arrived at school. I stared out the window, while the kids in the front rows got off first.

The school looked just like it had when I left it in June. The red-orange bricks were evenly compiled with concrete, creating a large, rectangular building where all the teenagers in Ashwick had to spend most of their days learning about things they thought useless. The frames of the doors and windows were painted white to contrast the dark colors of the building. Just by looking through the windows, you could tell which class was inside. The science lab, on the second floor, had a skeleton standing near the window, and the fluorescent pale lights were barely visible as they fought against the reflection of the sun on the smoke-stained glass.

I felt a tap on my shoulder. When I turned around, I met a girl's cold glare.

"Are you going to move, or should I cut?" she asked rudely.

I looked at the hall that ran between the rows of seats of the yellow school bus. It was empty, and everyone else had poured out onto the sidewalk, dragging their feet up to the entry's stairs and pulling themselves by the railing. If the students were covered in green with blood streaks, they could all pass for zombies.

I slung my backpack over my shoulder and grabbed my lunch sack while scooting out of the seat. The girl with the cold stare had a fake smile pasted on her face. I simply ignored her and made my way down the aisle, grabbing the backs of the seats.

When I stepped out of the bus, I could smell the fresh morning dew, one of my favorite smells. I could tell that the grass had been cut recently. Light and dark green strips extended from the woods to the school's sidewalk. Some new flowers were planted on the edges of the steps and at the front of the building. I stood for a second, caught up in a daze, but I quickly snapped back to reality when a senior bumped into me, almost making me drop my lunch. I rolled my eyes, annoyed with how seniors thought they could be rude because they were older, and made my way up the hard stone steps to the main entrance.

The halls were already crowded. There were fifteen minutes before classes began, and the normal teenager would typically arrive late on the first day. I pushed my way through the mass of teachers and students, saying "Sorry," "Excuse me," and "Pardon me," until I found the front desk.

Stella, her name on a silver plaque on the dark wooden desk, glanced up at me as I approached. Her old green eyes looked at me from under the weighing wrinkles that seemed to fold over her face. Stella was a well-aged woman who had worked constantly as secretary for forty years; that's how she knew *everyone's* name.

"Hello Nicole, how are you?" She didn't pause for me to answer. "It seems that this year we're going to be a bit crowded. All of the new students are freshmen, except for one." She made sure she had the number right, pulling her glasses up to her eyes, checking the list and then dropping them again. They hung by her neck with a fine, beaded string.

I entertained my fingers by picking at the cracked paint on the surface of the desk. Stella hardly seemed to notice. "Yeah, it's pretty stuffed up. Do you have the schedules for juniors?"

Stella puffed up her grey hair and opened a cabinet to her left. I could see her pearl earrings shining brightly through her thin hair. Each year, it looked like more hair shed off the top of her head, creating a bald spot that made her look older than she was.

"I think I left it here. I made a lot of copies. For freshman year, I made a huge number of copies, and that still wasn't enough!" she exclaimed, laughing.

I chuckled nervously. I didn't really care about freshman year. I hardly knew anyone, and she knew that. I shifted my eyes to the doors, searching for long dark curls, but since I didn't see any, I looked back at Stella, who also seemed to be searching the crowd. Guessing her thoughts, I shrugged.

"She got here before."

Stella's hair bobbed up and down exaggeratedly as she nodded.

"Ok, here's your schedule," she said, laying the paper in front of me and quickly slamming down another one on top of it. The paper had three numbers on it: 126. "Your locker number." After I gathered the papers, she waved me away, letting the next kid in line take my place.

As I weaved through the hallways, I found them less crowded. The aroma of recently cleaned floors was keen beneath the disgusting odor of nerves and excitement given off by old and new students alike. It was the first day of school for crying out loud; there were hardly any new people. Every year was exactly the same, except for the content of the classes. I read the locker numbers engraved with black paint: 124, 125, and 126. I stopped in front of my locker and inspected the outside. This was a step up from last year's locker. The metallic door wasn't scratched too badly, but there was a big dent in the bottom right corner where someone had clearly kicked it. I grabbed the bright green lock from my backpack and slipped it onto the lock hole. Then I looked at the schedule: I had art and then chemistry. I slipped the books I wasn't going to use into my locker; it was hard trying to maximize space with only two narrow shelves.

I zipped up my backpack and made my way back through the corridors. I recognized faces from last year. I smiled at the twins from science class; the ex-cheerleader who I had found in the bathroom last year, crying because she didn't make it on the team; and at the chess club, making their way down the middle of the corridor as if they were "all that." Usually the cheerleaders did that, but they made themselves more exclusive by walking through the halls after the bell rang and the halls were deserted.

I turned right when I reached the lunchroom's double doors. Pulling them toward me, cold air blew in my face and slightly lifted my hair. The light breeze smelled like coffee and freshly baked muffins. A small smile twitched at the corners of my mouth. There was little room between the tables, and many kids were already lined up near the cash register with their hot drinks and breakfasts.

"Over here!" Violet sing-songed from the table we had claimed since we were freshmen. She waved and pointed at the two cups of hot chocolate. It was pretty coincidental that neither of us liked coffee.

I walked to the table and lifted myself onto the stool. "Thanks." I held the warm cup in my hand and let the heat creep up my arm, slowly tickling me. "So, how was your summer vacation in Italy?" I asked her, admiring her lush, black curls, which fell over her shoulders to just below her waist. She still fashioned her hair in the same style, hanging down on one side and occasionally flipping it when it bothered her.

Her smile was broad and bright. "It was great! I'm completely speechless." She sighed. "I did so many awesome things, I couldn't possibly tell you now. I have to process it first."

I laughed. She did this with every trip. The first few days after she came back, she didn't speak much of her vacations;

then it was two months of nonstop talking. "Fine. What was your favorite thing, place, activity, etc.?"

She thought for a second, closing her eyes. When she reopened them, I saw a soft glimmer. "I would have to say..." she laughed nervously. "Venice!"

I nodded, taking a sip from my hot chocolate. It didn't really make sense that I was drinking it in summer, but it was kind of a back-to-school ritual. We always drank hot chocolate or orange juice in the morning before classes started. We liked to talk about more private things here instead of walking down the halls. "Why Venice?"

Violet gazed wistfully over her shoulder and out the window. She shrugged. "I don't know, maybe the fact that everything is so beautifully simple, and there are boats everywhere."

I nodded. "Tell me more. Did you go to a masquerade?"

She smiled. "Yeah, I did. It was great. I saw the best handmade masks *ever*. They were awesome; some had tons of feathers and glitter. I kept it simple." She scratched her arm with her long nails; they were painted with different animal prints. Ever since Violet found a special store in Florida, she had fallen in love with nail art. Almost every month, she came up with a different way to paint them. Last time, she painted them with flames, and on her ring finger's nail, she delicately painted a golden mockingjay pin—the symbol of our favorite book.

"And...?"

"And I met a guy." She blushed and looked down at the table to conceal it. I raised my eyebrows. She usually fell for the

S. Elizabeth Dover

ones who lived far away or were too famous. "I saw him for the first time on the day the festival began," she explained. "I supposed he also had an eye on me, or my mask, because he found me the day after. At first, we just talked about friends, school, careers, and other stuff, but then on the last night, he ..."

My mouth dropped, I looked at her now with my eyebrows lowered and pure suspicion. "You didn't make out, did you?" I shoved a strand of hair that had managed to loosen itself from my ponytail eagerly behind my ear.

When she shook her head, I sighed. "He made the move on me."

I slammed my hand against the table. "He did not! What happened after that?"

"I didn't see it coming. We were having a pleasant conversation crossing the bridge to get back to the festival, and he planted one on me. I shoved him away a bit, not knowing what to do, but then something came over me. After that, I just walked really quickly back to the festival without saying anything or waiting for him to catch up. I got lost in the crowd. I seriously don't want you to mention this to anyone. I didn't even tell my parents. It's just something that's in the past now." She paused. "But...I can't believe I'm saying this. I really liked him Nikki. I wish he had followed me through the crowd..."

I nodded and sat silently. I could feel her reading me. Understanding my lack of words, she jumped in to start the conversation rolling again.

"What did you do the rest of the summer?" She played with her straw's paper wrapping just to keep her fingers busy. A curl fell straight in front of her face, but since she was looking down, she didn't mind.

"The same old thing," I replied.

She assented with her head and smiled. "Read, eat, sleep; the best way of living." Her hands went to her large purse that she used as a backpack and pulled out an iPod. She tapped the screen rapidly and occasionally laughed quietly.

I pretended to be entertained by the transparent lid of my cardboard cup, turning it and pushing down on the plastic, watching it web wherever I dug in my nail.

"So, I hear that there are a lot of new freshmen this year. When you got here, were the halls crowded with them?"

Usually the freshmen were the first to arrive, so they had more time to get their bearings and organize themselves. Most of them came with their parents and didn't want to be seen with them when the whole school was full of other students.

She shook her head. "No. When I got here, this place was deserted."

"Wow, you actually woke up early." Violet rarely made the effort to make it to school for our morning chit-chats, but this was something. Who could blame her, since she usually packed her free time with extracurricular activities?

Violet placed her iPod on the edge of the table. "I didn't sleep well. I suppose I fell asleep at three, and then I woke up by myself at six. Even though I wanted to sleep more, my brain was already thinking too much, so I got ready and headed for school a bit early. I decided to have breakfast here and wait for you."

She grabbed her iPod and saw me staring at it, so she just shoved it in her purse.

I snickered. "So, the great Violet was actually nervous the night before school?" I teased her. "I thought you were never nervous about little things like that, I mean, to be able to get on a stage..."

"Oh, just shut up, will you! It doesn't help. Plus, the stage is just the place where I feel best and can communicate the easiest." She smiled, pleased with her words.

I sipped my hot chocolate. "Is there something you're not telling me?" I smoothed my jeans and retied my hair in a high ponytail. My chocolate brown hair fell past my shoulders to about a quarter of the way down my arm. It was plain and very frizzy.

Violet traced the curve of her jaw on her round-oval face. She tried to act as if there was nothing she wasn't telling me, but she wasn't a very good actress. "Oh, nothing of your concern."

"Yeah right."

Violet usually acted hard to get when she really did care about something. This either meant that I should leave her alone or prod. Just now, she suggested that I should squeeze the information out of her, but it wasn't necessary.

She shrugged. "Just choir, drama, and band auditions."

My mouth curved into a smile. "The three-in-one day!" When she nodded, I felt like laughing, because it was sort of foolish for her to worry about these goals she would definitely achieve. But I wanted to reassure her that she was going to get in; no one wanted to lose the opportunity to have Violet in his or her club when she was the best singer in town. "Really, you shouldn't worry about it."

Violet looked at me over the rim of her cup and then put the cup down softly, swallowing hard. "I know I shouldn't get worked up, but still, the thought that I might get rejected still gnaws at me."

I laughed. "When was the last time you got rejected for singing?"

She sat without words. Her answer was zero. My point was proven.

"So, about the guy in Venice...did he at least give you his number or name? Or was it more of a mystery guy, romantic chick flick movie thing?"

She grabbed her cell phone, scrolled through some files, and then handed me the phone. His hair was dark chocolate brown, and he had intense brown eyes that slightly glimmered. He wore a well-ironed tux and a mask covered most of his facial features. You had to know the person to actually identify him from behind the mask. All I could glean from the image was his hair, eyes, and clothes. But there was something strange about the lighting. It was as if the picture was taken in the dark, with only one light to the boy's right, illuminating half of his face, neck, and shoulders. Or maybe it was taken during a sunset, when the light is dim and he was half in the shadows.

"His name is Henry, and he's eighteen." Violet smiled. "I have his phone number, but I don't know if I should call him. Maybe it would be a bit awkward with the whole incident and all."

"Has he called you?" I asked

She shook her head and slipped her phone into her purse. "No, but I hope he does."

I tensed when I heard the bell ring. Sometimes, it could really frighten me; it was very loud, plus the table was right under the shiny metal bell that hung on the wall. "Gosh, I'll have to get used to that again." I laughed. Looking at my schedule, I said, "Hey I have art now, what about you?"

Violet unfolded a paper and frowned. "I have to start the week with algebra. You are *so* lucky." She said the "so" with a soft hiss, almost cat-like.

"I'll see you during recess?"

"Deal." And with that, she turned and snaked her way through the tight spaces until she reached the door of the cafeteria. You could tell now that some kids began to pour out of the lunchroom and into the halls. She turned around and smiled at me. I raised my crossed fingers at her, our simple sign, wishing her luck. She turned and disappeared in the wave of passing students.

As I felt the cafeteria, it was hard to make my way through the halls. Flowing rivers of students were pressed together as they followed the current and divided when the hall split in two. I nearly had to ram into a kid to get into the crowd. But as other students filled the classrooms, slowly the halls became less compressed and it was easier to breathe.

I turned into the art studio. Tall easels were propped up in rows where desks should have been. Streaks of paint stained the light brown wood and the white walls. Clearly someone had

had a paint fight or couldn't make out the difference between paper and walls.

Some students already sat behind easels, their backpacks hung on the rack at the back of the room so they wouldn't get dirty. I sank onto a stool propped up in front of an easel in the back corner of the room. I leaned my head against wall and sighed. I liked the smell of paint, paper, and brushes, but usually everyone got noisy in art, and it gave me a bad headache that I had to bear for the rest of the day.

I heard a soft cough next to me. I turned my head, still leaning it against the wall. "Hi Emma." I looked at her hair. It was cut short over her shoulders. She looked great with her new style. Emma's hair used to fall in long, wavy, light brown sheets.

"Nice hair, is it recent?" I asked.

"Well, I cut it two weeks ago, but yeah, you can call it recent." She shrugged and rolled her eyes. "So, how's Violet?" She grabbed a paintbrush from the small boxes attached to the wooden frame of the easels and lightly combed it.

I sat up straight and turned to my right, facing her. "She's fine. You can talk to her, you know."

Emma tensed. She was the kind of girl that was capable of nice acts but preferred to do the contrary. During freshman year, she and Violet were crushing on the same guy, Nathan. He was the average hunk, blond hair, blue eyes, and a smile that could win over a whole crowd of angry wolves and turn them in to soft puppies. Of course, as a freshman, when you liked a guy, you thought you'd marry him, and he used that to his advantage.

Nathan played with them and Emma couldn't stand the fact that she was competing with Violet for the same guy.

At that time, Violet still wrote in journals. Emma somehow found them and photocopied every single entry. Then she posted all the copies in the school paper for everyone to see.

Violet realized that Nathan wasn't worth the whole rivalry and stopped talking to Emma. I couldn't blame her. I would hate the person who made my personal secrets and writings public, especially when most of them were dedicated to said guy. After the whole scene in school, Violet asked me to help her to bury all her journals in her backyard. Later, we planted some alstroemeria flowers over them to hide the mound of recently dug up, dark black earth.

"No thanks," Emma responded. "Violet probably hasn't forgotten."

I shrugged. "It doesn't matter if she forgets, only if she forgives." I turned to face my easel as I heard the teacher walk in.

Mrs. Harrison set her purse down on her paint-stained wooden desk. She sighed, and since not many noticed her arrival, she clapped her hands.

"Good morning, juniors!" The students in the front rows were the last to turn around and face her. "I'd like to give you a warm welcome back after three lovely months of vacation. But even though you have just arrived back from wherever you went, I will not go slowly and my expectations will be higher than ever. So, a little word of advice...do not slack off in my class." She smiled warmly. Mrs. Harrison was the kind of teacher who was friendly after giving you an F on a project and smiled in your face as if mocking you.

A hand in the front row shot up. "Mrs. Harrison, what's the main project this year?" A student called from the back of the classroom.

Mrs. Harrison grinned, showing her pale yellow teeth. "Good question, Jared. I haven't really decided on our project this year, but I was hoping we could paint a mural on the front wall of the public hospital." When she finished, he nodded, approving her decision.

I stared out the window on the other side of the classroom. It was sunny outside. I knew it was going to be warm, but now, judging by the sun, it was going to be boiling. I noticed Emma looking at her nails while the kid in front rocked his stool back and forth. *Thump. Thump. Thump.* Then I heard something out of place. A voice. I looked up at a kid in the doorway. Well, more specifically, a familiar looking teenage boy, with dark chocolate hair and soft brown eyes. He held a paper in his hand, looking completely lost, but his eyes were fixed on me.

"Oh, may I ask who you are?" Mrs. Harrison walked to the door and stood next to him. He was tall, much taller than her, and I bet taller than me; but what gave him the impression of being big was his massiveness. I could tell he was strong.

The boy nodded. "I'm Skyler." Since he saw no reaction from his teacher, he continued. "The paper here says that I have art."

Mrs. Harrison looked around the classroom, a bit annoyed. "There's an empty seat. You can take it. And next time, don't be late." She walked to the whiteboard behind her desk and began to write on it. I could hear the marker squeaking as it moved over the smooth surface of the board.

Skyler walked through the small passageway that crossed the center of the room and slipped behind his easel. The way he moved, the way he dressed, and even the way he had spoken seemed normal, but there was something in the way he stared at me. Ever since I looked up, he had been holding my gaze. It wasn't curiosity, no, more like intimidation? I positioned myself so I could hide behind the heads of the other students.

Emma seemed to have noticed. "What's up with him? He looks at you all the time." I could hear the tension in her voice. She didn't like it either. "I bet..."

"Okay, class," Mrs. Harrison instructed, "the first task today will be painting in pairs. Since this is the first week, we won't be working with so much intensity, but I want you to combine objects from your vacation to create an image. There are no rules with this one, so you can use any style you desire. I will choose the pairs, and I don't want to hear anyone whine about their partner, am I understood? However, you can trade partners only if both partners agree."

The whole class chanted "yes" simultaneously.

While Mrs. Harrison began to choose the partners, I held my breath. She was mixing people from different lines and rows. I heard my name being called. "Nicole." Skyler was still looking at me. I tried to act as if I didn't notice. "You're paired up with Emma."

I exhaled with relief, "Thank God."

Emma smiled at me.

"Skyler, you're paired up with Jade."

Jade was Emma's best friend. I could see her longing stare from across the row, asking her to trade. All I could think in my mind was *no*.

Emma turned to me and bit her lip lightly. "Do you mind?" She ran her fingers through her ponytail, knowing that I also read the look on Jade's face. She also knew that I would say no.

"Seriously?" Disbelief made me speak slower. These were the little actions that made me loathe her.

Emma nodded with a mischievous smile and stood up. She walked over to Jade and whispered something in her ear. The corners of Jade's mouth pulled up into a smile. She nodded at me in approval and told Skyler to sit in the empty seat next to me. He stood up and offered her the stool. She sat down and giggled as he made his way over to me. I was so going to kill that twerp.

"Hello Nicole, "he said, extending his hand.

I didn't answer. How the heck did he know my name? Probably Jade or Emma told him before they switched partners. I turned to face the blank canvas in front of me, ignoring his hand completely, as he slumped on the stool. Not that I wanted to be rude, but I wasn't about to shake hands with this creep who kept staring at me. His gaze had been constant since he came in, buzzing in my head like an obnoxious fly. All I could possibly think about at the moment was how much I despised Emma.

"So, we have to do this..." I began.

"What did you do on your vacation?" Skyler asked, his emotions suddenly switching. He quit glaring at me as if he wanted to slit my wrists; instead, his head tilted slightly to the side, making his face look absolutely gorgeous. I bit the inside of my mouth. Did he care that he just interrupted me? Or did he really not notice that I was talking?

I observed him a bit closer, since he was sitting right next to me. Highlights in his hair shone copper under the bright classroom lights. The green flecks in his dark brown eyes looked as if someone had grabbed a tiny paintbrush and added hints of green near his pupils, like microscopic shards of emeralds tangled in brown vines. I wondered if his pupils expanded, would I be able to see the hidden emeralds in his eyes?

"Hello?"

I sat straighter, realizing that I had looked at him for too long. Skyler's lips twitched at the corners, as if he wasn't allowing himself to smile. "Sorry, I sometimes get distracted." He didn't believe me. Neither did I.

"What did you do on your vacation that you want to paint?" His knee brushed mine. I should have felt heat rising in my cheeks, but the heat from my body was drained out in a matter of seconds, leaving me cold.

"I didn't do much, mostly read and walk outside."

Skyler smiled. In a normal situation, I would have thought that he was insanely hot, but the way he was acting totally threw me off. After reading so many books, I knew that the normal teenage reaction should be sweaty palms, heart jammed in my throat, and butterflies in my stomach, not cold blood, a twisting stomach, and trembling hands.

"Well, I would have never guessed that you are an introvert." He grabbed a paintbrush and opened one of the paint tubes. He pressed it. At first, only air came out, but then black paint stained the palette.

I didn't know if I should be offended or just uninterested. Prejudice much? I stopped looking at him and ran my fingers over the edge of my long shorts. My mother had cut a pair of jeans to make long shorts, so I didn't have to wear pants to school in the summer. I pulled at one of the loose strings and wrapped it around my finger until the tip turned dark pink.

"Do you want to paint? I'm not very good at it," I said, passing him the large, blank canvas.

He accepted it and ran his hands along the corners as if he were smoothing them out. I noticed that his hands were large, and there were several scars across the tops of his palms. The scars looked like thin white lines delicately drawn across his skin. I suddenly longed to ask him what had caused the scars, so I began to open my mouth but rapidly shut it. The question was probably too personal, or maybe I didn't have the guts to ask him.

Skyler picked up a dab of paint with the brush and stroked the paper lightly, leaving an even black trail behind. I observed him while he painted. His head was slightly tilted, and his eyes were focused on the canvas. It seemed like he had separated himself from the world; all he could see, hear, or smell could only come from him, the brush, or the paper that gave slightly under the pressure of his hand. His gaze was fixed on the canvas when his mouth started to move. "You're staring at me," he stated indifferently. "Again."

I turned away quickly. I had never been caught like this—*never*—watching a guy. And I definitely did not want to get caught doing it twice. "Who says I was looking at you?" I tried to answer bitterly, but my voice came out weak.

He chuckled, shaking his head, and continued painting without looking at me. I sucked at lying, and you didn't have to know me to see that. After all, he definitely didn't know me, yet he could tell. He laid down the paintbrush and turned to look at me. I observed what he had painted: a single hand grabbing a book. The book's cover was blank, but swirls came out of the pages as if the story were pouring out. I knew which question was coming now. "So which books did you read this summer?"

I could hear the kid in front of me still rocking on his stool. *Thump. Thump. Thump.* "I don't see what that has to do with our assignment. Any cover will do."

"I didn't ask for the assignment." His eyes were steady on me.

Okay...this was awkward.

I thanked him silently when he began to paint again and didn't push the conversation any further. He drew a half-moon with bold lines over a rowboat sitting in the water. The waves curled softly against the boat's underside. He added more and more details. I tried to watch him without him noticing.

"Ok, I think we should start adding the colors," he said.

"It's beautiful," I whispered.

Skyler smiled furtively, looking proud of his artwork. "You like it?"

I could feel my eyes enlarge the more I looked at it. "I love it."

My words didn't seem to have much effect on him as he pulled different colors of paint from the box. He lined up the tubes on the small ledge "Do you know how to add the colors?"

"Sure, but I can't guarantee anything good."

"Here, you'll need this." Skyler pushed the paintbrush into my hand, his fingers rough and calloused, and squirted different tones of blue paint onto the palette. "Mix some of the black paint with the blue, but just a drop." He watched me closely as I had him, while I mixed the paint colors. I tried to do it in the most elegant manner so it didn't end up all over my clothes, but I gave up quickly and continued to mix carelessly.

I was careful to paint within the bold lines Skyler painted, because I didn't want to them as I painted water beneath the boat. My hands slightly trembled, even though I ordered them not to; but, as always, my body was highly disobedient.

I could hear him shuffle on the stool. "You're doing great." His voice, soft and warm against my neck, sent shivers up my spine. I didn't like people breathing on me, their hot breath running over my skin. He held his breath when I dragged the brush across the paper and exhaled whenever I picked it up. I almost played a game to see how long he could last without breathing and if he could keep up with my short strokes. I pondered, *Could I make him pass out?*

When I finished painting, the waves had lighter tones of the same blue, so it seemed as if the moon were reflecting off the water. I put down the paintbrush and observed my work. I stayed in the lines, and the paint was evenly distributed. I felt a hand lean on my shoulder and peer at the canvas.

Mrs. Harrison smelled like jasmine and wet paint. She observed our work steadily and nodded. She patted Skyler on the back and left. We could hear her mumble something like, "Well done," but we weren't sure.

He was looking at the floor when he spoke. "Looks like we make a great team." Even though he was complementing our work, his face contained as much expression as the canvas had before we painted it.

I moved to grab the paintbrush, but Skyler swiftly took it instead to paint the sky a purplish-blue and add what looked like the Milky Way crossing just underneath the moon. His artistic talent was amazing. It actually looked as if the paper contained some sort of magic that allowed the sky to suddenly appear.

While he ran the brush over the canvas, I peered over his shoulder to see Jade and Emma laughing their heads off while they painted. Emma's short hair made her face look rounder than usual next to Jade's heart-shaped face surrounded by sleek, red-brown hair. I got so caught up watching the two friends laugh together that when the bell rang, I almost jumped out of my seat.

I turned to look at my art partner, but his seat was empty.

I looked frantically around the room, but there was no trace of the new boy. There was no way that he could have disappeared like that. Skyler was getting weirder and weirder with each passing second. I looked at the empty stool and the canvas painted with the beautiful night scene on the cover of the unidentified book. He had painted all of this with unbelievable speed, and the outcome was astounding. He even had enough time to wash the paintbrush and put inside its holder—the only thing that reassured me he existed. I wrote our names in the bottom corner of the canvas, so we could reclaim it after it dried and work on it in the next class.

I grabbed my backpack and walked down the hall to my next class. I kept an eye open to see if I could find him, but he had vanished as quickly as he had appeared. Part of me was glad that I couldn't find him. Despite the feelings of fright that he provoked in me, and the constant desire to flee, there was also something that made me feel like I could trust him.

Chapter 2

Violet walked three paces in front of me as we made our way through the basketball court to the grassy fields. There was also common space where a large oak tree stood tall on its large roots and extended wide branches adorned with frail leaves. The tree had been sick for a while now, but it still provided great shelter from the wind and cover from the sun.

Violet sunk down, leaning against the wrinkled trunk and sighed. She turned her face up to the sky and closed her eyes. Her breathing deepened, as if she was sleeping, and her vanilla perfume lightly scented the air. She opened her eyes and turned to me. "What are you eating?" She pointed her chin to the paper bag I held in my hand.

"Peanut butter and jelly sandwich, with an apple for dessert," I respond after looking inside. "What about you?"

She peered into her lunch box. "Chicken sandwich, a tomato, and some grapes." She looked up at me again with her brown eyes. "I'll trade you the grapes for the apple."

I picked up the glossy red apple from the paper bag and handed it over. "Okay." I tossed the bunch of grapes into the bag and unwrapped my sandwich from the foil paper. After taking a bite, I cleared my throat. "So, how were your first few hours of school?" I took another bite. Violet and I usually didn't share our lunch period. We used the time for homework, or she went to band, choir, or drama meetings. Even though band and choir hadn't started, they frequently set up auditions during lunchtime.

Violet's eyes were glossy and vacant. "Other than boring, fine. At least the teacher isn't mean, but he still gave us homework. Did you know that extracurricular activities start in two weeks? Isn't that a bit late, I mean, they usually start the second week of school." She continued talking, but my head turned to the lunchroom.

It was filled with people. And when I say filled, I mean packed. The small lunchroom wasn't designed to hold so many students and teachers. I could even see some pouring out to the fields. It seems that we weren't going to be the only ones eating outside this year.

"Are you even listening to me?" Violet shook my arm abruptly.

I nodded but then replaced the nod with a shake. She caught me, and I wasn't going to lie to her. "Are you going to join the yearbook committee?" I changed the subject and steered clear of looking at the students taking seats on the grass and unpacking their lunches. There was one person I really didn't want to interrupt my lunch.

She ran her hands across the grass to brush off the crumbs. "I don't think so. I'm gonna have a pretty tight schedule and our Friday nights are irreplaceable."

"It must suck to be so busy. You don't have time for anything else."

"You make time."

I laughed. I wasn't capable of sacrificing sleep so I could do other stuff. It just wasn't worth it. But Violet did have the capability to sleep five hours and feel perfectly fine the next day.

Violet nudged my knee with her elbow. "Who's he?" she asked, staring at someone who was making his way to a lonely spot on the grass.

I turned my head. Skyler. "Oh, he's just the new kid in our grade."

"Why didn't you tell me about him before?" she whispered as if he had bionic hearing. I mean, it is kind of rude whispering while staring at someone. It makes the other person feel...judged.

I shrugged. "He didn't come to mind-"

"What is he like?" She tugged on the sleeve of my t-shirt.

I shifted in place and looked at her, bothered. "Is it really necessary that you interrupt me?" I asked, lifting one eyebrow. He was looking at us. I could tell. I could feel his gaze on me and feel his warm breath against the back of my neck, saying "You're doing great," like in art class.

What the hell was wrong with me? I wasn't used to thinking of guys, that's what. And especially not guys I had just met.

Violet threw her paper napkin back into her lunch box and grabbed the container that held a neatly cut tomato. She ate it as she thought. " I feel as if I've seen him before." Her eyes were fixated on some shards of grass and her hair hung, untouched, over her shoulder.

I sat silently as I usually did when she was thinking. I glanced at my watch. She'd been philosophizing for five whole minutes. Why was she thinking so much? Only tests could take hold of her mind for so long.

She fidgeted; her first sign of breaking free from her five-minute trance. Finally, she spoke, "Nope, I can't remember. That's strange because I usually remember everyone I meet; if not the name, the situation or a fragment of a conversation." Her eyebrows knitted, and for the first time, her memory failed her. Her face suddenly went neutral. "Whatever. So, tell me about him." Her eyes were obliquely fixed on him.

I began eating the grapes. "Well, we have art class with Mrs. Harrison, and I was paired up with Emma. But, of course, she wanted to be with Jade, who by the way, is also in art class, so I ended up with him." I avoided eye contact with Skyler, but I could still feel his eyes on me. This guy had some serious manner problems.

Violet's face was expressionless. "You were paired with him?" She clearly didn't believe me. "Tell me more. This is the first exciting thing that happens in years and, if it weren't for him sitting there, I would have never found out." She stopped trying to look at him and firmly planted her gaze on me.

I shrugged. "I didn't think it was going to be so important, but I was going to tell you anyway; he just beat me to it." I threw the leftover grape branches into my paper bag. "Well, he got to class late, so it's not like we could talk before class; but once he came in, he sort of stared at me."

"How much?"

"A lot. It was getting really uncomfortable, and then Emma wanted to trade partners, even though I didn't want to. She sent Skyler over to me, and we had to do a project together. At first he acted creepy, then fazed into stuck-up and finally he turned into a pretty normal guy. When the bell rang he just disappeared."

Violet laughed. "He couldn't have disappeared. Anyone can leave art early without other people noticing."

I shook my head. "I swear he simply vanished."

Violet laughed harder. Her hair fell into her face, and she grabbed her stomach. "Oh my God, I can't believe you might have fallen for a practical joke he's pulling on you." Clearing her voice, she continued. "And if he really did disappear, you can go over there, sit by him on the grass, and ask him how he did it."

Was that a dare?

"No way! I'm not going over there so I can look like an idiot." I crumpled the paper bag and tossed it from hand to hand.

Violet smirked. That smirk only meant one thing. I could already feel the weight of the question she was about to ask, and I knew she wasn't going to take no for an answer. "Do you like him?" she asked slowly.

"Have you gone crazy? Have you lost your mind?!" I said a bit too loudly. Skyler turned to face us, startled by my exclamation. "There is no way I'm falling for Skyler." My voice was hushed, as I did *not* want him overhearing.

Violet tossed her hair over her right shoulder. "I don't believe you." Her brown eyes searched mine for any signals. "You suck at lying."

I rolled my eyes. "How can I suck at doing something I'm not?"

She sat still.

"Fine, I don't know! It's not my fault this guy comes on so strong. It's weird. I feel terrified but at the same time intrigued."

She smiled. Why would I blame her? She loved to win. And who didn't? "Ok, I have to go to drama auditions, and then I have to get my books and run to the farthest wing. Promise me that you'll walk home with me." She stood up and patted the back of her jeans, making any leaves, blades of grass, or twigs fall off.

I stood up and did the same. "Deal."

She smiled. "Deal." Before taking off, we both glanced in Skyler's direction. To our surprise, he was gone. The only trace that showed he had been there was a small dent in the ground, where he had sat on the green grass and squished it under his weight. Violet raised her eyebrows. "Wow, that is creepy."

* * *

I sat on the edge of the low brick wall that separated the sidewalk from school property. My back was hunched, and I leaned over a notebook, doodling, while I waited for Violet. At first, I just drew tornadoes. They were easy to draw after all; you just sketch circles, one on top of the other. As you reach the bottom of the tornado, you make the ending a bit smaller and TADA! The only thing missing was a flying cow, a witch, and a farmhouse lifting from the ground.

Something hit the cement steps hard. It was a bone-breaking kind of noise that chilled my spine.

I turned around quickly; my ponytail whipped the base of my neck. It was Nathan, who had just pushed a kid. I wasn't sure who it was, but I definitely had seen that face before. The kid's books were spread all around him on the ground, and Nathan's voice was hard. "And don't you ever hit on her again!" He threw the last of the books at the poor kid, who surely didn't know that Emma was *his* property, and marched back into the building.

The kid caught the books and began to pick up everything that had fallen out of his hands and poorly closed backpack. I dropped my notebook and backpack and walked over to him.

He looked at me with glossy green eyes. "You don't need to...His shaggy black hair made him look like a skater. He wore jeans and a plain green t-shirt with some logo on it that I had never seen before. He had metallic braces that covered his upper teeth and what looked like rubber bands hooked onto the molars and the teeth right above them.

"I know." I cut him off before he got to the speech. I shouldn't be doing this, not if I didn't want to get in trouble with the lacrosse team, but I had to. I remembered when this had happened to me, being bullied, and no one had been there to help me. I had felt horrible. "Are you all right?"

He muttered something under his breath, surely insulting his aggressor, and grabbed the book I was holding out to him. "Yeah, I'm fine, but I don't know about my folders." We both looked at a transparent folder at his feet. The hooks had opened with their impact with the ground, and all of the sheets of paper were strewn around him. He shoved them back into his backpack. "Um, thanks." And with that, he left me kneeling on the ground alone, where a just moment ago, all the contents of his backpack were on display.

I stood up and brushed off my pants. People were staring...at me. I didn't mind. If it was me who had fallen, I would have run away completely embarrassed, but now I didn't mind much.

I walked back to the brick wall where I had left my stuff. There was only one thing different with the way I had left things. I'm pretty sure that I didn't leave a large seventeen-year-old guy standing next to my backpack and looking at the deformed tornadoes I had been drawing. "Told you I didn't draw that well."

Skyler lifted an eyebrow. "In this," he chuckled, "you hardly showed any interest. I bet you can do better." He looked at every doodle I have ever drawn on that pad. "What you just did was nice." He dropped the notebook back on the wall and sat by my belongings.

I took the liberty to sit next to him and stare at the houses in front of the school. They were all simple, typical Ashwick houses with white picket fences surrounding green gardens with colorful flowers and wooden paneling. In one garden, a grandmother was bringing out cookies to some sophomores. And to think that some years ago, most of them were chubby, friendly little girls who liked playing dolls and pretended that the backyard was a completely different world. I sighed and ran my fingers through my ponytail.

Skyler followed my gaze and looked back at me. I guess he couldn't figure out what I was thinking. He cleared his throat, evidently wanting me to notice him again. "Would you mind if I walk home with you today, Nicole?" For the first time, his voice showed insecurity.

I looked into his eyes, searching for the green I had seen in art class. Thank goodness Violet had asked me to walk home with her. Not that I didn't like him, but I didn't really like the fact that he still looked at me in that creepy way. "Sorry, I already promised Vi."

He nodded and said good-bye in a hushed voice, as he slowly began to walk away...in the same direction Violet and were headed. His head was lowered, and if he had a tail, it would probably be between his legs. Was he trying to make me feel sorry for him?

"Ok, I just couldn't interrupt. What did you tell him to leave him like that?" Violet appeared from behind the wall, making me jump. Sometimes it was scary how well she could sneak up on me.

I looked toward Skyler; he was still walking *extremely* slowly. "Nothing much, he just asked me if he could walk me home, but I told him I was walking with you today."

Violet looked up at me with her dark brown eyes. I knew that look. "You should go with him; I'll stay close behind watching, keeping an eye on you." Her curls were less fluffy now than they were that morning. Her large purse was slung over her shoulder and hanging down her side. Her arms were filled with books, and her cell phone was propped on top of them.

I nodded. "We'll talk later tonight, ok?" And after, that I jogged up to Skyler. His head was no longer bowed, and there was a small smile on his face. His chocolate brown hair looked messy, as if he ran his fingers through it, shaking it, the way guys usually did. "Let me guess. You saw this coming."

He laughed; of course he did. "Violet's your best friend? I've seen her before." His hands were in his pockets, his backpack was over one shoulder, and his pants were torn at the bottom. If he didn't always seem to be hiding something or know my next move, I might actually have fallen for him.

I raised my eyebrows. He knew what I was going to ask. The only thing my mind could say was 'two can play this game,' and that gave me an idea.

"Good for you," I commented with a shrug. Of course he had seen her before, at lunch.

"Don't act as if you don't care."

How did he know me so well? And where had he come from? You didn't just meet a guy, and he randomly knew everything about you. Something was up, and I was determined to find out. "How come you know everything?"

His eyes squinted and he knitted his eyebrows; finally, he didn't understand something or at least didn't expect it. "Excuse me?"

"I mean, how come you know what I'm thinking and how I'll respond to stuff?" I steered away from him, near the edge of the sidewalk. We were surrounded by some houses and mostly woods—dark, dangerous, and mystifying woods. The underbrush was thick and made good cover for anyone sneaking around, and most of the trees had very thick trunks. Now that I was next to Skyler, I suddenly realized that this was the perfect place for a crime. You could kill someone, and no one would ever notice. Even though this was a small town, people didn't make an effort to include each other in their lives. That meant there would be fewer witnesses of a disappearance.

Skyler smiled, and I think I could tell his chin rose a bit. If I was right, the feeling he was having was called pride. "You could say that I am smart enough to figure it out on my own, or maybe you're just an open book." He nudged me with his elbow. Oh no.

I walked straighter. "I've been told..." my voice trailed off. I would let him think what he wanted. "So, why did you come to Ashwick? What made you move *here*?"

He rubbed his hands as if it were cold outside. He sure was enjoying this conversation. "My job sent me here."

"You have a job?"

"Yeah."

Never in my life would I have guessed that he had a job. Ever.

"What do you do?"

We were rounding the corner into the most deserted part of town. Only a few houses were scattered here and there. Violet and I lived pretty close to each other, about two or three blocks away, and we lived in houses farthest from the center of Ashwick. My mom and dad had bought my house because she said she preferred the quiet. She was sort of a closed person and didn't like nosy neighbors with loud kids.

Skyler shifted his backpack from one shoulder to the other. "I'm sorry, I can't tell you yet." He looked down at the ground and then up at me. "It would ruin everything."

What the hell was he talking about? My mind raced. What job could he have that would ruin *everything*? The only jobs I could think of were secret agent, serial killer, or undercover cop. I really didn't like the idea of him being any of the three. "Okay, be all mysterious and stuff, like I care." I started to like playing hard; it was like a modern way of playing chess.

He began to kick a small rock in front of him, but when it fell into the sewer, he stopped and smiled mischievously. "Of course you care, and it'll haunt you until you figure it out or I tell you. And guess what? I bet you're going to figure it out before I even get to tell you."

I rolled my eyes. Before, I had admitted that he was being sort of fun, but this was too smart aleck. "Whatever. Tell me more about your life before you moved here." I retied my ponytail with a black elastic band that had a silky blue bow.

"Told you, you care." His smile turned into a grin, a very nice one, I had to confess. "But first, I want to know this: Do you have a boyfriend?"

Wait, what did he just ask me? That is a question guys pose before they ask you out. "Nope, no boyfriend."

"Lover?"

"Pretty sure I don't have one."

"Crush?"

"You tell me." I answered, feeling a blush rising in my cheeks. I tried to conceal my answer since I knew he could make me admit everything. I'll bet if he asked me to jump off of a roof, I would.

He laughed, almost mocking. He knew. I was screwed. "Not sure. I would probably be able guess who he was if you were to have one," he taunted, grabbing my hand and pressing it like he would if I was his girlfriend.

I quickly, but smoothly took my hand out of his and threw a punch at his arm. I think it hurt me more than it did him, but I had to do it. "Jerk. What makes you think it could be you?"

The way he laughed made me hold my breath. "I never said it could be me." He had just fooled me. I would really have to be careful with my words around him; he was like the devil, transforming them, giving them a new meaning or slapping them back at my face.

Suddenly, he took hold of my shoulders, his eyes wild, and challenged, "Race you to your block." And with that, he took off in the direction of my beloved home. He left me behind, standing on the sidewalk and feeling like an idiot, as I tried to process everything he told me with his eyes.

When I regained my senses, I ran behind him. Man, he was fast! The only thing I could hear was my breath and my feet stomping on the cement sidewalk beneath me. My feet were quick. I was on the track team, but my speed wasn't worthy compared to his. He was a lightning bolt.

I slowed down. I wasn't much of a cross-country runner, more of a sprinter. I crouched down, trying to catch my breath. My heart was racing but not because of the sprint.

I could see Skyler standing still on the street corner. Was he laughing? No, he was regaining his breath just like me. No, wait. Yep, he was laughing. I stared into the forest next to me. Hardly any light leaked through the leaves above, making it seem darker. Something jumped out of the woods. My heart stopped, and I screamed. But when I turned around to see who it was, all I saw was the white tail of a deer jumping back into the forest on the other side of the road.

I laughed at myself as I approached Skyler. He was also laughing. Great, I just embarrassed myself in front of him. "Let's get going; I need to finish some homework for tomorrow."

We walked together, talking about nothing really, just teachers and classmates. Our pace was slower than before, but my heart didn't stop pounding in my chest. Finally, we reached my house.

"So, this is it" Skyler stopped in front of the walkway that led up to the steps of my porch. "It looks really warm and rustic." He stared at it with his big brown eyes. "I like it."

My eyes were on him, but I knew my house so well that I didn't have to look at it to describe it. It had white-paneled walls on the outside and a green-framed door. The porch was painted the same washed-out green as the door and window frames, but some of the paint had already peeled off, revealing the light brown underneath. Most of the first floor was covered with ivy that had been crawling up the wall since...forever. There was a big willow tree in the front yard and flowerbeds scattered here and there. One bed bloomed with colorful anemone flowers, one with orange wallflowers, and the last with hollyhock. The walkway that led to the porch was cracked in several places from untamed weeds.

My voice was soft as I stared at him. I was surprised he let me stare. "See you tomorrow?"

"See you." Before he left, he playfully but softly punched me on the arm. "I owed you one." And with that, he left.

I beamed as I walked up the steps, which squeaked in protest, and opened the screen door, which also needed oiling. I set my backpack on the bench in the entryway and yelled, "Mom I'm home!" I began to walk to the kitchen where surely she'd have my snack ready. But when I reached the living room, I froze.

My brother was looking out the front window, with my mom and dad behind him.

Chapter 3

"What are you guys doing?" My voice squeaked in a high-pitched tone. I didn't have to ask. Of course, I knew what they were doing. My rotten family was spying on me. My face automatically flushed a deep shade of red and heated up like fire. I think my brain liquefied with so much heat.

My brother, who was five years older than me, smirked. "The question is, what were *you* doing?" His hair was a similar color to mine, not too light and not too dark, with a hint of wave in it, unlike mine, which was very straight. Because his hair was buzz cut, you couldn't see the waves. He also had brown eyes with hints of honey in them, which looked great with his angular face.

I didn't want to answer, afraid that I would stammer or my voice would dissolve into an unnaturally high pitch that only dogs could hear, but I had to say something. "Just bug off, Steven, he's only a friend." I used the same tactic I had been using with Skyler; act cool but not too noticeable. I turned to my father. He shouldn't be here, not unless..."Dad, what happened? Why are you here? Are you hurt?"

My father chuckled. Never in my life have I been able to make him crack a hearty laugh the way my mother did. His dark hair was cut short like the army ordered, revealing deep-set eyes—eyes that had suffered, that had seen things he will never be able to forget. My mom always said that I had my father's eyes, but his were different because he had seen all of those things, and I hadn't. Yet. "Sugar, I'm home because I finished work. I have a two-week vacation before I have to leave again."

My heart leaped. I had forgotten to keep counting the days, but that didn't matter now. I wrapped my arms around his neck. He smelled like lead, dirt, and death, but that didn't matter. "I am so glad you're back home," I whispered in his ear.

He hugged me even tighter. "Me too." This made me smile, and I bet my mother, watching all of this, smiled as well. I hadn't noticed, but she was wearing her pretty flowered dress, the one she saved for special occasions. Dad had bought it and given it to her on one of his visits.

He finally let me go and insisted that we all go to the kitchen, grab a snack, and talk. I still couldn't believe that my dad was actually here. I was so happy that I couldn't keep still. I decided to work off my extra energy by twitching my foot rapidly once I sat down.

My mother's even waves spilled down her head and ended right above her shoulders. Her grey eyes, which were always filled with grief, pain, and worry, were now filled with love. She was the only one in our small quartet with light eyes.

She set the table gently, as always, and often smiled at herself or let out a soft sob. I could tell that this was more than she could bear. She had been waiting for some time now, but that time always seemed forever. Having my dad back home with us was a dream. "How was your day, sweetheart?" she asked.

"Sweetheart" and "sugar" were my parents' pet names for me, just as "darling" and "kiddo" were for my brother. Instantly, I knew my mother was talking to me. I munched on a chocolate chip cookie that I grabbed from a basket on the table. "It was fine, pretty normal, nothing out of the ordinary," I answered with a shrug.

Steven's eyebrows rose as she placed cookies on his plate. "So, you call it normal to walk home with a guy?" Even though he was twenty-two, he had the maturity of a teenager. It's funny to see a guy like him, large in size and muscle, dipping his cookies in chocolate milk.

My father smiled, his white teeth standing out against his tan skin. He had gone to war to defend our country a few years back and then chose to spend the rest of his life training young soldiers. I supposed sun block wasn't on their list of priorities. "Who is he?"

"I didn't recognize him; I bet he's new." Steven commented.

My mother finished setting the table and moved her chair next to my father. She held his hand between hers.

"Yeah, he is. We both had art first period." I ate another cookie. They were so good. "Mom, did you make these?"

She nodded, keeping her eyes on my father.

My brother swallowed hard like he always did when he really wanted to talk but had food in his mouth. "So, what is he like? He seems strong. I bet he plays football or swims. I bet I can beat him if we ever fight each other." He sat up straighter, proud of his own size and strength. My brother wanted to follow in my father's footsteps. After finishing college, he had decided to sign up for the army.

My father slightly frowned at him. "I thought you already knew that size isn't important, the tactic is. My partner was half my size, but he could take down a six-foot-tall man in five seconds. In the end, he never taught me how to do it. I guess I will have to force him the next time we meet." He smiled at my mother. I loved when he looked at us over the rim of his mug when he drank.

My mother caressed his cheek. "I'm glad you're back. We're all glad you're back." She laughed because he made a face. That was typical of my father. Every time you gave him a compliment, he made a funny face so he didn't have to say "thank you."

Steven perked up. "Now you'll have to help me with training." He was obsessed with keeping fit in preparation for the day he would go to boot camp.

My dad's lips curled into a grin. If I weren't his daughter, I would be intimidated by his sinister smirk. "Don't expect it to be easy."

"Oh, I don't."

My father laughed. "We'll see in a few days." He rubbed his stomach and stretched his arms. I rolled my eyes; it was the typical guy move. He grabbed my mother and held her close.

I'd seen this image before. It was the same image as the picture over the chimney. They were both younger, before Steven and I were born. Stress and work hadn't yet made them tired every night. But now, there was a big difference. The picture was no longer in black and white, mom wasn't fashionable, and both of them had wrinkles at the corners of their eyes and on their foreheads. It surprised me how young they looked twenty years ago and how quickly they aged.

I pushed my plate away and sighed. This usually caught my parents' attention and made them begin asking questions.

"So Nikki, tell me more about your boyfriend. Where did he come from, and why did he move?" I hated the nickname my brother had given me. It all started in third grade when he bothered me by saying that I had a guy's name. It was funny how he couldn't remember my age, but he always managed to remember the nickname I hated. Too bad Violet picked up the same habit of calling me Nikki.

I bent one leg and sat on top of it in a strange, yet comfortable position. "I don't know where he came from, but I do know that he moved because of his job." When I looked up, my entire family was looking at me with wide eyes and eyebrows lifted. They had the same reaction as I did. How stupid I must have looked!

My mother's mouth was slightly turned downward. "But he's just a child! He shouldn't be working. What does he do?"

This comment was typical from my mother. She was against child labor. She didn't even let me sell popcorn and lemonade on the street corner with Violet.

I shrugged. "I didn't ask."

I grabbed three more cookies in one hand and balanced my mug on my plate in the other. My parents looked at me as if to say, "Aren't you going to stay a bit longer?" I brushed away their gaze with a flip of my ponytail.

I carried the plate and mug to the sink and unfolded a white napkin with the word *love* written in the bottom corner in red ink. I folded the napkin around the cookies and tucked them in my pocket. The kitchen drawers and cabinets were made of a dark wood whose name I didn't remember. They looked good with the soft yellow-orange color of the walls. My mother painted them herself. It was the first hobby she took up when my dad left with the army. Several not-so-professional paintings my mom created hung on the walls with nails and copper wire. Unlike most mothers, mine had a lot of free time. Violet's mom, Monica, had taught my mom the basics of painting. They met twice a week to paint together. Of course, Monica's paintings were exceptional and looked like framed reality.

I looked at the last painting she created for the kitchen. It was a simple, silver kettle next to a teacup on a plate. Both the teacup and the plate were rimmed with red, purple, and gold flowers that curled and met perfectly.

I made my way across the kitchen to the door that led to the tiny hallway. "I have to do my homework. Afterward, I'll help you with dinner, Mom." I let the door close softly behind me with a *click*.

I walked through the narrow hallway and ascended the spiral steel staircase. I ran my hand over the cool metal and looked down at each step. The staircase was painted black, but since it hadn't been painted in a while, there were patches of its original grey color. I stood on the landing and looked at the doors that were positioned opposite from each other. There were four doors, all the same color, and all with an equal amount of space between them. I tilted my head to the right. I couldn't believe I had just realized that my house was almost perfectly symmetrical. Nothing really caught the eye because everything was where it should be.

I opened the last door to the left and inhaled. My room always smelled like a library. That's always how I wanted it to be. Pages and pages of stories, adventures, romances, and conversations that could never be mine lined my walls like bars of a cell, a cell I would love if I were ever a prisoner. I tossed myself onto the light blue bedspread and stared at the ceiling, which was covered with small glowing stars. Violet and I had painted them with glow-in-the-dark paint. Now, they looked messy and uneven, but they were breathtaking when I was younger.

I turned over onto my stomach and hugged the pillow. I forgot I still had the cookies in my pocket. While unwrapping the napkin, I was careful to keep the crumbs off of my bed. After stuffing my mouth, I grabbed my small pink diary, which was covered with love stickers, and opened it. I loved reading my old diary. When I was younger, I decided to copy Vi by writing my thoughts and feelings in journals, diaries, notebooks, and anything else I could find. We hadn't been "official" friends yet, but I thought about giving it a try. Everything went well until I started to forget and, well, I just stopped writing. I began reading an entry from a few years ago..

February 12th

Dear Diary,

I can't believe the day after tomorrow is Valentine's Day! I mean, I hope Connor gives me a card with hard candy, the ones I love—the sugar hearts. He was looking at me today in math. I know it. I could feel him looking at the back of my head all the time. If I didn't like him so much, I probably would have told him to look elsewhere, but I find it sort of cute.

I tried to explain to Mom today that I needed her to buy red-colored paper so I could make him a heart. But she said it would be too obvious, and that everyone at school would laugh at me for making such a big heart for a boy. Why would I expect her to understand? She's old and probably was born holding dad's hand. It's as if destiny already had their names written on the same page. But now, destiny has a whole lot more people to take care of than back in the old days.

Wish me luck on capturing Connor's heart,

Nicole Henderson

I rolled my eyes. I couldn't have been that stupid just a few years ago. I tossed the diary into the corner of my room, the only corner that was dark. I used that corner to put the stuff I wanted to throw away, and that diary was a definite must go. I would've kept on reading it if my younger self didn't disgust me so much. I hated to admit it, but I used to act like the popular bubbleheads I now read about in books. Destiny had taken me down a whole different road. Now I had real friends, not the empire I had built up in my imagination.

I was thinking stupid again. I sat up straight and walked over to my desk. I turned on my laptop, and it began to hum with life. While it loaded, I looked up at my bulletin board. There was a list of books I wanted to read, some pictures of Violet and me, a picture of my dad in his military uniform, and several drawings I had made. After sharing art class with Skyler, they looked dull and childish, but I still kept them pinned to the board.

Beep.

The computer turned on. I quickly typed the password into my computer: *Nicole Henderson.* It wasn't the most original password, but it was easy to remember. My hands flew over the keyboard.

I ran my finger over the mouse pad and made the mouse hover over the screen. I logged into my email and checked the chat.

Friends on chat:
No contacts online

I couldn't help feeling a little disappointed. Violet usually was online, unless Skyler had caught her spying on us and...no. He couldn't have figured it out. Violet was good; she wouldn't let anyone catch her.

I threw myself on the bed again and glanced at my bookshelves. I had organized them by series and favorites; from what I could tell, nothing was out of place. I considered reading my diary again, but it didn't tempt me enough. This was a typical moment for me. I didn't know what to do. I wouldn't mind altering my normal routine, but my body refused to move. It felt good to waste time and let nothing bother me.

I tensed. I heard something. A voice? Where is it coming from? I looked down the hallway. All clear. No one was standing, walking, or going into a room, and the voice became weaker. That only meant one thing. It was coming from my room.

I walked around my room, trying to figure out where I heard it the loudest. I looked out the window, hoping children were outside making the soft whispers that were driving me crazy.

As soon as I looked down, I quickly dove under the window frame and out of sight. Why did he always show up out of the blue? It was starting to get on my nerves! Skyler was creeping the hell out of me. He paced back and forth on the sidewalk in front of my house. The guy was nuts.

I peered over the edge of the window, reminding myself that I didn't have to be seen. Skyler continued to pace the sidewalk nervously, back and forth. He occasionally looked up, stopping for a second, and then went back to wearing down the sidewalk. His hair was ruffled like it had been when we walked home from school, but now his clothes were messy and muddy. It was as if he had run through the forest for a long time and just came out.

I tried to make sense of his words by slowly opening my window, making sure he couldn't tell that I was eavesdropping. At first, I could only hear the soft whoosh of the wind blowing into my room, but then Skyler's voice became clearer. I shook my head. It was still no use. I could hear him, but I couldn't make sense of his words. I looked over the windowsill again and down at the sidewalk. Skyler was still walking back and forth, but now his face was filled with frustration and anger. At who? Himself?

I remembered Vi had taught me how to read lips. I tried now. It wasn't working as well as I expected, so I tried to mimic his lips.

"How could I..."

"Stupid thing..."

"I should know..."

"Before it's too late..."

"She knows too much..."

None of his sentences were complete. He talked too fast. Maybe I was getting it all wrong, but the last sentence I deciphered before ducking below the window did, in a certain way, chill me to the bone. "She knows too much" couldn't mean *me*. I hardly knew him. Even though I was falling for him...no I wasn't; I wouldn't fall for him. Not when he paced in front of my house like this. Maybe my neighbors couldn't hear, but they could definitely see.

Oh my God. My parents could be watching and listening. Then they'd think he was a freak, a complete psycho. I leaned against the wall and buried my face in my hands. My hair fell around my face, hiding it from the rest of the world like cascading brown curtains.

I checked my computer to see if Violet was online. Nope, still no sign of her. Through the corner of my eye, I noticed my cell phone on the night table. Should I text her? She did say she was going to log on. I mean, I knew it irritated her when I got impatient, but I needed to tell her about Skyler.

I looked out my window again, even though I knew it was stupid to do so. He would still be down there. But maybe, just maybe, when I looked, he would be gone. This was so typical of Violet, leaving me hanging, waiting for her, when I needed her most. I needed to hear her reassuring voice that I wasn't crazy and that Skyler was normal.

I shrugged. Who was I kidding? The guy was definitely not normal.

Chapter 4

Beep. Beep. Beep.

My hand slapped around my night table, trying to find the alarm clock. The noise was too loud for my ears. I couldn't find the clock. The noise beeped louder. I knew that it would keep on beeping for three minutes and then end, but my head couldn't take it.

When the realization hit me, I wanted to punch myself. I didn't have an alarm clock! How could I have been so stupid? No, asleep. I poked my left arm out of the covers and looked at my watch. Now that it wasn't muffled by the covers the alarm blared. The bright green rubber band wrapped around my wrist left a red mark on my arm. I must have fallen asleep on top of it.

I turned off the alarm and slipped out of bed. Despite the fact that it was fall, the air was still taking its time to cool down. I stood in front of my mirror and looked at myself. My eyes were squinted, because I had forgotten to close the curtains last night, and now my room was flooded with light. My oversized orange t-shirt read *Nobody's perfect. I'm nobody*. The way it hung over my body and my messed up hair made me look like a hobo.

I put on my dinosaur slippers and headed downstairs. When I got to the kitchen, I could smell the eggs frying. That meant that my brother was up and about to come down. He usually wasn't home, but college hadn't started yet, and he liked taking a five-mile run in the morning.

My mother was dressed in white pants and a soft lilac shirt with ruffles near the neck. She wore her large pearl earrings and a thin silver chain around her neck. Her hair was tied up in a bun pinned in place with a flower. "Good morning, Sugar. How did you sleep last night?" Her voice was clear. She had woken up a while ago.

I slumped onto a stool next to the kitchen island. I looked down at the bowl my mother placed in front of me. It was filled to the rim with oats and honey wheels. My favorite. "Thanks." My voice croaked. I hated it, but it always happened when I just woke up.

"So, today's your second day..." Her voice trailed off, leaving the sentence unfinished. She wiped her hands on the front of her apron. Her damp hands left darker trails on the white fabric. "Remember not to miss the bus. Unless you're walking, then you have to leave early."

"Good morning, Ashwick!" My brother marched into the room and swung himself onto the stool next to me. I was surprised that it didn't break or that he didn't fall off the side. His hair was combed, unlike mine, and he wore a blue tracksuit with three white stripes down the sides. "Yum, I could smell the eggs from the stairs." My mother set down his plate in front of him.

There was a soft knock on the front door. We all perked up in our seats and looked at each other.

"Well, that's a surprise." My mom took off her apron, folded it neatly, and shut the drawer. After touching up her bun, she went to see who was at the door, leaving Steven and me alone.

Steven smiled mischievously at me. Uh-oh. "Can I ask you a question?" He turned his whole body to face me. This wasn't good. It's never good when a brother suddenly wants to talk.

"Sure, what's up?" I smiled sarcastically at him, as if I would be delighted to answer any of his weird, strange, or gross questions.

He rubbed his chin. It made a scratching sound, so I supposed he hadn't shaved. "You know that boy...what's his name...Skyler? Can you explain why he was walking in front of our house yesterday?" Even though he was trying to act mature, he took way too big of a bite from his eggs, which made me gag in disgust. When would he grow up?

I shrugged. He saw. If he saw Skyler, I wonder if Mom and Dad had seen him too. This was bad. Steven would probably tell them whenever he got mad at me. Or worse. He'd probably invent some creepy story that would make Mom and Dad never let me see him again. But what did I care if I didn't see him again? It wasn't as if I had a crush on him or anything. I might have had mixed feelings yesterday, but after the pacing scene, it was a definite *no*.

"And you think that I know? Steve, it's not like I know each and every single move he makes. He's not even a friend."

My brother shook his head. "Well, he certainly thinks that you're his friend. If not, I don't think he would have walked in front of our house yesterday as if he were Romeo waiting for Juliet to open her window. Oh, and I forgot that your window has a view to the front yard. Isn't that a coincidence?!" He laughed at his own joke.

I didn't find it funny. His jokes were always bad. If Steven were ever to work as a comedian, well, he would probably starve to death. "Think whatever you want. I don't mind. And he is sort of attached."

My mother walked through the door and pointed at me, looking confused. Her eyebrows were knitted together, and her eyes were vacant. This usually meant that she couldn't find an explanation for the situation at hand. "It's for you."

I walked to the entryway, hoping my mom would follow, but she didn't. I opened the front door, the knob warm to my hands. Skyler stood on the other side of the screen door, his hands in his pockets, his backpack hanging on both of his shoulders, and a helpless smile on his face. Was he trying to hide laughter? I froze. I was still wearing my pajamas. Oh my gosh. "I...I didn't know that it was going to be you."

He looked around. "Well then, I think I'm going to have to change my name when I come here." He laughed at his own joke. I would have too, but the heat was rising to my cheeks at an incredibly fast rate. "I came around to ask if you want to walk with me to school. I don't mind waiting for you to change, unless today is pajama day."

I nodded and opened the screen door. As weird as this situation was, my mother would have never allowed rudeness. "Sure, in the meantime, come inside..."

"No, I think I'll wait on the steps. Thank you, anyway." He sat down on the porch steps, his back facing me. I bet he was smiling.

I went back into the house, shutting the door behind me but not locking it. I stayed there for a second, leaning against the door, and looked down at myself. I was in my freaking pajamas, and I opened the door for him. I looked around to see if anyone had been looking at us while we spoke. No one. I was sort of hoping that Steven was spying, so I had an excuse to go marching up the stairs angry.

I changed into some jeans and a peach t-shirt that looked pretty and girly with my brown hair. I put on some makeup and combed my hair. I looked at myself in the mirror with satisfaction.

"Mom, I'm walking today!" I yelled at my mother, who surely was in the kitchen with Steven, and ran down the stairs. I opened the front door and closed it slowly behind me, as if I hadn't hurried. Skyler was still sitting on the steps when I turned around. "Let's go," I said in a peppy mood.

We began to walk together down the concrete sidewalk. There were some paw prints embedded in the concrete. Apparently, an animal had crossed the sidewalk when the

S. Elizabeth Dover

concrete was still wet, and then the concrete hardened with the tracks in it. It was funny how essential those random paw prints were. They gave me something to stare at when there was nothing to talk about with the stranger I walking with to school.

Skyler spoke first. "I promise, I won't tell anyone about your pajamas." He looked at me under uncut hair. I wondered what he would look like with trimmed hair. He usually ruffled it and looked through it as if trying to look cool.

"Why would I be concerned about my PJs? They're perfectly normal." I moved slightly to the side. His hand bumped into mine for a millisecond, and I blushed. He drew his hand away.

He raised an eyebrow. "'Nobody's perfect. I'm nobody.'?" He muffled his laughter by covering his mouth discreetly, lifting his shirt slightly and showing his flat stomach. I tried to look away.

I said I tried.

I swayed from side to side as I walked on the curb. I tried not to fall from that narrow edge of concrete that only permitted one foot to go in front of the other. "What? That shirt is so true. 'Cause I am nobody; I bet half the school doesn't even recognize my existence. And because I am perfect." My smile was smug. I stuffed my hands into the pockets of my sweatshirt.

Skyler's eyes looked greener today. Maybe it was just because of the morning light, but I've heard of people whose eyes slightly change with the weather. "Ok, wait. You're perfect?" He laughed. "If you're perfect, then I'm a unicorn."

"So majestic." I batted my eye lashes.

"Exactly."

He walked strangely, sort of like the way he looked at me, steadily closing in. His feet moved silently against the ground, and his arms seemed to set pace for his whole body. He looked like a hunter. His arms showed it. Hard muscles padded his upper body. He could crack my neck. The task would be as easy as eliminating a small insect.

When he looked at me, I tensed.

"What are you afraid of?" His head tilted like it did when he was painting.

Goosebumps crawled over my skin, and a cold feeling spread throughout my body, making me shiver. He couldn't read my thoughts, but he sure acted as if he could. "I'm afraid of heights."

His expression changed. He didn't believe me. His eyes were still locked on me. I bet he was wondering how to use it against me. "You must be kidding."

I shook my head. "I've never been able to climb higher than the second branch of a tree. Guess I'm afraid to fall. What about you? What are you afraid of?"

"Nothing."

I felt like laughing. Not a normal laugh, but the outbursts that make you look insane. I held it back. "Why don't you tell me anything? I mean, I don't even know where you come from. A town, a city, a farm?" I grabbed a leaf from a nearby branch and traced the small veins that stuck out on its backside.

His hand was in his pocket now, no longer grabbing the strap of his backpack. It looked as if he were holding something not too small, bigger than a pocketknife, but not too big like a large wallet. He twisted it in his hand but kept it out of my view. "I moved from a relatively large city. I'm going to have to go back again sometime...maybe you'll come and visit?"

"Maybe. What's the city called, or is that also classified information?" I looked up at him for a second; we locked eyes, and then I went back to the leaf. Since I was a young girl, I always found it quite addicting to trace all the fine lines of a leaf.

He kicked a rock, I believe, in attempt to control his impulses. I could see he really wanted to take the object he was holding out of his pocket. My stare dared him to take it out and show me, but he wasn't looking at me directly in the eyes. "It's called Arcane. I'm sure you haven't heard of it."

He was right. I had never heard of the place until now, but it sounded sinister. "It has a strange name. Where is it? Maybe I could find it on a map at school."

"It would be no use. It's not on any map." He looked at me now. Maybe it was a cell phone. Did he have to call someone but didn't want to be rude? Or maybe he got a text message, and his phone was vibrating.

"What do you mean, it isn't on a map? It has to be. Every little town is there, even Ashwick!"

He extended his hand to me, palm up. "I'll bet you. If you lose, you have to overcome your fear tonight." His voice was filled with danger, causing red flags to appear in my mind. This guy could really change his mood quickly.

I knew that I should say no. Every single part of me screamed that. I shouldn't..."Fine, but what do *you* do If I win?"

I tossed the leaf aside and watched it linger in the air before silently resting on the grass.

"I won't lose, so I don't have to do anything," he said matter-of-factly. "But if you insist, I'll eat three worms." He took hold of my hand in a firm handshake. His hand was large and the thin scars felt like the ripples on water under my fingers. His handshake was strong and felt like he was never going to let go. But eventually, he did, and we started making our way to school again at a faster pace.

I hadn't realized before, but now I did. My hand was throbbing and shaking. I stuffed it in my pocket, hoping he wouldn't notice. I looked at him through the corner of my eye. He wasn't paying attention to me.

We turned the corner. Now, the school was in sight. We could be watched. I could feel him walk a few steps ahead of me. We were on opposite sides of the sidewalk, which was pretty far away compared to our previous positions. I didn't mind, though. I think I liked this better than bumping hands.

"How will you make me overcome my fear if I lose?" I asked.

"So, you do admit that you'll lose."

I shook my head. "No, I'm just curious, that's all."

"Well it's for me to know and for you to find out." He opened his mouth to say something more, but then shut it when he saw a short figure running toward us.

Violet stopped a few feet in front of us and looked at me wide-eyed. "I was waiting for you, but then the bus came and you didn't get off. I thought something happened to you, 'cause you know, you never miss a day of school. Ever!" Her eyes shifted to Skyler. "Hey, Skyler." She shrugged and raised an eyebrow. She was trying to act as if she didn't care he was there.

Skyler smiled with a little laughter and stretched out his hand. "I think this is the first time we've met, and you already know my name. Hi. You must be...?"

"Nicole told me you are really cute...you have a really cute name, and... Did you know your face reminds me of my... cousin? So yeah...hi, I'm Violet." She looked at me nervously. Her brown eyes screamed, "Help me!" She was talking too fast—that was the problem. And when Violet talked fast, she would just blurt out whatever was on her mind. She still hadn't noticed that she should take his hand and greet him properly, so I eyed her and nudged my head in the direction of his outstretched hand.

When their hands let go, Violet stood, petrified, as if she had just seen Medusa and looked into her snaky mane. Skyler sensed it and swayed slightly from side to side. "We better get going if we want to make it to class."

"You should walk with us." I blurted out. I could hear Violet sigh.

He nodded, his brown hair bobbing up and down. "I don't mind."

Violet walked by my side as we made our way into the familiar hallways, too small for the number of students pushing their way through the crowd. We tried to stay next to each other, but sometimes we had to form a single-file line in order to move.

Even though Violet was small, she was the one who most people noticed. People turned their heads to look at her long trailing locks, which bounced behind her as she walked, and her fashionable clothes.

I looked at my friend who was trying to avoid my gaze. "The words just fell out of my mouth. I really couldn't stop them," I whispered, hoping he couldn't hear.

She shrugged it off and smiled, relieved. "Good, now we're even." She looked past me at Skyler. "So, where do you come from?"

"A city."

"You don't say. Which one?"

He looked at her, straight on, fearlessly. "You don't need to know."

She looked at me with her eyebrow raised. *Really?* She spoke to me without words. Clearly, she was irritated. I had to admit, I was also a bit hurt and annoyed when he played hard. Weren't girls the ones to play hard to get? Weren't we the ones who should act mysterious?

"Okay, and where are you staying at now? And who are you staying with?" Violet was more insistent now. She wasn't the kind to shrug it off. She was cautious and careful, an excellent human polygraph.

"Why do you care?" Skyler snapped back. He didn't look at her. He was smart enough to realize that it would have been a bad move. But something deeper was hidden in his attitude.

Violet touched up her hair and rolled her eyes. "Because I'm getting to know you. I mean, isn't that what people do when they don't know each other? Ask questions?"

I rested my hand on Violet's shoulder and pushed some locks of curly hair out of the way while I got close to her ear. "Maybe you should act a bit softer." My eyes pleaded with her, waiting for an answer.

Violet looked past me at him. "I just want to keep my friend safe." I turned to Skyler. I knew by the way she said it that she wasn't talking to me, but to the boy whose presence disturbed her. And to think that yesterday she was asking me about him like a cat drawn to a canary.

Skyler gazed into the crowd with a troubled look. "I have somewhere to be." He excused himself politely and disappeared down the hall.

I shut Violet up before she could yell something at him. "You really didn't have to do that." I felt like my mother when I was five years old, telling me to stop drawing on the walls with my favorite magenta crayon. Of course, her tone had been much more imposing and strong, mine was just a warning.

Violet shook her head. "I don't care. But what I do care about is that he is a freak, and you shouldn't be alone with him, ever. Do you understand?" She smiled at me sadly. "I'm scared."

"About what?"

"I'm not sure, but he has weird vibes. Anyway, I gotta go. My locker is in the other direction, and I need to be in class on time, okay?"

"Nothing bad will happen, Vi. I promise," I reassured her with a soft and calm voice as she scurried away. Why did she suddenly leave? She never cared about getting to class on time...

Chapter 5

Violet's voice hushed the noise around us, dimming it like the last embers in a campfire. The words she sang were clear, and I recognized them immediately. How could I miss them? She had been singing this song since the age of seven.

I listened as her voice faded into a soft piano and then ended with a hum, which slowly turned to silence. The birds didn't dare sing yet, nor did any animal nearby in the woods dare to move or crack a twig. I didn't dare speak and interrupt the calm atmosphere Violet had just created, so she spoke first. "I don't like it when the clouds move so slowly. It bores me because they hardly change." Her head was tilted backward as she walked. She still hadn't told me anything about the real reason for her sudden escape that morning. I wasn't going to push her to tell me, even though I was dying to know why. It was related to Skyler, that I was sure.

I kept looking at the ground, but occasionally I glanced into the dense forest and thought that maybe Skyler was following us, like Violet had done yesterday. I shivered at the thought. Perhaps telling her something about Skyler might encourage her to share her feelings. "Yesterday, Skyler was pacing in front of my house, where *everyone* could see him, and he was talking to himself. I could tell because his lips were moving." I realized how fast I had spoken and looked at Violet to see if she had grasped anything I had said. I wasn't sure, so I repeated the last part. "He was walking in front of my house, talking to himself or something like that."

Violet nodded with a half chuckle but didn't look up. We hadn't made eye contact the whole day, something that reconfirmed my suspicions. "I understood your gibberish, Nikki. I'm used to it, but what I don't understand is why he would be there if he had already left. I watched him leave."

But he came back.

He knew that Violet was following. But how?

* * *

I sorted Mom's chocolate chip cookies from smallest to largest. I touched the rough surface of the cookies, making crumbs fall onto my bedspread like tiny boulders freeing themselves from the flat, edgy surface. There was a soft ping from my computer, and the conversation box popped up. Violet. I didn't get up. Not that I didn't want to talk to her. No, but because I was watching the strangest boy on earth pacing in front of my house, *again*. But this time, I brought a snack along for the spectacle to see how long he would stand, walk, and mumble there. Then I would tell Violet. First, I had to see how long he would last.

I heard the beep again. The computer screen flashed one more time, illuminating my room for a brief second, like lighting illuminating the dark sky. The lights of my room were off. I didn't want him to see me watching or suspect that someone could peer down at him, putting at risk whatever he was doing or trying to do.

He looked up at my window. I froze. Could he see me? We held each other's gaze for seconds that passed after an eternity of silence. I could feel him watching me, looking past the reflection of the window. I was far enough away to stay hidden but close enough to have the best view. I exhaled with relief when his eyes fell to the sidewalk, and he began pacing again.

I heard footsteps approaching my bedroom door. Soft steps. Too soft to be my brother or my dad, so that only left one person. But her feet didn't stop in front of my door. My mom only came in to leave clean clothes or to clean. She walked past my door, opened hers, and shut it behind her with a *click*. My mom's footsteps were the only sound I had heard in a while, besides the constant beeps from my computer. I think it had been...what, fifteen minutes since someone broke the haunting silence? I crept a bit closer to the window and placed my fingertips against it. They squished up against the glass, and when I removed them, small ovals were left where my fingers had just been.

I slid open the window; the afternoon air was less humid than before. Now, a soft breeze replaced the ever-present pressure. "You know, you should stop doing that," I called down to the startled boy. "My parents will think you're stalking me. My brother already thinks you're a creep." I spoke from the edge of the window.

Skyler reddened but quickly regained his composure. "You saw?"

"Busted," I sighed.

He shook his head and ran his fingers through his hair, shaking it, messing it up. "This is..."

I cut him off rudely, but not intentionally. Lie—very intentionally. "Awfully embarrassing? Yes, it really must be for you. Do you want to come inside and get a drink?" My hair was tied up in bun that weighed down on me as I stuck almost half of my torso out the window and looked down, waiting for an answer. I could feel myself wanting a yes, but my guts told me no.

Skyler looked up at me again and smiled. "I wouldn't mind." Did I see a wink when he finished? I didn't hang out any longer to find out. I closed the window and jumped from my bed to my computer in an easy leap, landing in front of the desk. I typed quickly, telling Violet that Skyler showed up, and I had invited him in. I waited for an answer, but none came in the short time that I waited. I quickly threw on a sweater and ran down the stairs, skipping every other step as I went down.

I landed on the wooden floor below and made my way to the front door. I opened the door and shut it immediately behind me. Skyler looked confused. I already guessed what he was going to ask before he said it.

S. Elizabeth Dover

"We're going through the back door," I said without explanation. "By the way, why were you walking in front of my house again?" I didn't look at him; instead, I led him over the short picket fence that separated the front yard from the back. My parents had put up that fence when I was a child, so I couldn't escape and wander off into the woods like Steven had done so many times.

Skyler rubbed his hands together and jumped the fence as if it were a mere stump. He looked at me and smiled. I guessed he was waiting for some kind of compliment, but he didn't get any such thing. I took advantage of the moment to look down at his pocket, the one that held something he wouldn't show me. His right pocket sagged under the weight of a medium-sized object. He followed my gaze and turned to his side, walking into my garden as if he were admiring the view. What he really was doing was hiding the pocket from my view.

I showed him into the kitchen. My hand glided over the stone countertop and opened the overhead cupboard to grab a cup. The glass was cold against my somewhat tanned skin. I hardly tanned in the summer, and now the minor track of summer was fading fast.

"What do you want to drink?" I asked politely, without looking at him. He mumbled "anything," so I opened the fridge, pulled out a jar of water, and filled the cup. I closed the fridge with the small *thump* and handed the cup to Skyler.

Our fingers touched as he took the cup with his firm hands. He held his hands still, as if wanting to touch my fingers. I looked up at him with one eyebrow raised. His smile was dashing. But then, he let go and took a sip from the cup, looking over the rim with his strange eyes. He put the cup down on the counter and walked toward me.

"Thanks." He stopped only inches away. Suddenly, everything was silent, and the only thing I could hear was my heart. I could feel the pulse in my neck, the very same spot he had breathed on in art. I looked away to hide the heat that was rising in my cheeks.

He had a strange effect on me. He freaked me out like hell, he read my thoughts, and he made me feel strange inside. I had to come up with something to say. The silence was too loud for me, and it was getting uncomfortable. "I lost the bet." I looked back at him. His eyes looked greener now.

"I know."

I moved to scratch my left arm but accidentally bumped my hand on his stomach as it made its way up. I mumbled "sorry," but he didn't seem to be bothered much. Still, I was more concerned about how I was going to face my fear tonight. I remembered perfectly when I went to the library this morning. It had been silent; almost no one was there except for the librarian, two teachers, another student, and me. I had crept to the very last computer and Googled "City of Arcane." That's when I realized I had lost. There were no matches, only related names, but no City of Arcane. "So, how am I going to overcome my fear?"

He grabbed my hand and began to pull me toward the back door. "Let's go." I tried to resist at first, and then I let myself be led.

"Nikki . . . I'm sorry. I didn't know you had a friend over, sweetheart." My mother stood, immobile, in the kitchen doorway. One of her hands was holding the door open, and the other was playing with her necklace, a nervous habit she had.

She looked down at our hands. I blushed and quickly pulled my hand out of his and dropped it to my side. "Mom, this is Skyler. He's...new at school, and I invited him in to have a drink." I looked at the bridge of her nose, because I didn't dare look in her eyes. I felt fiery embarrassment run through my veins. "We were just leaving," I added quickly, walking toward the back door. My mom regained her composure and obliged me to stay where I was standing with an icy cold stare.

"Don't usher him out like that." Her voice sounded sweeter than ever. She was trying to act as if it didn't bother her, which clearly it did. She had, however, underestimated Skyler's skill at reading people. "Hello, you must be Skyler. We've heard wonderful things about you."

My mouth dropped. She did not just say that! "My name is Karen Henderson; I'm Nicole's mother. How are you?"

Skyler walked toward my mom and shook her hand. "I'm fine, thank you." He looked at me and then at my mother. Uh-oh. A smile spread across his lips, showing his remarkable white teeth. "Now I can see where she gets her looks."

My mother nodded, grinning. She touched her hair, another sign of nervousness. "Thank you, Skyler, that's very nice of you. Do you have to leave now, or can you stay a bit longer? No wait, I just had the most wonderful idea. Why don't you stay for dinner?"

* * *

"I can't believe you told my mom that she has looks. Do you really think she's pretty?" I asked, as Skyler and I walked down the sidewalk to the place where I was going to face my fear. The forest looked different at night. Instead of all these shades of green and different textures, there was only one dark shade of green that hid the beauty from human eyes.

Skyler walked closer than ever now. Next to me. On the sidewalk. In the dark. I shuddered. There was hardly any light, and his features cast shadows on his face, making him look forbidden, dangerous, and beautiful. His voice was lower now, as if he had been sleeping for a while. "No, I think you're beautiful." He was dead serious, but I felt that there was sarcasm hidden underneath.

I shook my head. "You wish."

He grabbed my arm as he has done so many times. "Look over there." He pointed to the school. I should have known; I walked or rode the bus down this way practically every day! "You're going to climb up to the roof all by yourself."

I shook my head. He couldn't make me. "You're nuts!" I laughed. But inside, really deep inside, I knew that I shouldn't be laughing at all. I was terrified and knew that soon I'd be shaking.

He looked at me with stern eyes, which looked pitch black in the darkness. "You bet and you lost. You should be more careful when you make promises." He grabbed my hand, just like he had done at home, and made me run until we crossed the road and rounded the school. "There aren't any cameras here, so we'll be fine. Oh, and remember, I'm going to be right behind you." He spun me around, and I was facing the wall.

"I must inform you that I'm no Spiderman," I said, turning my head to the side so I wasn't talking to the wall.

"Look harder." There it was again. His breath on my neck. But this time, it wasn't warm and pleasant but cold. Ice cold.

I patted the wall with my hands and found a slippery ladder rung, which was more like a handle. Then I felt a bit higher and found another step just like the first, just as slippery. I tensed. No way. Over my dead body was he going to get me to go up there! I would have to climb up two stories. What if I fell down?! That would definitely kill me. But I had lost a bet, and I couldn't chicken out in front of Skyler. No, I had to be tough. My body trembled, and my heart raced. I grabbed the first rung and pulled myself up, helping myself by pushing off the wall with my feet. My mind told itself only one thing. *Climb up, don't look down. Climb up, don't look down. Climb up, don't look down.* I repeated it so many times that it became a chant and the rhythm to my ascension. One rung after another; I was climbing pretty fast and to a constant rhythm.

It felt like an eternity, but I kept on going until no more rungs were left. I threw myself over the edge of the wall and gasped. *I made it. I made it.* I smiled on the outside but inside, I was worried about the way down. It's always easier going up. I felt a hand on the small of my back that pushed me into a sitting position.

Skyler smiled a real smile. I'd never seen it before. He was proud and shocked. I bet he was thinking that I was going to chicken out on the first few rungs and plead to him to let me down, but I actually made it all the way up. "I think you lied to me, Nikki." It startled me that he used the nickname only my brother and Violet used. "You went faster than I ever could have gone. Congratulations." He helped me up to my feet but didn't let go. I thanked him for that, because if not, I would have fallen back down. I was running out of air from breathing too much of his scent.

Slowly, Skyler pushed me down onto a folding chair. "Where did this come from?" I asked. I had already gotten my breath back; my skin was flushed and my heart steadied. The folding chair looked like the ones golfers took onto the course as they waited. The rough cloth had a camouflage design, and it gave under my weight, making it more comfortable to sit on.

Skyler pointed to the center of the roof. It was flat and made out of cement. The school's roof made the perfect place for hanging out, or in his case, I discovered, a temporary home. There was a small portable oven, the kind people use when they went camping, that shone silver under the soft glow of the crescent moon. Next to it, there was a foldable table for one or two people and a tent, which surely had a sleeping bag, a pillow, and a bag with his clothes. "Welcome to my humble abode."

I raised my eyebrows, looked around, and then looked back at him. "How did you get everything up here?" He could have strapped everything onto his back and then climbed up the ladder, but how did he get the freaking table onto the roof? His arms showed that he was strong, so did his grasp, but *that* strong? I wiggled my way out of the chair without bumping into him. He was leaning a bit too close.

He stepped away, getting my indirect message, and walked by my side as I stepped nearer to his strange campsite. "I brought it all up here. How else?" It was a stupid question to ask, of course, but I had to ask. As I rounded the table to get closer to the tent, I ran my hand over the plastic tabletop. Skyler imitated me, walking close behind and covering my hand with his. I drew mine up quickly before he caught it, and I spun around to face him so it didn't seem so noticeable.

"Can we go down now? I'm not feeling so comfortable up here. We're so far away from the ground." I ran my fingers through my hair, which was still tied up in a loose bun. I saw him look at my hair and then tilt his head.

He came closer, still looking at my hair and then his eyes dropped and stayed steadily on mine. "I've never seen you with your hair loose. Can I see it before we go?" Really? I was going to say no, but no harm would come from it. I nodded, and he slowly pulled the rubber band out of my hair before I could do it myself. Creepy.

My hair cascaded over my shoulders, blown by the soft breeze that was more perceptible from the roof than the sidewalk below. "Where are we going?"

The clouds above moved faster now. The soft white puffs of cotton candy stroked the sky and occasionally hid the moon from sight, creating a dark curtain over the small town underneath. "You partly faced your fear," he commented, ignoring my question. "Now I want you to walk with me and sit on the edge."

My stomach fell. No.

"Come on." He read the fear on my face, the tension of my body.

"I'll walked to the edge but no sitting on the ledge," I stated as we walked slowly toward front of the roof. I didn't want to look down. I instinctively shut my eyes and grabbed Skyler's hand tightly. I was willingly taking his hand. This was a moment that should go down in history. I could tell we got to the ledge, because we stopped moving and he pressed my hand lightly. I peeped through my still-shut eyelids and looked down. I could see green, yellow, white, and red. I opened my eyes a bit more and saw what I was really looking at.

The ground looked so much farther away than just two stories. I could hardly make out the tiny flowers on the large bush that covered the principal's office window, and the grass was a cheesy shade of green still marked by the lawnmower. The building's bricks were a dark terracotta color because the street lacked illumination. I could feel Skyler's arms around my shoulders, and he slowly, but softly, pushed me forward.

I screamed. I screamed as loud as I could, but he covered my mouth when he pulled me back onto the roof. For a second, I thought he let go. He might have if I hadn't screamed. He could have killed me. I panted. "You could have given me a freaking heart attack! Have you gone insane?! I could have fallen!" I punched him on the chest and collapsed onto the roof, shaking. "You could have killed me," I mumbled to myself, but loud enough so he could hear me. My stomach was lodged in my throat, and all the blood in my head had drained down to the rest of my body, making me feel incredibly chilly and dizzy.

Skyler sat next to me and nudged my arm. "Oh come on, don't exaggerate." He ran his hand over mine so I would look at him, but the results weren't as he had expected. I still wasn't looking at him, but he figured out that my skin was cold. And since he was *such* a gentleman, he fetched a sleeping bag and draped it over my shoulders, so I wouldn't freeze to death. "It's too cold for the beginning of autumn, don't you think?" he asked. He clearly didn't know Ashwick.

I shrugged. "It usually gets cold at night." I could feel the heaviness of the sleeping over my shoulders. Skyler squirmed next to me, taking the free end of the sleeping bag and wrapping it around him. Our shoulders touched as we sat silently on the roof. This was one of those awkward moments when no one had anything to say; nor did anyone want to talk. I didn't like sitting so close to him, so I silently thanked whoever was calling me on my cell phone that vibrated in the front pocket of my sweatshirt. "Hello?" I brought the device to my ears and waited for an answer.

"Where are you?" It was Violet. "You sent me a message like three hours ago, and you haven't spoken to me since! What are you doing?" I could feel her suspicion of Skyler grow immensely. She must have thought that I had been kidnapped.

I scooted away from Skyler, stood up, and walked to the farthest end of the roof, away from him, maintaining my space from the edge. "I'm at, no, on the school's roof."

"What?!"

"Yeah, it sounds..."

"What are you doing there? Who are you with? You're not with *him*, are you?" she drilled her questions at me with impressive speed. I could already picture her pacing around her room, dragging her feet on the white carpet, or sprawling across her bed with a book thrown open at her side and fiddling with the large dream catcher hanging above her bed.

I lowered my voice so Skyler couldn't overhear, which I highly doubted. "No, I'm up here because I lost a bet and I needed to face my fear of heights. And yes, I'm with him." I combed my hair with my free hand. I was getting cold without the sleeping bag wrapped around my shoulders.

I heard her sudden intake of breath and waited for her to exhale. She never did. "Get off of the roof."

"Now?"

"Yes!" she demanded. I could hear someone call her. "I'm coming down in a bit!" she yelled back. "Sorry, I'm at a family reunion, but if you seriously don't get down now, I will go and make you come down." There was a short pause before she added something else. "Remember how I thought that I had seen Skyler somewhere else?"

I looked at the split ends of my hair with the little light the moon provided. I twisted them in between my fingers and watched them spin. "Yeah."

"He's not who he says he is. Just wait for me, and I'll explain everything." After a short silence, she hung up.

S. Elizabeth Dover

I walked over to where Skyler was sitting. He had turned on the camping oven to simulate a bonfire. "Sorry, it was Violet, she just called because she had a problem and needs me to go over to her house. Plus, my parents must be freaking out that we're taking so long." I tried to cover the lie and make it sound real.

He stared at my blank face for a while, deciding whether or not to trust me. He stood up, folded the sleeping bag, tossed it into the tent, and turned off the oven. We walked together toward the metal ladder that was our only way down.

"Ladies first." He signaled with his hand. I turned around and tried not to look down as I stepped onto the first rung. When I put my last hand on the rung, he touched my shoulder.

"Good-bye." I smiled and nodded, but he touched my hand once more, making me look up. I couldn't shake off his hand, because I would fall. I glared at him and asked what he wanted. "I'm so sorry I have to do this." We looked in each other's eyes for what seemed like forever. What did he mean? He put both his hands firmly on my shoulders. I waited for the reason for his apology. No reason came, just the force of two hands pushing me away from the ladder. I tried to regain my grip on the rungs, but they were too far away.

I was falling. Fast.

I clawed the air for something to grab and stop my fall. Of course, my efforts were in vain. The building was too far away. No tree branches softened my fall, just empty space between the ground and me. With a bit of help of gravity, it would all end soon.

I felt hopeless, a small baby bird that hadn't yet learned to fly and just jumped to test its wings. But I knew I wouldn't make it. My mind flashed. My vision went black...and then saw reality again. I was closer to the ground now. I could feel it. Skyler was looking at me with a grin on his face. Bastard. The world turned dark for another second.

I heard a thump, no, a crack.

No, both.

Pain spread all over my body like electricity through water. My brain, head, bones, lungs, heart—everything hurt. I couldn't breathe. The air had been violently pushed out of my lungs. When I tried to inhale, something pinched me. I wasn't getting any air, so I stopped trying.

All I could do was lie flat on the recently trimmed grass and await my death. The clouds moved strangely above. They curled and danced around the moon but never hid it. My imagination was mocking me. I heard a thump nearby. Skyler. I would have tensed if it didn't hurt so much. Why was this taking so long? Why couldn't I die and end this? I should have known. There were so many signs.

He stopped next to me and knelt down. He was going to pray for me! I would have laughed, but my body was already beginning to suffer from oxygen deprivation. His face showed repulsion when he saw that my eyes were open. His eyes looked tauntingly green. I made out something of what he said. "How did you survive...?" and "They warned me they get harder to kill each time...."

This was planned? I managed to get a bit of air. Just half a breath, but that was more than enough. My lungs ached even more just storing this tiny bit of oxygen. My thoughts were crushed by a huge headache that hammered my skull from the inside and made my brain feel like goo. I tried to move. Oh, crap. It all hurt too much. So I went to the smaller body parts. My eyes were the only things that didn't hurt at the moment, but I tasted a raw, metallic flavor in my mouth. Blood. I must have bitten my tongue when I fell. It hurt but not as bad as it would if I had sliced it with my not-so-sharp teeth.

I tried to move a toe. It hurt. My head. Deadly pain took over my movements and froze me on the spot. Skyler was still looking at me, surely trying to figure out what to do now, how to end me since the fall failed to do so. I managed to move one finger that wasn't in terrifying pain. I tapped the soft green grass beneath me. Now it felt soft; before it had felt like solid concrete.

I took in jagged breaths. My heart hammered belligerently in my chest. It seemed to say, "I'm alive. You're alive too," but I wished it would just stop and end this once and for all.

Skyler stood up now. He heard something. So did I. I had heard this expression in a book—it was called being "icy." It's when all of your senses were prickling and awake, as if the fog had been lifted and you suddenly saw everything clearer, the way it actually was. Everything was much sharper. I heard the sound of a car door shutting. There was no engine starting, so I supposed someone had seen me and was coming to my rescue.

Skyler left my side and pulled an object from his pocket, the same object he had hidden from me this morning. I heard a soft whimper and then a *snap*. I closed my eyes, afraid he had just harmed my rescuer. When he spoke, he reassured me that the person was very much alive. "Did you call anyone?" he asked. There was no answer, and he wasn't in the mood for patience. "I said, did you call anyone?!" His voice was filled with frustration.

A soft sigh followed the sound of someone getting knocked down.

The person had answered, and now Skyler didn't need them, so he disposed of him or her. I began to cry, my tears like acid against my skin. I began to drool involuntarily. The smell reeked of blood.

Skyler came back to my side and smiled weakly at me. He grabbed my arms and pulled. I screeched. The sound was horrible, like a dying animal. I was dying. There wasn't much difference, was there? One of my arms hung in a strange, unnatural position and now screamed for the pulling to stop. The most probable explanation was that my arm had been dislocated from the socket when I fell.

My legs felt like sand bags that weighed down my body and resisted the rough pull. I felt tiny needles prickle my back and make my legs go numb as I was dragged into the forest. The tall trees looked like giants now. Their large trunks and broad branches loomed overhead. The leaves filtered the moonlight and hid the stars from view. I moaned. The sound that escaped my lips made more blood spurt out. It trailed along my chin and dripped down the side of my throat onto my shirt.

I felt Skyler's disgust at my condition. He thought he could kill me just by throwing me off a roof. He thought I was weak. He stopped dragging me. One would think this would have relieved some pain, but the pain only increased.

"There we go." He spoke to himself and reappeared in my vision. "You really don't want to die, do you? But I guess I'll see you soon." He winked at me and pulled out what he had been hiding from me that morning—a long, shiny knife. It was stained now. He had apparently used it against the other person and hadn't cleaned off the blood. He put the flat side of the blade against my skin and ran it down my arm until he got to my wrist. He stopped there. I moved my fingers in protest. He couldn't do this! But it was already too late to do anything. It had been too late when I got onto the roof, when I had made the bet.

His knife bit into the soft flesh of my wrist. He cut the main artery. I would be dead in seconds. I could already feel the numbness tug me to an endless rest. My heart raced, its beat unsteady and unsure as liquid poured from my wrists, emptying my body for good.

The last thing I saw before darkness enveloped me was Skyler, Skyler kissing my cheek and closing my eyes. I wish I could have fought back. I could hear my father's voice telling me that I was a fighter. My dad was wrong. I was never a fighter. I had been weak from the beginning. I had fallen quickly into the net of emotions I had created and, consequently, I killed two people, one of them being myself.

I heard Violet's voice, "I don't care. But what I *do* care is that he is a freak, and you shouldn't be alone with him, ever. Do you understand?" She smiled at me sadly. "I'm scared."

"About what?" Now my voice echoed in my head, filling the hollowness I felt.

She didn't answer now. Her presences vanished slowly.

Now the silence stayed. It felt cold, excruciatingly cold and empty. Now I knew what death felt like—an eternity.

Chapter 6

I wandered in the darkness, without the slightest clue about where I was headed or in which direction I was moving. There was no way to keep track of time, since no sun rose over the horizon, warming the abyss in which I was stuck. No moon gave off its white glow to break the impenetrable darkness. The icy, motionless air bit me to the bone and, despite my tiring attempts at regaining my body temperature, the cold stuck to me—a constant reminder that I was dead.

I was dead.

Or at least that's what I thought. I could feel my body, even though I couldn't see it. The only real difference was that I tired easily, which forced me to sleep on the solid ground until I had enough strength to pick myself up again. I had lost my ability to hear, with the exception of a high-pitched ringing in my ears, and I couldn't feel the normal vibrations of my voice.

I had never thought that I could take my body to heaven, hell, or purgatory. I had been taught that the body was merely physical, and only the soul survived death. I couldn't be sure, so I supposed that I was stuck in some sort of limbo, my soul unable move on. I was screwed.

Not only was the vast darkness cold, but it also gave me the sensation that I wasn't alone. Someone, somewhere, was watching me make my way through the emptiness. I couldn't hear, and I couldn't see. Since the air stood abnormally still, no scents were carried from place to place.

I kept on walking in the same direction—forward. Only two things kept me going; hope and the voice inside my head that kept me busy with conversation. Speaking to myself not only was comforting, but it also helped me pass the time.

Do you feel it? It whispered deep within my mind, echoing inside my skull. *Yes,* I answered. Something had felt different when I woke up, like some sort of calling that made me change direction for the first time since the fall. I didn't have anything else to do, and it was the first time I had felt something that strong, so I followed it. I felt stupid at first. Following an attraction...who was I kidding? But my obedience to my instincts was soon rewarded when I sensed light for the first time. Yes, sensed it. My eyelids seemed to be glued closed, allowing me to make out the orange glow, but I felt the warmth that came from it.

I started running without worrying about my footing. I knew the ground by heart—solid, flat, and even. This could change everything. The soft glow grew stronger as I got closer. So I kept running until the light was blinding, staining the thin skin that covered my pupils a bright red. It pressed my eyelids even harder now, and I brought my arm across my face since it was so strong. The stiff breeze around me turned into a sturdy gale, whirling and spinning my body around, waltzing with my hair, pulling me toward the origin of the wind. My ears rang even louder, but the sound came from inside my head. I fell down, slipping forward and banging my forehead against the hard ground. I couldn't move. The gale pushed me back down, pinning my arms next to my sides and my legs parallel to the ground. I was too close to the light to give up now, but my only option was to stay put in fear of getting blown farther away from the glorious glow. The wind felt like a tornado, and I was at the very end of it. It ripped the hair out of my scalp and sucked the life out of me.

Then, the wind calmed.

The ringing subsided and softly beeped from somewhere near me...*Beep-beep. Beep-beep.*

I gulped in air with one heavy breath. My hands went up over my face only to hit a hard surface above me. Anxiety took over. The smooth roof wasn't very far above. I hit the roof again, harder this time. The sound echoed around me as if I were in a small, enclosed space. What the...?

Beep-beep. Beep-beep.

I tried to open my eyes, but something was over them, sticking my eyelids together. I peeled off the soft covers that had been pasted over them. Luckily, the glue didn't rip off my eyelashes. I opened my eyes just a crack and waited until I got used to the light. After spending so much time in the darkness, I felt my retinas burning up, but eventually, I was able see again.

Beep-beep. Beep-beep. Beep-beep.

Wasn't I dead? If so, then why was I looking up at faces? None of the faces were familiar; however, they looked almost the same: brown hair, brown eyes with flecks of green, and perfectly white teeth. Shock hit me as I realized they all looked just like Skyler. His name popped bitterly into my head. I opened my eyes again after a long blink, hoping the faces would change. They didn't. I saw the same people hovering over me with serious expressions, taking in each detail of my face. Were they doctors? Could I have actually gotten to a hospital? Maybe I had been in coma. I tried to sit up, figuring that the walls around me were the last parts of my dream, but I bumped my head against something clear. I patted the air around me. I was in a box.

I was in a box! I pushed up on the lid above, but it wouldn't budge. I hit it with my fists. "Let me out!" I yelled. I could feel my lungs taking in as much oxygen as they could, wasting the precious gas. A two-story fall on my back didn't kill me, but suffocation definitely would.

Was I at my own funeral?

The people above me quickly moved away from the box to some panels on the walls that contained many labels and graphs, pressing buttons and talking to each other. One stood next to a small table and stared at me with deep curiosity. They were all women, I realized. Not one man was in the room. There must have been a reason. I looked down at myself and panicked. I was bare; no clothes covered my skin. I covered myself as best I could by folding over myself. A woman on a phone hung up and walked over to me. She opened the latches that held the lid shut.

No fresh air whooshed into the confined area, so that meant that I must have been put in the box recently or it would have been stuffier. She pointed at a hose at the end of the transparent coffin. "This renewed the air so you wouldn't ever run out." Her hand extended toward me as she answered the question I hadn't asked. Once I was outside, she grabbed a thin pile of clothes and gently handed it to me. There was a towel on top of it. I immediately felt wet. When I looked back at the box, I noticed that it was filled with water or some other strange liquid. I also noticed that the beeping had stopped. A screen that monitored my heartbeat was connected to the box and had stopped emitting sounds once I was out.

"Here, you change into this and knock on that door when you are done. Someone will fetch you." The woman's voice was tired as if she hadn't slept in days. She had probably been checking up on me the whole time. The difference in her clothes and the way she held herself surely meant that she was in charge.

It took me some time to actually get my voice out, and when I did, it caught the woman by surprise. "Am I dead?"

She turned to the rest of the women in the room, who just stood there, watching. Apparently they weren't expecting me to make a sound. She turned back to me. "No."

"What am I doing here?"

"Waking up."

I tried to hide my confusion. Waking up? I thought I was dead, and now they told me I had been asleep? Maybe I should run. No, first I should change and then sprint for my life. Where would I go? I didn't have a clue about where I was, and who knew how long I'd been out? First, I had to make a plan. I placed the clothes on the lid of the transparent coffin, wrapped myself with the towel, and pondered silently.

Everyone left the room promptly, and I was alone. None of them glanced back, except for the woman who had given me the clothes. "Remember, knock on that door." She pointed again to the only door that wasn't white. The dark wood stood out like a portal to another world.

I turned around and observed my surroundings.

On the wall to my left was a large coat rack filled with white coats and goggles. There were several screens on the table and the walls. All of them were off at the moment, but I could imagine the "whir" sound they must make when activated. Some kind of collage on the wall featured framed inscriptions, giving the room just a touch of color. Black. I wasn't interested in reading the inscriptions, which related the origins of something, so I continued to observe my surroundings.

The wall in front was covered in touch screens and buttons. It almost looked like a control center. It was completely different from the third wall, the one to my right. That one had glass desks lined up against it with papers and pens scattered all over them.

I remembered that I was still undressed. I dried myself with the towel, running it over my skin and through my hair. My skin looked a lot paler than before, probably because I had been indoors for a while. But what I found strange was that I couldn't see the intricate designs my veins used to make on the insides of my arms. When I touched my wrist to feel my pulse, I withdrew my grip—my skin was ice cold. It was pale and freezing to the touch. If it weren't for the constant thumping in my chest, I probably would have thought I was dead.

I tied my hair in a knot at the back of my head and grabbed the clothes the woman had left for me. It was a black jumpsuit with silver etching on it. Silver threads were sewn into a curling design that I couldn't quite describe. I ran my fingers over the hard fabric and then ran my fingers on the inside, hoping that it wasn't as hard as it was outside. I was right.

When I put it on, I felt it expand and then tighten, as if it were adjusting to my figure. I wished I had a mirror to look at myself. I felt slimmer, maybe because I hadn't been eating. How had they been feeding me?

I knocked softly on the dark brown door, as instructed. I let my hair down and combed it a bit with my fingers while I waited for an answer. No one came, so I knocked harder, almost pounding the door.

It opened with a swift movement, and a huge man stood on the other side. He blocked the whole view of the hallway—he was massive. His large chest and arms were padded with muscles. He must have had to go through some intense training to look like that. His voice was thick and deep. "Follow me," he said, as he turned and walked away quickly. I had to jog to keep up with him; my legs felt weak after not being used in quite some time. The burn I felt in my thighs and the creak in my knee was the least of my worries at the moment. Somehow, I had managed to keep my emotions under control, but then I slowly began to hyperventilate, making me extremely lightheaded.

I was alive.

The man halted suddenly, and I crashed into his back, caught up in my own thoughts. I mumbled "sorry," but I wasn't sure he heard me. He turned around without a trace of anger or annoyance. His hair was trimmed so short that it was barely visible, which made his head appear incredibly round and fat, which looked strange, especially on him. He opened a set of double doors and signaled me to go inside.

I nodded a silent thank you and stepped inside the room. Inside was a large oval table, possibly meant for formal presentations, surrounded with leather chairs. The walls were a faded gold rimmed with dark brown wood, except for one wall was fully covered in a large mirror. Two adults sat next to each other and invited me to take the seat in front of them. They looked the same as everyone else, except that one was a middle-aged woman with a bun so sleek and tight she probably suffered with a major headache. The other was a man wearing a dark purple suit.

The moment I sat down, I lost all interest in where I was, how I was going to escape, whether the purple suit looked horrible on the man, or if the woman was as stiff as she seemed. I cried shamelessly, not caring if snot ran freely from my nose or if my face was blotching. The expression of the two adults in front of me showed no sympathy, but they didn't insist that I stop, so I continued to cry my eyes out.

I remembered falling...and bleeding. I remember Skyler kissing my cheek as if he had any right to do so before I left the world...only to return again.

When I managed to stop crying, the two adults in front of me took advantage of the moment to start talking. The woman intertwined her fingers as she spoke. "I imagine you are wondering why you are even alive at the moment. I can tell you that, but first things first. Please stop crying. Once you realize what you have woken up to, I doubt you will want to waste your tears."

The man pushed a box of tissues toward me. "Before we get to the questions, we want to draw a big picture of it all. You might have heard of the four elements of the earth." He paused, waiting for me to nod or respond, but I was wiping my face with the soft tissues, hoping they would just get to the point. I tucked my hands under my legs to stop them from trembling. When the leather made them sweat too much, I pulled out my hands and balled them into fists.

"Well," he continued, "people say that it is just matter that makes up everything. On one hand, they are right, because it does make everything up. But mostly, they're wrong. You see, every fifty years, four elements are reborn. What does it mean to be reborn?" he asked himself. "You, along with three others, have been chosen from birth to continue to live in the advanced society of the elements. This is just the training center. We don't want to get into this now. At the age of seventeen, you are 'reborn.' The room you woke up in is one of the transformation chambers. You represent one of the four elements—earth, water, air, or fire. You might imagine by your looks what you embody." He scanned me, with his eyes showing a bit of admiration. "You, my dear, are the element of air." He slid a compact mirror over the table.

I picked it up.

I almost dropped the mirror on the table when I saw my reflection. "What have you done to me?" There was no way that the girl I saw in the mirror was me. My hair, once a frizzy light brown curtain that fell straight down past my shoulders, had been replaced with a silver-blonde cascade of wavy silken hair. It was incredible and disturbing. I hardly recognized myself. But my brown mane wasn't the only thing that had changed. My irises were light blue, the kind of pale blue one only saw on washed out t-shirts, with small flecks of silver. The silver flecks, like captured tears, reflected the light as if tiny mirrors were caught in the twist of light blue that darkened to grey near my pupils. My porcelain skin looked as if it could combust if it was touched by sunlight. But I was no bloodsucker. I was an element.

"You have always been this way," the man said simply, taking back the mirror.

I couldn't look at myself. That was not me. "What do you mean, I have always been this way? I have never looked so…"

His eyes softened when he recognized the distress and confusion I felt. "We'll get to that momentarily, but first we need to proceed with the briefing."

The woman shot me a glance as if I were wasting her precious time but decided it would just be wiser to continue with the task at hand. "About your old life—you can never go back there. The people you knew are lost now, irrelevant to the true sense of your life. I doubt you will ever have the chance to speak to them again, since they don't belong to our world. However, if you do, apart from being punished, it would be in vain. We have selectively wiped their minds, not of everything, but just the memories they share with you. So, to prevent you from ever retriggering their memories, and for other cultural reasons, we changed your names to more symbolical ones." I tried to soak up all the information, but how could I accept something as a fact if my brain kept telling me that it wasn't real?

What did "our world" mean? "If I'm not on Earth, where am I?" My voice came out hoarse and weak.

The woman rolled her eyes, irritated that I had ignored the "questions later" rule. "Well, it isn't a different world; it's the same one, but we are in a different realm. You have been living in the mundane realm, and now you have been transported back home where you belong. Our land contains no human corruption, a land fit for your existence. Let us continue with the briefing, and then you may continue asking questions." She signaled her partner.

I inhaled deeply when it hit me like a brick wall. I was an element. How had this happened? A strange smell hung heavily in the air. It was a mix of cleaning products and antiquity, almost like mixing a library with a hospital. Looking back at how I got here, I felt stupid for falling for the tricks Skyler had played on me. I had fallen for each one of them. Would it have been possible to avoid this fate? Somehow, if I hadn't involved myself with him, could I have kept my old life? Or would he have hunted me down? *You were selected from birth*...No, there was no way of out-running that.

The man pressed the tabletop with his fingertips, and suddenly, icons began to appear, as if it were a computer screen. He swiped the surface a couple of times and then looked up at me. "Nicole Henderson, you will now be known as Aurora." His self-satisfied smile suggested that the name was creative and that he had come up with it. I bet a computer had chosen my name at random from a large pool. I was named after Sleeping Beauty? Great. He waved his hand over the table, turning off whatever had appeared before, with a superior look on his face. "Now, do you have any questions?"

I put my elbows on the table and held my head. My brain hurt, but it had clicked. They weren't lying, but how could I believe this outrageousness? "Why me?" My voice was heavily weighed down with desperation. I couldn't see my family ever again, or friends for that matter. I would have to start a new life, living in a new race, completely unknown by mankind. The least I could ask for was the reason. Yes, I knew I was selected from birth, but why?

The nameless man didn't budge. "The first four children conceived every fifty years get the chance to live a fraction of eternity. The rest, well...aren't so lucky."

"What happens to the others?"

The woman, who had been picking at her nails and looking disinterested, pushed the imperfections back into her sleek bun. She wasn't as pretty as she assumed. "Well, they don't get transformed. They don't even find out who they really are."

I wouldn't have minded being one of those. "Why can't we go back to our family or friends?"

They didn't hesitate; it was as if they had practiced all the answers to every question I would ask. "Humanity cannot know about our existence. It would be dangerous. You might not see it now, but elements have 'gifts' that any mortal would kill to have."

"What gifts?" My nails dug into my scalp to stop myself from crying again.

"Elements have powers," the woman continued. "Everyone obtains them at an early age, usually right after they are reborn, and they develop them into their thirties. By then, most elements have mastered their power. Of course, some special cases do exist; these elements don't even get powers, or some have two. But that rarely happens. The first case is more common than the second."

Silence fell over the room. I could be one of those cases or not. I tapped the table lightly with my pale fingers to soften the sound of silence. We have powers. At least there was one advantage of dying. "You say humanity can't know of our existence, and that elements are distinguished by their looks. Then what are you guys? Why can you know and not our families? And why do you all look alike?"

"We're not purebred like you, but we're superior to humanity as well." The woman spoke as if she was some sort of distant royal decedent, and I was the child of the king. "There was once an incident in which an element and a human had a child. They raised a family, and all the children looked similar, like every individual element of the same kind, but they didn't look at all like their parents. They had brown hair and brown-green eyes. Zach and I belong to that line. Of course, now it's forbidden for an element to have any sort of relationship with humans or my kin, the same for our race. We're all decedents from the children of the element and the human."

"Do you have powers or gifts like us?" The more I asked and the more I knew, the less I paid attention to my feelings. Besides, it would help me understand much more about the world I was about to enter. I had to be prepared.

The woman shook her head. "No, we are able to live longer, but not as long as you and not in the same conditions. We age at a faster rate."

Age at a faster rate? What was I? Immortal? "What do you mean?"

Zach now reentered the conversation. "I'm going put it this way. For every fifty human years, you only gain one year. So, you live for about three thousand one hundred sixty-seven human years if you don't die before."

"Why that number of years? Why not longer? I mean, not everyone dies at the age of what..." Three thousand one hundred sixty-seven years was a very long time to live. What did we have to do that was so important? Most of the girls at Ashwick thought that immortality would be wonderful, since they read a lot of vampire books, but I always thought of it as a burden.

"Eighty? Well the Golden Four don't permit more than eighty years of life. It gets too long for some, and it's unnecessary to live longer because you can't serve your vocation anymore." Zach continued, "You see, your sole purpose is to serve the Golden Four, and once you lose your purpose, you must pass on your spot to someone who can continue where you left off."

"Who are these Golden Four?" And why did they sound like a dictatorship?

The woman, who still hadn't given her name, looked shocked. As if I could have known already...Her eyes widened and her lips parted slightly, turning down at the corners. "How could I have missed mentioning that information?" She touched up her hair as if someone important were about to walk through the door. A grin suddenly lit up her face, because just talking about them made her happy. "One of each element, no matter what age, can be chosen to represent his or her element in the government, of course, only when needed. First, this element is examined by the Circle of Seven of their element, which is a small group of governors that propose laws and regulations. After the whole circle agrees, they recommend the element to the remaining three of the Golden Four. If the element is accepted, then the search is over. If not, they continue the search. How do they choose the element? I have no idea. The criteria they use is kept secret, so no one can try to manipulate his or her way into the Golden Four."

Zach nodded in approval. As I sat silently, he could see that I hadn't understood his companion's explanation, so he pressed his lips together, clapped his hands once, and smiled. "Any more questions?"

"I don't get the 'realm' thing."

The woman began to answer, picking up where she had left off. "The easiest way is to imagine it is that our realm is inserted into the human one. They cannot enter into our realm, since they do not have an essence. They cannot see the passages between realms because of their ignorance. Half-elements, like us, cannot see the gateways that connect the territories, but we can cross it as a consequence of being a distant child of an element parent.

"There are two ways of entering our realm, and that is through the natural gateways that the spheres created when they gave us this realm or with the use of talismans. Talismans are rocks that have the ability to create natural, momentary passageways with the use of any threshold, doorframe, or arch. Talismans are extremely rare, and they are kept under lock in the Golden Hall, the home of our monarchs, the Golden Four."

"What are the spheres?"

The woman waved away my comment with a swipe of her hand. "Your creators, but we don't want to get into that now."

"Now you shall be shown to your quarters," Zach said, looking at me now. "And you will meet your protector." He called for my "escort" with a button on the metal band he wore around his wrist. "No more questions will be answered at the moment."

I was led out the door behind my assigned escort, my eyes glued to the floor. My brain couldn't possibly handle looking at anything else while it tried to process what I had just learned. We walked down the halls for some time; it gave me the feeling that the place was larger than I had thought.

Finally, raising my eyes, I observed my surroundings. The halls were monotonous and plain. Everything looked sterilized and untouched. The gleaming silver doorknobs that showed up every now and then broke up the white gloom of the place. These were the only touches of color I had seen since the conference room. I remembered the conversation with the strange allied human-elements. They had said "every fifty years." No wonder the room's walls were faded gold. I wondered how many years had passed since they had painted them a strong, vibrant gold that awed whoever looked at it, as shiny and reflective as a mirror overlooking that truth-breaking, dream-crushing, family-tearing, hollowing, and frightening room.

I bumped into my escort as he halted without warning in front of me. "Sorry." I meant it, but he just smiled. He might have thought that I was stupid from the way his eyes pitied me: brown, green-flecked eyes. The same eyes that last saw me in my human form. I probably never had been a human. I had always been an element, but I needed to die first to show my true colors.

I shivered.

What a morbid metamorphosis.

My escort pointed at the door to his left and spoke to me for the second time. His voice now had a bit of comprehension. How could he know what it felt like? I was still in shock, waiting for my emotions to drown me like a tsunami. "Here's your room. In a moment, you'll meet your adviser and then your protector." With a swift movement of his wrist, the door slid open at his command, and he ushered me in. Once I was inside, the door closed behind me.

I turned around and leaned against the wall helplessly. I closed my eyes, sticking out my lower lip, and blew, so the small strands of hair that had fallen in my face flew around and drifted. I began to feel some of the heaviness I had been waiting for. I wouldn't be able to see my family again. Ever. The last time I had spoken to a human that I cared about was when I told my mom that I was going for a walk. My last words were a lie. I banged my head against the door. I banged it again. Somehow, even though it hurt, it cleared my mind a bit. It wasn't my fault; it was Skyler's. He did this to me. But then again, I had been chosen from birth for this.

I opened my eyes and explored my new room. It was white, of course. Well, it seemed white but it was actually a light shade of silvery blue. *You are an element of air*, it reminded me. There was a bed tucked into the left corner of the room, with a headboard against the back wall. The bed was almost big enough for two people. I ran my fingers over the thick grey covers. They were soft and silky but smooth. I sat down on the bed and rummaged through the only drawer of my glass night table. There was a book, more like a journal, with a pen hooked onto it. The leathery cover smelled like new shoes and clean horse saddles. I checked the pages of the journal to see if anyone had written in it. Three words were written in neat handwriting: *I did it.* I wondered who had written it; probably the air element who had been here fifty years before me. What seemed out of place was that the journal smelled new. I flipped through some more blank pages and found a second trio of words written in the same writing: *So can you.*

I shut the journal and went back to observing my room. A lamp was on the night table. It had no buttons save for a small black screen, which I guessed was a sensor. I didn't try it out because I suddenly became distracted by the view from the window that comprised the whole wall. On the other side of the thick glass was a garden—a magnificent, huge, striking, colorful garden. I saw plants of all sorts, some I didn't even recognize. I pressed my face against the cold glass. The sun was high in the sky, so I guessed it was a bit before or after lunch. I didn't have a clear view of the outdoor space, since my view was limited by a small grouping of trees near my window. Nonetheless, what I saw was wonderful.

I heard footsteps walk down the hall and stop at my door. I stood straighter, but they kept on going in the direction they were headed, so I slouched again. Somehow, I felt disappointed. I didn't know why.

There was a large mirror on the wall next to the window over a set of dresser drawers. It was rimmed in glass, just like the night table, the bed, and the dresser. I avoided looking into it, since I wasn't prepared to face the beautiful monster I had become.

I was an element.

"Beautiful, aren't you?" A woman had entered, unnoticed, while I was caught up with my thoughts. "My name is Era. They should have told you that I was coming. I am your adviser." She walked over to my bed and sat on it. She signaled for me to sit down next to her. I followed her orders and sat down. "What's your name?"

She looked young, maybe four or five years older than me, but in element years, that would be somewhere between two hundred and two hundred fifty years.

"Aurora." My voice sounded more confident than I felt. There was something about her that made me feel more secure about everything and that she was here to help me.

Era smiled. Her pale colors gave away the fact that she also belonged to the element of air. "The name fits you. I think it's a first-timer, never been used before." Era ran her fingers through her hair.

I looked down as I thought of home. I would never be able to see it ever again, unless I found a gateway or a talisman. Somehow, I would try to find a way out. I had to tell my family about who I was, that I existed, that I was alive, and that I was not dead. But hollowness filled me when I realized that they didn't know I died. They would never mourn, since they had been forced to forget me. "When do I get out of this building and into the city?"

She looked startled by the question. Maybe she thought I was going to act mute, maybe not. "Well, right now you're not in the city. We are rather far from it, actually. We're in the training center, but you'll be able to go there once your training is over."

"City of Arcane," that's where Skyler said he was from, but he didn't look like any of us just transformed. Instead, he looked like the escort, the people in the transformation chambers, and Zach and the woman in the conference room.

"Why am I in a training center? What do I need to be trained for?" I ran my fingers over the stitched curls that ran all along my jumpsuit. The thread was thin and felt nonexistent under my fingertips but gleamed bright silver when the sun hit it. The tracing movement was what kept me sane at the moment.

Era's blondish-silver bob had nice small waves near the bottom. "You have to be trained for the testing that takes place the day before you go to the city. It's meant to determine your position in the city. Still, try to give the best of yourself. If your results are good, let's just say that your assignment is much more comfortable. The training also gives you basic knowledge that our leaders think is essential."

"How hard is the training?"

Her pink lips curved into a smile as she stared at my face. There was something motherly about her, as if she already had a child. She looked too young, but then again, elements age slowly. "That depends on how much effort you put into it."

I nodded and crossed my legs on the bed. "What is your job?" I didn't really care much about the answer, but I was hoping to learn things that could help me in the future. I also was afraid that after she went away, I'd be stuck here alone. I was afraid to be alone.

"I work as an entertainer. I'm one of the most renowned entertainers in the city. I even put on shows for the Golden Four. But I also work at one of the hospitals." Her smile contradicted the look of shame and embarrassment her eyes displayed. "I want to hear your story now."

Silence filled the room. I didn't want to talk about my life, not now, and I was pretty sure not ever. My silence gave away my hesitancy for sharing my past.

"Well, whenever you feel like talking about it, I will be all ears. Before I go, I promised the head of training that I would present you to your protector. I bet they've already told you about the 'mix' between the elements and the humans and how that whole story goes. Well, long story short, a protector is someone from that mix who was born on the same day as you, just a year earlier, and has vowed at the age of twelve to protect you with his or her life from anything that can harm you. I find it a rather young age, but rules are rules." Era pressed a button on a band around her wrist, similar to the one worn by Zach in the conference room. It was thinner and more delicate, more appropriate for her way of being. The button flashed when she pressed it.

The door opened some seconds later. I looked up and in the doorway stood a boy. Well more specifically, a teenage boy with dark chocolate brown hair and soft brown eyes with green flecks. He had been holding a paper in his hand the first day I saw him, and he had looked completely lost, but his eyes had been fixed on someone. Me. His name broke the bars of the cage that contained my rage and sadness. I had been holding up relatively well until Skyler came in.

He smiled dashingly. It was the smile he had used on me so many times. It didn't look that dashing now. "Hey, I thought you might have missed me." His voice purred in the back of my head, saying the last words I ever heard as a human, *"I guess I'll see you soon."* The whole night played itself back in my head with him popping the knife out of his pocket again and again before cutting the soft flesh of my wrists.

I launched myself at him after the door closed, and he looked at me with the fakest smile I had ever seen. I pounced like a cat, using the balls of my feet to cushion my fall as I landed on top of him. My body was weaker than I thought, and my unused muscles strained, but I couldn't stop. I wouldn't stop. I pinned him against the door using the momentum in my favor. My face was inches from his. In my human life, I *maybe* would have kissed him, too late for that now.

"You..." I didn't know what to say. What did one call her killer? No one could possibly create the name. Instead, I punched his nose with the force of adrenaline that, strangely, coursed through my veins. I'd heard of adrenaline appearing in dangerous situations or when someone got really scared, but I wasn't scared. My brain went completely haywire, triggered by the image of his face.

He flinched, his head facing the left because I had hit him with my right fist. Blood dripped out of his left nostril like a sickly worm and crept over his lip. "You do know how to throw a punch." He smiled with a red tooth, stained by the blood that poured out quicker now. I winced at the sight. "What are you going to do now? You already broke my nose." He laughed and spit on the floor of my room, leaving a scarlet blob.

"I didn't...bu–but you're the one who pushed me off the school roof!" I screeched harshly, a tone that escalated each time I added another word. "And you made me bleed to death! And don't forget that other person! Now you're laughing? I don't know how you can live with yourself!" He deserved to feel discomfort, which was nothing compared with my pain.

Nothing. I went for another punch, but Era grabbed my arm with more strength than I expected from a woman of her size.

She looked at me with stern eyes and knitted eyebrows. "What has gotten into you?" She spoke as if she were my mother. I guess advisers were some kind of replacement. "He hasn't done anything against the law." I opened my mouth to protest, but she quickly shut me up. "Our law." She pressed another button on her wristband and brought it close to her mouth. "Yes, I would like to request three security guards and a nurse to the reborn section, room zero eight." She looked at me with shame then turned to Skyler. "You didn't tell us someone else got involved. You know very well anything you hide from us can do great harm to your reputation and you could receive punishment. You do know that, right?"

I let Skyler go at Era's request. He nodded and covered his nose with his hand. "Yeah, I know." He walked to a closed door, which I hadn't seen before, and entered the bathroom. I would have to check that out later, because I was curious to investigate the newly discovered part of my room. Era had her eyebrows raised and forced me to remain seated on my bed. Skyler came out again with toilet paper stuffed up his nostril and some more in his hands. He winked in my direction, but I shot him a warning glance. While he cleaned up the spit blob on the floor, he asked me a question in the most casual tone ever. "So, how was the waiting room?"

Waiting room? "I haven't been in one." I said without looking at him. Instead, I stared that the white wall.

He smiled underneath the curtain of thin absorbent paper. "Oh, come one. The whole time you were out, you didn't go anywhere? I mean, the study books make it sound dark and vast and cold, ending with a sign of your element, so you probably woke up to a tornado or strong winds."

They called limbo the waiting room? "If you know so much, why do you ask?" I growled at him in the most hostile way. My short, cold words usually had the desired effect, but they seemed to slip right off of Skyler.

He shrugged. "The same situations can cause different experiences and feelings in people." After cleaning the floor, he stuffed the used paper in his jeans. I rolled my eyes in disgust. He seemed to notice my reaction. "Well, if your highness thinks this is disgusting, I might as well leave the bloody toilet paper in your trash can to creep you out, and so you can think thoroughly about what you just did."

"I had a reason."

"I had a job."

"I have feelings," I finally said. I instantly regretted saying the words aloud. Era looked at me with satisfaction, comprehension, and bright eyes. Skyler was staggered. Way to dig up feelings. Idiot. "It's over now. Dead," I added. The room stayed quiet.

Three large security guards barged in, and the nurse, a woman in a light-green dress with dark brown hair and an angular face, hurried after with a medical kit. She began to check Skyler. Meanwhile, the three massive security guards, who looked like clumsy teenagers, stood in front of Era, waiting for orders.

Era was quick and organized, giving commands while keeping an eye on me as she controlled the situation. "One of you has to call the Head of Training and ask him to meet with Skyler, so he can tell us what really happened the night Aurora was transformed. Then the other two have to take shifts guarding her room. The rules say that she can't roam freely in the training center without first having agreed to Skyler as her protector. You can have two shifts of twelve hours each or four shifts of six hours. You choose. If you want to include some other companion, you may, but I don't want the training center or its permanent residents unattended at any time."

"Yes ma'am," they answered in unison and headed outside. I heard four shuffling feet walk away and imagined the last security guard stayed behind to start his shift.

Era sat down next to me on the bed. "I'm sorry we have to do this, but rules are rules. You can only exit your room to eat and train, but the rest of the time you have to stay here unless you agree to have Skyler as your protector. That would simplify things a lot."

I looked at Skyler. He was looking back at me, through all the movements of the nurse, with the same steady eyes he had in art, but without intimidation. He looked at me, for the first time like someone he actually cared for, like a human...element. I shrugged it off and turned back to Era, turning my back to him.

I played with my neatly cut nails. "No, I want a change in protector. I don't want someone who killed me to 'protect' my life when he already took it away from me."

Era nervously ran her fingers over her arm, clearly irritated by my stubbornness. "It sounds logical, but you see, protectors are chosen once they are born. You can't get a new one, because you are only allowed to have one." She laid her hand lightly on my shoulder and pressed it. After a meaningful look of warning and caution, she headed outside, along with Skyler and the nurse.

I was left alone in my room again. I didn't hear the click of a key after they left, but that didn't mean they hadn't locked the door. I went to the door but didn't find any knob. I ran my hand over the smooth, cold surface, which slightly caved in from the wall. There must have been some sensor or button, or even control to open it from the inside, but mine had been turned off. I guess they actually took things seriously. I sighed heavily and threw myself on my bed, finding nothing else to do besides look out the window. I saw purple-ish flowers that reminded me too much of Violet and her favorite color.

I shut my eyes and imagined her. But that only made my homesickness worse. I wouldn't be able to hug my parents again, fight with my brother, or tell my family how much I loved them. I wouldn't be able to hear Violet sing, get married, have children, or see the people I loved—ever again.

Before I realized it, small rivers rolled down my cheeks and fell on the silky bedspread. It had the tiniest stitching I'd ever seen, with the same design as my black jumpsuit. I ran my fingers over it, tracing the design until I could trace it with my eyes closed.

My eyes felt heavy and my head felt light, made out of helium, making the bed spin when I closed my eyes. My breath was slow, constant, and silent. Soon enough, the only thing I could hear was the sound of my heart beating against my chest. Something I forgot I had...I had pleaded for it to stop. Now I was happy to have it back. I swore to myself, whether it was in my dreams or in real life, I would never lose the ones I loved.

Chapter 7

Someone or something must have shut the blinds over the window, because the breathtaking view was gone. I pushed off the heavy silken covers and slipped off the bed onto the ice-cold floor. As soon as I walked to the dresser and stood in front of the mirror, the blinds, like hard wall-like curtains, opened and revealed the same view as yesterday. Many flowers were still opening due to their light sensitivity.

It was not that late then. Still dazed, I looked at my reflection. My eyes were ringed with red, surely because I had been crying, making my irises seem whiter than ever. I looked at them closely and saw a darker ring of silver around the edges. I pulled away, taking in my groggy face. I had to wash it off.

I headed toward the bathroom. The lights turned on automatically as I stepped inside and lit up the large room. Enclosed in a glass box was a large area where five showerheads pointed toward the middle. A bathtub was next to it, sunk into the floor, so all I had to do to clean myself was take off my clothes and walk down a few steps. There also was a normal-looking toilet and a glass sink. Over the sink was a long mirror. The walls were painted like the erosion of sand dunes, but instead of being a sandy color, they were a silvery light blue. The design on the walls moved, barely, but it was noticeable if I stared at it long enough. Next to the sink was a small shelf with holes of different sizes; in the holes were a comb, toothbrush, toothpaste, a pack of elastic bands for tying up my hair, and some other objects that I couldn't quite identify.

I grabbed the comb, which looked as if it were made of crystal, and stared at the buttons on the side. It had different "modes": shine, massage, straighten, and unknot. I pressed the largest one, unknot, and ran the brush through my hair. I looked at the mirror as I combed it and stared in awe how the comb unknotted my hair without even tugging the delicate strands. After my mane looked like hair, I pressed the next button: shine. I would find a use for massage and straighten some other time.

After my hair looked as polished as it could get, I walked back into my bedroom. Something was different; there were clothes on the dresser. Not just one pair of fresh clothes, but a whole stack. They looked like the jumpsuit I was wearing, but instead of being black with silver stitches, they were a dull grey with pale blue stitching. I placed my clothes in the dresser drawers and quickly changed into one of the new jumpsuits, which seemed to be made of tougher material and padded at the knees and elbows. I glanced at myself in the mirror. I looked like a piece of paper dipped in grey and light blue. I shook my head, disappointed with the depressing lack of color around me.

Surprisingly I found two black boots by the front door. They looked like the moss green military boots both my brother and father wore, although they had a feminine touch to them. Heels. They weren't high heels, as training in them would be too difficult and uncomfortable, but the heel was a more noticeable elevation. I slipped them on and laced them up. I could almost imagine my brother mocking me about how stupid I looked dressed in a color that wouldn't camouflage me very well unless I were in snow-covered terrain.

I wondered if I would be able to get breakfast. Era had said I could get out of my room for meals, but the door slid open before my balled up hand struck the painted metal. I poked my head out and looked down the hall both ways.

No guards.

I chuckled. Great security system they had here. Only for the tiniest second did the idea of being filmed cross my mind. Maybe they had security cameras, but that was out of the question because of the obvious answer. Of course they were filming me; they were filming everyone. Still, they took precautions by hooking me up with personal room guards who failed to do the task. Maybe the cameras worked as well as my guards. I recited "eeny-meeny-miny-moe" in my head to choose which side was going to lead me toward the dining room. Right. I started down the hall in hopes of finding some clue of where to find the food. I hadn't eaten anything since I was pushed off the roof. I was hungry.

Every hall looked the same, and every door did too. I was making too much noise as I walked, but the boots were heavy as hell and made it difficult to raise my feet from the ground. I looked at the different numbers on the doors as I tried not to make so much noise. My room was 08 in the reborn section. I guessed it was relatively close to where all my reborn partners were, as well as my adviser, who treated me like a child. Her child. But these numbers were much larger than 08. I had already passed some rooms with numbers from 620 through 613. I must have been getting closer to the main rooms of this section. There weren't clear divisions between sections, something I found strange, not even a glass door or a sign. Or perhaps this was created so you could only memorized the route to where you had to go and how to get back, or you got lost. It stopped you from wandering. Or maybe it stopped an enemy or unwanted person from knowing where to go. I shuddered. I felt included in at least one of those categories.

When I heard footsteps, I looked up. I shouldn't have been wandering in the halls by myself, but I was searching for food. Far away, I saw a boy turn into the hall ahead and begin to walk in my direction. His head hung downward, and his hands were in his pockets. The image of Skyler walking down the sidewalk with me popped up clear in my head. He was playing with the knife in his hands. The image flashed forward to the night he pushed me off the roof. He had already dragged me to the forest and pulled out the blade. It was covered with dried blood as it slit the insides of my wrists.

"No!" I cried out, grabbing the inside of my arm. I swear I could feel blood dripping out of me, staining the floor beneath me red.

"Help!" I called to the figure who ran toward me, but my voice was just a whisper. My hyperventilation made me feel light-headed and too dizzy to stand straight, so I knelt on the ground and pressed my arm harder. The blood didn't stop pouring out. The boy finally reached me and took hold of my shoulders. "Blood, everywhere!" I cried. Tears streamed down my face, blurring my vision so that I couldn't see who was in front of me.

The boy held my face with both hands and looked into my eyes. "Look at me." I tried to turn back to my arm and stop the bleeding, but he forced my head upward. "Look. At. Me." I did. The tears blurred my vision, only allowing me to see a cloud of gold. I tried not to blink so the tears would dry up faster. Soon, I was staring at the golden irises of the boy in front of me. I felt my blood pressure drop.

"I need you to match my breathing, okay?" His eyes were the only objects I could see, but I knew he was loosening my grip so he could feel my pulse on the inside of my wrist. His breathing was loud and slow. As I imitated him, my heartbeat slowed and I focused my vision on the floor around me. It was white.

There was no blood.

There never had been.

My face turned red when I realized what had happened. I had hallucinated the whole thing. "Are you better?" he asked in a low voice, so as not to overwhelm me. I took in his appearance. His hair was light brown, but with strange natural highlights in it that shone red in the light. They went well with the warm tone of his skin.

"Thank you." I held onto him as we stood up together. My knees buckled underneath me, so he wrapped my arm around his shoulder, bringing some of my weight over to him. I didn't know him, and I didn't like getting so close to strangers, but I didn't want to risk falling and looking like a fool again.

His face was red, but I couldn't tell if it was because he was embarrassed or because he had just been crying. The area around his eyes was as puffy as mine, but fresh blotches surrounded them. When he raised his large round eyes to mine, I inhaled sharply. His irises stared at me with so much intensity, I was about to combust right in front of him. He belonged to the fire element. He had to.

"What was that, by the way?" There was no harshness in his voice, only concern.

Most likely he also had experienced flashbacks, but I couldn't be sure about how or what triggered them, but he had been killed too. "Flashback."

"Yeah, you shouldn't worry about that, we all have them. They might feel real now, but in a few days, they will be gone." He held me for a second before a look of realization took hold of his features. "This is kind of an awkward question, but given that it's the first time we've met...what's your name?"

"Aurora."

"Cool. My name is Aiden. So, where were you going?"

"I was headed toward the dining room." He led me toward breakfast, back down the way I came.

"That's great, I was just heading that way." Aiden smiled softly and began to carry me toward the food. "So, what took you so long to finally decide to come eat breakfast with us today?"

"What do you mean?"

Aiden stared straight ahead. He didn't even look at me when he spoke. "Well, the other two elements and I have been eating breakfast together for about three weeks already, and we never heard any news from you until today."

Three weeks? Why had I taken more time than the rest to "wake up"? "I only found out about all of this yesterday. I didn't know that the rest of you were waiting." He didn't answer; he just held me up and pressed his lips into a thin line.

When we walked past my room, walking in the other direction, a question began to surge in the back of my mind. If the newborn section of the building was here and the lunchroom was toward the left, where was he coming from when he bumped into me? Training hadn't started yet, and the dining room was on the other side of the building. He could have been walking around, just to clear his mind, but then why had he been crying? Aiden said he had gotten over the flashbacks quickly. Was he homesick? I tried to free myself of his grasp so I could walk on my own, but he resisted.

"I can walk on my own, you know," I insisted.

"I don't doubt that, but I don't want you to fall." He had a point. I didn't feel very stable, but I didn't like hanging on a stranger either. When I didn't answer, he held me a bit farther away than before.

We reached two large, polarized glass doors. I felt like retreating, running and hiding back in my room. I did want to meet the rest of the elements, but not now. Fire boy pushed open the door with his free hand. It swung with ease, revealing a large, school-like cafeteria filled with half-elements. My eyes bulged until they were about to pop out of their sockets. I had no idea that we would eat with the rest of the training center.

"Where are they?" I tried to find the other two elements, but I didn't know what to look for.

Aiden pointed to a small table for four in the far corner. The rest of the room was filled with crowd of larger tables that could seat up to ten. The long tables were joined together and made long rows occasionally interrupted by spaces so the half-elements could circulate with ease.

"We're going to have to go get our food first," Aiden said, as we made our way through the tables toward the line. Many half-elements turned around to stare at us, and most of the stares lingered, since I was holding onto a male element for support.

Once we reached the line, I unhooked myself from the Aiden. There were few people in front of us, and the line advanced quickly. I grabbed a blue tray that looked as good as new, a big contrast to the ones I used to grab in high school. Those were scratched and scribbled on with permanent marker—*Jade=hot bod, F+G*, and *gay* came to mind. I slid my tray over the rails, slightly pressing down, so I could release a bit of the tension in my body. I waited as a skinny old woman with white hair tied back in a hair net handed me my breakfast. She wore a white apron over her light green working dress. It was the same dress and color the nurse had worn the day before. The woman looked at me, noticing my great difference in pigments, and turned to call to someone in the kitchen. A young girl walked out holding a transparent container about the size of a small plate. It opened outward and held food covered with a transparent lid. My name was scribbled on top of the lid in blue marker. The girl gazed at me in terror as if I were holding a gun to her head. She handed the container to the old woman and quickly retreated to the kitchen without looking back. The old woman, unaware of her coworker's behavior, handed me the container and looked at the next person in line. He showed her his wristband, and she scanned it. After checking something on a screen, she walked over to a machine where she sent the information, placed a container under it, and watched as brown and green mush poured out. I gulped hard. It looked like vomit.

I walked over to my table, right behind my escort, where I was greeted by silence. The other two elements had already arrived and were busy eating their food. The female had lively coral-colored hair that sprung out around her head in curls. Her high cheekbones and almond-shaped eyes gave her a very feminine look. Her irises were the same color as the ocean. The deep blue intertwined with green, and she had the same mirror-like reflections in her eyes that I did. A smile appeared on her pink lips, and she greeted me, inviting me to sit next to her.

"Thank you," I said, as I put down my tray. Her jumpsuit was blue with darker etchings on it. I was positive she was a water element.

"Who is your girlfriend, Aiden?" The earth element, the last one left, gave me a glance that made me shudder. His skin matched the dark color of rich soil making his ivy green eyes stand out. His muscles were tensed as he gripped the plastic container that looked too small in his hands.

I blushed and fumbled while trying to open the little box that contained my food. Aiden paid little attention to my reaction and didn't seem very affected by the comment. "I'm not—we just met." My voice was small.

"I'm Ren," the water element extended her hand toward me. I shook it and smiled back. "This here is Juris; don't pay much attention to what he says. Most of the time, he's in a mood." She spoke this second part in a much lower voice before speaking aloud, talking to the rest of the group. "But I do agree with Juris that both of you guys looked a bit too comfortable to be strangers. Perhaps that is why we haven't seen her before..."

Aiden swallowed the brown mush before speaking, "Flashbacks."

"Oh my gosh, those are terrible! I remember when I had those. I still do sometimes, but they aren't as bad as they were before. Don't worry; you'll get over it soon. Anyway, I suggest you start eating your breakfast before it gets cold, then it tastes even worse." She wrapped a curl around her finger as she spoke and played with her food when she wasn't eating it, smoothing it out and drawing in it.

I broke the bag that kept my cutlery clean. When I stuck the spoon into the mush, my stomach churned. I was very hungry, but my appetite was gone when I felt the thickness of the paste as I scooped it up. I took a brave bite. The taste was overwhelming and disgusting. I didn't want to swallow, but I forced myself, since it would be much worse to have it sitting on my taste buds. "This tastes like…"

"Like crap," Ren finished my sentence.

Juris looked up again, shooting everyone a menacing look. "This food is supposed to give us sufficient energy for training, so if you don't want to eat it, even better. But if you *are* going to eat it, why don't you just shut up?" He stuffed a whole spoonful in his mouth just to prove that he was stronger, probably trying to show off, but I didn't care. All I wanted was not to throw up in front of the whole cafeteria. "And why haven't you been eating with us lately? Preferential treatment? Who are you? A Golden Four's child?"

"I woke up yesterday." I didn't look away when he glared. I met his gaze and waited for him to turn away first, but he didn't.

Finally, I turned to eat my food. A smile of victory crept over his face. "Anyway, I was thinking of our outfits, and…" I shut out Ren's voice, as I wondered why Aiden wasn't talking. He seemed nice and easygoing in the hallway, but now he kept his head down and ate his food without complaint. He didn't speak unless he was involved in the topic. He sat at a diagonal to me, which made me notice the hard shape of his jaw. It made him handsome. "You haven't told us your name. Hey!" Ren elbowed me to catch my attention.

"Sorry."

"Don't sweat it," she said as she evaluated the moment. She had caught me staring openly at Aiden, and now there was a wicked glint in her eye as she slowly put it together in her head.

I had completely forgotten about presenting myself to the other two. "Aurora."

"No way!"

I knitted my eyebrows, not quite getting it. Aiden looked up momentarily, meeting me eyes with a subtle smile

Ren flipped her hair and beamed. "My favorite Disney princess was Sleeping Beauty! Isn't that like a totally awesome coincidence? And you kind of look like her except for the extremely white hair and your eyes, and well, your skin of course. You probably will get skin cancer if you try to tan, so you might as well just use spray-on when summer comes. Do you think they have a tanning salon in Arcane?" It wasn't hard to picture Ren as a human. I could just see her—popular, probably up for homecoming queen, a pretty vague future, which probably involved studying at a college selected by her parents and plenty of partying.

"Could you just shut up, or will I have to stick my fork down your throat?" Juris snapped. He sure was hotheaded, ironically, since he wasn't the fire element.

Ren shrugged off his comment. "Gosh, and they call girls hormonal."

His nostrils flared like those of an angry bull until he managed to calm down. "What I want to know is why my protector went to your room yesterday. He told me that the whole training center knows what you did." He looked at me

S. Elizabeth Dover

now, choosing me as the next victim of his harsh words. His jaw was set, and both Aiden and Ren looked at me with deep curiosity. Juris smiled with satisfaction. He was turning them against me. Well, he was trying.

"Yeah, we had a minor issue. No biggie." I filled my own mouth with food to have an excuse not to talk. I didn't want them to know about the incident with Skyler. It was a personal matter that I had to solve myself. The only thing I could really do now was act polite. It would help...a bit.

Juris began to talk again, but I didn't listen. I searched through the crowd of brown and green eyes. They all looked the same. It had to be boring not to be able to find anything different, besides the shape of your body, in your class, family, boyfriend, and coworkers. Something stuck out, though. Something white. I turned my head to see if I could get a better view. The white something was a bandage on an oh-so-familiar face. I winced. It was Skyler, of course, the guy who had popped up everywhere in the last few days of my human life and now here. If there was one thing I thought was good about being killed or waking up and turning into some unknown creature, it was that there was no Skyler to bother me or kill me again. It seemed someone had chosen him to follow me during this period of my life, with him as my protector and me as the protected. His nose was wrapped in a white cast, and his eyes were searching the crowd. They stopped on me, as usual, no surprise there.

I turned back to the table only to realize that they were all looking at me in silence, and then followed my gaze into the crowd. I slurped up some more food, trying to look busy. Then all their eyes rested on me again.

Juris smiled slyly. Oh no. Ren looked confused, and Aiden had a weird expression on his face. I wanted to pound my head against the table. The silence was overwhelming. I wished someone would talk about something, anything. I pushed away the transparent container and stared back at them with hollow eyes. Everyone seemed to mimic my actions in silence. No one ate; we just had an intense staring contest.

Thank goodness, soon enough, two large men with the same hair and eyes as everyone else led us away from our exclusive table, through the uniformed crowd, and into the white hallways. I looked at the other elements walking with me. If it hadn't been for them, I would have killed myself in this plain building where everything looked the same. Ren smiled at me and pushed her curls away from her face. Those curls reminded me so much of Violet.

"I can't wait to start. It's going to be so fun," she said excitedly.

"You won't last a second," Juris commented. "Your weak muscle structure won't even allow you to kick a person and knock him down. I, on the other hand, could probably hunt someone down and snap his neck with minimal effort." He flexed his muscles while he spoke. I rolled my eyes and avoided speaking to him. I made a mental note that the more distance I could put between us, the less friction there would be.

We all stopped in front of two large metallic doors. No one had dared to make a sound. We were all too anxious, or in

Ren's case, scared, to say anything. Our escorts typed codes into keypads on both sides of the doors. They held up their wristbands to a sensor, and the doors began to go up instead of swing open. Juris looked at Aiden eagerly. Our escorts didn't say anything; they just stood next to the doors. Juris didn't hesitate and strode in confidently. Aiden followed, then Ren, and I took the rear. We walked into what seemed like one of the largest rooms I had ever seen. It looked larger than an indoor football stadium. It was filled with small stations that varied in size. A large area in front of the stations was left open in order to make room for the large box.

An assistant had us form a horizontal line; it was the same nameless woman who had greeted me in the conference room. Her hair was tied up into a sleek ponytail. "Welcome to the physical training room. You will be spending most of your mornings here, training at the different stations, and then you will spend your afternoons in short breaks and intellect training. Here you have all the stations where you can practice. At first, you will have to try them all, and then you will be able to choose your area of specialization. But first..." She called over a man who had been standing next to a large transparent box. There was always a "but." "But first we have to do a test required by the Golden Four." She smiled. "Who will volunteer first?"

A hand shot straight up. Of course everyone knew who it was going to be.

"Your eagerness and positive attitude is much appreciated, Juris." She eyed us all, walked him over to the box, and pressed against the glassy surface. The door opened, and she shoved him inside. He looked back at us, proud, with his chin held high. The man pressed a few buttons on a control panel. There was a soft rumble, and then a huge rock came out of the ground. It was flat with a sharp end. That end was facing Juris and suddenly shot through the air toward him. The man was watching, seeming to have the time of his life. Juris pressed himself against the glass, and, seeing no escape, raised his hands in front of his face.

That's how it happened.

When Juris raised his hands, a huge rocky shield rose from the floor and shattered the oncoming boulder. We stared in awe. He looked at his hands, aghast. The woman couldn't resist clapping at the impressive demonstration of power.

It was exciting to watch a human, I mean an element, do that. Juris pounded the glass, euphoric with his newfound gifts. He dodged and threw boulder-like stones at the targets that were threatening to take away his life. He moved as if each step had been choreographed. Juris's movements came to him naturally and with shocking grace. He persisted through the test until a bullet-sized clump of earth struck him on the shoulder. When his body fell to the ground, he covered himself with a rocky shell.

That's when the man decided it was enough. "Good. Good. Very good," he mumbled, as he scribbled on a clipboard. Then he opened the door with his controller and waited for Juris to break though the shell he had made and come out. He had little clumps of dirt and stains all over his hair, face, and clothes.

The woman called for the next person to volunteer.

Juris looked at the three of us and pushed Aiden forward. Aiden approached the box, wiping his sweaty hands on his trousers. He looked nervous. Ren took my hand and breathed in.

He was fire.

The door shut soundlessly behind him. He didn't look back.

The man pressed a button on his control panel.

A soft glow rose into flames, which grew greater as they crept toward Aiden. He backed up, his features twisted, as he realized he had nowhere to go. The flames were three feet tall when they reached him, hiding half of his body from view. He turned around and banged desperately on the glass. His yells were muffled by a sound barrier in the box. Ren dug her nails into my arm. The flames chewed on his clothes, climbing up the cloth like fiery claws that dragged him down. He fell back, engulfed by the inferno, and disappeared inside a mix of orange, yellow, and grey.

I ran to the box.

Aiden was drowning, lost in a sea of fire.

I reached the furnace and banged on the glass walls, shouting his name. The box was unnaturally cold, although its interior was scorching. "Stop it. Stop it now!" I yelled frantically. Someone grabbed my arms and pulled me away from the box. I tried to fight it. They were killing Aiden, and Juris and Ren were just letting them do it! I turned my face to see who it was. Juris. A strange, low growl escaped my lips.

"Let him out!" Juris yelled from behind me. He almost left me deaf, but I didn't mind, he was on my side. He lessened his grip on me. I squirmed my way out but didn't run back to the box.

The man at the control panel waited for the conference room woman to give him the signal. It took an eternity for him to finally press the button and kill the flames. He pressed another button, which made white foam spray over the spot where I guessed Aiden was laying, lifeless. The man called for someone on his wristband, something a lot of people seemed to have.

Two men barged in, wearing the same light-green clothing as the nurse, carrying a stretcher. My heart plummeted.

I turned to Ren, whose intense blue eyes seemed to be tearing up. I hugged myself. He was dead. But when I looked back, they lifted some black, burned, and struggling boy who didn't at all look like Aiden. His hair had been burned off, and his skin was scorched. It was stained coal black in some places, while others had blisters or directly revealed the raw meat under the tan skin he used to have. They laid him on the stretcher and pulled him out of the room. Strangely enough, his clothes had resisted the heat. Aiden lifted his fingers as they took him away, giving us a small signal that he was still alive. My heart gave a little leap at this sign.

He was alive.

The woman turned to me, disappointed. "I see you have a soft spot for this boy." I wanted to strike her across the face. So, wanting to prevent the death of an innocent person, which could easily be prevented, was having a "soft spot" or showing a preference? This place, this woman, had it all wrong. "You're next."

What were they going to do with me? I wished I were made out of concrete. That would make it harder for them to drag me in there and harder to break me. "Why?" It came out a bit scratchy.

"Why not?" The woman walked placed her hand in the small of my back. She eagerly pushed me forward toward the spotless box. What was this box made from? It looked almost magical. It's a magical torture chamber. I sighed. This place was going to be the end of me as well as my sanity.

The door closed quickly behind me. Well, quicker than I wanted. It didn't give me any time to stick in a hand or arm to stop it.

Something began to whirl in the center of the box. I only heard it, but soon enough, I began to feel it too and how it lifted my hair, making it hover around my face. It was similar to a small tornado, like when I had woken up from my deep slumber after Skyler killed me. But it didn't go around and around. It just lifted me off my feet and suspended me in the air. I was immobile and glued to the spot, but at least it wasn't anything that would kill me.

It was a strange sensation to float in the air as if I were about to rise into the sky, through the roof, and back to a safer place. My body began to rotate once I was suspended, setting my body in a horizontal line, face down. If I fell, it wouldn't kill me, but it would hurt terribly. Soon the wind was impelling me higher and higher, pressing me against the ceiling. I was being suffocated, as my ribcage slowly and painfully closed in on my lungs. This is what it had felt like when I fell off the roof. But instead of the air inside my lungs escaping quickly and abruptly with one blow, it was strangling me slowly.

When I closed my eyes, I was falling off the roof again. Skyler was sneering above me, and the ground approached me from below. When I hit the floor, I fell face down. I opened my eyes and touched the floor below me. I wasn't on my back on the school lawn but in the crystal-clear testing chamber. The flashback had seemed so real. I felt something cold drip down the side of my face. Tears. I stretched out my hands and realized that there were small, dark pink moons on them, since I had dug my nails into the soft flesh. I could almost see Skyler standing next to Juris and Ren. He was haunting me. It wouldn't work. At least Skyler was here, far, far away from the people I loved most, where he couldn't hurt them.

I sat up in the middle of the box inside the large room. Everything was big, plain, and symmetrical. The man with the control panel was scribbling more things on his clipboard, but he didn't open the door.

Instead, the air became heavy and thick. I had to take larger gulps to satisfy my body's need for oxygen. I tried to stand up, but I stumbled on my feet. My hands caught my fall, but I could no longer breathe. I tried to swallow the air. Everyone outside of the box watched me as if I were a fish out of water, twitching inside a boat, waiting for a knife to slice into my brains. There was no knife, but I began to twitch and shake as my vision fogged and darkened.

I was going to pass out.

Fshhhhhhhh...the oxygen quickly diffused. I gulped in air, and once I knew I had enough, I did it about six more times. When the door opened, I wanted to run to the man and smash his face in with his stupid clipboard. Instead, I slumped toward Juris, while Ren took my place. I walked toward the back of the room where I slouched against the wall to breathe in more air. I felt light-headed, and Aiden wasn't here to help me get through it again, so I had to do this on my own.

The water element took her place as the last to enter the box. Ren began to swim as the water in the box of doom began to rise. She was swimming, and she wasn't bad at it either. Her coral hair flattened with the weight of the water. But the water was rising too high, and soon enough, the box was filled to the top, and there was no place left for oxygen. Unless she could hold her breath for a very long time, she wouldn't last long.

I closed my eyes. I didn't want to see it. I hated this place. I hated these people, and I wanted to go back to the place I called home. To the rough, warm bedspread I had in my room, which was littered with books and clothes. Where Violet and I would talk for hours without end, and my dad would play games with me that he learned while he was on duty. I swallowed back the tears. I didn't want to cry, but I couldn't help it. I wept in silence and curled up on the floor, hugging my knees. I pushed back the tears. I couldn't cry here. No, I would cry in my room by myself. I would mourn alone. I would mourn the living. When I reopened my eyes, Juris was staring at me with...compassion? Whatever feeling he had seemed to disappear in an instant. He sternly looked back at Ren, who was being carried out of the box.

She hadn't gotten her power yet. Only Juris had. This would make him feel even more proud of himself. Great.

Ren coughed out water. She was half sitting against the same wall I was leaning against, while the man with the clipboard wrote some more. I scooted over to Ren and helped her sit up. Her blue eyes looked lost and hazy. She held my hand and pressed on it lightly. I wrapped my arm around her shoulders. This was the fastest I had ever bonded with someone. She looked at me to thank me. Without even needing to say a word, just a glance, I returned the look.

The man with the clipboard was gone now. He had left without making a single sound. That only left Juris, the woman, and the rooms. Juris took in Ren and me with hateful eyes, as if we were going to start a conspiracy against him.

The woman who had let us regain our strength, slightly, now ushered us to stand. "Now, you'll have training. Don't waste your time; you can't fight against each other, since only one element can be in a box at one time. Oh, and you must go through all the stations." After her command, she turned and left, with her clicking heels and black pencil skirt. I realized that each person's jobs or ranks were classified by color. The highest one here at the training center must be black; the trainers were dressed in dark blue, and the rest were in light mint green.

We walked slowly to the stations that were behind the box.

Juris quickly walked into one, disappearing as soon as the door clicked behind him. He had looked like an arsonist with twenty matchboxes in his hands as he walked in. The door was marked with two axes; one had two handles, while the other had a double blade.

Ren, unlike Juris, approached the obstacle course. That compartment was larger than most of the others, and the sign on the door was a person jumping over a wall.

I chose the archery station, since it reminded me of the main characters of so many books I had read. As I suspected, I was no good at archery. The arrow would soar over the target, hitting the padded wall, or clatter against the floor, escaping the bow before I could launch it. The trainer, a twenty-year-old half-element, reassured me that once I learned the right technique, practice would make perfect. I kept trying, I but as my time at the station neared its end, I only got worse.

The more I failed at hitting the target the more I wondered why I was even practicing archery. Why on earth would I have to know how to shoot an arrow?

A whistle blew, and we had to change stations. Juris went to practice javelin, Ren chose one-handed weapons, and I chose knives.

The practice knives were made out of blunt metal with a flexible end. They were much easier to handle than the bow and arrow, and they wouldn't hurt the trainer if I hit him accidentally. I swished a knife around and struck the trainer only once in the throat. It would have been a quick kill, but he had already gotten me nine times in the heart, back, throat, leg, arm, and stomach. So before I would be able to kill someone, I would already be dead. The new trainer, a small elderly woman, saw my disappointment and decided to change to throwing knives—

real knives. She taught me how to balance the knives in my hand before I threw them, how to make the sharp end dig into my opponent, and how to aim. These knives were sharp and could easily bury themselves in someone. When I hesitated, the trainer decided it would be best to give me a demonstration. She threw three knives swiftly and struck three of the six dummies in the center of the face.

I glanced at her and raised my eyebrows. "You want me to do that?" There was no way I could hit them in the head. Well, maybe if I missed one and accidentally hit the other.

"Just try. Perhaps it would be best if you aim at the torso." She reminded me of the throwing position once more before I could take another shot at humiliating myself with a weapon. The glint of the light on the sharp edge made me nervous. What if it slipped and cut me? I couldn't think like that if I were in a dangerous situation. It would only make me hesitate, and I'd be dead in a matter of seconds. I pretended I was one of the heroines in a book. I was defending something or someone, and I had to kill one person, just one, and we would be safe. I gave my opponent a personality, a serial killer who had momentarily exposed himself, giving me the chance to end his work. Yes, this way it was easier.

I inhaled.

I threw the knife and waited to hear it clang on the floor or drive itself into the soft wall behind the dummies. But there was no *clang;* instead, I heard a soft *thump.* I searched on the wall for the knife, but it wasn't there. Instead, it had stabbed the dummy on the top left side of its torso: right where its heart should have been.

Chapter 8

I slumped after my escort. My feet ached, distracting me from all the negative thoughts that stormed around my brain. They shuffled noisily against the polished floor. I moaned inside my head. At least now I would be able to lie down, cry alone, and sleep off the pain. Due to my lack of energy and willpower, I would have to take a shower tomorrow morning, even though I smelled terrible. I moaned again, this time audibly, realizing that I would have to sacrifice the nap I craved for the intelligence training I was forced to attend. A strange impulse told me to slam my body against the wall, slide down to the floor, and sleep or break down in the middle of the hallway; but I resisted the urge.

I looked around. There was nobody to be seen. Weird. The only places where I'd seen people, and in quantity, was when I had woken up in the rebirth coffin and in the cafeteria. My escort stopped next to the door to my room. The two numbers *08* shone unnaturally under the fluorescent lights. I mumbled a soft "thank you" under my breath and walked inside. About to throw myself on my bed, I halted. There was already someone on it. "Do we have to talk now? I wanted to be alone."

Era signaled for me to sit next to her like she did yesterday when we had first met. I obeyed and sagged against the wall. "I came here to tell you that Aiden is all right." She looked at me with eyes identical to mine.

I shook my head. "He's not all right, and neither are the rest of us. I know you've probably been through this, but we just lost everything, everything we knew, had, loved, absolutely everything. And to top it off, we've been killed, and now we've been tortured, and no one moves a finger. Everyone acts as if it's perfectly normal and natural! I just saw someone get burnt alive. That's an image no one forgets, ever, and now you just pop up telling me he's okay? I mean, you and all your little..."

"Aurora! Don't speak like that ever again. I've been through this and you will see, maybe not now, that this is your real life. You are an element from birth, and you can't change it. You can pretend, but you have always been different; you have always been special. You have been chosen out of millions to keep on living as yourself, not some human you were pretending to be. Those who don't get transformed, even though they are elements, aren't as lucky as you. If you're grieving because you won't be able to see your old family and friends, I recommend you stop. You'll find new and better friends soon enough." She grabbed my hand and held it tight.

I wanted to cry. I wanted to cry so badly. I had been so naïve, and now had I lost it all, my whole life, and would have to start again, from scratch, without anyone familiar to help me along the way. I cried. It was a relief that I didn't have to hold back in front of Era. She didn't understand and would probably scold me or tell me that this was better, this life of training and weird tests in which we had to prove ourselves. But the only thing I wanted her to do was help me and hug me. I sobbed silently, while my eyes blurred with tears. She pressed my hand. I didn't know whether she wanted me to stop or if she was trying to sooth me.

"Don't cry, Aurora." She moved closed and embraced me. Her slim arms wrapped around me and cradled me. Era ran her fingers through my hair. If it weren't for our different figures and faces, we could have been identical twins. "You didn't get your power, did you?" She sounded disappointed

She knew and she probably thought I was crying about that too. The tears slowed, my eyes were rimmed with red, and my hair felt tangled. "No, I didn't." Era looked down at her feet. I let her down. "Juris got his, but the rest of us...nothing."

She forced a smile, pushing up her cheeks and trying to fill her eyes with happiness. "You'll get it soon enough." She was about to stand, but I grabbed her wrist.

"Why do we have powers? Why do we have to test and train? Why do we have to die?" The questions blurted out of my mouth. If someone in this large building would answer me, it would be Era. She could be trusted, for now. "Why can't we go back to where we grew up? What if our old family and friends swore to never tell anyone? Who are the Golden Four?"

Era sat down again, her eyebrows furrowed. Did she actually get what I had said, or was she still processing the gibberish only my mother or Violet could understand? "Our powers exist so we can fulfill our job, controlling the elements of nature and keeping the natural balance. You'll soon see that they come in handy in your assigned job. In the past, they served as a means of protection when elements weren't organized; but that was a long time ago. The test allows us to give you full physical training, to help you develop those underused muscles of yours and acquire new skills and strategies for self-defense. It is always good to know how to protect yourself. As elements we are a very scarce race and we must be able to defend our lives in case of an emergency. You are given a job based on your talents and powers. That's why you have the test. Everyone passes it; it's not as if you get kicked out for failing, because you can't.

"As for getting killed to transform, we do this to educate you and so you can return to your body when it's fully functional and well developed." She walked over to the large window, her back facing me. "You see, elements don't have souls, only humans do. We have an essence. Some of our researchers discovered that we place part of that essence in a scientifically prepared human body, with its own fingerprints and identity, for the seventeen years in which the element body remains dormant. This helps us gain the years we would have spent on education and gives the element general knowledge. When we kill the scientifically prepared body, which contains the small fragment of essence, the portion of that essence goes back to the element body and completes it. It's only natural for your essence to want to return to where it came from. And hopefully, just in time to wake up."

I waited for her to continue answering my questions, but she just stood silently with her back to me. She let me take in all the information before I asked another question.

"We would have years to educate ourselves, because we can live for a really long time," I ventured. "If it weren't for the Golden Four, we could live even longer. Can you tell me exactly who they are?" I leaned against the wall, my knees up, as I watched Era closely.

She turned around, nodding, and leaned back against the window. Her neatly trimmed nails tapped a rhythm against the cold, transparent glass. "The Golden Four are four elements, one of each, who have been chosen because of their better-than-average behaviors, talents, and powers. You have to stand out to be noticed by them. When one of the Golden Four is kicked out because of improper behavior, conspiracy, retirement, or so many other things, the other three choose between the possible candidates. There is an age limit, though; you have to be older than twenty but younger than forty-five to be chosen. Then, at the age of sixty-five, just like in the human world, you retire because of old age. After retiring, elements are already considered old, and they take up an important hobby or acquire a less demanding job. The Golden Four are mainly there to establish order and make decisions on very important issues, assisted by the Circle of Seven." She raised her grey eyes to me and noticed my clueless expression. She continued, "Seven of each element are chosen to form the Circle of Seven of air, water, earth, and fire. The Circle of Seven have important input in the discussions that take place in the Golden Hall, where the Golden Four live. They also help choose the next Golden, that's the nickname we give to members of the Golden Four, by presenting elements of interest as candidates. Of course, they can't present themselves as candidates."

I laid down on my bed now and hugged the pillow. Era sat next to me, untied my ponytail, and combed my hair with a comb she grabbed from the bathroom. Her strokes were even and steady, like Skyler with the paintbrush. I began to cry again. I felt helpless not being able to stop this. I wanted someone like my dad, someone who could understand everything I felt without my needing to speak.

Era's fingers ran through my hair and massaged my scalp slowly, stopping the tears and slowing my heartbeat, which raced every time I thought of Skyler. "You have to accept him if you want to be let out of your room," she whispered. Her voice echoed off the bare walls, making it sound louder.

I shook my head. "No." I would never accept him. He made me lose everything. Why should I give him anything?

"Why? Why do you have to be so stubborn? I already explained everything," Era stopped combing my hair. I thought she would have understood. It was hard to let someone back in who had taken so much from you. I had trusted Skyler. I had been genuinely open with him, but he didn't deserve it.

I stirred. "You know why."

Era left the room without a word, closing the door behind her and leaving me alone. I closed my eyes, taking advantage of this short moment before I must go to lunch and more training.

It must have been five minutes since I had closed my eyes, when I heard the door open and close again. I opened my eyes with great effort and stared at the doorway.

"Do you mind if I come in?" Ren pushed a set of curls behind her ear. This was something she regularly did, I realized.

I pushed myself up on the bed...and lied. "No, come in." She took a step in and stood awkwardly. She gazed out the window and tried to act comfortable. "Come sit," I invited, gesturing her toward the bed.

Ren sat down on the bed and took in the stitching on the fabric. Her finger ran over it lightly, like I had done yesterday. "How did training go for you? I am so exhausted, I can barely pick up my feet to walk, but I'm getting kind of lonely. Juris is a pain in the ass, and Aiden's silence creeps me out. Besides, he got burned up." She propped her feet up against the wall and smiled at me. "That left you."

"Third choice, I am honored."

"I don't really know you...Anyway, I thought I would try now. So, how was training?"

I pondered on how much I should tell her. What if we were competing against each other? They would have said something if we were; if not the woman, Era would have mentioned it. "At first it was frustrating, but when I got to throwing knives, I got better."

Ren blew a large pink bubble. How had she gotten bubble gum? "Well, I found out that I'm really good at dodging and I'm pretty resistant, so when I did the obstacle course, I completely aced it. But when I tried weapons, I was only good with firearms. That's it. Have you ever practiced throwing knives before?"

"No. Weapons were more of my brother's hobby. He was into military training and loved practicing with melee weapons."

Ren sat silently.

"I bet you were pretty good too. Have you done any obstacle courses before?" I threw the conversation back at her. For all I knew, she might be telling everything to Juris afterward, but I doubted that would be the case. That's what she would want me to think, though. I didn't like this way of living and not being able to trust anyone. At least I knew I was not going to fall off any more roofs, and that was a major plus.

Her bright orange hair blinded me at first. It flew out of her scalp in perky curls, creating a halo around her head. "Well, I am agile. I was always good at dodge ball, but I guess we won't be playing that anymore." She laughed gracelessly, trying to hide some tears that were gathering in her eyes. She scooted discreetly toward me, making me a bit more uncomfortable. I had hugged her during training, but that was different. It seemed like we were all sent to die there.

I had to change the topic—fast. Something was bothering her, and I didn't want her to break down in my room like I had already done, luckily, before she came. "So what about Juris?" I asked.

She shrugged. "I have no idea what is up with him. I mean, the only thing he does is talk about himself, brag about the life he'll never have again, and share his dreams for the life he'll have as one of the Golden Four." She mimicked his voice and posture. "They'll have to choose me if I stay surrounded by all of you jerks. I'll look like a god." She transformed back into herself. "He's not even that hot. I bet he won't even have an admirable job. But that's what I thought before he had his power. Now surely, they'll put him at the top of the list, way ahead of all of us until we get our powers. Now that I think of it, he would really fit as the boss of the army, ya' know?"

"How do you know there's an army?" Why hadn't I been told about any of the jobs that we could have? Why was I the only one who knew next to nothing?

Ren looked up at me. "I know because I asked my adviser about the jobs. He told me the ones I should go for. I was thinking of professional athlete, maybe an ice-skater. I love the elegant dresses, with all the glitter, and the how gracefully skaters glide over the ice. It's like flying. And what are you planning on doing?"

I blinked. I found that the only thing I could do at the moment. "I have no idea."

She nodded and raised an eyebrow, a grin spreading across her face. "And what do you think of Aiden?" Her eyes looked playful like my brothers had when he had asked about Skyler.

I wanted to bury my face in my hands. And what about him? "He seems much nicer than Juris." I tried to make my comment sound nice without insinuating anything. I remembered when he soothed me in the hallway. *Look at me.* His eyes had seemed so surreal. Juris, Ren, and I did have shocking pigments, but they could have been an intensified version of any human's. The world was filled with light-blue eyes and shocking greens, but never had I seen someone with pure gold eyes. I found myself blushing at the thought of him.

Ren braided her wild hair, not noticing the bright color on my cheeks. "Yeah, I know, right? But the distance he puts between himself and the rest of us reminds me of my younger brother. I had two brothers and a sister. We all looked alike, with our dark hair and green-blue eyes, but my sister was sort of the oddball. She had reddish hair like my mother, but we still had the same eye color. She was beautiful. And now, I look more like her than ever, except for the really intense blue eyes and wild curls. But other than that, we look similar. And maybe it sounds weird, but I feel much closer to her than I used to as a human. I also feel whole. Didn't that happen to you? That, as a human, you felt something was missing, but you couldn't quite figure out what?"

"I had never thought of that. It had never occurred to me. But I did shelter myself a lot in books." I had to admit that Ren did seem to have a bit more depth than what I had originally expected from her.

"The awesome thing about being an element is that we're going to look so good for so long. Just imagine all the fashion trends we're going to be able to wear." She kept on braiding, and even though her hair protested and jumped out of each twist, she managed to keep the braid going after repositioning them. "Anyway, are you hoping to enter the more modern half of the city or the less advanced side?" She continued talking when she saw that I wasn't helping the conversation flow. I wondered if she would be able to remain silent for more than five minutes.

Less advanced side? More modern half? What in the world was I getting into? "As I told you before, I have no idea whatsoever about Arcane. I only know that there are two bodies in the government—the Golden Four and the Circle of Seven." I began to play with my hair too. I wasn't good at braiding like Ren; instead, I just twisted the strands around my finger until I almost cut off my circulation. My finger reddened as I tightened the hair around it and then went back to a strange pale color as soon as I let go.

Ren bit her bottom lip. "Well, what if you ask your protector about it? Or maybe your adviser." She had good intentions, but I knew she hadn't found out about my punching Skyler in the nose. He could have blocked it easily, or even dodged it. He let me punch him. Oh my gosh, he let me hit him on purpose! Why? Did he think he deserved it? Did he think it would make me feel better? He was right on both counts.

"Yeah, I started on the wrong foot with my protector, and the relationship we have is pretty cold. I can be blamed for things I did, but he took advantage..." My voice trailed off, leaving the sentence unfinished.

"Wait, you have a boy protector? That is so cool." I guessed she had been assigned a girl protector. "Ours could be best friends for all we know. He told me that he had trained here with the other protectors and said some were pretty neat."

"So you have a male protector too?"

"Yeah. Too bad I can't date him. He is *so* cute." She grinned, showing her radiant white teeth. They could have been used for toothpaste commercials, but I highly doubted that elements would have large billboards with advertisements. There would be too much competition, and all the commercials would look alike.

I opened my mouth to say something, when someone walked into my room. I seriously didn't know what was going on or how many people had access to my room, but it seemed like an open house. There was no privacy and definitely no knocking. That was another thing I missed from my old life.

"Ren, we have to go." He was handsome, Ren's protector. His beauty was strange because he looked like every other half-element, but he had his own style.

Ren winked at me and smiled. "So, I'll see you later?" I answered with a quick nod, and she strode happily after him, bouncing with each step. Once she got past the corner of the hallway, I realized my watch guard was holding something out to me.

It was a package. It was covered in black paper and tied with a golden string. I took it and waited until the door shut before opening it. I placed the box on the dresser, untied the string, and carefully unwrapped it. Under the paper, whatever they had sent me was secured inside a bright metallic box. Its luster was blinding. There was a small hook on the side that I unlatched to open the box. I saw a white envelope with my name written in cursive and what looked like a tablet. I opened the envelope first, hoping it would explain how to use the mechanism I had received. I read the letter carefully.

Dear Aurora,

I'm dreadfully sorry I can't be there right now, but I will be with you in the evening, hopefully. I should have given this to you while I was with you, but this box hadn't arrived. This tablet device is something we call the PF2, or Person Finder 2. It's the second model and has higher image quality, more information, and finds people in seconds.

You can turn it on by pressing the button with a transparent circle on it, at the top left corner of the tablet. A white bar will appear in the center of the screen. Tap it once, and a keyboard will pop up on the touch screen. You have to type the person's full name; no nicknames are valid. Then, a list of people will appear on the screen, and you must find the one you are looking for. To make navigation easier, the device has been adjusted to only find people you knew in your human life.

Once you're in the person's profile, you will be able to see his or her general information. The buttons at the bottom of the screen will show different information about that person, and you will see two other buttons labeled "Video Watch." With these, you will be able to watch footage of the person in actual time, or you can choose a moment from his or her past life, and then search for someone else.

I hope this helps you feel better. Your element friends, the other newborns, will also receive tablets. Do not lose yours, because you will not be able to get another one. Don't mix it up with the rest.

I hope to see you during the evening,

Era

I laid down the letter and stared at the PF2. I slipped it out of the box and pressed the power button at the top left corner. It glowed as the device turned on. When the bar appeared on the screen, I tapped it once as I had been instructed, and the keyboard popped up. I thought for a second about who I should search for first. The first person who came to mind was Steven, my brother. I typed in his full name, Steven Henderson, and waited for his profile to load.

Name: Steven Henderson

Address: Logway Road

Age: 22

Biological Parents: Karen Greywater and Nigel Henderson

Gender: Male

Race: Human

School: Jenrake Military Boot Camp

Brothers: -none-

Sisters: -none-

Children: -none-

What did that mean? No sisters? He still had me. Even though I died as a human, that was only one part of my essence, not the whole thing! Or maybe the information registered was what he thought he knew. If they erased his mind, it would make sense that he wouldn't know I was actually his sister. All of his memories of me were gone. The only comfort I had was that my family wasn't suffering any pain about my "death." But I think that hurt me more than anything else. Yes, it would be awful if they had suffered, but it was worse to be forgotten. I imagined that my funeral would be filled with people that went to say their last good-byes, but knowing that no one would remember me left a big hole. Everyone who had loved me didn't anymore.

I wondered how hard this was on Aiden, Ren, and Juris. Juris would try to hide the pain and act as if he didn't care, but I knew that deep down it would somehow affect him. Maybe it would soften his heart a bit.

I looked at the picture of Steven on his profile. It was a picture of his face. His expression was neutral and his eyes seemed to be looking straight into the camera. In the reflection of his pupils, I could see the road in front of him and nothing else. How had they taken this picture? He looked handsome, handsomer than I ever gave him credit for, but he wasn't superstar material. No one in my family was until I got the extreme makeover. I looked like a ridiculous superstar who tried to gain popularity by wearing crazy outfits or having an extreme haircut. I didn't look that bad, but the different colors were a shock to me. My hand instinctively reached for my hair. I caressed it and then began to read the buttons Era wrote about.

The different buttons read: Biography, Personal Information, History, Moments Shared with Element, Camera, and Search.

I didn't really want to read Steven's biography, and I already knew History and Moments Shared with Element. The camera option didn't tempt me. What if I got him showering? He never had a schedule, and he would do anything at any time. Instead, I pressed Search and typed in Violet.

Her profile popped up instantly.

Name: Violet Becker
Address: Fernwood Drive
Age: 17
Biological Parents: Monica Stellar and Eric Becker
Gender: Female
Race: Human
School: Ashwick Public High School
Brothers: -none-
Sisters: -none-
Children: -none-

I already knew all of Violet's information, so I ran my gaze over it and quickly pressed Video Watch. I wanted to see her. The screen went black, and then it suddenly burst with color. All the information had been in black and white, so I thought the video would too.

She was curled up in the turquoise hammock she had hanging in her room. It slightly swayed from side to side as she softly pushed herself from the wall. Her eyes were shut, and a broad smile played on her face. The phone was pressed to her ear. She was listening to the person on the other the end. I couldn't hear whoever it was. I didn't even know if I could hear her either until she spoke.

Her voice was just like I remembered it. "Yeah. I mean, I hope we can do that, but I was thinking about going to the movies tomorrow. I don't feel like going out today. Maybe you could come over? We wouldn't be able to hang around in the garden, because Mom and Dad decided they want a pool in the backyard, so..." The person on the other end of the line cut her off. People in Ashwick had manners, so this person must have been close—as close as we had been. I felt heaviness rain on me. I knew I shouldn't be sad, because they had erased her memory, but the fact that she'd replaced me, well, hurt.

"Of course!" She laughed so spontaneously, I was about to cry. My surroundings were hushed, and I leaned in closer to the tablet. "Maybe we could read a while, do our homework together. And, oh my gosh, I didn't tell you! Remember the guy I told you about?" There was a pause. I knew which guy. "Yeah, the one from Venice! Well, he called me yesterday to talk about stuff and how sorry he felt for not following me that day. He said he's been up to a lot of things, and this was the first moment he had to get to a phone and talk to me. I honestly thought that he..." The other person cut her off again.

Outside her window, I could see her father with some men next to him. They were pointing around the garden, maybe trying to see where the pool would fit best or look the nicest. I could see some of the bright flowers that her mother had planted. I also saw the ones we planted, the alstroemerias, above where we buried her old journals.

Violet began to talk again, but I clicked on "End Video" because I didn't want to hear what I was missing or what she should be telling *me*. I've never been the jealous type, but this enraged me and made me want to cry for two different reasons: I missed her, and she should have remembered me.

Something also caught my attention. When she called me, the same night I had been killed, she had wanted to tell me something about Skyler, about him not being who he said he was. But how could she have known him? They hadn't met anywhere else. I concentrated on our previous conversations. She recognized him at lunch the day before, or thought she recognized him. But how could you not remember someone who looked like him? Perhaps his face had been covered and...no...Skyler was Henry from Venice? That was impossible.

I went on and typed my father's name to forget about these thoughts. The only way I could be sure was by asking Skyler, and I would rather just forget the whole issue until I was certain. I read my father's history. There were so many things I hadn't known about him, about his past, like how he lost both his parents at the age of nineteen. I knew my grandparents died really young but not that young. I also learned that my mother would have had five children without counting me, but three had been miscarriages. All the names of the children, born or not, were listed: Susan, George, Josephine, Carol, and Steven. None of them were mine.

Why wasn't my name on the profiles? Why wasn't I listed as Steven's sister?

Chapter 9

I stepped near the door, hoping that it would slide open as it usually did. But this time, it didn't. I stepped in front of it again, but it remained motionless. I even jumped, but all my efforts seemed useless. If the door was locked, it meant that there was someone out there. I looked down at my boots. After slipping them on again, I knocked on the slab of movable metal.

There was a soft click from the other side, not the sound of a key but one more of a switch, and then the door slid open. The guard on the other side looked at me indifferently, like another animal locked up in the zoo. "What do you need?'

I ran my fingers through my hair and raised my eyes to his. All my guards seemed strangely gigantic. "I want to see if you could ask for Era, or if I could go to Ren's room. You know, to talk."

He looked at me with raised eyebrows when he heard the name Ren. "I beg your pardon?"

"You know, the water element? The girl with orange curly hair?" I tried to explain, acting innocent and brainless.

He pressed his wristband and spoke into it after giving me a second glance. "Air element heading for your station. Watch her after she passes the limit, and make sure she stays on track." He pointed in the direction I had to walk in order to get to Ren's room. "Just go straight, and then turn right. After the second break in the hall, turn right again and go straight until you find the room zero three."

I nodded and walked in the direction where he was pointing. I wasn't really going to go there. I was going to explore and then make it look as if I had gotten lost on my way. I would turn right at the first break in the hall and then go my own way. It was stupid of the guard to let me go alone, when I could easily do as I chose once I was out of sight, exactly what I would be doing in a few moments. Maybe he was fond of me. Maybe I had won a bit of trust. But all I knew for sure was that he was going to get into a lot of trouble.

I shrugged my shoulders. At least he'd learn from his mistakes. I turned on the balls of my feet and immersed myself in the bleached walls. This training center was strategically planned. I knew that I would soon run into a watch post, which was hidden behind the walls. Equipment was concealed all over the place, so they could determine where I was and when I left. Worry began to bubble in my stomach. This was wrong. I completely abused of the guard, telling him the fattest lie I could think of at the moment without arousing too much suspicion. I whisked away the worry.

My paces echoed in the empty halls. Weird how there was absolutely no one around when I walked through the halls. There was something off about the echo. I lazily caught on after a while. I wasn't the only one walking. It was like there was some sort of counter beat to my walk. The sound had seemed faint before, but now it felt as if it belonged to someone who was walking alongside me.

Aiden appeared around the bend and jumped slightly when he saw my figure appear against the white of the halls. "Aiden!' I exclaimed, hugging him tightly. I was overwhelmed with relief, but I suddenly withdrew myself from the embrace, realizing that moments ago, he had been terribly burned. "I thought you would be dead or in a coma. How did you survive the burns? You look great now."

I recalled his burned body on the white stretcher. He had looked so damaged with his soot-stained skin and dark red, exposed flesh. He had looked like a bomb victim, but now he was intact. His hair had miraculously grown back, even at the same length as before, perhaps a bit shorter. His clothes had been untouched, but that was the only thing that had kept him from looking like a frying hamburger.

Those flames had been so tall.

He smiled after regaining his normal expression and color. "I think I should roam the hallway more often if I'm going to bump into you each time."

I would have blushed at the comment, but I was too busy looking at the bandages that covered his arms. They were a slightly different color than the tone of his skin and had little holes to let air reach the scorched skin underneath, helping his skin regenerate. His eyes fell to his hands as he turned them around, looking at the twists in the cloth. The corners of his mouth turned downward into a frown. "I was taken to the medical wing where some doctors took care of me. A bit of fake skin here and there, but they said I would be all right. I have to apply ointment all over my body three times a day, and they said I should be good as new for the test. I've been told that the jury favored the flawless." The small scars on his face would soon be invisible.

I remembered when I was a young girl, I had burned myself with a frying pan. My mom had been frying eggs for breakfast. I had been too eager to get them out, too impatient, and grabbed the pan by its edge. It had taken me three seconds to completely remove my fingers from the hot metal, three whole seconds to realize that I had been burned. The balls of my fingers had swollen up and turned the same color as exposed tissue. It had taken many days of ointment to make the swelling go down and some weeks for the burn to completely heal.

I looked at Aiden's face, then his arms, and then his face again. Astonishment took over me as I realized how much he had improved in such little time. "Well, I'm glad you're okay. You had all of us worried sick."

"Aurora," he tested my name for the first time. Even I wasn't used to it yet. But it felt like me in a way, unlike Nicole, which felt provisional. Aurora sounded graceful and elegant; two things I really needed to work on, but if I did, I could live up to my name.

I took a step back, allowing some space to settle in between us. "What are you doing out here, Aiden?" I called him by his name as he had done with me. All noise was suspended, and I could only hear my breathing and my heartbeat steadily drumming inside my chest. He stared at me straight on. I could hold his gaze without feeling awkward.

"I was walking back to my room. What about you?" He returned the question to me. I wished he could be a bit more creative and ask another question. What was I really going to answer to this? Yeah, I wanted to escape my room, because I was being held captive until I agreed to accept Skyler as my protector.

"I wanted to escape," I told him ironically, hoping he wouldn't catch on to the reality of my words.

Instead, he nodded. He understood? He must be feeling it too: the loss, the pain, the loneliness. He looked down both directions of the hall and then turned back to me. "Well, to be honest, I don't think I can help you with an escape route, but we can talk if you want. I doubt my room is the first place someone will go looking for you." He extended his arm to show the way.

I considered turning down his offer, but I wanted to talk and he didn't seem like such a bad option. "Why not?"

I followed him down the halls until we stood in front of his door. He let me walk in first and invited me to sit on a comfortable sofa.

I felt the brown leather under my fingers. Leather reminded me of my father's knife collection. My dad had wrapped the knives in their cases with their sharp ends protected by small sheaths that smelled like a saddle or really old books. Actually, everything old smelled the same. I curled up in a ball against the armrest and leaned against the back cushions. The leather squeaked and groaned as I nestled into it.

Aiden sat on the floor against his bed, facing me. He observed me silently as I moved restlessly on his sofa and made too much noise. So much for grace and elegance. He grinned as he watched, his teeth perfectly white and straight. He shuffled a bit himself, but nothing could compare to me. His golden eyes flashed in the dim light. Funny how moments ago I was wishing for sleep, and now I was wide awake, searching for someone to talk to about the information I now knew.

"Do you mind if I ask how it was?" I asked.

Aiden's head tilted to one side. "How what was?"

I didn't know whether I should ask about it or not. "The fire, healing, all that."

"Don't take it personally, but I don't want to talk about it at the moment. How was training, though?" Aiden's room looked a lot like him. The bedspread was a reddish-brown that looked as if it had golden detail on it, and the walls were painted black. The illumination was a simulation of candlelight that cast dark shadows across the room. Aiden had his shutters closed so light from outside couldn't come in. There was also the possibility that he didn't have any windows to provide natural light.

I relaxed my head on the sofa cushions and exhaled. "I have never trained with weapons or at such an intense rate. We got to pick the stations we wanted to practice, so I went with knives, archery, personal defense, and the obstacle course. I don't think I've worked my muscles this much for a long time." I rubbed the back of my legs automatically. The ache was already coming back. I had been too distracted by the tablet and Ren that I had forgotten all about how tired I was. I saw a slim, shiny silver lid. "Aiden, can I ask you a question?"

He looked up, intrigued. "Ask away."

"Did you get a tablet?"

"Yeah, why?"

I kept my eyes on the silvery box. Maybe it had happened to him too. "Did you search for your parents and your siblings?"

He shook his head. "I didn't get the chance to do it yet, I just got back from the medical wing." He kept his head up, holding it with his hands, which were propped up on his knees. His hair shone red now more than ever. "Did you?"

I hid my face in my hair. "Yes." Underneath my hair I could see him, divided by all the silver strands, leaning back and looking around the room. I didn't quite understand what this meant.

"And what happened?"

"I'm not considered a child of my parents or the sister of my brother."

He nodded and sat down next to me on the sofa with a quiet sigh. "What if our parents aren't our real parents, our biological ones?"

My eyebrows shot up, and I couldn't feel anything else but offended. "You're saying that my mother, who wouldn't be my real mother, could have adopted me and not mention it to me?" He opened his mouth to justify his argument, but I didn't let him go on filling my head with nonsense. "You know nothing about my family, and you don't know that my mother would have told me I was adopted if I were—which I'm not!" My arms waved around me, almost hitting him in the exact spot I had hit Skyler.

He grabbed my arm just before I could punch him in the face. His grip was soft and secure around my skin. He lowered my arm slowly and took his time letting it go. The ghost of his touch remained on me. My cheeks flushed. He looked away.

"It's true that I don't know your family," Aiden began, "but I was suggesting it as a possibility. Don't you wonder why none of our brothers or sisters is an element too? Two humans cannot give birth to an element. A human and an element give birth to a mixed race. This only leaves the possibility that we were born from two element parents. There is no other explanation. And if this is true, with the few things that I know about the community, I am sure that they must have placed you with your family in an unobtrusive way, like changing their real child for you when she was born." He fiddled with the transparent clasps they used to hold his bandages together.

"Why would you think that? Why would you doubt everything? Even your own family..."

"Because things are different now; I can't expect to have died and only a portion of my reality be a lie. I have to consider every detail that they could have altered." He slumped back down and made a dismissive motion with his hands, signaling me to forget it. I definitely would.

My legs ached and protested, because they were cramped and I was balled up. I slowly shifted into a regular sitting position, facing Aiden. "What was your life like before all of this happened? What was your family like?"

Aiden looked lost in thought for a few minutes, as if he was caught in a daydream, his eyes fixed in place.

"You don't have to answer if it's too personal."

He ran his fingers through his hair, returning to the real world. I didn't think he would answer, as his was face expressionless; but suddenly he began speaking. "We were ten in my family: my mom and dad, six sisters, and an older brother. I was the third child, Phillip Nolan. My father usually left Turrell to work in the city. A small-town job wouldn't earn him enough money to raise all his children, so my eldest brother took care of us when mom was busy with housework. It was hard to hire cleaning staff in town; no one wanted to come and work at our home." He laughed at the memory. "We once had this maid who quit because she was tired of making nine beds every day and cleaning up after the girls."

As he turned to me, the face of Philip Nolan filtered through for a brief second. Aiden cleared his throat and ran his fingers over a pink line on his face, touching a patch of skin. Or it was a piece of fake skin that they had added? Perhaps it was one of the few pieces that were really his. His gaze traveled to the small space between the wall and the ceiling from where the candlelight glowed. His eyes were eroded sand dunes, warm and golden, in the sunrise of a warm day. I could almost feel the warmth of the sand in his gaze, the tan of hills in his skin, the roughness in his hands, and the beauty in his smile. "Is it a habit of yours to stare?"

I really didn't mind anymore. What's wrong with looking at someone? "You could say that."

"What a shame. I kind of like feeling special." I couldn't quite figure him out. His smile vanished slowly, and he sat up straighter before tackling the next topic. "I heard, well, I have been told that you have an issue with your protector."

How did he know? His face was dead serious, and he didn't appear afraid or distant. How much did he know? "He didn't kill me straight on." I decided to volunteer the least amount of information and only answer if he asked.

"And how did he kill you?" He played with his hands while he watched me.

"My protector got me to climb to the roof of my school, and by the way, I am terrified by heights. Then he pushed me off. Apparently, I survived the two-story fall, so he dragged me into the forest and cut my wrists so I would bleed out." I just told the whole story in two sentences, as if it was all right, but my voice cracked a bit when I spoke.

"That must have hurt."

"Yeah."

"Is that why you punched him?"

Aiden knew I had punched him. How did he know? What if Juris and Ren found out too? "Yes, and also because he..." I didn't know if I should finish the sentence. What would I say? Yeah, I sort of had a crush on him, but then he crushed my bones. No way. "He toyed with me before killing me."

Aiden frowned and his eyebrows furrowed. "You mean he..."

I turned away, afraid to blush or even turn red in embarrassment. "No. NO! He would never do that. I said it wrong. He played with my feelings." I needed to set things straight. I didn't want to be bothered about this, and hopefully Aiden knew how to keep a secret.

"You must have a really good arm, because you broke his nose. He's supposed to know how to dodge those kinds of attacks." He watched me roll my eyes and instantly guessed my conclusion. "Unless he let you hit him."

I nodded. "That's what I thought."

"At least he assumes the consequences of his actions."

I pressed my forehead against the heel of my hand. "People can always tell what I'm feeling. I'm not good at hiding my emotions. And I didn't really mean to punch him, but I guess my impulses got the better of me," I confessed in a low voice, but not low enough so he couldn't hear.

Aiden shifted on the couch, seeming uncomfortable, but not because of his position. "I get what you mean. It's hard, especially now, to know who you can trust."

"So, how were you killed?" I inquired softly, knowing that the topic could be touchy for him too. I suddenly noticed my mistake. I shouldn't have asked him. His expression shut off completely, and he withdrew into a small shell. This only made my curiosity grow, but I wouldn't ask again. Why was he like this? One moment he was open and smiling, and then he was silent, guarded, and withdrawn.

Silence began to creep in, filling in the distance between us, when the door slid open.

Skyler quickly marched into the room. He looked at Aiden. "Where is...?" Then he looked at me. His distressed eyes seemed to relax a bit. His nose was covered in a white cast that covered most of his cheeks. "You escaped from your room again, when you know it's wrong until you accept me. Why did you do it?"

I glowered at him. "Because you killed me!"

I could feel Aiden standing back, observing the situation. I wanted to see his reaction, but I didn't want to back down.

Skyler touched his nose and glanced at Aiden. "I wasn't talking about the punch; I was referring to the fact that you left your room without permission again." His teeth clenched as he said it, and he avoided my stare. He could purposely take a punch, but he couldn't look me in the eye.

I smiled misleadingly. "I'm pretty sure the guard outside my room let me go. You can even ask him."

Skyler stared me down. I could feel his hard breath and see the purple and green bruises peeking from under the white cast. "Tell that to Era." He grabbed my hand, pulled me surprisingly gently off the couch, and quickly led me out of the room.

I wish Aiden had said something as I was being pulled away, but he just sat still with his mouth shut, as if he were glad that I was being hauled away. Maybe he was just pretending to like my company.

"Let go, I can walk on my own!" I resisted his pull, but he gripped my arm firmly.

"No."

I was back in my room in an instant after nearly jogging after Skyler. My legs burned with the pain from training this morning. Lunchtime never seemed to arrive. Era was pacing around my room, her eyebrows drawn together, and her gaze lowered. When she saw us arrive, she thanked Skyler and he left us alone. "What got into you?"

"I asked for permission," I protested weakly. Era should already know if she had asked the guard outside my room.

She rubbed her temples with her middle and index fingers. "You asked permission to go to Ren's room, and then you just disappeared. Where were you, and why didn't you go to Ren's room when you said you were going there?"

I stood uncomfortably next to the door. "I got lost. The guard didn't give good directions, and then Aiden found me and we began to talk. It's not my fault that every single hall looks exactly the same."

Era walked over to me. Her pale figure blended in with the white, silver, and light-blue room. If only I were home...Steven would be downstairs talking with my dad, and my mom would be cooking something tasty for lunch, not barf-looking slop. Everything would be so much easier.

"You can't leave anymore, unless you leave with me or Skyler or ask for an escort," she insisted. "Aurora, this is really bad for your reputation. You should be taking better care of yourself. Everything you do is registered and accounted for when you do the test. As your adviser, I advise you to clean up your act and behave your best. And as friends, I want the best for you. I want you to go to the modern side of the city.

"You see, there are different positions, as you may have realized, which are indicated by the color of the uniforms people wear to work. Some working positions have better benefits than others, but all are equal. I want you to have a good position, live near me in the modern city, and go to parties, wear the best dresses, and have the opportunity to go to a council with the Golden Four. Maybe we could arrange a meeting. Oh, and you could meet some of my friends. Some of them are younger. In Arcane, you don't have friends of the same age, except one of your fellow newborns. You and Ren will end up apart, and so will Aiden and Juris. Only two elements, one female and one male, can go to each side of the city. Impenetrable walls separate both sides, along with a river."

I could only end up with Aiden *or* Juris? Honestly, I preferred Aiden. "What if I go to the less modern area? Will you be there too?"

Era shook her head and headed over to my night table where the silver box was laying on the journal. She moved the box and grabbed the journal. "What is this?" she looked surprised when she read the three words on the page. *I did it.*

"That was already there before, probably from the element that came before me." She inhaled sharply and almost dropped the journal onto the floor. I had no idea what she was thinking, but she was staring blankly at the wall.

After a moment, she snapped out of it. "All of the advisers are chosen from the modern side of the city. So we wouldn't see each other regularly if you went to the less modern side." Her eyes gazed straight back at me with concern. "That's why I don't want you to go to the other side."

I leaned against the wall and crossed my arms. Era didn't look happy. I couldn't figure out if it was because of her tone, word choice, eyes, or just plain intuition. She turned away, and I sensed her tension. She wasn't telling me everything there was to know. What did this previous element have to do with all of it? Did he or she manage to avoid the less modern side of the city? And what was so wrong with it that she didn't want me to go there? "Are you sure that's the only reason?"

Era's mouth turned downward, and her eyes were glued to the floor. Her fingers wrapped around the edges of the book she held in her hands, crumpling the corners in her firm clutch. Her usually joyful personality was now solemn and reserved. She opened her mouth to say something and then closed it. She moved close to me and spoke in a low voice. "You don't have to decide now, but you will have to make the choice."

"What choice?" I found myself straightening up and inching toward her.

She raised her chin as her hands trembled. "If you want to know, it is your obligation to assume the consequences of that knowledge. It won't be easy, Aurora. If you prefer to have an easy mind and restful nights, that is your right. I will not impose this on you. Just take into account your strength and how far you are determined to go."

She was already imposing this on me whether she realized or not. It was the journal that had unleashed this. But did I want to know? Was it useful? There was only one way to find out. My head was already muddled, it had only been twenty-four hours since I had woken up, but I sensed this could benefit me considerably. The only question I needed to answer was: Was I willing to take the risk?

Chapter 10

"Here. Don't tell anyone about this, or it will mean a death sentence for both of us." Era fumbled with the key in the almost invisible door. Without a huge sign that read *Do Not Enter* on the hidden access, it would have been inconspicuous and a bit tricky to find. After mishandling the key for a while in the door, we could hear the sturdy *click,* and the door opened.

Everything wasn't as dreamy as they had described in the briefing. "You can have death sentences in Arcane?" I asked.

She turned to me as she entered the black hall and gestured me to follow. "Only if you do something very bad." She was swallowed by the darkness, and her footsteps echoed rhythmically in what seemed a black pit.

Once I stepped into the dark hall, I waited for the lights to turn on. But the only light, the one that came in through the threshold from the other side, disappeared as the door slid shut behind me. I didn't like this at all. I felt the wall to guide me. It felt solid and slippery, like humid bricks. A soft glow pulsed in front of me. This was like dying all over again. I half expected a tornado to come and blow me away. But no tornado came, just the eerie glow from a white torch that Era held in her hand.

"Where did you get that?" I could see the floor now and the walls too. They were, indeed, made out of stone bricks, and the floor was earth. This sector of the training facility seemed old and untouched. "Where are we?"

Era, who had waited for me to catch up, looked like a ghost with the torch only illuminating the left side of her pale face. The irises of her eyes caught the light of the ashen torch. She smiled and looked at the white flame. "Remember when I said that I was an entertainer?"

I nodded.

"Well this is my power—to create illusions. This torch is an illusion. I can create almost anything. I can make you feel as if you are in another world, in another part of this world, and many other things. The only problem is that the illusions I create are just that—illusions. They are not real. You cannot touch them or hold them. They're temporary. The bigger or more beautiful the object, the faster I get tired and the faster it disappears. This torch," she waved it in front of her face, "hardly takes any power at all. I could use this all night and not feel a thing. But it also depends on the frequency, how often I create the illusions." She grinned and turned around, taking long strides to the other end of the passageway.

I had to follow her quickly to be able to see the ground beneath my feet. It was a tiled surface, the same color as the walls, with dust cluttering the sides. Someone had swept recently because some places looked relatively clean. Trails of dust created a lane that was so packed, it almost seemed as if the floor were a light shade of grey.

"So, where do you perform? And who do you perform for?" I asked, as I tried to avoid some large mounds of rocks. Heaven knows where they came from. The conversation served as a distraction from what waited ahead.

"I do private shows and public shows at events." She kept on walking, also avoiding the random mounds. Her hips swayed in a delicate movement and she hardly looked down, as if she had memorized the entire path, as if she had been here so many times she already knew every crack, mound, and pile of dust by heart.

Era was a professional then. My hands remained on the walls, sliding into every fault and hole. I felt a bit claustrophobic. The whole place seemed to be built in the middle ages, but Era wouldn't want to put me in danger. She was my adviser.

She paused and looked to her left, holding the torch close to the wall, or more accurately, to a gap in the wall. "Going down." She vanished into the side of the wall.

"Where are we going?" I felt like I was in the story *Sleeping Beauty*—the stone walls, the uncanny light, the secrecy of it, and most of all, the silence. The echo I had heard was now gone, and a bloodcurdling stillness made the hairs on the back of my neck prickle. I put one foot after the other and lowered myself deeper into the ground. The steps were uneven, just like the rest of this sector, and my boots didn't grip well on the stone. I pushed my arms against the walls, as if I were trying to separate them, and lifted my upper body, not letting my feet rest on the steps until I was sure the steps were stable.

Era turned and glanced back every now and then and frowned, as if she knew that what I was about to go through would leave me scarred for life. The flame danced around in the small space, its bright light swaying in the darkness. I took in deep breaths of the humid air.

The stairs unexpectedly opened up into a large chamber. I could only tell because the walls drastically turned outward on both sides. My steps echoed, and Era shouted from afar to be careful. I stood quietly wherever I was and waited for the light to come on. The room had a lingering sense of emptiness that made me feel uncomfortable.

"What are you waiting for?" Era's voice was not very far away. "Here we go." The sharp sound of a lighted match was followed with the roar of an expanding flame. The walls had little dents in them where there were trails of oil that, once fully covered in flames, lit the room. The large space between the four stone walls was practically empty, except for a wooden post fixed into the ground. Two tarnished silver rings hung from the post. Both the post and the floor around it were stained with large, dark splotches. I started to approach, it but Era halted me with one gesture. "I wouldn't get close to that, honey."

"What is it?"

"Blood."

I drew away quickly and stuffed my outstretched hand under my arm. That was blood? What had they done here before? It hadn't been cleaned in ages. I gawked at Era, waiting for an explanation.

In deference to my emotional state, she tried lay it all out, simple and clear, without freaking me out. "This place is pretty old and untouched. There used to be a lot more elements in Arcane, which is why there are so many buildings, though most of them are filled with half-elements. When there are so many people, it's hard to keep an eye on all of them. If anyone broke the law, that person would spend some time here and learn. Also, humans that had found out or were involved in suspicious activities were brought here..."

"To die?"

"Sort of..." Her voice trailed off, as she pulled me away and off of the dried puddle of blood. No wonder it reeked down here. The air smelled like metal, rust, dust, and death. We bordered the room together, avoiding every little change of color on the floor, afraid that we could be stepping on some dead person's blood. "Just right through here, and you'll see." She spoke to herself in a lower voice, too loud for me not to hear her.

The fire that glowed on the walls seemed to flow to the next room, and then the next, and so on. We walked in silence, and the ghost flame Era had been carrying was long gone. It remained only in my memory, like everything else from my past life. I touched the still damp stones and leaped over some rotting planks, fearing that I would fall through. "Were you here when the other elements tortured and murdered people?"

Era turned around, stunned by the question. "You are a pretty curious element." She sounded offended, and her chin slightly pointed itself higher. "And yes I was, but right at the end of it, when the Golden Four forbade it." She turned around and led me past the empty cells, which had pristine floors. Why would they clean the cells and not the floor of the bloody torture room? I opened my mouth to ask, but I stopped, cautioning myself not to risk offending Era any further.

I withdrew my hand from the wall, remembering the amount of dried blood on the floor. Who knew what else could be in the rest of these underground tunnels? "Could I know where we're going exactly?" My voice sounded hollow within the large space. "You owe me at least that much after making me stand in a puddle of someone's blood." Using the word puddle minimized the situation.

She reached the barred door first and lifted the thick metal plank that blocked the entrance before I could help her. She set it aside and pushed the bars open. I heard scuffling sounds from the far corner as we entered, and Era lit a match. The faint glow from the tiny flame expanded as she touched it to the head of a torch. She walked alongside the wall, stopping at each torch to light it.

"I brought her to you," Era said. "Should I leave you two alone, or do you prefer I stay?" She bent down to the hunched figure that sat on a flat, dirty cot.

The voice was gruff... surely it belonged to a man. "I think we'll be fine." He waved Era away and extended his bony hand toward me. "Come, I won't bite." He signaled for me to sit next to him on the beat-up cot. I came closer but leaned against the wall, not wanting to sit on the floor or near the man.

The closing door trapped me in the small room.

We were alone.

"Was that blood yours?" I blurted out the question without thinking. He seemed startled by my blunt question. I looked at him closely, since the lighting in his room was far better than in the halls. My eyes adjusted quickly.

His scrawny hands peeked out from the long sleeves of his oversized shirt, like two forks from a drying rag. His skin was almost translucent, and I could see all of his purple-green veins bulging out underneath. His head, covered with thin silver hair, looked too big for his body. He was in bad conditions, very bad, and the lack of good nutrition was obvious. "Yes, every single drop." He looked at the door to check that no one was there and then turned to me with brown eyes that had little flecks of another color, surely green. "My name is Zareh. What's yours, child?"

"Do you want to know my human name or my element name?" My body tensed. There was no real threat to him. He was definitely too old to fight well, and he wouldn't have enough strength anyway. My only fear was that someone important might find out about my presence on the lower floor.

He smiled with crooked, rotten teeth. They were brown and chipped; some were even missing. "Both, if you like."

I hesitated to answer. "I was Nicole Henderson, and now I am Aurora." I shifted my weight from one leg to the other. Things were getting uncomfortable, and I was hoping that this wouldn't take too long.

"Aurora," he echoed. "It has several meanings, depending on the origin. It could mean good wind or dawn. Usually, they pick a name that does not vary much in meaning." His face was solemn, and his young eyes were hidden behind pain and deep wrinkles. Dark shadows hung beneath the orbits in his skull. Zareh smiled again, showing off his rotten teeth. "I see you're an air element then." He stated the only obvious fact he could about me. "And I see that Era is your adviser. She's a good woman, has plenty of tricks and secrets hidden behind that pretty face. You're in safe hands, but you must listen and obey her."

I nodded, finding it the only thing I could do at that moment. "May I ask you a question?" He sat in silence. "Why are you here?"

He moved to the edge of the cot. His backbones stuck out of the thin cloth of his ragged shirt. "I see. Well, you might have guessed that I did something very wrong. I'm actually down here because I did something right."

I laughed. "Yeah, right."

Zareh spoke with both eyebrows raised. "You don't believe me, naturally. If I did something so bad, why do you think Era would bring you down here?"

I stopped smiling. He had a point. "Mostly because I'm doing things how I want to and not how the 'law' states it. Maybe she wanted me to come down here so I could see the consequences of not obeying the law. To see how I would end up."

"Elements don't get this punishment. And no, she brought you down here because she sees potential." He ran his tongue over his cracked lips, but his tongue was also dry. "I got this punishment because the Golden Four found out that I betrayed them. I found out the truth and spoke up. So, what do you think they tried to do with me?"

This sounded like a trivia question. How many points would I get if I got the right answer? "Silence you."

He clapped. "Very good! And how do you think that's going so far?"

I couldn't help smiling. "Not very well. Wouldn't it have been easier to cut out your tongue if that were the case?"

Even though Zareh scared me slightly, he was kind. He seemed much younger than he looked. Could it be possible that the torture made him age faster in body but not in soul? I sat down next to him on the cot. Not too close, but I sat down. All he needed was company and a shower, along with fresh clothes and a toothbrush.

"They don't have bright ideas like yours, I'm afraid, though it would be best if you didn't give them any. Now, tell me what you want to be in Arcane."

"I have no idea, but Era wants me to be on the more modern side with her." I rubbed the back of my neck and craned it from side to side. My stomach grumbled with hunger, and my limbs still ached. I couldn't believe I was still experiencing this exhaustion and not fainting in the middle of the room.

He nodded, surely expecting more of an answer. "Well you shouldn't have to be worrying about that, because it's not your choice. But it would be so much easier for Era to have you in the same half of the city."

"Why were more elements in Arcane in the past, and why only one of each element each year?"

"Back then, the Golden Four didn't realize that it would be much easier to control two hundred and fifty-two elements than many more, and if they let two of each element wake up every fifty years, then there would be at least five hundred and four elements, not counting all of us half-elements," he stated clearly. "There are a lot of people on both sides of the city, about one hundred and twenty-six elements on each side." He paused in order to change the subject. "Have you ever wondered why the city is named Arcane?"

The randomness of the question aroused my curiosity. "No, why?"

"It means secrets, the city of secrets."

"Of course, the whole element race is being kept a secret from humans; it would only be logical to use that name," I replied quickly, trying to find the reason Era had brought me down here. Conversing with a prisoner didn't seem like it.

He turned to me now with a serious face and a hard expression. "That's what they would have you believe. Aurora, you can't believe everything they tell you." I leaned away from him and stared at the floor. No. I couldn't believe him. "I know it may seem hard to understand now, but the whole city, especially the Golden Four, is infested with lies."

I rubbed my head and tried to make sense of what he told me. "But...why would they want to lie to us? We have nothing. They have no reason to lie."

Zareh cracked his knuckles. I flinched at each crack in fear that his fingers would snap off. "You don't believe me."

"No."

"Tell me about the fire element. He was left in the clear box, almost experiencing death, just to see if his power was showing itself. I'm sure they did the same thing to you." Zareh selected the words carefully, searching for the tiniest reaction displayed on my face. "You think that is normal?"

That had been the question I had asked myself. "I am not normal."

He took in my words and weighed the meaning, leaving a moment of silence between us. "But I assure you, a government that is willing to put their own children in danger, their own future, just to see their potential, is twisted. We do not grab babies, newborns, and throw them out of windows just to see if they sprout wings.

"You may have noticed how elements tend to set themselves apart as a race with more rights than humans, with more intellect and talents. They are correct in one way, but they have ceased to think like elements. They imitate the very creatures they despise, releasing their young to learn from humans. And after the transformation, they blame them for being too human, too latched onto their families and their past, the only thing that they have ever known.

"And the power of the Golden Four has increased in the last few centuries because of their control over the citizens. To gain that control, they had to reduce the number of elements living in the city. They've killed thousands of half-elements and hundreds of your own kin. Just add this information to the fact that they roasted your friend alive and then compare it to their speeches of 'safety,' 'protection,' and 'truth.'

"It may not seem clear why they would lie, but it shows how contradictory they are. I was the adviser of one of the four elements that came before you. I helped them escape. That's why I was put down here, just like you said. I will not be silenced. You will escape as well."

"What?" I looked back and forth at both of his eyes.

The bars swung open, and Era darted in quickly. "Aurora, we have to go *now*." Her voice was filled with warning. Her eyes darted to the flames on the heads of the torches and finally landed on Zareh. "Turn them off."

I turned to Zareh before passing the through the doorway.

"Come to me again if you wish to know more," he offered. "I can give you the answers they do not want you to have." His voice carried through the air. His words entered my ear, ran through my skull, and exited thought the other side, only giving me seconds to register his offer before it vanished into thin air. He had given me a whole introduction just to get friendly and then sucker punched me at last moment. Had he timed it? Possibly. He wanted me to reflect on this before we met for a second time. If we met for a second time. I could return the blow by not coming back. My mind kept on replaying the five last words he had spoken. *You will escape as well.*

Chapter 11

My wet hair stuck to the back of my neck. The relaxing bath salts started to kick in, making my muscles ease from the morning training and the exhausting sitting position in the afternoon intellect training. My feet didn't drag on the floor, and my back stood straighter. "Hey again," I waved as Ren turned into the hall followed by her protector.

She beamed, following my gaze. Her protector seemed relaxed and walked unhurriedly behind her. "Isn't he, like, so adorable?" Her voice was hushed as she smiled back at him. His eyes smiled back. "So, do you know where they're taking us?"

"No," I looked at my wet hair then at Ren's.

Hers was tied up in a braid that I would never have been able to tie up by myself. It twisted from side to side, ended at the base of her neck, and then cascaded down her back. She noticed me looking at her hair and looked at mine. "I could totally braid your hair one day, or I could try to teach you."

I shook my head. "I don't have good hand coordination when they're behind my head, thanks though."

Era pushed the door open and yelled back toward us, "Girls only!"

Ren looked at her protector and blew him a kiss. He stood next to the door with his back against the wall.

The door slid shut. The room looked like that of a seamstress. Round steps stuck out from the ground, and a large table was positioned in front of them. The steps were in a semi-circular position in the middle of the room. Fabrics of different colors and textures were piled high on the table, along with sprawled pencils and papers. It looked like my room in Ashwick. A large shelf offered an endless supply of different colored pencils. The bright curtains that hung on the walls were merely decoration, since there were no windows.

Ren jumped up on one of the pedestals and twirled. "We're going to get dresses!" Her face lit up when Era nodded and knocked on the door on the other side of the room. "Why isn't my adviser here?"

"She is at the same meeting I was two days ago. Advisers have rules, and we also have to make reports." The door opened and a woman came out. "Hello, Glitter."

Glitter gazed at her from behind rectangular glasses and then at us. "I can work with this." She fanned her fingers in the air and made her way to a large padded seat behind the table. She had a full figure, brown eyes, and black hair with light-brown roots peeking out. She made herself comfortable, organized the table a bit, and invited Era to sit after ordering me to stand on one of the pedestals.

"What are the dresses for?" I asked. I hadn't been told about any celebration so important that I needed a new dress.

"The celebration for the end of training and the new beginning in the city," the designer replied indifferently. Her glasses were set near the end of her nose so she could see over them.

A pair of men came out of the same door Glitter had come, fully decked with measuring tapes around their necks, pencils behind their ears, notepads in their pockets, and weird wristbands with needles stuck in them. They flew to us without delay.

Ren held her chin up high and her arms out wide so the man that was measuring her small waist wouldn't have any difficulties. I felt the measuring tape tighten around my own waist, and I looked at the man who was measuring me. He was wearing full black contact lenses. He looked drugged, as if his pupils had dilated way too much and were now stuck like that forever.

"So, what do you think we should do with her?" Glitter asked Era, looking at me as if no man was measuring me. She stared me down. "Maybe like this?" Her pencil scratched the paper underneath and left a black trail. I couldn't see much of what Glitter was drawing, because she was evidently hiding it from my view.

Ren called to me from her pedestal. "What do you think yours will look like?" Her eyebrows were raised and her blue eyes were bluer than ever.

"I don't have a clue, but I bet yours will be blue."

Era caught on to our conversation and wore that motherly gaze she usually had before explaining something about elements and Arcane. "Dresses are very important in celebrations. They represent your element and your personality, usually. There are always exceptions. The dresses have to be made for each body type. It's not valid to copy anyone else's design or make it almost the same. There's no rule, but of course, it's a guideline that us women follow. And each dress has to be different. No dress can be used twice in the same year."

"You only wear a dress once?" Ren asked the question I was thinking.

"Basically. It's an old tradition we have. The origin of this tendency started when Nina, the Golden of Fire, was crowned. She stated that no woman could use the same dress twice in a year. She imposes all the fashion trends. Of course, you can reuse it, but for some other occasion."

Ren turned to me and whispered, "I think that woman is totally awesome."

I disagreed with that. It sounded like a waste of cloth. If you had thirty parties in one year, you already had thirty dresses. And the next year, you wouldn't reuse all of them, so that meant more dresses. Shouldn't there be some sort of way to reuse the cloth for another dress? I could already picture the closet of a seventy-eight-year-old female element wondering how she was going to fit in at least two more dresses. "How many parties a year are there where we would have to make dresses? And why is this party so important? Shouldn't we celebrate after we're chosen for sides?"

Era looked up from the drawing and nodded at Glitter. "We should make this wrap around and then tie it up to her..." Her finger pointed to someplace on the paper. I was dying of curiosity to know what the dress would look like. "What, Honey? Oh yes, um, well we might have around three major parties a year, but you don't have to go to all of them. Then there are the parties that people arrange, and you only can go if you receive an invitation. But at first, you'll rarely get invited to any of them. As you grow a bit more, you'll become essential at the parties. There is also a party after you get selected, naturally, but don't you think that the end of training for our newborns is a matter to celebrate? We only get to do this once every fifty years." She looked back down at the drawing.

The man who had been measuring me was writing down the measurements and passed the paper to Glitter. What an odd name for her. I've never actually heard of the name Glitter, but if I had I would have associated it with a naïve, blonde, size zero, popular girl, not a heavy, black-haired woman wearing thick glasses.

Ren looked down at the floor and balanced her weight on the balls of her feet. Her smile vanished. "I wish we could go to the same side of the city together. It's gonna be such a bummer to start in a new city without someone I already know." Her braid fell over her shoulder, and she played with the curled end.

I looked at her with sympathy. She knew we weren't going to be together, and I really hadn't thought about being separated and how I would have to make new friends again. "I know, I bet we could visit each other." I didn't really know her though, so it didn't really change the situation. What I was worried about was being stuck on the same side with Juris. He hadn't even put effort into giving a good impression.

Her face lit up. "Yeah, and..."

"Aurora, could you come over here for a second?" Era called to me from the doorway.

I nodded and jumped off the pedestal, making my way to Era. "What?" My voice was low and casual.

"Look, I need to stay here with Ren and Glitter, working on Ren's dress. We already finished yours. Would you mind going to your room alone?" Her head tilted downward, as if she were assigning a very difficult task. "And when I let you out on your own, please go directly to your room. I don't want to organize a search party for the third time."

I rolled my eyes. "Of course, I will go directly to my room without delay." She didn't look convinced. "I promise." She still didn't look convinced, but let me out the door.

I couldn't believe they still trusted me walking alone down the halls. I thought they would have sentenced me to a total lockdown. And the fact that Era had taken me to meet Zareh caught me off guard. It had been only two days since he told me that I was going to have to escape. I still hadn't decided what to do with that information. What he had said terrified me. They had killed hundreds of elements in the past, what could stop them now? This made me wonder even more why we were training with mundane weapons. Yeah, they allowed us to use all of our muscles, depending on what we chose, but regular gym did that as well.

The whole place was as secure as a prison. How did he expect me to run away from here? Somehow, the four elements before Ren, Aiden, Juris and me had escaped, but that was fifty years ago. Now, unquestionably, the security had been doubled, so it wouldn't happen again. No one would want the only four new citizens to run away every year. And why hadn't they found them? Didn't they have the best technology?

I walked down the never-ending hallway, while these thoughts ran through my head. Thinking too hard made my forehead throb. Suddenly, I heard footsteps coming from behind. "Ren..." I stopped in mid-sentence, because the person running behind me wasn't Ren. My face paled.

Of course, he wasn't running. If he had, his boots would have sounded like thunder a mile away. Instead, he was marching determinedly down the hall toward me. "Aurora," Juris hissed as he got closer.

I stood my ground. I had heard that if I ever encountered a wild animal, I should never look it in the eyes. That would only mean I was defying the predator. I forgot about this as I turned around.

"I'm going to say something, and you are going to listen."

Juris stood in front of me as straight as a column and looked down at me. He was taller, yes, but not huge. He was only half a head taller, at most. I breathed in to puff up my chest. I must have looked like a blowfish. "Hello, Juris. How are you?"

"When we are at training, I want you to step down. Got it?" His ivy green eyes looked like entwined stems of a creeper. They flashed green when the light hit them and darkened when they were in the shade, expanding the pupils into deep wells.

I touched my still-wet hair and took a step back, just to gain distance between us. I could feel his breath when he spoke.

"Now, why would you want me to do that?" I countered. I was intrigued to hear the stupid reason why I should throw away my training. I had to do my best so I would be better prepared for the test, better prepared for my escape.

"You know why."

"Is it because you don't want to end up on the same side of the city as me? How do you expect me to do that? And I won't do it. You cannot tell me what to do, so if you don't want to end up on the same side, as if you knew the criteria they use to select us, I advise you to step down."

He glared at me with rage, his hands curling up into fists at his sides. "You will step down, because you know I'm doing it for your own good."

I rolled my eyes. "If you really wanted the best for me, you would be encouraging me to do my best. Why do you want me to step down?"

"Shut up."

"Do you want to be with Ren? Do you like her?" The words slipped out of my mouth like soap from buttery fingers. I couldn't believe I had just said that to Juris. Of course he didn't like Ren.

The space between us was suddenly consumed with his large body. I looked up at him, leaning my head back against the wall. The space felt too small; I could almost touch his chest. His hands pressed against the wall on either side of my head. "Take that back."

I raised my hands and tried to set some distance between us, but he didn't budge. "Come on, Juris, it's not like we're in third grade. What's..."

"Take it back." His left hand grabbed my shoulder and pinned me to the wall. I couldn't shake him off or push him away.

I struggled, knowing it would be in vain. "Get off!" I yelled at him. My voice echoed throughout the empty hallways. Juris's dark, strong fingers curled around my shoulder and dug into my back.

"Juris, please," my voice was more persuasive, but still not as convincing as I wanted it to be.

Juris grabbed my neck and began to squeeze, slowly suffocating me. I tried to reach up and claw his hands away, but he grabbed them and pressed his body against mine. "Listen to this. You will step down because I say so. Because that way and only that way, the watchers stop watching you. It's the only way to look weak enough, so you don't catch their eye and their undivided attention. Keep your talents hidden, your questions hushed, and your eyes on the ground. The less they know, the harder it will be for them to track us down."

We heard a scream.

He let go.

We looked at each other, puzzled, and ran in the direction of the scream.

It had come from Ren's room. She stood in the hallway, looking at her hand, with her back against the wall. She was wrapped in a light blue towel, and her hair was tied up in a braided bun. She was wet, as if she had just ran out of the shower because a spider was hidden between the tiles. But of course, there were no spiders here.

Juris got to her first. He had longer strides than I did, and even though I was faster, he was more persistent. "Ren..."

"Don't touch me." She kept looking at her hands, horrified.

My feet ached. The boots were new, so my feet felt as if they had been compressed between walls of leather, and my bones were about to shatter. "What's wrong, Ren?" I looked down at her hands. They were perfectly normal, a bit shaky, but the same color and size they had always been. I couldn't find an explanation for her sudden, fearful outburst.

"My hands...My hands..." She stammered. She looked her hands with absolute terror. "Aurora, Juris. I...my hands, they were..." Her voice trailed off, as if she didn't know what to say or how to explain.

Juris took her hands in his and turned them around. After deeply analyzing them, he let them fall to her sides. "Nothing is wrong with them." He shrugged and looked at me as if Ren were crazy.

I didn't look back. "Ren, what happened?"

"I wanted to take a bath, so I turned on the shower and undressed. When I stood under the water for a while, it began to turn into something..." Her eyes were wide. She rubbed her temples and looked back at Juris and me helplessly.

I grabbed her bare arm. Her skin felt cold under my hand. "Could you show me, please?" I could feel my heart beat in my feet. *Thump. Thump. Thump.* The beat was as steady as the rocking chair in art class, when I first met Skyler, when I didn't know that he would betray and kill me...

Juris and I followed Ren into her bathroom. She stood in front of the sink and waited until Juris and I flanked her sides to turn on the water. She nervously turned the wheel of the faucet, and water gushed out in a steady stream. She slid her hand under the water and looked away, closing her eyes. Juris and I observed steadily.

Ren was right.

After only five seconds, the middle of her hand began to turn light blue, which darkened as the color webbed across her hand, covering every inch of it. Her nails turned silver as the water cascaded over her skin. The blue kept expanding until it reached her fingers. It dripped down them as if the pigment were paint, paint that moved under her epidermis. Ren cried out silently. She was watching too but kept her hand under the current for our benefit. Her skin was changing texture. The soft flesh of her hand was now covered with reptile-like scales. They shone in the bathroom light. Once her skin came in contact with water, it seemed to wash off, revealing the scales.

Ren's protector made his way past Juris and looked at her hand. "Holy shit, you got your power!" His smile was broad and white. He put his arm around her and shook her lightly. She forced a smiled, but I could sense the tension in her body. "This is great!" He didn't seem to be disgusted or scared or distressed. I bet he was used to seeing this kind of transformation. I didn't think I could ever get used to it.

Everyone stayed quiet in the bathroom. Ren's protector's enthusiasm diminished after he noticed our reactions. He slipped his arm away from Ren, taking it off her shoulder and silently placing it at his side.

Chapter 12

Moments after my shoes were off my feet, moments after the awkwardness settled for good between us in the bathroom, Ren's room seemed to fill up quickly. Skyler was in the crowd. He was there. Why was he there? My head drummed at the same speed as my feet. I walked barefoot among the people who were asking Ren questions. I really didn't care if they were doctors, researchers, or whatever. I walked straight toward the guy I had been avoiding for a three whole days.

He was staring at me through the mob as he usually did. His eyes looked darker than the rest—a darker shade of brown, a darker shade of green. "Aurora." The one word he said reminded me that I used to talk to him when my name was different, and that this new name, Aurora, felt strange but somehow fit perfectly. Then I thought of Aiden slowly testing my name. He had said is slowly and gently, while Skyler spoke it as if it were a formality.

"Skyler," I answered back, trying to avoid looking at the white bandages on his nose. "Do you mind if we talk somewhere more..."

"Private?" He was surprised that I wanted to talk to him. "That sounds good."

We both turned into the white maze. My mind had already memorized the turns and paths to different destinations. The only path I didn't quite remember was the one I took with Era to see Zareh. I didn't know if Skyler knew about Zareh or even the cells that rested a few feet below the very floor on which we stood. "Something happened to me."

His eyes were concerned, his body tensed. "What happened?"

"Nothing..."

"Aurora, I want you to be up front with me. What happened?" Why was he overacting?

I shrugged my shoulders and told him that I wasn't feeling very safe. I left out the part that Juris had been the one to attack me.

He looked at me from a distance, respecting the boundaries I had set ever since I punched him in the nose. "What do you mean? Did someone threaten you?" My gaze implied the obvious. "Who did this to you?" He touched my neck lightly where I supposed there were marks that Juris's fingers left behind.

"You name the sin, not the sinner," I remarked. "The name isn't important. I just wanted to tell you that I accept you as my protector. Maybe I prefer being followed by you than him..."

"You mean Juris?"

"How did you know?"

"Everyone takes the pain, the emptiness, or whatever they feel for their loss differently. You took it out on me—one punch and your head cleared. Juris is trying to secure his future. He wants to be sure he can be in control of his life, since recently everything whirled out of control. He makes himself look hard, tough, but I can assure you that something inside him is crumbling." His explanation left me speechless. He usually never gave me any information. Then again, that was when I thought I was human. He remained on the far side of the hall.

"How can you be so sure?"

He paused outside my door to let me walk in first. "Aurora, you must understand that though you aren't humans anymore, you still have feelings." He slumped and sat on the floor, while I sat on my bed. He could tell I still wasn't convinced.

I crossed my legs and looked out the window, avoiding his gaze. "You should know more than anyone, shouldn't you?"

I could see him press his lips into a thin line through the corner of my eye. "You should know that that was my job. I threw you off the roof for your own good. If I hadn't been there, if you hadn't been chosen, you would be dead or living with the most insufferable pain ever. And if you had died, you wouldn't wake up to this. God, you're never happy with anything. I even let you punch me in the face! I let you break my nose! I made sure that somehow you wouldn't get in trouble for escaping your room. I even brought this back to you." He pulled a piece of paper out of his pocket and extended his hand toward me. I was forced to look at him.

I crept silently toward Skyler, afraid to see what was on the paper. As I got closer, I realized that he wasn't holding a piece of paper. It was a picture—a picture of my parents. My dad was dressed in his military uniform, his backpack hung over his shoulder and an arm around my mother's waist as she kissed his cheek. She was wearing the flowered dress Dad loved, and her hair was tied in a twisted bun. Her red lipstick looked good on her. She looked younger. I couldn't help smiling. This was the picture mother kept on her night table and kissed every night when she prayed for her husband to return home safe and sound.

"Where did you get this?" I asked.

Skyler smiled. "As your protector, I'm sort of in charge of clearing all your memories from anyone who knew you or possibly knew you. We almost had to go through the whole town erasing everyone's memories. As we were clearing out the pictures, I saw this one and thought you'd like it. I made a duplicate and put it back where I found it, but this is the original. No one can know, so this is our secret, okay?" His fingers didn't let go of the image until I tugged a bit harder.

I looked at the photo and remembered the nights when I had wished for my dad to come back home. "Thank you."

"Wow, I never thought that I was going to hear that from you."

I could feel Skyler watching me as I carefully placed the picture in the PF2's silver box. I hid the box in my drawer. "When you said that the others who don't get transformed suffer, what did you mean?"

"Have you ever heard of Alzheimer's?"

"Yeah."

He met my gaze to intensify the message. "Well, the scientifically prepared body doesn't last forever, just as long as any human would. Old age isn't what kills it. After a while, the essence in the body recognizes that it doesn't belong there. Usually, this starts at a later age. Once the essence recognizes that it isn't at home, it starts breaking down the body. How? It starts in the brain. That's where the Alzheimer's part comes in. It's much more painful for an element than it is for a human. When the brain is too damaged, the body shuts down, and the essence travels back into its original body. But this one is already gone, so the essence transforms itself into its purest state. This last part happens to every element when he or she dies. In your case, your body will turn into air."

"You have to be joking."

"Nope."

"And what do you turn into?" If he was half-human and half-element, did he have a soul or an essence? And if he did have an essence, what would he turn into? Probably a pile of dirt...His irises contained green, and I only knew one element with that trait. He didn't answer. There was so much I wanted to know, but I didn't know what to ask.

"So..." The conversation fell into an awkward zone, as neither of us knew what to talk about. "You had a crush on me?"

I wanted to hit him. I wanted to hit him again so badly. I wish I had just shut up when I blurted out that unnecessary fact. I sat in silence, hoping no answer was better than making a fool of myself.

"So, you did have a crush on me."

"Hard not to. You were the only guy who intrigued me. Now I know you are a complete ass. Problem solved. But am I that predictable?"

He shrugged. "You're not predictable, I manipulated you. You had every right to punch me, and that's why I let you." He walked over to where I sat on the bed. I tensed. He sat down, rested his head on his fist and looked at me. I looked back. "I shouldn't have...fooled you. I had no idea about your feelings. I'm sorry."

I enjoyed listening to those words. I savored them. He was sorry. He hadn't meant it. Or had he? I remembered Violet's words: "*He isn't who he says he is.*"

"The same way you manipulated Violet, Henry?" I asked pointedly.

Skyler drew in a breath. "That was not my intention. I never knew that she was going to take it so seriously...we were just fooling around."

"Just fooling around? Skyler, she was my best friend!"

He raised his arms in defense. "Nothing happened! I only made out with her once, okay? That's it."

"Why did you call her back then? Why didn't you wipe her memory clean from recognizing you? If it was just fooling around, I don't think you would have bothered to preserve her memory of Henry." I ran my fingers through my hair. He opted for breaking her heart when he had had the opportunity to make a clean cut. She could have had the chance to forget him and move on.

Finally, he turned to me. "Okay, I admit I screwed up. I do like her, a lot. And I know that I should have erased that memory from her, but I didn't want to take it away. I wanted to handle the situation the right way. Yes, I will call her to end it because that is how it should be done, not cutting corners to avoid pain."

I hated when he convinced me that he was right. He knew he wouldn't be able to have a relationship with a human, so why risk it? On top of that, she was my best friend and he knew that! "I want you to call her today."

"If I do, will that make you happy?"

"I don't care, but it is the right thing to do." I turned to him and added, "You're an ass."

He winked at me. "I know." That wink, his smile. He was driving me mad. We just spoke about Violet, and now he was acting up again? I moved to the other end of the bed. This made him laugh. "Do you still hate me?"

"Hate is a strong word; I prefer annoyed." I tried to remember how Aiden did that strange thing with his fingers to keep his hands busy.

"So, you mean I can't hug you or anything?"

"Don't you dare..." It was too late. Skyler was already at my side, wrapping his arms around me. "If you don't let go, I'm going to..."

When he backed away, I let myself breathe again. The air around me still smelled like him, like the blanket around my shoulders on the rooftop, like his hand holding mine in the kitchen. I despised him for reminding me. I detested him because he had taken my life away.

"Ary?" He said my nickname for the first time. Ary. It seemed so simple, but I didn't want my nickname to have anything to do with Skyler. I was only letting him be my protector so I wouldn't feel threatened anymore. He messed up his hair with his hand and gazed at me. I shuddered, suddenly feeling invaded. "Ary, are you okay?"

"Yeah, why?"

"You look a little pale."

Stifled laughter escaped my lips. He smiled. He wasn't dumb. He never had been. That's what I hated most. He knew how to make me smile, laugh, and feel good. It couldn't hurt to have at least one friend in this twisted world. "Tell me something..."

The door slid opened, cutting me off mid sentence, as a pair of large teenagers strode in. Skyler immediately stood up and moved closer to me. His jaw tensed as the boys wearing dark red suits approached us.

"You have both been summoned."

I stood up but remained behind Skyler as we were both led to a small room with three chairs and a glass coffee table. I wiped my hands against my pants to dry the sweat. A man was already seated in one of the chairs.

"Please, sit down." He invited us in with a wave of his hand. He wore a large golden ring on his finger, but I couldn't make out the design; it was hidden from view.

I followed orders and sat down directly in front of the man. His turquoise eyes followed Skyler until he was seated and then turned to me. "You do not need to be afraid." He smiled, noticing how my hands curled into my lap and the way I stared at the two boys dressed in red.

Skyler nodded his head toward the man and greeted him. There was a slight hint of restraint in his voice. "Your majesty, it is an honor to be seated in your presence."

Your majesty? I turned to the subject in front of me and suddenly realized who he was. His red hair was intricately combed to clear his face and there was an air of authority in his gaze. He wore a pristine, dark-blue suit, which must have cost double the amount of any college degree. The color matched his features well and made the golden ring on his finger stand out. The emblem on it could have only meant one thing.

I was sitting in front of one of the monarchs—the Golden of Water.

The monarch ignored Skyler's salutation and smiled at me, as if he realized what I had discovered. "I'll explain why you have been called for in a moment, but first, have a drink." The boys in read gave each of us a glass of water. The clear liquid sat eerily still in the glass. The cup was covered in golden details, which felt cold when I grabbed it. I took a shy sip since as the monarch stared at me, but Skyler didn't leave one drop.

The monarch smiled once more. "I heard that there have been conflicts between you two. Am I right?" Skyler cleared his throat, and I felt a chill run down my body. This felt like a trick question, even though I had worked it out.

I looked over at my protector. He set down his glass on the table and wiped the sweat from his forehead.

"We have already solved the problem, and I have accepted him as my protector," I announced.

Why was one of the Golden Four here? One would assume that the highest in power would only deal with the most important issues in the city, so why was he summoning us over a teenage drama? I took another sip from the glass before setting it down.

"Indeed." He watched us carefully. "Are you not thirsty, Aurora?"

I stumbled on my thoughts, as I tried to figure out what to say. "I feel like it's rude to be enjoying a beverage while you are not drinking one yourself."

"Such manners." His voice sent goose bumps crawling over my skin. "It is a shame, though, that you are so disobedient." His fingers played at the ends of the armrests, his ring flashing underneath the lights.

I suddenly began to feel warmer inside. The feeling trickled over me slowly, enveloping me in a warm embrace before turning ice cold. My eyes lost focus for a second. I turned to Skyler. His body shook and beads of sweat fell from his hair. "What?" I gasped as pain began to swell from inside me.

The monarch sat silently, watching us groan. "You both have disobeyed our rules. Rules are essential for maintaining peace and order. They are established to make life easier. And even though you do not believe we see you when you break them, we do. And because of that, you both must suffer the consequences of your acts. You see, I never make my citizens do anything. I always give them options. For example, I brought the glasses, and you chose to drink a sip while your friend drank the whole thing. He punished himself."

I stared at my glass of water and then at Skyler's. The pain was everywhere and nowhere at the same time. I didn't know where it began or where it ended. My breathing became harder, when Skyler screamed out. He had drunk the whole thing. The whole glass. What had they put in the water?

"Aurora, your cleverness is awarded; you shall not have to tolerate too much pain. The next time you think of stepping out of line, consider first what may come of it." I started freaking out, trying to stand up, but I found myself paralyzed. I longed to reach for Skyler, but he sat as still as ever and screamed. My eyes searched for an answer. "Do not worry," the monarch came to me and grabbed my hand, "the poison will fade eventually."

He stood and left the room, as if nothing had happened. His steps were slow and steady. I could hear him say something to one of the boys in red, who he directed to watch over us.

I needed to get the poison out of my system. I was thinking of solutions when I managed to break free from the paralysis. In one swift moment, I stuck my fingers down the back of my throat and made myself gag. If only I could throw it up, maybe I could reduce the effects and help Skyler.

I bent forward; my stomach churned and expelled its contents. The shivering began to stop as I wiped my mouth with the back of my hand.

Skyler screamed and his hands clutched the armrests. The two boys in red began to laugh. I shot them a daring look and then returned to my quest. I needed to make Skyler throw up. All the side effects I had felt fled from my body once all the contents of my stomach were gone. I took hold of Skyler's shoulders, but one of the boys tossed me to the side. My body slid on the floor.

"What do you think you're doing?" He stared me down. "You must think you're special because you're an element, don't you? Well, let me tell you one thing...I don't care what you are. When you break the rules, you receive the same punishment as the rest of us." He grabbed my hair, pulling my face upward. He made me look at Skyler.

Skyler's face was flushed with color and sweat covered him. He clenched and unclenched his jaw. Why were they doing this to us? *To* him? I admit that I hadn't been playing clean the whole time, but the things I did were minor, nothing that deserved this type of punishment. I tried to play back all the situations that could have angered the monarch.

My heart beat a little faster. He knew. The Golden Four knew that I visited Zareh. They knew that he was right, so they were trying to intimidate me and make me feel that if I left, I would suffer greatly. That only meant one thing—Zareh was right. And they would use Skyler against me.

But how did they find out? Era wouldn't have taken me there if she had known that they would punish me. I turned my eyes to the ground and tried to shut out the noise of Skyler's screams.

* * *

Once the poison wore off, we were escorted back to my room. I made sure the door was closed before I spoke. "Skyler, tell me about your childhood in Arcane." I moved closer to him and kept my voice low in case there was some type of recording device in my room.

He tensed. "It was pretty different from how you grew up."

"Skyler I need to know." I touched his arm lightly. Being this close to him reminded me of my family, of Violet, of the roof and the fall, but I pushed back all the imagines that popped into my mind and concentrated on the present. "Please."

"You met with Zareh, didn't you?" So, he was in on it as well.

"Yes."

Skyler ran a hand through his hair. "They know, or maybe only Wiley knows." Silence settled between us. "He's the freaking monarch of Water. Do you know how that can affect you if your king knows? You have to be careful, Ary."

I took a step back, frustrated. "Tell me Skyler, how was your life in Arcane?"

"I told you already, different. They way the elements move about is different. It's a place where duties and obligations are thrust upon you, and you have to carry them out because everyone else does. If you fail to complete your tasks, then the whole mechanism stops working. Harsh laws keep order and peace. But the main part of the city isn't that bad. The only things I know from the southern side are myths, that's why you have to speak with Zareh about it."

I could only hear his voice, as the picture of him screaming and squirming in the chair was emblazoned on insides of my eyelids. One of the monarchs had given us poison and didn't even flinch. "I did study about your origins and about some of the history. All I can tell you is that Arcane was built out of the ruins of the ancient ways. Elements were splitting up and leaking into the human world, so they created a city where they could use their powers and live in society. They shut the place down, so no one could go in or out unless he or she had been authorized by the Golden Four."

"Do you know about the massacre that happened not so long ago?" I asked. Zareh hadn't told me much about the past or why exactly I was in danger.

"The facts are vague, but supposedly it wasn't considered a massacre, it was actually a transition in which most of the population moved to the less modern side, or southern side, and were never heard of again. Not hearing from the elements of the different sector is quite normal, but a lot of things changed after that, and people became suspicious. Rumors spread that in the southern side, elements were tortured and used for experimentation. Our female monarch supports this because she considers it as a way to learn." He paced around the room as he spoke, trying to tell me everything in a way I could understand. "Why don't you go down and ask Zareh for clearer information and instructions. I can imagine you are considering leaving now."

I didn't speak a word. There was something that didn't make sense. I couldn't put my finger on it, but I was beginning to feel that what Skyler described wasn't the worst thing going on at the moment.

"These rumors...how do they spread? Where do they come from?" I asked.

He tried to smile. "A whisper."

"This makes no sense!" I threw myself on the bed and buried my face in my pillow. I screamed into it to release some of my frustration. "Everything is so confusing. I mean, why do I even have a protector if the city is so safe? Why did I get poisoned for seeing a prisoner? It only confirms that Zareh is right."

Skyler sat down next to me. "It's more of a tradition. In the past, when The Golden Four discovered that the race of half-elements existed, they made families give up their children to protect them from danger as they crossed back and forth between the elemental realm and the human one. I guess those dangers subsided, but the Golden Four decided to keep the tradition to demonstrate their superiority over my race. It also helps them keep an eye on all of you. I know I shouldn't be saying this, but I am their eyes and ears in your life. If I see anything suspicious, I have to report you. And if I side with you, I get punished. But we also have to help you and accompany you through your first years in the city. You'll probably lose Era in a couple of years, perhaps two or three humans, but me... I'm sticking around until I get old or until I die."

I blew some strands of hair away from my face. "How very nice."

"And as far as the poisoning...I think he knew that you weren't going to drink it all. He must have believed that by making sure I got poisoned, you would back down. If the Golden Four doesn't want you to know something, there is a reason behind it. If they figure out that you know something that you shouldn't, they punish you." He extended his hands toward me, showing little scars that webbed his skin. "It also may be a warning; if you leave, I'll suffer." He spoke the last sentence to himself.

I looked at the floor. Arcane used to sound like a magnificent place, but now the pleasures it offered were tinged with blood. If you lived the way you were told, you were safe, secure, and protected. If you decided to step out of the box they created, or even peep out, there would be punishment, death, and an overpowering government that didn't hesitate to show you your place.

"Do you mind if we change topic?" My voice was devoid of emotion. I didn't want to think anymore until I saw Zareh again.

Skyler looked straight at me.

"What?" I gazed back.

"You haven't done that since the last night you were Nicole." He tried to gloss over the fact that he threw me off a roof and then slit my wrists by replacing it with my old name. Surprising how such a smart boy didn't realize that my last night as Nicole had been spent in a clear coffin, "sleeping."

I raised one eyebrow. "Done what?"

He slid closer to me. I didn't like the closeness. I tensed again. My muscles were still spent from the morning training, but my body was getting used to it. No more clear box, thank goodness. Ever since Aiden had been scorched alive, we hadn't seen the glass box again in the training wing.

"You haven't looked me in the eyes without anger or resentment."

"And you know that because..."

"Because I know."

This made me laugh. "Do you now? Tell me some things about me." I sat up straight, curious about what he was about to say.

He smiled. I didn't know whether I liked him, despised him, or just felt sorry for him. He was stuck with me for the rest of my life, for his life, which would probably end in eighty years. I, however, would have turned eighteen and would already be halfway to my nineteenth birthday. "Well, you love to read. I saw a billion books in your room. You especially like fiction, action, and romance. But you don't mind reading science fiction, suspense, or drama. Your father joined the military, and you never got to see him much while he was away. Now he's back. You only have one brother. You're an element, air to be more specific, and you still don't have any power that I or any member of your crew..."

"I have a crew?"

"That's what we call the group of people that is constantly around you. And before you interrupted me, I was going to say that you don't have any power that we know of, which I hope you tell us before we find out on our own. Do you need to hear any more to prove that I know you?"

I shook my head. "What you just said is what you deduced about my room and what you already know. It's a poor answer, I'm afraid to say."

"I know that you hate black licorice."

My eyes widened. There could be no possible way he knew that unless..."You read my old diaries?" He flushed and ducked from my glare. "Answer me, Skyler."

He rubbed the back of his neck and smiled. "Only one or two entries. Not much...I swear I didn't read anything personal. I mean, the only entries I read were foolish comments about situations any seven-year-old writes about." I sighed in relief but didn't tell him I wrote most of the diaries when I was nine and ten. That would have just been embarrassing.

"Skyler you still don't..." I looked down at my hands. His fingers ran over mine. They didn't move away. What the heck did he think he was doing? I slipped my fingers from underneath his. "You are not doing this." I said louder than necessary.

"Doing what?"

I moved away to put some distance between us. "Don't act as if you just didn't make a move. Okay, I accept you as my protector. Follow me around all you want, but don't expect me to act like Nicole. Especially after what you did to Violet."

He rubbed his head with confusion as if he didn't understand. Maybe he wondered why he even placed his hand on mine. "Okay, that's fine with me."

"Good." I leaned back on the dresser and stared at the floor.

He stood up to leave. "Sure."

"No, don't go." I took his arm to stop him from leaving. "Look, I didn't mean to be so harsh, but you have to understand. We can still be friends. It's just that I can't feel that way for a person who killed me, besides, it would be against the law."

He looked up and took my hand. "Ary, I get it. Okay? Don't worry. I don't know what got into me; I didn't mean to make this awkward. I have to go." He turned around one more time before leaving. "Since when did you start obeying the law?"

Chapter 13

"This, somehow, is my dress?" I raised my hand, levitating the white cloth that was sewn together in something called a sleeve. My hair was tied back into a bun so it wouldn't get in the way of the white cloth that drenched my colorless body into less color. The only things that held the pieces of fabric together were safety pins and needles. If I moved too much, the needles poked my skin.

The man who had been measuring me the day before was now inserting more pins into the cloth that hung around me like an oversized cloak. "Stay still," he scolded me, and I let my arms fall back to a ballerina position. I couldn't tell how I looked or how the dress was going to fit. It was just a prototype, Era and Glitter told me as they slipped on the cloth. Now Era sat behind her desk, looking steadily at the drawing and then at me.

Glitter walked around me, instructing the man with needles to pin up the cloth, tightening it around my chest and abdomen. I had lost weight since I had transformed, or been born again, but the extra fat had slowly come back, as the slop we had to eat filled my stomach morning, noon, and night.

"No! I told you to bring up that piece to her shoulder...Maybe you could...Yes, I like that. We could wrap it around the torso," Glitter instructed.

A pin poked into my skin. "Watch it," I barked.

The stylist quickly pulled out the pin and then stuck it back in again, carefully staying clear of my pale skin. "It's hard enough with you moving around all the time," he spat back bitterly. I didn't like him. He didn't like me. Our dislike was mutual.

"Stop it, you two!" Era reprimanded us from the desk. She nodded and agreed with everything Glitter said, but now her eyes were fixed on me. "What are we going to do with her hair? It looks nice pulled up, doesn't it? It clears her face and it would show off the top."

Glitter took as step back, almost bumping into the desk, and admired her creation. "Yes, I think you're right. I was thinking that we could find a way to make it funnel upward into a ponytail, but I think the bun looks fine. It makes her look more angelic; whereas, the ponytail, with strong makeup, would make her look a bit more dangerous and modern."

"What do you prefer, Aurora, to look angelic or dangerous?" Era asked, as the stylist stepped back to observe his work.

I looked down at the loose skirt. The cloth prototype wasn't very pretty, and it was quite hard. "I don't want to stand out."

Glitter pinched her nose with her index finger and her thumb. "What is she talking about?" She acted as if it were some major drama. She looked back at me, trying to make me understand. "You have to stand out. You have to be noticed. If not, I fail as a designer. This is my chance, and I'm not letting some stubborn air element take it away from me. No, no, no, no. Now twirl." I rolled my eyes and spun on the pedestal until she told me to stop. I felt light-headed from all that spinning.

Era offered me a chair. I was about to say yes, when I realized that it would be dangerous to sit on a bunch of pins. I asked her if I could take off the cloth.

With careful fingers, the stylist peeled the dress off of me and hung it on a rack inside a black bag. It was strange that I didn't get to see my dress. Usually it was the guests who were intrigued by the gown.

I sat down and curled into a ball on the chair. I laid my head on my knees and thought. Spinning around wasn't the only reason I was light-headed. Everything that had happened in the last few days kept me wondering about so many things. I wondered what the exact date was. I didn't even know what month it was. I had woken up five days ago. Four days ago, I had started training. I had seen Ren drown and Juris use his power to defend himself. It sounded illogical that I was training with human weapons and had a protector, even though I was going to enter into the safest city. I had seen Aiden burn alive in a glass box. I had also met Zareh, who told me that I had to escape.

Two days ago, I was told that I was going to go to a party, Juris had threatened me, Ren had gotten her power, I had accepted Skyler as my protector, we got poisoned, and Skyler had held my hand. He had held my hand. I couldn't believe he had dared. Ever since Skyler held my hand, things began spiraling from bad to worse, despite what I had told him about just being friends. He walked me to breakfast, lunch, and dinner. He ate with me and waited outside my door. Sometimes, he would follow me everywhere, ask me about everything, and he would try to touch me...my hand, my arm, my shoulder. The walk to physical training today was nothing less than uncomfortable.

Training yesterday had been brutal, leaving me with several bruises after trying to disarm my enemy. Zareh's face had popped into my head. What if he was right? Maybe we were training so they could release us into an arena to fight to the death. Or maybe they were sending us on an impossible mission in which all of our critical thinking skills would become essential. But we wouldn't be doing any of these things. No, we were going to go to the city to live calmly and peacefully, so why did we need to know how to throw a knife?

Aiden had been burned, and nobody had reacted to this. Could it be that the end of training celebration is to celebrate our survival? Training could be the test. But who were the watchers? And how did they watch us? Could Juris be right? Lately, I had been avoiding him. We hadn't encountered each other again except at lunch, where nobody spoke. A haunted silence had taken over as well as exhaustion.

I tried to remember what Juris had said. He had told me that in order to lose the attention of the watchers, I had to play weak. I had to let them underestimate me. He had mentioned them tracking us down. Was it possible that he also knew about Zareh? Was he also going to escape? Did we have to escape together? If we did escape, what would we do with Aiden and Ren?

If Juris was right, then I had blown my cover. In the last four days, I had been trying my best and my hardest. Playing dumb would be obvious now. The watchers probably already knew my strengths and weaknesses. If they knew me, then it would be easier to track me down because they would be able to predict all my moves. I hadn't seen Juris "step down" either, though.

I couldn't believe that I was actually considering the idea of escaping. But what other choice did I have? I did not trust a place that burned and poisoned teenagers for fun.

That's when I accidentally heard the conversation between Era and Glitter.

"Is he going to do the same with her this round?" Glitter whispered to Era, as if I couldn't hear. She kept her voice low. I had been so caught up in my thoughts that I hadn't heard the earlier part of the conversation.

Era sighed. "I hope so. It would be tragic if he didn't. How do you think they'll... you know?" I felt as if I were eavesdropping on my parents' intimate conversation when they spoke "in code." But these weren't my parents, not even my mother. I felt the picture of my father become heavier in my pocket. No, he wasn't my biological father, but he was my father. He had loved me and cared for me.

"All I know is that it will be much harder than last time," Glitter whispered. "Surely the heads of security have doubled the cameras and all the security measures. I would be infuriated if someone did this to me, spilling my secrets and ruining the plans I had been working on for years." Glitter knew. Who else was in on it? Did the whole training center know that Juris intended to run away, that perhaps I would agree to join him? Wow, I never thought that I would ever agree with Juris, not in my lifetime.

"Yes, but he's only doing it for the best. He's wise enough to risk his life to save two other ones. He almost lost it the last time," Era replied.

"I wonder why they kept him alive. I wouldn't have found it useful to keep him. So, it would have been much better for him not to keep on living, if you know what I mean..." Glitter's voice trailed off. I acted as if I couldn't hear them, as if I were still caught up in my own thoughts. But they lowered their voices even more, so listening got harder.

"He is useful," Era continued. "He has helped with many innovations in the city—the neutralizers for out-of-control powers or for protection, the silhouette-tight silk, and much more. He has provided many things for our city when he should have been penalized."

"Did you take her down?" I knew what "down" was.

"Of course."

"Does she know?"

There was a pause.

I could hardly make out what Era answered. "She knows what he did and what she's going to have to do, but I don't know if she wants to. She hasn't spoken to me about it, and I don't want to push the issue. She's very sensitive about these things."

"She's sensitive?" Glitter asked, as if I didn't have feelings.

Era laughed. "If she can feel a needle, I bet she can feel the loss."

"I don't think it's much of a loss."

"You haven't been through it, that's why."

"Neither have you."

"Almost."

Silence settled in again.

"Ary, you know, you can go to your room now if you want." This felt like my old life. She was trying to act like my mother. Well, no matter how hard she tried, she wasn't my mother.

* * *

As I got closer to my room, I noticed someone standing outside my door. The man looked familiar with his large, oversized body and his arms and chest packed with muscles. He was guarding my door. He shouldn't be. I had already accepted Skyler. "What are you doing here?" I asked. "I don't need surveillance anymore."

He smiled shyly. The smile didn't fit his face, and it looked out of place with his proportions. This "stone statue" guard now smiled at me. "I just wanted to make sure you were okay."

"By guarding my door?"

He looked down at the floor, ashamed. He wasn't telling me something. He was being too nice. "What? Imagine if you get your power today. You would need assistance, and I can offer that assistance." Quick save, but I didn't buy it.

I didn't know what to say. I stood outside my room, awkwardly waiting for an interruption, for a chance to leave.

"Oh, I forgot to tell you. You have a visitor."

"Thanks." I excused myself quickly and entered my room. Aiden stood up when he saw me enter. A smile spread across his face, one of the goofiest I'd ever seen...not that I'd seen much from him. His smile was perfectly straight, the white teeth contrasted against his tan skin. His arms were no longer bandaged. No scars were left. He looked fine, if you know what I mean...

"Hi." It was hard for me to look him in the eyes for a long time, since I was afraid he would see into me. I didn't know how it happened or when, but he made me nervous and jittery.

"Hey, Ary." The nickname Skyler had given me had spread like wildfire. It made my name sound less formal though. "I'm sorry I walked in on you and all, but I really wanted to show you something."

His eyes sparked with excitement.

"No, it's fine. What is it?"

His smile. Oh, man.

"I got my power."

"That's great!" I exclaimed as I hugged him. "Congratulations!" This was a pretty big thing for both of us, since neither of us had gotten our power. Ren and Juris were already practicing how to control theirs.

I had been expecting the embrace to be short and friendly, but he held me there for a bit longer, not allowing me to back away when I intended. This extension made me feel his warmth and allowed me to smell the pleasant aroma that stuck to his skin. I felt my knees weaken and make the task of letting go become even harder. When we parted, I stared into his golden eyes. I wished I could touch the small flaws in his irises, the cracks in the golden halo. "What's your power?"

He held out his hands. It seems they could all do things with their hands. I couldn't do anything. I had no power. "Watch." He rubbed his hands together quickly and then cupped them, blowing lightly into a hole he formed with his fingers. I watched in awe. He looked up at me. His hands were still cupped and shielded everything that was going on between them. His eyes flickered with joy. Finally, he slowly opened his palms.

It was beautiful.

He held a tiny flame in the center of his hand. It danced around in an invisible current that came out of nowhere. It was light blue at the bottom, like the shallow end of the Mediterranean Sea, and as golden as his eyes on the middle and top of the flame. It was a small thing, puny, completely defenseless, but it could burn.

"Check this out." He pressed his hands together and exhaled slowly, emptying his lungs. Where the flame had once danced, lightly licking his hand, there was a little black stone. It was perfectly round and glowed blue in the light.

"What is that?" I asked, holding myself back from touching it and breaking it.

He shrugged. "I have no idea. I haven't told anyone yet. All I know is that if I press it long enough, this little ball becomes transparent, almost like a little diamond. Maybe if I learn a bit more about my power, I can make a bigger flame. Who knows?" He smiled and then looked down at the floor. He must have remembered that I still remained powerless. I would have felt exactly the same if I were in his position. "You still don't..."

I forced a smile so he wouldn't know that it hurt to be the only one without a power. I couldn't help feeling a bit jealous. "Don't worry, I'm a late bloomer. I mean, I did wake up later didn't I?"

"Yeah, you're probably right. You could get your power in a month or so, and that would be perfectly normal." He smiled and ran his fingers through his russet hair. Seeing him so open was a rare thing.

I managed a muffled laugh. As ironic as his comment was, it still hurt a bit. I might not get a power. I would get all the bad things of being an element without having the good ones. "And you say that as if you were perfectly normal."

"You're right." His face turned serious and he stepped back, but not too far away.

"What?"

"I'm not normal." He looked down, avoiding my gaze. I didn't mean to hurt him. The corners of his mouth didn't budge. "I'm...an element." He hesitated.

I nudged him. "You..."

He stood his ground and hardly budged. After a moment of uncomfortable silence, he began to laugh. Soon I began laughing too. I had almost forgotten what it felt like to laugh, careless of what just happened and what would follow. It warmed my stomach and spread the heat through my limbs. I savored the last feelings of it before it vanished.

"So, how does it feel to have a power? How did you know you got it?" I walked around the room, wondering why I didn't have a sofa. My fingers grazed the edges of my furniture as I passed them.

He stared at his hands, turning them over, inspecting every crease or wrinkle. "I don't know. You just...feel it. Juris got it by luck during the test, and Ren found out because she was about to take a shower. But I just began rubbing my hands together, don't ask why, and this tiny flame sprouted from my hand without burning me. I guess it was just this feeling that drove me to discovering my power. You might already have your power. You never know." I couldn't help looking at my own hands while he spoke.

"Couldn't there be some way, like a meditation sort of thing, that could help me discover my power, or at least help me get it?" I clasped my hands tightly together in frustration. The tips of my fingers turned red and kept on darkening as I held my ground. When I felt that I was about to cut off my circulation, I let go.

Aiden observed me passively. He looked at my reddened fingers and frowned. "Don't take it out on yourself. You have every reason to be a late bloomer. Or maybe you have such an especially powerful power that's taking longer to come out. Do you get what I mean?"

I nodded, but inside, I felt doubtful. I had no concrete reason why I woke up so late from the transformation and didn't understand how that could have any possible influence on my power. When I walked past him, he grabbed my shoulders and engulfed me in another hug. His breath tickled me as he spoke into my ear.

"Hey, you shouldn't be sad."

I pulled away and smiled at him, a silent thank you for understanding me without a lot of explanation.

"My power is quite useless for now. I mean, a tiny flame? The most I can do is burned an ant and hopefully piss off an earth element."

"Are you kidding? Your power is amazing! Soon you'll be able to set things on fire! Your skin is fireproof!"

He touched his arms as he pondered silently. "For all I know, I might only be fire proof as long as I am the one to light the flame. You shouldn't let powers define you. You are so much more than that."

Chapter 14

The morning passed in a flash.

I woke up to more nightmares in which I was falling and the severe pain of pins was prickling my skin. Somehow the stylist had left some of them in my clothes, and I couldn't help feeling that it was on purpose.

Breakfast was quiet and disgusting.

Training was intense.

The shower was too hot.

I couldn't feel any more tired. There was no time for rest, so both my mind and body were exhausted.

I sprawled over the bedspread, caressing my hair gently with the brush. My hair dried quickly and fell naturally in even waves. The shape of my hair was like a birthmark. No matter what you tried to do to change it, it never changed. The brush was neutral; I hadn't chosen a mode. My hair fanned around my head, and my knees loomed over my body, feet pushed up close.

S. Elizabeth Dover

There was a knock on the door. It distracted me from observing details on the plain white—no surprise there—ceiling. I tossed the brush onto my dresser, my aim flawless because of knife-throwing training, and rolled over on my bed. "Come in," I called casually.

Juris walked in.

"Get out."

He looked at me helplessly. "But I just..."

"Get...out...now, " I growled.

Juris remained in the doorway without moving. He finally began walking toward me, only daring to take a step or two. "Ary, listen to me!"

I raised an eyebrow. "Why should I?"

"Because you need to hear me out." he yelled. My eyebrow fell back into place. I looked outside the door, which still hadn't slid shut, to see if Skyler was out there. He had told me he was leaving to take a bath and then come back...where was he? "About the other day, in the hall..."

"I won't step down. I won't do it." I interrupted again. I stared at him sullenly.

"Shut up for a second, will you?" he yelled again. I hope he wouldn't make a habit of this. I felt small and defenseless lying on the bed. He paced around my room, agitated, as I cowered. "The other day, I really don't know what came over me, Ary. I've never felt this way before. I used to be a good kid, you know. I had good grades; I helped around the house; I made my mom happy. I would help my little sister with her homework, and I even volunteered for charity; but this..." He looked at his reflection in the mirror. "This changed me. It changed more than my appearance." He looked at my reflection, staring at my body. I wanted to stand up, cover myself with something not so tight and run. He ran his eyes over my face over and over again as if trying to read my thoughts. "These anger attacks are occurring more often than before, so I apologize for that, but we have a more important matter at hand. You haven't listened to me." He banged my dresser with his fist. The mirror trembled.

"And how would you know that?" I raised my chin a bit higher.

"I can see the..."

"Who are the watchers?" I demanded, since I knew where this was going.

He turned around and sat on the dresser. His boots grazed the floor. "They are the ones who watch us in training. They watch when there is a purpose. I can tell they're watching you. Every time we walk into the physical training arena, they watch you. Various times I've seen the trainers use their wristbands to send a message, and that is a clear sign that they want the watchers to observe your training and your progress. You may not see this as anything terribly important, but the progress you make in training affects the test. Now let me ask you one question: Why do you think they don't let us out into the garden?"

I glanced out the window to see if the answer was right behind the windowpane. It had never occurred to me to ask why they were keeping us cooped up. "So we are more concentrated on our training? So we can't hide in the garden when we want to skip training?"

He held his hands in front of him as if he was calm, but something about his face suggested the opposite. Where was Skyler? I wanted him to be here just in case Juris exploded again. "Remember that Zareh told you that he had helped the four elements before us to escape? Well, they escaped through the garden. That's why the authorities here don't want us to go outside, just in case we have a plan."

"Say we do have to escape. We don't have access to the garden. How the hell are we supposed to escape? Unless we can break the window, I'm sure there aren't many other ways to get outside." I held my head tightly as if I were squishing my brain so all the ideas would pour out, like juice from an orange. My instincts kicked in. Why was Juris suddenly being so open and unaggressive with me? Yeah, so he said he had anger problems, but talking about our escape—not that I had decided I would follow through—wasn't enough to make him control himself. "And how am I supposed to trust you?"

Juris did not seem a bit surprised by my question; he seemed to expect it. He exhaled softly. "We'll talk about the way out when I go down to see Zareh again, or you, if you want to get your own information and think of a different plan. And about the trust thing, just try to understand me. I'm sorry. I'm very sorry." His ivy eyes looked directly into me. I didn't want to get tangled in his vines because he changed too quickly. I didn't know if he had been faking his attitude before or if he was faking it now. "How can I make it up to you?"

"Why did you try to choke me?" I asked.

"Jealousy."

"Jealousy wouldn't drive you to pin me against the wall and try to choke me."

"I wasn't going to choke you."

I raised my eyebrows and pushed my hair aside, revealing small bruise marks on the side of my neck. I would have sought medical treatment, just like Aiden had, but I didn't want to be examined and have strange things done to me.

Juris rubbed his temples, disturbed. "While you were asleep, Aiden, Ren, and I hung out occasionally. As you can tell, neither of them is much of a leader, so I filled that role. They looked up to me, but Aiden wouldn't talk and Ren just loved talking, so it was hard to manage. At that time, I was struggling with the fact that I had lost everything, we lost everything, and we were dumped in our rooms without knowing anything. The day you woke up we had the 'talk.' And then the next day, we had training and a bit more freedom. All these good things began to happen when you arrived, and so Aiden suddenly began talking and Ren turned to you for company. This deepened the rift between us. You are also great in training, so I thought showing off the skills I had would bring me closer to them again, but they both turned to you and left me alone. This drove me nuts. I'm just not used to being left alone by my companions." He impatiently paced around the room while he spoke. I watched him pace back and forth, and then he stood still. His hands were balled up into fists again. I began to worry for myself, when the door swished open. Juris turned to face the newcomer.

"What the hell are you doing in here?" Skyler demanded. His feet were planted on the ground, and his eyes were like daggers aimed at Juris; one false move and pain would be inflicted.

Juris loosened his fists when he noticed Skyler staring at them intently.

"I just came here to talk to Ary," he replied.

"She doesn't want to talk to you, not after what happened."

"You told him?"

I was caught between Juris's and Skyler's stares. "He is my protector. You couldn't believe that I would stay quiet."

"But you still wanted to talk to me." Something changed in his posture at that moment. Had no one listened to him before?

I stood up and walked past Skyler to the door. "I never said that. Are you coming to lunch?"

"Yes," the two boys said at the same time. I could hear Juris growl silently in resentment toward Skyler, while my protector coolly met his gaze.

* * *

I sat down next to Ren who smiled at me widely. We always sat next to each other now; it gave us the chance to speak in low whispers. Aiden sat in front of me, and Juris sat next to Aiden. Skyler had gone to fetch my food, something he did regularly now.

"Hey, have you tried on your second prototype dress yet?" I asked Ren.

Ren smiled. "Yeah, this morning. Too bad we can't go together anymore. I know that it would totally spoil the whole surprise thing, but it would be nice, wouldn't it? I can't wait until you see my dress. It's looking so pretty."

I nodded and listened to Juris's conversation with Aiden. He was asking him about his power and how it felt. Aiden caught me looking and winked at me secretly. I couldn't help smiling. Ren said something to me, but I was too distracted. "Sorry, what did you say?"

She rolled her eyes. "What's up with you? You've been really distracted lately. I said that Juris seems more himself now, less uptight. Remember how he was before? That is what I call a pain in the ass." She took a spoonful of the brown flavorless mush we were forced to eat morning, noon, and night.

I looked at Juris. He still seemed hostile. I knew that being resentful about the hallway situation wouldn't be right, but I just couldn't get the image out of my mind. He wanted me to step down so we could escape and have a better chance of not being found, but while he said that, he was choking me. My head spun. Nothing was right since I had awakened; I wished that I really had died and that I had been a human mistaken for an element. "I don't know. He still acts strange."

"Here you go." Skyler left my food on the table in front of me and pulled up an empty chair to our table. He was the only protector who ate with us.

I opened the transparent box and watched the predictable white puff of vapor float toward the ceiling. "Thanks." I filled my mouth quickly with the spoon so I wouldn't have to say anything else.

Skyler's nose cast was off, and he looked perfectly fine, just like the first time I saw him. Knowing him better made me change my opinion about him. He wasn't mysterious; he was upfront, honest, and overprotective. "So, what was the whole issue with Juris in the room about?" He ate his different kind of food on a plate where I could actually recognize the different ingredients—sliced carrots, lettuce, mashed potatoes, and meat. His food looked so much better than mine. "Do you want some?" He pushed his plate toward me.

"No thanks," I denied politely and pushed his plate back to him. He received it gladly with his fork ready. "Juris just wanted to tell me something, but you arrived at the right time."

He smirked. "You know I'm trained for that."

"For what?"

"For saving the damsel in distress..."

I couldn't help rolling my eyes. "Whatever." He laughed, turning the heads of many of the other half-elements in the room. They planted their gazes on me. I tried to avoid them, but I couldn't help it, so many eyes, all the same with miniscule differences. I thought of the pain it must be to be one of them. I couldn't even imagine having a boyfriend who looked exactly the same as another person, my parents, or even my brothers. I would go crazy.

Juris called my name. I turned to face him. Everyone at the table was looking at me. "Ary, I have a question." I remained silent. "Is it true that you're good at throwing knives?"

I shrugged. "Yeah, kind of."

"Yeah, about training. Skyler, do you know why we have to bust our butts instead of taking it easy?" Ren cut in.

Skyler ignored her question and faced me. "Well, well, well. You never told me about that skill."

Ren's raised her eyebrows, and her mouth fell slightly open.

"There are lots of things you don't know about me, Skyler. And would you mind answering Ren's question?"

Skyler looked at me, confused. Of course, he hadn't heard her.

Ren smiled ironically. "Why do we have to train so much, you know, with weapons and the intellectual training?"

"Ary, tell us something we don't know about you," Juris jumped in, suddenly very interested. Ren mumbled under her breath and ate more of her food. I couldn't tell if Juris just ignored her completely, or if he just didn't hear her. But Ren had spoken louder this time.

"But Ren..." I squinted my eyes as I spoke.

Aiden looked at Juris skeptically and then looked at Skyler. "What's going on?"

Ren slammed her transparent container shut and pounded her fists on the table. "I can't take this anymore! Can't you see that I am also trying to speak?" she shook her head, piled the paper napkin and spoon on top of her container, and grasped them in her hands. "You guys are totally annoying," she snapped bitterly at us. And with that, she marched off to eat in her room.

The boys stared in humiliation at each other. The conversation ended suddenly with an incredible amount of awkwardness. I stared around the rest of the cafeteria. Some boys were looking my way; not at the table or Ren's sudden outburst, but at me. I could feel them analyze my every virtue and flaw. They didn't look at me like they did before. Before, I felt like they stared at me as if I were some sort of freak, something so wrong that looked right; but now, I felt warmth from them as if they, in a way, cared for me.

Juris broke the silence. "You never told us."

I shrugged. "There's nothing much to tell you."

"Of course there is," Skyler contradicted.

"You know because you pried." I couldn't believe they didn't care about Ren's exit. "I think you should apologize to Ren; she didn't look happy."

Juris hardly flinched. "She'll get over it. How does Skyler know so much about you?" He stared at Skyler as if he held the secret to finding a hidden treasure. What was up with them?

Skyler raised his eyebrows and grinned like my brother would. "Oh, I have my ways."

I stood up to leave, but a hand caught my wrist. I looked down, and Aiden's eyes met mine. "Do you want me to go with you?"

I shook off his hand. I didn't want to do it, but I also didn't want to sit at a table and act dumb as three guys competed. "I don't want anything else to eat, and I'm perfectly capable of walking alone. Thank you."

The three boys were about to say something, but I shut them up with a quick motion of my hand. It was impressive how obedient they were. "Thank you." I marched away, not sure if the buzz I felt in my cheeks was because I was proud of making such an exit or because I felt humiliated.

Chapter 15

"So, what do you know about all of this?" Zareh sat next to me on his cot. After the lunchroom scene, I had gone to speak to Ren. Then I asked Era to take me to Zareh. I wanted to know more. She tried to get more information out of me as we walked down the steps, but I remained silent as I scrambled to gather my thoughts.

"What do you mean by 'all of this'?" I asked him.

Zareh looked worse than the last time. His hair disappeared at an incredible rate, and dark purple bags hung under his eyes. He was consumed by hunger and lack of sleep, and his skin showed a sickly tone in the dim light. He hadn't been out since he was imprisoned.

"Let's go little by little. What do you know about the training?"

I tried to remember the weak explanations I had been given, but it didn't seem convincing. "I know they are watching, analyzing our progress, or so I have been told. We were put in a transparent box to test us and see if our powers would reveal themselves. But ever since Aiden was scorched, the box never appeared again."

Zareh tensed. "What box?"

"A huge glass box that tests us with our element. They sent flying boulders for Juris, massive flames for Aiden, drowning waters for Ren, and whirling winds for me. Of course, only Juris was able to save himself. He was the only one with power at that moment."

"And now?"

I picked at the dead skin near my manicured nails. "I'm the only one without my power. I think it's because I woke up later from the transformation than the others."

Zareh rubbed his hands together. "You woke up later than the others?" I nodded. "That isn't the reason why you haven't gotten your power yet. You might have it, Aurora; maybe all you need is to discover it. Anyway, the training is for the test, obviously, but why do you think you need to pass an intelligence test as well as a weapons test?"

His question echoed in my head. "I don't get it."

"You're not supposed to. Next question. What do you know about Arcane?" The sound of his dry hands rubbing together irritated me, but I managed to keep calm. It was like listening to two pieces of sandpaper scraping against each other.

I ran my tip of my tongue over my teeth. "Let's see, well, Arcane is divided into two halves; the less modern side and the more modern side. The government depends on the Golden Four who are four elements, one of each, selected with the help of the

Circle of Seven. As I understand it, there is one Circle of Seven for each element, so that would make twenty-eight elements. What else?"

I tried to bring back all the memories of my conversations with Skyler, Era, and Ren. "Oh, Arcane's location has remained a secret; only very few people know where it is, not only because it is hidden from the rest of the world, but because it belongs to a different realm. Your race also lives in Arcane, along with the elements. That's pretty much it, I think."

Zareh nodded. One of the torches Era lit sputtered out. "Everything you know is just half of the story. I don't know how you can be satisfied with such little information."

"I'm not."

He began to pace around the room. "Then why didn't you ask for more?"

"You think I didn't? Everything here is rationed. Information, taste, even color."

There was something on his leg, but I couldn't tell what it was in the dim lighting. It could have been a cast or a bandage. It was stained red, and with each movement he made, the color spread. When he sat down on the cot, he sighed with relief. "I have no idea what's become of the training center. I've been stuck down here for fifty years"

"Fifty years!" I exclaimed, shocked. He had been down in these rooms, tortured, for fifty years. "How do you keep yourself alive? I would have killed myself long ago."

He huffed disappointedly. "That's not a positive attitude. You gain nothing from losing your own life. And one thing kept me going—helping you."

"Helping me escape."

He grinned, showing his brown, rotting teeth. I tried to look away, or at least not look so repulsed.

"You catch on quick, just like my boy. My advisee was much like you; I bet he still is. He was my favorite out of the whole group. He was a quick learner and couldn't be stopped if he set his sights on a goal. We were great friends, even though I killed him for the transformation. It's common for the relationship between protectors and their elements to be rough, especially when the elements first wake up and realize that they are stuck with their murderer. You can't call us murderers unless we kill—all we do is transform. But the friendship I shared with my assigned element was always strong and stable. We were best friends." He stared at the wall longingly, as if he could see his protector if he stared hard enough. "Back to the reason why you're here...you have to escape, and apparently you want to."

I hated to admit that he was right. Skyler was no murderer. He was a...transformer. No, that made him sound like a robot. "Yes."

Zareh stared at me intently, squinting his eyes and creasing his forehead. "You don't trust me."

I couldn't lie to the old man. "Not entirely."

"But you chose to come down here again."

"I had no other option than to come here to get the information I need," I stated dryly. I didn't want the idea of me escaping getting into his head. I was going to learn about my possibilities, and then I would make a choice.

He smiled. "The fact that you came down here means you still trust me."

He was almost as stubborn as I was. I inhaled the dense and humid underground air. "I'm guessing that if you told Juris, you must have already spoken with Ren or Aiden."

"No, I haven't."

"Why is that?"

"If I knew, I would tell you."

Was it just coincidence that Juris and I had come down here, or was there a purpose? I supposed that I wasn't going to escape along with him, but I asked just in case. "We have to escape with the other two as well, right?"

Zareh nodded. "You will have to escape through the garden, though. It's the only way out."

"Wait, before we get to the details, I want to know the real reason why I have to escape." I stood up and walked over to one of the glowing torches. I glared into the fire as long as my eyes permitted.

The old man propped up his leg on the mattress and checked his wounds. I tried to act unaware of the disgusting process of unraveling the bandages and exposing the hideous sores. Zareh must have been tortured for the same reason I was poisoned.

"Well, I hope you remember what I told you the last time you came here. There are not only contradictory, but they fool people into thinking that something bad can be good. You have also fallen for this. A clear example is when they told you that the city has two sides, an underdeveloped one and an advanced one. That is one of the first lies. Both sides are equally advanced in technology. One side is devoted to developing it—the supposed 'less modern side,' while the other one uses it to make life easier. That's why once you're actually in the city, they will refer to the northern side and the southern side. The northern side is what you know as the modern side. The southern side is the less modern one.

"I do not know why they call it the less modern side, but I can assure you that what goes on in there is not as pretty as they make it seem. You are escaping to avoid falling into that sector of the city. Having two elements escape isn't enough. Even if two of you are left, one would be going to each side. The safest move is for all of you to run for it."

"You still haven't told me what we are running from. I want clear reasons." I spoke softly, since my voice echoed off of the stones.

The old man turned to me, annoyed. "If I told you, you wouldn't believe me. And if you want to know, child, then you should let me finish. To make the message clearer, I will divide the city into residential and industrial. In the industrial side, they learn how to create new things; they experiment. The working conditions for elements are very hard and often, they will not live past the age of thirty-five. I don't want to scare you, so I won't go into details. Is this enough for you? For your first reason?" he inquired as he readjusted the stained cloth on his leg.

I still didn't look at him. My heart was racing, and I felt something bubbling inside me. I couldn't quite pin down the emotion, but it was agitating me, and I didn't like it. What Zareh described matched what Skyler had told me. They were developing technology and experimenting on elements to achieve advancements.

I walked along the walls of the room until I reached the bars of the door. I grabbed them and pressed the metal. It didn't give in, as I had expected, but it helped release some of the energy inside of me. "Why do they do this?"

"So they can learn more about themselves and advance even more in technology." His voice was uneven and deep. "Another reason is that once you enter the city, there is no way out of it. You just become one more puppet for the Golden Four to control. Your privacy, your life, is gone. Lately, things have been stirring, Aurora, and it would be best for you not to be there when it finally blows."

"What is stirring?"

Zareh remained silent, until I turned and demanded an answer with my imploring stare. "It's hard to say. The last time I was in Arcane, I was eighteen, you must forgive me, but elements are opening their eyes and searching for solutions."

He had given me two logical reasons for escape, even though they weren't complete. If this was true, why had they tricked us into thinking that Arcane was the best thing that could happen to us? It sounded as if the city was inhabited with ignorant people who didn't realize what was going on around them, while the other half suffered. From what? I didn't know.

"So, about escaping... how are we supposed to do it?" I turned just in time to meet his triumphant grin.

"You have to jump the wall that surrounds the garden."

"Yeah, about that, we aren't allowed to go into the garden."

"Don't worry, that's where Skyler comes in." Zareh fiddled with the loose strings of his clothes. His hands were webbed with thick veins that crossed each other like overlapping ropes. "I should have guessed that the garden wasn't going to be open for you, since they don't want you to leave, but there are always other ways out. To get out of the building, you will have to create a diversion. Skyler could help you with this. I'll try to get the message to him, but if it doesn't reach him, please tell him yourself. The party will be the best moment for you to leave... yes. You should escape then, in the middle of the party, with your companions."

"You make it sound so easy."

"It is."

I laughed. "Yeah, in a fancy dress and high heels." This wasn't a movie. Running away wearing a bright dress would be hard to conceal, and the high heels meant that I would have to run barefoot, not a good idea no matter where I was running.

Zareh thought silently for a few moments. The cool, muggy air chilled my bones. "Couldn't you wear your boots?" He stared at my feet.

"I would have to go to my room first if I wanted to escape with them. You see, they don't go very well with a gown." I stretched out my feet before me and stared down at them. I could feel Zareh's curious gaze on my feet. "How am I supposed to get out of the garden? Isn't there a security system or something?"

"Yes, but I'm not sure about it now. I know that the watchmen don't stand still on the walls; they are always moving. So there must be a small window where you could jump. And there are stairs on the wall; just try to find the ones less used, where plants grow over them. Not everything is what it seems in the garden. Don't touch, taste, or smell anything unless you're one hundred percent sure what it is. Many flowers have...secondary effects."

I nodded. "And let's say we did get out. What's beyond the wall? How would we traffic supplies and find our way? What if we cross the wrong side of the wall? How could we ever get to the other elements?" I tried to think of all the possible questions I could, so I would be prepared for whatever happened. I was finally accepting the fact that we had to escape.

Yes. I would escape, if it were the best thing for all of us. If it would protect us, I would do it. I had to trust someone, so why not Zareh?

"What lies outside is uncontaminated nature...living organisms that thrive in their natural habitat, enough to help you survive while you're on the run. I do not know where your destination will be, but if my kid, and the rest of the elements that went with him, could do it, I know you can.

"The training center is surrounded by a semi-circular garden. All you have to do is climb up the ladder located in the middle of the wall and climb over it. Once you're out, you'll have to run for it. Be sure to search for some manmade markers on your way. When you reach the largest weeping willow, you'll know you hit the stash. Dig on the eastern side of the trunk, and you should find a hidden door. Open it and you will find four backpacks filled with supplies. I made Al promise to refill the supplies so when you escape, you won't starve to death running in the wrong direction."

"And how are we supposed to find Al and the rest of them?"

"There will be a map inside. A line will mark your trail. On the back you'll find the natural landmarks to guide you."

There was one small detail that bothered me. "How do we escape the party without attracting attention? Glitter, my stylist, said that she's going to make sure I attract attention with my dress, and that I need to catch everyone's eye. I think that's a great disadvantage."

Zareh walked over to a torch and blew it out. One corner of the room was now completely drenched in darkness. "Once you find a way out to the garden, you must explore it quickly and get out of there as fast as you can. Hopefully, the distraction Skyler comes up with will last a while." He blew out another torch, leaving another corner drenched in darkness. Half of the room disappeared into nothingness. "I'm just saying this in case you have second thoughts. You can't back down now; you already know too much, and it's better to be caught rather than live with the guilt of knowing that you, Aurora, could have done something to save your friends, but you didn't." He blew out yet another torch. The only one left ablaze was the one nearest to me. "I assume that you have already guessed that you must leave with the other elements of your age as well. Tell Aiden, only Aiden, right before the party, so he doesn't have the chance to back out."

* * *

I looked out the window. The wall that I was going to jump in a few days looked small and dark under the shade of the looming trees. It was already evening, and the time flew as I planned how I would escape, how I would tell Aiden, what distraction I could ask Skyler to create, how I was going to get into the garden to search without looking obvious, and where we were supposed to go. After we jumped the wall, we would still be in the elemental realm, which would allow them to find us faster since I supposed it was a limited amount of space.

"Hey..." Era spoke after sitting down next to me. "How have you been holding up? You haven't told me much."

I shrugged. "I guess I'm not that talkative."

She nudged me with her shoulder. "Oh, come on. I know you better than anyone here in this building." I was about to correct her. Skyler knew me better. He knew me much better, so well it scared me. He knew me because he snooped around my room and read my diaries, while Era waited here for my awakening.

"Well, I don't know what to say. You probably know what it's like to be in my spot," I justified weakly. I wanted to tell her how I didn't know how to react with Skyler and Juris evidently giving me too much attention, and the way Aiden made me feel. My mind had never been so flustered over one person.

"Every experience is different. I've been working on an illusion, human illusions, and I would love to try one with you. May I?" Era asked.

I nodded and accepted the hand she offered to help me up. She led me to the center of the room, and then she walked over to one corner. She closed her eyes and inhaled deeply. She moved her hands in the hair, keeping her eyes closed.

Sparks flew out of her hands, quickly surrounding the room and transforming it. My old room suddenly appeared, surrounding me—my bed, my window, my desk with the open laptop, my pile of books in the corner, and the shelves with my series-ordered books. I looked at my surroundings longingly but didn't dare touch any of it in case it would dissolve in a rain of light blue sparks. A little tornado began to whirl in front of me, settled at a shorter height, and took a human form. I gasped. "Violet!"

"Wow, Nikki you look so different." I could hear surprise in her voice, but there was acceptance in it too. She was smiling.

I couldn't help glancing down at myself. "I know, but it's still me."

She walked around me, taking in my appearance. Her brown eyes were steady, and her hair was tied up in a bun as if she had been in her house the whole day. "Is this permanent?"

"Yep." It felt weird talking to something who wasn't real. She looked real and spoke just like Violet. Maybe this really was her, but I had seen the blue sparks from her figure.

"Talk about a makeover. It doesn't look bad, you just look...strange." Violet walked closer to me and read my face; she never needed to read my face to figure out my emotions. "What's wrong?"

I couldn't tell her. She was fake, not real. "Nothing." My voice got caught in the middle of my throat. Why would Era choose to imitate her?

Violet frowned. "I know it's been rough, but you can tell me anything." She was dead serious and was about to grab my hand. Instead, she wrapped her arms around me. I could feel the warmth of her skin on my jumpsuit.

How could it be? Illusions were untouchable. How could she hold me? Perhaps I couldn't touch her. Her usual vanilla scent hung in a concentrated cloud around me, suffocating me. I didn't wrap my arms around her; I just stood there and began to cry. Why was Era doing this to me? She knew what would happen, but why? If she was looking for a breaking point, she found one. I tore apart the illusion, and Violet turned into a hurricane of blue and white sparks. I fell to the floor on my knees and covered my eyes. I didn't want to see it.

"Era, stop!" I cried. "Stop..." My voice was becoming fainter with each word that left my lips. I couldn't help the tears from streaming down my cheeks. They blurred my vision, and no matter how I hard I tried to wipe them away, new tears fogged my vision again.

Era ran to my side and held my shoulders. She pressed me to her chest and apologized over and over again. "I didn't mean it, Ary. I just wanted to practice, that's all. Sometimes, I get so far in that it's hard to come back to the surface until I'm completely out of energy." She caressed my hair. The repetitive motion soothed me.

I shouldn't have burst into tears like that, but something inside me ached terribly. Violet was like a sister. Her embrace had felt warm but hollow, like there was something missing.

Chapter 16

Three.

Two.

One.

Little squares on my screen popped up. Thick lines interrupted the squares and made their way to the center. The instructor, a well-aged man with thick glasses, had told us to find the most efficient route from one sector of the city to another. This was one of the many exercises he loved to use to test our abilities. Juris, Aiden, Ren, and I were separated by short yellow barriers that stuck out of the desks so we couldn't copy each other.

I ran my fingertips over the smooth surface of the touch screen desk. Finding the fastest route wasn't as easy as it sounded the first time. After each level, the city divided itself into more and more roads and walkways. I tried to concentrate and looked at the space in between the two spots, which blinked furiously. There was a small timer at the top of the screen. I began to run my finger over the screen; I had found the route. Then I heard a sudden mumble from Juris.

"Hey, Ary, you mind coming to my room afterward to talk?" He was concentrated on the task at hand, but he seemed too eager to wait until the exercise was over. There was a bit of frustration in his voice, as if he still couldn't find the fastest route, and I could see small beads of sweat gather at his hairline.

My finger didn't flinch as I answered. "No, thank you." When my finger connected the sectors, the screen blacked out and another city grid popped up. It seemed as if the grids had zoomed out on the map and two more sectors were instantly added.

"Please?" Juris whispered.

I wanted to shut him up so badly. I gasped. In my growing annoyance toward him, my finger moved, slightly, but it moved and led the route into a dead end. The city grid turned red and became fuzzy. I growled lowly at Juris.

"Aurora, could you please come here one minute?" the instructor called in his withering voice.

I stood up, staring with disbelief at the screen. How could I have twitched? This was the first mistake I had ever made in this exercise, and now he was calling me to his desk. My head hung low as I walked past the other elements to the elevated platform where the instructor sat. I always wondered why the instructor's desk was perched on a stage-like platform. I raised my face to meet my instructor's gaze. What would he say?

"You are wanted elsewhere. Just go through that door and you'll be fine," he directed.

I turned away from his modern grey desk. He could be wearing only his underwear and no one would notice. He never moved from behind the desk.

"Oh, and Aurora..." I stopped and turned my head. "I'm shocked you made a mistake just now..." His voice trailed off, and he left me standing there. Everyone could hear his comment, so why say it so loudly?

I slipped outside the door, trying to avoid Juris's and Aiden's gaze. I leaned against the door, closing my eyes and slowing my breathing. Most of the exercises kept me on the edge of my chair and required all of my attention. When I opened my eyes, I saw a woman staring at me.

No.

It was the woman who had decided to remain anonymous. I had last seen her in the training room when the big glass box waited for us. I scowled when she grinned with pure wickedness. "Sit down, Aurora. I insist." She gestured at the chair before her, across the table. The images she was watching quickly vanished as she swiped the smooth surface of the table. The room was probably made so she could monitor our performance in the intelligence training.

I thanked the table with all my might. If it weren't there, I would probably have been forced to sit next to her. My stomach turned. I knew why. She always showed up when something bad happened—when I realized that I wasn't dead and when Aiden had been burned alive.

"Do you know why you're here?" She asked in a not-very-nice voice, not that her usual voice was nice.

I shook my head. I was clueless.

She leaned in, resting the weight of her body on her forearms. We were completely alone; there was no third person here to be a witness of what was going to happen. "I think you do."

I think I did, too.

The last time I had been summoned, I got poisoned for visiting Zareh. I couldn't wait to see what they would do to me now.

"Tell me, Aurora, about life as it is now."

I shrugged. "I suppose, in a way, normal."

She smiled at my irony. Her lips were slathered with lip gloss. The thin pink lines shone whenever her lips moved. I couldn't help staring; it was too distracting.

"Really? You think all this is normal?" she asked.

"In time, I guess. This is my new life, and I will be stuck with it for quite a while."

"But is it normal?"

I chuckled. "Nothing's normal here."

She backed off. I still didn't know her name. "I want to know if anything unusual is happening right now."

I could smell her false attitude. She already knew. She knew that I had seen Zareh. She knew that I would be escaping soon, and that I would be helping Ren, Juris, and Aiden to escape as well. Was she trying to make me confess or intimidate me? "No, not really."

Her eyebrows arched. "Really?"

Her sarcasm was quite noticeable.

"Why do you even ask? I'm sure you've been keeping an eye on me." This woman was making me feel frustrated and trapped. Was it really necessary to interrogate me just to receive the answer she already knew?

"You're quite quick."

"You're quite obvious."

"Touché." She looked at me through the slits of her eyes; obviously, she didn't trust me. "But let me ask you one thing, Aurora..."

"Not that you haven't been doing that already," I mumbled under my breath.

She grimaced. "And I expect you to answer with absolute truth," she continued as if she hadn't heard me. Her eyes locked on mine. Her gaze was too potent; I was forced to look down. I don't have a choice, do I?

"Now, are you sure you don't know why you're here?" Her voice remained dead and flat.

I looked down at my hands that were stretched against the smooth surface of the table. "Enlighten me."

She rolled her eyes and pushed her hair behind her ears. "Aurora, you already have your power. And my theory will be proved if you answer this next question with full honesty. Please don't feel ashamed to say the truth, because it is very important." My mouth dropped. I already got my power and I hadn't realized, just like Aiden had said. "Have you been trying to call attention to yourself lately?"

I shook my head quickly. I wanted to know my power. I was terribly excited and scared at the same time. Why would they bring me here to deliver such news? I must have done something.

"Do you know what the word involuntary means?"

I nodded. Get. To. The. Point. My mind insisted.

She delayed as much as she could, but my gaze seemed to be quickening the process. "You see, Aurora, you have something called an involuntary power. It means you have no control over it whatsoever, and you never will. Most of the elements that possess this kind of power never know they have it until they are told."

Was I jumping in my seat or trembling? Was I feeling excited or terrified? I was sure that I felt a pang of anger for not being able to control my power like Juris or Aiden. "So, what is it that I can't control?"

She sighed. "We haven't been able to determine what you do to other people yet. We'll need to observe you more closely, ask some personal questions, but all of that comes after the test." I didn't like the sound of this. "You are attracting the attention of many male students at our training center. We can't tell you in what way you are affecting them or how, but you have had a great increase in brain activity these last days in regions which usually remain unused."

Skyler, Aiden, and Juris all spoke to me more frequently. Skyler didn't surprise me since we were in a good place; Juris did kind of shock me, but I thought it was because he was getting ready to escape. However, Aiden was the rare case of the three;

he held back a lot, so when he began participating in the conversations at lunch or dinner, I was baffled. No wonder they were acting strange in the cafeteria, and all the other "mixed races" were staring at me. Who could blame Ren for getting so irritated? I sat silently.

"You see," the woman continued, "we have studied the brain activity of elements with similar abilities, and your brain's activity has matched their patterns. How about I tell you a bit about them?"

I answered with a single nod, since I couldn't find my voice.

"The first element to have an involuntary power was one of the first elements ever. He was a water element and quite a charming man. He had the involuntary power of truth. This didn't mean that he only could tell the truth, no, it meant that every element, half-element, or human could say only the truth to him, and they couldn't even avoid saying things. If something was being hidden, it would be blurted out. This man later was chosen as a Golden because his powers were of much use to solve conflicts and interrogate people. His fellow companions could only be honest with him.

"The second element had the involuntary power of destruction. Everything she touched, sooner or later, would disintegrate, burst into flames or, well, fall apart. She killed more than twenty people before we could stop her and destroyed over one hundred objects. The only way to solve her problem was making special gloves for her hands. Our technology was more advanced when she discovered her power, so we were able to stop her, but she was very useful. She also was a member of the Golden Four and one of the most important, most lethal, fighters the elements have ever had.

"The reason why having involuntary power is so grand, despite not being able to control it, is that your power is so much stronger than the rest. We still haven't discovered why, but we suspect that it is related to the portion of the brain being used."

"So, this makes me the third element to have this kind of power?"

"Yes."

I pressed my lips together and felt the weight of my future fall over me. I would have stronger power and would probably be a recommendation in case of a missing Golden. I could be a Golden. It seemed such an unattractive job, to be in charge of a whole city of elements. One wrong move and you would have hundreds of deadly powers pushing you up against the wall, but I wouldn't have to worry about that. I was going to escape. I didn't plan on telling her. "Can my power be stopped?"

She shrugged. "The problem with your power is that we don't know where to stop it. I mean, the female element that could destroy everything with her own hands was an easier problem to solve, believe it or not, because all we had to do was create gloves with neutralizing crystals sewed in them. The neutralizers made her involuntary power inactive unless she took the gloves off. But you are a different story."

"Are you sure there isn't any way?"

"Maybe we could take away your power, but all your other veiled powers would run a great risk of being lost. You see, elements only possess one power but there are rare cases, like yours, where your involuntary power is not the only one you have. Your power is so great that you can use it in different ways. Having said this I repeat the risk of losing your other powers if we remove the involuntary one and I'm sure you wouldn't like that, would you?

I shook my head. The answer was quite obvious. "How did you realize that I had this power?"

She grinned. "Oh, like I said before, we've been monitoring your brain activity."

I slid down in my chair and slouched. "How did you do it?"

"We have our ways."

"And I have to put up with this until when?"

"Until we solve this and until you take the test. Where you end up determines what treatment you receive."

"How come?"

She froze. "Never mind." She had said too much, gotten too relaxed, and spoken carelessly. She changed the topic quickly. "You can't tell anyone about your power."

What? "Why?"

"Isn't it obvious? Would you like knowing that someone is influencing you? No, so don't say a word about your power or this little talk. Once we solve the issue, you can tell everyone."

"What if someone asks?"

"Lie."

I knitted my eyebrows. "You want me to lie to my friends?"

She was openly encouraging me to lie. This attitude, the way they spoke, it all fit in with the description Zareh had given me of the city.

"Do you think they would believe you if you told them? They would think you've gone mad, inventing stories, because you haven't received your power."

I couldn't believe I was having this conversation with a woman I had just met, and I had to trust her. If every time she came around something bad happened, then keeping this from other people could end badly. "I don't even know your name."

"If there's one thing that you should know, it's that identity doesn't matter. We all serve the same purpose, and because of that we are family. I think it's the fifth or sixth rule that says, 'You stand with us or you stand against us.' That's why you have no last name. You belong to the city."

"So, your point is that you don't have a name?" What was her problem? Why couldn't she tell me her name?

She sucked in her cheeks and shook her head as if I were a lost cause. "Teenagers... I do have a name. It's Mae, if you are dying to know."

I leaned back in the chair and plastered a grin on my face just to tick her off. "Thank you."

Mae waved a hand at me as she touched her wristband, lighting it up. The buttons appeared, and as she selected one of the symbols, she told me to show myself out. Without a word, I left the room.

Out in the hall, Skyler was waiting to walk me back to my room. I hadn't asked him to walk with me, but he felt compelled to do so. Now that I had discovered my power, I knew that there was more to it than duty. "Hey," I said simply, just to acknowledge his presence, but I didn't want to lead him.

"Ary, there's something I want to talk about..." Oh boy. I waited for the car to crash, but he didn't confess what I expected. "I'm gonna leave for a while, but I'll be back for the party, hopefully before."

"What?" This completely caught me by surprise. "Where? Why?"

He smiled slyly. "I knew you would miss me."

I turned my head to the side and raised my chin. "I said nothing of the sort. Why would you think that? I'm just curious to know where you're going and what your assignment is, that's all."

"Yeah, you're just curious..." He stared at the floor with a solemn expression, despite his words. "I can't tell you."

Oh, please. "What is this? Old Skyler again?" We turned the corner. "Fine, leave, go wherever you need to go, but don't expect me to like you when you come back. You are leaving me basically alone in a training center full of people I don't know if I should trust."

"You can trust me."

Aiden was standing outside my door, waiting for me to arrive.

Skyler stuck his hands in his pockets and swayed from side to side. "Well, I guess I'll see you when I come back." He stood in front of me, not sure of what to do next.

My door opened. "I hope the plane crashes."

"Oh, I'm not going by plane."

I shrugged. "Then you don't have to worry about the plane crashing, do you? Come on in, Aiden." The door closed between us before Skyler could answer. A smile of victory crept onto my lips—I had always wanted to say something frisky. I gave a small jump of joy and then heard a cough behind me. Aiden...Oh God. I turned to meet him with a red face and my eyes glued to the floor. How could I have done that in front of him? Why do you care? I didn't exactly know the answer to my own question, but when Aiden was near me, I felt a bit self-conscious.

Aiden gave me a lopsided grin. "You two really love each other."

"Nah, we just get on each other's nerves sometimes. So, why did you come around?" My bed had turned into one of my favorite spots ever. I grabbed a pillow and placed it against the wall before resting against it.

Aiden sat down on the floor near my bed and cleared his throat. "Well, I just came to hang out, if that's okay with you."

Oh. Warmth spread through me as I recognized that the feeling was mutual. "Of course. Now, if you don't mind..." I unlaced my boots and began massaging my feet, which were killing me.

He leaned back on his arms and stared straight at me. What the hell was wrong with me? Why was I observing every move he made, how he was not playing with his hands, how the light played on his features? "So, where is Skyler going?"

I let out a sigh of tiredness and leaned back into the pillow, hoping it would swallow me up. "I have no idea. But that's how things are with him. You don't find out until it's too late."

"That's pretty comforting. You look exhausted." Aiden tilted his head and observed me. I thought I must look like a mess. My hair was tangled, I had dark bags under my eyes from lack of sleep, my jumpsuit was stained, and I must not smell good after the long, hard training we had that morning. I had decided to practice more in the obstacle course and knife throwing. Those skills would serve me well while escaping.

My hands ran over the swirls stitched into the bed cover. "I am."

Aiden stood and shook his pants. "I'll leave you to rest then. See you at dinner?"

"Wait." I raised my hand to stop him. "I need to tell you something." He stopped in his tracks and turned. I knew Zareh had told me to tell Aiden on the same night we were to escape, but I felt as if I had to tell him now, perhaps since he was under the influence of my power it would be better. "Don't leave." I insisted softly, reaching for his hand. His warmth ran up my arm. When he looked down at my grip on him, something changed. His breathing faltered. I stared down at myself surprised I had grabbed him. I let him go. "You can't say a thing to anyone else...promise me."

"What are you getting me into?"

"Trust me, will you?"

"Will it get me killed?"

Seriously? "I don't think so."

He took hold of my hand and curled his fingers around mine with reassurance. "Fine."

Thank goodness. I thought it was going to take forever to persuade him. But what if he acted like this when I told him about the escape? What if he used the extra time I was giving him to think of a counter plan? Would he turn us in? These were risks I was taking by letting him in on the secret beforehand. He wouldn't do that, though. Something in me told me that it was safe to tell him now. I followed my instincts, hoping that I wouldn't be sorry. Pulling him closer to me, I tried to lay out the situation as simply and sweetly as possible. "We're going to escape. I know you'll have a lot of questions, but I can't answer them today. I promise I will tell you everything you need to know or want to know when the time comes. Just don't tell anyone." He stared at me blankly. "Please."

He ran his right palm over his mouth, chin, and neck as if he were trying to solve the jumble that was going on in his head. "I...I...I have to go."

When he detached our hands, I knew I was wrong to tell him too early. "Aiden..."

He looked at me once more before leaving. His eyes were sad and frustrated, as they ran over the length of my body, making me shiver. He opened his mouth to say something, but then quickly shut it. Aiden turned quickly and without another word, he left.

When the door closed behind him, I slid down on the bed until I was laying flat on my back. What had I done? I had not anticipated his reaction. I thought he would have agreed or fought against me, but nothing like this. Not silence. And the way he looked at me before leaving... the mere thought made me shudder again. I couldn't believe I was admitting it to myself, but I liked it. He wanted to be with me, but I scared him off.

What are you thinking, Aurora? How could you possibly like a guy that may not even like you if it weren't for your power? What was I going to do with my power? How would I even be able to run when everybody outside the walls would be influenced? As a human, I would have considered it a blessing, but now, when it could change an already dangerous situation, it was a curse.

Chapter 17

The bitter stylist who loved pricking me with pins combed my recently dried hair into a hairdo that I couldn't see. He pulled my hair viciously, without heeding my soft whimpers. A woman I had never seen before was painting my nails. She grabbed my hand with her fingers and carefully glued small gemstones to my nails. The little transparent rocks stuck to my nails and didn't budge.

"Your skin is magnificent. I've never seen such natural glow!" the woman complimented my appearance again. At first, I thought she was being nice, but then it just became annoying. She was complimenting everything about me. First my eyes, then my face, then my figure, and so on and so forth.

Humph. The man didn't like agreeing with the woman. They were so different, opposites actually. I could feel him tug my hair harder. "Pass me the clip."

The woman stopped her work and passed him a silver clip. He played with my hair and secured it.

"Pass me another one."

"Imagine what it would be for you to go to parties!" she laughed. "No girl would be able to stand next to you without feeling intimidated." She handed him the whole pack of silver clips so he wouldn't ask anymore. "Maybe you could be the next Nina! You must know her, Joe, don't you?"

He let go of my hair. I could hear him take a step back. Joe, the stylist, was looking for something in his bag. He sprayed something on my hair. "How could you ask me that? We *have* to know her. She's as graceful as any queen could be, but she doesn't abandon her fiery fierceness." This was the most I'd ever heard out of him.

"Would you like to be in the Circle of Seven?" the woman asked me after applying the transparent coat on my nails. She fanned them so they would dry quickly.

I shrugged. I wouldn't have to think about that. I wasn't going to be in Arcane if everything went well. The escape must be successful, and if not, I couldn't imagine what the higher authorities would do to us. "Hopefully," I said it only because I knew she wanted to hear it, and she didn't want any discussion.

She smiled and patted my hand with false emotion. "Maybe you could go even higher. A girl like you could go far." She said it as if she had known me for a very long time. Fifteen minutes of listening to her talk felt like forever for her, just as it had for me.

The door slid open, and Era strode in on high heels. They clicked with every step as she made her way to stand in front of me. Since I was facing the window, I didn't see her walk in. Her white silk dress with diamond buttons on the shoulder was simple. She only was wearing the colors of our element out of tradition, but the ones who really needed to attract the crowd's attention were the four newborns. Her hair fell loose around her face.

"Oh, Ary, look at you!" She analyzed the makeup the woman had applied. She smiled, her red lips revealing even more white. "Lillian, you did a wonderful job on the makeup. And those nails!"

Lillian blushed at the compliment. "Thank you, Miss."

"And Joe, thank you for doing such a great job with her hair. I think I can manage her from here. Thank you both for your great effort." Era shooed the stylists from my room and turned back to me. She picked up a black bag that was lying on my bed and unzipped it. She pulled out my dress and held it high above the ground, making sure the bottom of the skirt didn't touch the ground. "Here, go ahead and change."

I stripped off the robe I had on and slipped into the dress, making sure not to rip it. It felt so light. It was like wearing a spring breeze but much softer, smoother. "Can I look at myself in the mirror now?" I looked down at the dress that had been designed especially for me. I wanted to see how I looked with it on. It was beautiful by itself, but would it look as pretty on me? Era nodded and smiled widely.

I turned around and took in the stranger who stared at me from the mirror. My hair was pinned up in a simple bun with the silver clips that matched my hair perfectly. The spray that Joe used on my hair had thrown the finest glitter onto the hairdo like a thin layer of broken diamonds. The makeup on my face could be summed up in two words: silver and pink. The eye shadow that covered my eyelids started out white and turned silver. My pores were concealed, and my skin appeared flawless. A light pink blush made my cheekbones look more noticeable. I wore no jewelry. I didn't have to; the dress was enough. The corset-like top made me look skinnier and emphasized the curve of my waist. The skirt was floor length, sweeping lightly on the ground with the most minimal effort. The cloth used for the dress went from light blue to white and had the slightest silver glimmer. I gave a small gasp, my soft, shiny pink lips parting. This couldn't be me. I turned to Era.

"More beautiful than the first day I saw you." She looked outside the window and hesitated but finally spoke her mind. "You won't be forgotten after tonight. Someone with as much potential as you will be searched for."

Every man would notice me anyway.

Era could feel my thoughts and sighed. "I found out about your power. You are very lucky; elements would give anything just to be in your spot. I think this will help." She dropped a long crystal in my hand. It was attached to a chain. "This should neutralize your power. But at least it stops the effect and may make it a bit easier out in the wild. When you think you are ready to try to control your power, you may take it off, but let's not make it an obstacle in your plan."

"Thanks," I said softly. I wrapped the necklace around my wrist. I let the crystal dangle; it reflected rainbows on its surface, which captivated me. It had been a while since I'd seen these colors.

Era turned to the bed and reached for another small bag. She turned around with a cheerful grin. "Every dress must have shoes to match." I looked at her hands; they held two pearl white pumps. The tips sparkled with silver pixie dust that vanished slowly as they reached the ankle. The heel was shining silver in Era's hands.

I took them and slipped them on carefully. "I don't know how I'm going to be able to walk around with these shoes, let alone jump a wall."

Era's eyes fell to the floor. "You should practice walking around in your room. Get used to them." Her false cheerfulness was hiding something that was troubling her. I couldn't tell how much was fake and how much was real. She noticed my concern. "Don't mind me."

I eyed her as I paced from one end of the room to another. "Why didn't you leave?"

"I beg your pardon?"

"Why didn't you escape?"

She held her face in her hands. "Because it's too late for me. I already have my place in society, so instead of escaping myself, I want to guarantee the escape of younger elements. Maybe one day, they'll come back and rescue me." She chuckled as if the idea of her escaping were absurd.

I walked up to her. With my heels on, I was taller than her. It felt strange looking down on someone at least one hundred seventeen years older. "How old are you?" I couldn't help asking.

She looked up at me, startled by the abrupt change of topic. "Well, I'm twenty-five years old." That made four hundred and seventeen years of living and yet hardly any aging. I couldn't help wondering if living so long would be wonderful or terrible.

"Doesn't life get boring?"

She shrugged. "The days may seem similar, but they're all different."

There was a knock on the door. This startled her and a sad expression washed over her face. "I guess this is it. I have to say good-bye now."

I shook my head. "I'll see you at the party, right?"

"Yes, but we can't say good-bye there—it would look too suspicious. It was a pleasure to be your adviser. Please don't forget me. Someday try to come for me, but only if it's possible; I don't want anyone risking their lives." She embraced me, wrapping her arms tightly around my body, standing on the tips of her toes so she could reach.

I hugged her back. "I promise." I was unsure about this promise. I had been making too many lately, to myself, and I wasn't keeping some of them. I promised to see my family again—Steven, Mom and Dad, and Violet, whom I liked to call my half-sister because we were bound together by friendship. I promised I would escape successfully with Ren, Aiden, and Juris. And now I had promised this, three big commitments that could probably never be fulfilled.

Someone knocked again.

Era rolled her eyes. "I'm trying to have an emotional good-bye and someone won't let me." She moved away from me. The door slid open and she walked out, letting Aiden walk in.

"Hey, do you know..." He stopped in mid sentence, mouth slightly parted, and his eyes widened. "Wow." He shook his head and smiled. "Ary, you look..." He stood across the room, while I blushed heavily. It made him smile even more to see me blush. This was nice after last night's silent dinner. Neither Juris nor Aiden had spoken much despite Ren's efforts. We had all been thinking of tonight. I turned around, showing my back to him and breathed in heavily. The intensity with which he stared at me was too much. So this was how it felt to be hopelessly head over heels for someone. My senses were tuned in to him as he walked closer. "I'm sorry about yesterday. I just didn't know how to react. I need to know everything you can tell me."

"I don't think I can tell you everything now, because it could take a while, but Zareh said..."

"Who's Zareh?"

I stared at him over my shoulder, eyebrows raised.

"Sorry, I won't interrupt."

"Zareh is a protector from the generation of elements that came before us, and he helped them escape. Now he has to do this with us, but only to protect us from what awaits us at Arcane."

Aiden stood next to me. His shoulder brushed mine ever so lightly. We both stared out the window into the night. It was utterly black—great coverage—no one would see us leave if we could make it outside.

"And what's so bad about Arcane that we have to leave?" I could feel him asking himself the same questions I had asked myself when I had the conversations with Zareh.

I hesitated. I didn't really know what say to convince him without it taking an eternity. I had to be quick and efficient. "Two of us will earn a respectable place in the city, while the other two will be condemned to suffer. We can't stay here, Aiden, none of us deserve this."

"How do you plan on escaping?"

I tried to make out what was sitting outside my window. I knew there was a tree and the deadly flowers, but I needed to see one last time. "We have to jump the wall and run."

He contemplated the sentence. "What's on the other side?"

I looked at him. "A green meadow filled with unicorns."

"No, really." His face was stern and serious.

I sighed. "Nature, directions, and a map. All Zareh told me was to make sure Skyler creates some sort of distraction while we jump. Once we get over, we have to follow manmade markers to the largest willow, and then dig on the eastern side of the trunk to find backpacks with supplies."

Aiden stared outside, remaining immobile. "Sounds easier than it probably will be. Do Ren and Juris know this?"

"Juris was in charge of telling Ren, like I was in charge of telling you yesterday. We weren't supposed to tell you about this until today, so you wouldn't have a chance to say no, but I thought you might need a bit more of time." I hesitated, fumbling with my hands. Aiden seemed too calm. "Do you trust me?"

Aiden shifted his vacant stare to me. This time, it was he who reached for my hand. "What other option do I have?"

Chapter 18

We stood in front of the wide double doors, waiting for our grand entrance. I felt Aiden fidgeting next to me. He was nervous, even though he didn't admit it. He kept tightening his grip on my hand and then suddenly relaxing. We remained linked to comfort each other. I relaxed as I watched him get worked up. He finally spoke. "Ary, there's a problem."

"With what?" My voice sounded eerily calm.

He played with his hands and stared at them. I could watch him from the side of my eye. "I don't think it would be good for me to run away with you tonight."

I shrugged, feigning indifference to the feelings of concern that welled up inside me. "As you said, you don't have much of an option."

"But it would be dangerous."

I stared at him. His golden eyes were uneasy and couldn't hold my gaze for more than a couple seconds. "We're all willing to take the risk. And what's the worst that could happen?"

He twitched. "I'm not talking about that, Ary. What I mean is, I can't leave; there's something that's..."

Aiden was cut off by the large swinging doors. They had opened, and across the room another set of doors revealed two more elements. Ren and I looked at each other from across the room. Her hand was on Juris's arm; she smiled at me. She looked beautiful with her hair knotted in a twist of braids all over her head and some strands falling in loose curls down her back. Her dress had a deep cut down to her waistline filled with light fabric studded with white pearls. The dress itself was simple. From top to bottom, it changed from white to dark blue, and the sparkling transparent sleeves were delicate and elegant. They fit her body perfectly.

Aiden swept me into a graceful walk toward the center of the room where we met up with Juris and Ren. Ren was also wearing high heels, and she reached Juris's shoulder.

Everyone's eyes were on us. Glitter was right about calling attention, but it didn't necessarily have to do with the dress. We were the only teenagers that looked different from the rest. There were murmurs as our quartet stood in the middle of the room, waiting for some kind of direction.

A voice came from the speakers. "Let us please greet our four new elements with a round of applause." Some people, though none were human, were happy to comply. "Now, you all may know that these lucky four will have the test tomorrow, so they can be assigned to their proper spot in the city. It is a tradition to change the rules every year. The examiners have decided to include the opinions of our guests. At the end of the party, each and every one of you, except the four who shall be tested, will take a question card and answer it. These will be read prior to the decision making. Thank you."

And with that, a string quartet began to play.

I had to be nice to people; I had to talk to them. This wouldn't help at all. It only meant that people would be even more aware of us than before.

Aiden's momentary calmness soon fell apart. He didn't like the idea. He turned to me nervously. "This is bad."

I rolled my eyes and laughed. Trying to sound light and happy, I said, "Oh, don't say nonsense, just enjoy yourself." My eyes cried, *I know, I know.* The crowd, which had made a ring around us, broke apart. Finally, we could stray from our awkward position in the middle of the room. I felt jitters in my stomach. Skyler wasn't around. No surprise there; he had been absent for the past few days. I had thought that maybe he would show up.

Ren and Juris walked over to where we stood. Ren's back was straight, and her chin was held high. She was smiling, even though she was nervous. "Why do they have to complicate things?" Her hair shone brighter than ever under the crystal chandelier.

Juris slowly and subtly dropped Ren's hand to her side and gawked at my dress. I thought the pendant Era gave me would stop this, but with Juris's inability to control his emotions, it was clearly not working right or, hopefully, yet. "Ary, you..."

Rolling her eyes, Ren turned him. "Shut it, Juris, or at least wait until I'm not here." She tapped her heel against the marble floor. The sound quickly concealed itself among the other clicking heels of walking half-elements.

Aiden looked around and stuck his head into the middle of our tiny reunion. "We better move aside. How about we split up and meet each other in half an hour? We'll mingle so we're not divided in two obvious groups, but no one can be alone." He glanced swiftly over the three pairs of eyes watching him to check that we agreed.

I could feel Juris's stare heavy on me. "I call Ren first!" I said swiftly, so Ren wouldn't be left with the boys. She looked as if she needed a break. I guessed that she wasn't use to not getting attention from guys; and I wasn't used to receiving so much attention.

I scanned the room once more, searching for any traces of Skyler, or at least Era so she could help me find him, but all I could see was the room covered with draped cloths and some tables at the back offering all sorts of appetizers. I nudged Ren in her ribs lightly. "How about raiding the table?"

A grin spread across her face. "It's as if you were reading my mind. We should eat well tonight in case we don't have enough for later..." She let her sentence trail off with the growing music of the string quartet coming from the corner of the ballroom. She didn't need to finish her sentence. In fact, it was better to be left incomplete in case someone was listening.

We walked to the tables, matching the pace of the half-elements around us. They wore simple black dresses and tuxedoes. Only the elements were allowed to wear color. This made the "end of training" party look more like a funeral. It seemed strange that they could only wear black. Maybe it was so we could stand out, making it more noticeable if we went missing. It also made it harder to find Skyler. I kept scanning the crowed in vain.

Ren and I looked hungrily at the food—so many unknown delicacies. It was difficult to identify what was on each platter. I went for what I thought I knew, while Ren tried the unknown. "You should try this. It's awesome." She pointed at the roll in her hand. It was filled with greens and browns.

I grabbed a roll and took a bite. The flavor exploded so forcefully in my mouth that I couldn't help but cough. I could feel the flavor in my nose. It tasted like tender, juicy meat, maybe lamb, and the green leaves added some spice. The spices tickled my throat as I swallowed. The same experience repeated itself with each bite. "It's strong. Not bad, but I don't like feeling the food in my nose."

"I don't care. It's the best appetizer I've ever eaten." As Ren took another roll, we stepped away from the table. "Oh, look," she pointed at a man in his late twenties walking around the room. His hair was a dark red-orange color, and his eyes were two small circles of blue, a cloudless sky at midday. He snaked through he crowd, gracefully greeting everyone who crossed him. My stomach slammed into my throat. "Don't you think he's special in a way? Just look at the way everyone tries to get his attention." It was true. People seemed to line up behind him, but he just kept on walking, ignoring them or not realizing they were there. "He's coming our way." I resisted the urge to flee.

This was the very man who had poisoned Skyler and I, the Monarch of Water. I looked at the table, longing to grab another bite, so I could keep my mouth full and not scream. Why was he here? Why not any other Golden?

The man stopped in front of us. "Good evening, ladies. I just wanted to congratulate you on your work, for I know you have been training hard, and wish you luck for tomorrow. My recommendation is not to go too strong with the seafood at the end of the table, just in case. You never know when your stomach can be...fragile. Better safe than sorry. And try to go to sleep as soon as possible." He held a crystal glass in his hand that was covered in golden designs and half filled with water. He spun the liquid inside the cup, taunting and warning me.

"I'm Ren, and she's Aurora," Ren said weakly. She was running her eyes all over his suit. If only she knew who was standing in front of her...I stared at the floor or at the crowd behind him, since I could not look him in the eyes. I didn't know if what I felt was fear or repulsion.

He nodded in our direction, a discreet bow, but his face remained neutral. "Ren, Aurora, it is a pleasure to meet you. How have you been enjoying your stay at our training facility?" He looked around the room, admiringly.

I hesitated. This could be another test; perhaps he was giving me a second chance by acting as if I hadn't done anything.

"The rooms are very comfortable, well at least my room. Oh, and the view of the garden is beautiful." I decided not to emphasize the garden. If he knew about Zareh, he probably knew that I would try to make a run for it through the garden.

He beamed for the first time. "Yes, the garden is one of the highlights of the building. The gardening apprentices tend to it every day. The best gardeners are sent to Golden Hall in Arcane, and the rest work in the garden." Silence settled between the three of us, making me fidget and search for a good conversation topic. He fished up a topic before I could. "Aurora, would you mind giving me the pleasure of one dance?"

I turned to Ren. She smiled and walked away, leaving me alone with him. "I don't know how to dance." He took my hand and pulled me toward the circle of well-organized couples, ignoring my warning. He gave some random person his glass, and when the women all spun on their heels, he took advantage of the moment to engage me in the dance. I had no other option but to follow his lead.

He placed one hand on my waist and held my hand in the other. His grip was tight, holding me in the dance and guiding my movements so they followed the rest. "Just follow me." The music kept playing, and he brought me closer to him. I could smell his cologne. My dress fluttered around me, as he made me spin again. The heels I was wearing made it hard to keep up with his gaining speed, and the soft music was now rising in a subtle crescendo. The man slowed the dance, bringing his mouth close to my ear. "I know what you're doing." And as if the room had suddenly burst with music, he guided me into the hasty pace once again.

I could see people leaving the dance floor and standing nearby, watching the stranger and me moving flawlessly together. More people crowded the appetizer tables, watching, staring. I fumbled, almost breaking the swiftness of the dance; but he was there, his arm around my body, shifting my weight, separating me from his body and then bringing me back.

"What do you mean?" I asked, breathlessly.

"You know what I mean." He brought my face close to his as he said this. I could feel his breath on my lips. I wanted to pull away, but he held me in his tight grip. The crystal wasn't working at all. I could sense the soft scent of alcohol on his breath.

"Oh, please, refresh my memory," I managed to get out as the direction of the dance changed. I was dancing backward.

He laughed and turned me so my back was against his chest, and his arms were wrapped around me. His cologne choked me. "Don't act dumb, Aurora. You know perfectly well what I'm talking about." He definitely knew.

I turned around and placed my hands on his shoulders. "No, I don't." My voice was filled with frustration and faked confusion. I stared into his eyes. What was his power? Could he read minds? Essences? He fixed my hold on him, putting one hand on his shoulder and the other in his hand.

We began to spin, twirling uncontrollably with the rest of the dancers. My dress was a heavenly cloud that shone under the dimming lights. They were dimming the lights. My mind could think of only one thing. The song was about to end. The other women dancing were half-elements, and they were dressed in black. I felt like Cinderella in the middle of the dance with my flawless dress and hairdo. I was missing the glass slipper. He would just have to look for me without it and follow my trail to wherever I escaped. I wouldn't let him find me.

The Golden lowered me into a smooth dip. I tilted my head backward, spotting Aiden in the crowed. His jaw was tensed, and he stared at the man. Juris was standing beside him; his green eyes flashed before they fell, diving to the ground. I could hear my dance partner's voice as the lights went out. "I'm watching you." He ripped me away from him in the darkness. When the lights turned on again, he took my hand and kissed it lightly. We both bowed, thanking each other for the dance. Finally, I walked out of the group of dancers toward Aiden. Juris had already disappeared into the crowd.

Aiden's hands were buried in the pockets of his suit, and he glared at me with his golden eyes. "What was that all about?" Something in his voice sounded off. Jealousy?

I slipped my arm in his to steady myself. He didn't mind, and I needed to hold myself upright with his help. My mind still spun from the dance and the man's warning. "The guy just wanted to dance. Do you know if we can go outside? I really need to breathe some fresh air." The Golden's cologne remained in my nostrils. If I didn't get fresh air soon, I might throw up.

Aiden walked me to the double glass doors that led outside. When he turned the knob, the door didn't budge. "I guess we won't be able to go outside," he stated nonchalantly, but deep inside there was disappointment woven into his words.

A half-element approached us when he noticed that we wanted to go outside. "There is an internal garden through those doors. It isn't a big at this one, but it will have to do." He guided us to a second set of doors.

"Thank you," I said ,when it seemed the half-element didn't intend to leave. He watched us as we wandered into the enclosed area.

"This is nice," Aiden said at my side. The interior garden was larger than I thought it would be. Ivy crept up the walls, flowers dotted the darkness with color, and Victorian lampposts hung over the cobblestone walkways. I shivered, the fresh air hugging my bare arms and forming goose bumps on my skin. Aiden noticed my shuddering. "Here, have my coat." He unhooked his arm from mine and began to take off his coat. I put my hand on his and stopped him.

"Don't, I'm fine," I said weakly.

He didn't care. He ripped off his coat and placed it over my shoulders. He kept his hands on my shoulders longer than necessary, and I could feel the heat emanate from his body. "I don't need it anyway." He played with his hands once more. It seemed that his nervous tic was this game he played with his hands. I still couldn't figure it out despite its simplicity.

I pushed the coat off of my shoulders and handed it to him. "I don't need the coat. *Really.*"

"But your skin is cold."

"As yours is warm." He finally accepted the coat with evident irritation. My heels clicked on the cobblestones as we walked slowly into the heart of the garden. The stones were spaced evenly on the ground. It wasn't the most comfortable surface to walk on, but it could have been worse. Few people came outside, perhaps since the food was inside.

"Over here, Ary!" Era waved her hand. She was smiling, earrings dangling, as she held the hand of a man next to her. He was much taller than her, with blonde hair and white eyes. The only thing that distinguished the iris was the fine grey line at the edge. His pupil was dilated due to the lack of lighting. Judging from the way he held Era and how he looked at her, he was probably her husband. "This is Ellil. He's my partner." Her voice was filled with pride. She pressed his hand.

"Partner?" I couldn't help sounding confused.

Ellil smiled down at me from his towering height. "Elements don't have husbands or wives, they have partners. Matrimony is a celebration that unites souls in love and life, but we don't have souls. Pleasure to meet you, by the way." He extended his hand, and I shook it. He turned to Aiden. "You must be…"

"Aiden, sir."

"Yes, thank you, pleasure to meet you too. Now Aurora, may I call you Ary?" after my nod, he continued. "I've heard many good things about you. Era has been telling me. But of course, I would like to get to know you myself. I know maybe one day you might come and visit Era and me in our home and talk over dinner." He tucked Era closer to him and kept caressing her hair.

I smiled at him. If he kept on talking, we would never be able to escape. "I would love that. If you don't mind, Aiden and I were hoping to take a glance around the garden…"

Ellil nodded and gestured for us to continue down the path deeper into the heart of the garden. "A pity it's nothing like a real garden. Anyway, we wouldn't want to keep you two here talking with your elders. Go enjoy yourselves!"

Aiden grabbed my hand and pulled me after him as he walked over the path. We passed small bunches of the transparent, blue, and orange flowers that I had seen from my room before finding a small marble bench hidden near a small fountain between two leafy trees. Two stone statues dressed in robes held up a jug that poured water into the pool. Fire boy took my hand and pulled me down onto the bench next to him. "I'm nervous."

I looked at him; the shadows created haunting angles on his innocent face. "You think I'm not? You'll be all right. We'll be all right. Just trust me on this one."

He shook his head and grabbed my hands. His wrapped around mine easily and provided enough warmth to stop my constant shivering. He looked down at them. "What are we running away from, Ary?" His eyes didn't meet mine. "Please be honest."

"I already told you. The city has two sides, the northern and the southern side. Those who live in the northern side have a blissful life, while the rest in the south are condemned to experimentation." We sat side by side, in silence, as he flattened my palms against his chest, the white fabric providing almost no coverage from his unnatural body heat. "Please stop doubting." His uncertainty made me doubt Zareh.

S. Elizabeth Dover

A sarcastic chuckle escaped his lips. His breath was shallow and agitated. "I don't know how we can trust one man. What if he's wrong? What if it's okay for us to stay here?"

My hands rested just centimeters from the buttons of his shirt. I had to control myself to stop thinking of unbuttoning them. Why was I thinking of that now? My future hung in the balance, and here I was wanting him to lean in and kiss me.

I could feel his heart beat faster through his shirt.

He had a point, but Era was my adviser. She was supposed to give me good advice. "Why would they tell us to escape if it wasn't true?"

He paused. "It could all be some sort of test, a part of it."

I began to slip my hands down and away, but he grabbed them before they parted. I was trembling. I hadn't realized. He held my hands and reassured me that everything would be all right.

"The worst part will be crossing the wall. After that, it's pretty easy, or so they said." My nerves started kicking me in the stomach. He finally looked up at me. "What can I do to make you feel better?" I whispered to myself, but I guessed that Aiden had also heard me speak.

Aiden searched for something in my eyes. He slipped his hands from mine and set them on my waist. He brought me closer. I wrapped my arms around his body and rested my head on his shoulder.

"Just don't get mad at me, no matter how stupid I act. If I do something irrational, I want you to know that that's not how I am," he whispered into my ear. I raised my head to ask him what he meant, but when I was inches from his face, I found myself short on words. What was I going to say?

He stared back at me, taking in every detail of my face as I memorized all of his angles. Our lips were just inches away. My eyes began to close. He moved toward me and then suddenly inhaled, withdrawing himself. I balled up my hands into fists and sat up straight. When I opened my eyes, Aiden wasn't looking at me but at someone behind us.

"Hey," Skyler's voice made me jump, and Aiden stared at him irritably. "Ary, I know about...you know, and I wish the best of luck to all of you." He eyed Aiden but then turned back to me. "You look beautiful."

My nerves were about to snap again. How could he do this? He played with my emotions, threw me off a roof, let me punch him, and then acted all goodie-goodie. He left for days and then reappeared at the worst moment possible.

"Where have you been?" My cheeks flushed pink.

He stuffed his hands into his suit pockets. "I've been working some things out. I see you've been busy too." A smirk crept over his mouth.

I wanted to stick my head in a hole. "Four days is quite a long time to work things out. Was it because of lunch? Were you avoiding me?" I said it up front and didn't mind at all that Aiden was standing next to me, listening. He scooted over and grabbed my hand, giving it a light squeeze. I pressed it back. Skyler dropped his gaze to where we held hands. He stared with indifference.

"Why would I want to avoid you?" His voice remained steady. "I'll think of a distraction. But my question is whether you have a plan for getting to the main garden." Aiden shook his head. "Well, I guess in that case, we only have one solution. You have to wait until I create the distraction. Once I do, you have to go straight to your room. Break the window and run to the wall. There's a ladder behind the rosebush."

Suddenly, he left, looking once more at my hand in Aiden's. I slipped it out carefully and stood up. I managed to see a small grin creep across his face before he turned. "Oh, and Ary," he called from a distance. "Fifty seconds." He looked down at his watch and walked away at a faster pace.

Fifty seconds until what? The distraction?

"We need to get Ren and Juris."

Aiden and I walked as casually as possible, searching for them. It didn't take as long as I thought. They were walking in the same direction we had, appreciating the beauty contained within the four walls. Ren was laughing and Juris's facial expression looked happy. That was something very unusual. His chest fell and rose rapidly in silent laughter after Ren commented on something. She saw us first and whispered into Juris's ear. His face turned solemn in a matter of seconds. My crystal was definitely working.

Ren pushed a strand of hair off of her shoulder and down her back. "Did you find any way to the other garden?" She kept her hand on Juris's arm.

"We have to go back in," I said dryly. I didn't know how much longer we had until Skyler implemented his "distraction."

In a matter of seconds, we were standing inside the large room where music, laughter and loud conversation hung in the air. I could see the Golden of Water glance at me once, but after that, no one paid us special attention. We sent Juris to grab some food for all of us while we waited. I tried searching for Skyler, but I couldn't find him in the crowd.

"Here, take these." Juris handed us each a sandwich. I took tentative bites, while the boys swallowed theirs whole. "What are we waiting for?"

Aiden rubbed the crumbs off of his hands before stuffing them into his pockets. "Well, we're waiting for Skyler to do something." He spoke softly, but his irritation was still palpable. Was that the reason why he still stood close to me and watched me closely through the corner of his eye? I smiled at him, hoping this would make him relax, but his expression didn't change. No, then he wasn't that upset about Skyler...it was something else.

Ren shifted her weight from one leg to another. "Ugh, I hope he does something soon, because these heels are killing me."

Right then, I heard a yell followed by another one. Black smoke curled toward the roof as one of the curtains and tablecloths caught on fire. The line of fire moved to the next curtain and the next table. That was our signal. People fled through the double doors where we had entered, while some men in dark blue suits hurried toward the blaze. This was our chance.

We mixed in with the rushing crowd of panicking half-elements that flowed into the rest of the building with linked hands. When Ren recognized her room, she got closer to me. "I'm going to get my boots."

"Go to my room afterward. Take Juris," I said quickly, as she dragged the earth element into her room.

Aiden and I followed the thinning crowd until my room, 08, appeared. Once inside, I followed Ren's example and put on my boots. I longed to change into the jumpsuit I had in the dresser, but I was afraid that it might contain a tracking device. "How are we going to break the glass?" I asked, as I laced up the second boot.

Aiden paced around my room, searching for something that could break the glass, when he reached my nightstand. He had to be kidding. He crouched down and grabbed it. It was clearly heavy. He threw it at the glass, but the glass didn't break. The nightstand just hit it and slid to the floor like a helpless bird trying to fly through a window. "Dammit." He grabbed it once more and aimed at the exact same spot, the center of the window. This time, he ran a bit before tossing it into the air.

The window cracked.

Juris and Ren ran into the room. Juris quickly helped Aiden with the nightstand. They decided to grab the legs and ram it in continuously into the glass. With each impact, I cringed, but the crack became bigger.

Finally, the window shattered. Ren screamed.

"We're okay, you don't need to yell," Juris grumbled as he shook off the broken glass from his shoulders and hair. Small shards of glass covered the floor and gleamed mischievously like little diamonds that would kiss and mark your flesh if you dared to grab them.

"Hand me the bed cover," Juris ordered. I handed the heavy large cloth to him. He extended it over the hole and kicked at the glass to make an even bigger exit. "Who's going first?"

"I'll go," Aiden offered himself. He looked too big to come out the other side unhurt, but somehow he managed to fold himself and remain standing on the other side.

Ren walked up to the exit and hesitated. She held up her skirt, and with Aiden's help, made it to the other side. Juris went after her, leaving me for last.

"Why don't you guys find the rosebush? Skyler told us that the ladder is behind it. I'll help Ary, and we'll be right there." Aiden sent them off, as I struggled to keep my skirt from tripping me. "Give me your hand." I did. With him to steady me, I was able to pass through the sharp shards. My dress wasn't so lucky, though. It caught on the glass and ripped when I pulled.

I stared back at the pieces of cloth caught on the broken window. What a shame; it was a pretty dress. "Why did you send them away?" I inquired. We had to stay together in case we encountered something or someone on the way.

He brought me to him in one swift movement. The small distance that had been between us was now gone. My hands fumbled from my sides to his neck. When our lips joined, my first reaction was to pull away, but I didn't. His lips moved slowly on mine, allowing me to predict his movements and follow.

My heart skipped a beat, as his fingers traced up my back. The heat that came from them intensified. My stomach, which was brutally beat up by nerves, now lay quiet and enjoyed the sensation. Flames engulfed me. All I could see was yellow, red, orange, and Aiden. He was standing in the flames with me, still locked together. His lips parted from mine, so he could inhale. The shadows of the night hid us from everyone else, but the stars shone on us, drenching us in a soft glow. I kissed him freely, knowing that no one was watching. My head burst into a million sparks, stripping every thought from my mind.

"Aiden," his name escaped my lips as fire boy kissed me harder.

Millimeters away, I could feel his breath on my skin and smell the cloth of his tuxedo. We stood still in silence. The flames that had been surrounding me were now small embers under my feet. They rested with their warm glow, waiting to be ignited again. "I needed to have this last moment alone." His voice was hushed and started spreading sparks. He was going to ignite the embers underneath, closing in on me once more, but he kept me waiting.

My eyes closed. I gathered the small strips of my mind and reassembled them, clearing my head. I threw a bucket of water on the embers by kissing him on the cheek. "We have to look for a way out." Aiden nodded but took a while to let go of me. I stepped forward and followed the direction I thought Juris and Ren had gone. Aiden followed behind.

Cobblestone walkways snaked around the plants. The back walls were hardly visible, as large trees shaded the barriers that separated the training facility from the outside world. Who knew what could be on the other side? Plains? Mountains? Jungles? No, definitely not a jungle. It was too dry outside.

There were no lights, but the moon was full and bright. After passing rows and bushes of flowers, we finally reached the wall. It was tall but not as tall as I had expected. The steps of watchmen were audible from where we stood. Trees packed and lined the wall, so it was hard to see it. Nonetheless, it was concrete. The grey tone gave it away. We continued walking parallel to the wall until we found the other two elements murmuring near the rosebush.

The rosebush was not hard to find. It was immense, creeping up the wall almost to the top. Red flowers bloomed, dotting the dark green leaves. "This is it." Juris kept his voice hushed because of the watchmen crossing overhead on the wall.

I reached out to touch the wall behind the rosebush, but long, sharp thorns stopped me from advancing. I pulled out my hand and studied the prick on my finger. Blood oozed out of the small puncture. "We're going to have some problems climbing this." I said after I sucked off the blood. I didn't mind the coppery taste.

Aiden studied the plant. I could still feel the ghost of his body holding mine. "These thorns are huge. Can't be normal. I remember when my mom had to remove roses from our home, and I had to help her cut the thorns; they were half this size." He stuck a hand in the plant and felt around. "Here we go...a thorn-covered ladder. If we manage to escape somehow and not get captured again, we'll have a path of blood behind us as their yellow brick road." He ran his fingers through his hair while he thought.

"So, we time the gap between each watchman, and it's about fifty seconds to a minute." Ren twirled a strand of hair on her finger. We were escaping, and I had no idea how she kept her cool. I was agitated because of the nerves, and because I had just kissed a boy for the first time. I glanced at Aiden. His face glowed in the moonlight.

"Ary..." Ren pulled me back into reality.

I looked at her with wide eyes. "Yeah, fifty seconds," I repeated. That's when I remembered. Skyler had mentioned that number.

Juris gave me a skeptical glance and then huddled us together, like a quarterback with his players before a football game. "We'd have to go over the wall in some sort of order. Since we're going to have to cross one at a time, we have to have some sort of plan." He spoke in a hushed voice.

Aiden thought next to me. I could see it on his face. "I could go first. I don't mind. If something goes wrong, I'll make sure you know it; and if not, I'll help the rest of you get over. I think you should go last, Juris. If something bad happens, you won't have a problem facing whoever or whatever is there."

"I want to go third," Ren continued, "so two people can catch me. Ary, that means you're up second." I shrugged. As long as I got over and out safe, I didn't really care about the order.

"This is it," Aiden signaled to the plant. We all knew what we were going to do next, so we stood in silence.

I counted in my head silently right after a watchman passed overhead. One. Two. Three. Four. A soft cold breeze blew, announcing the winter. It was pretty warm for winter, though. This climate reminded me of Thanksgiving with cold nights, thick clothes, a turkey, and a fireplace. In Ashwick, we would have a large dinner with Mom and Dad's friends. This year, Dad would be eating with us, but now I was the family member who left an empty seat. Of course, there wouldn't be an empty seat. They would carry on as if I never existed, because for them, I never did. I felt the breeze lift my skirt and make it ripple.

"Fifty seconds." Ren's soft voice interrupted my thoughts. Skyler had announced the timing to me.

Aiden nodded. He pulled off his suit's jacket and wrapped it around his hands. "Going up."

I had to find a way to cover my hands for the climb. I reached for the hem of my dress. I didn't want to rip it, but it was already tattered. The sound of the ripping cloth was fragile but haunting. I ripped it so the end would be even. My boots and ankles were fully exposed now. I had plenty of cloth to cover my hands. "I hate doing this."

Ren mimicked my actions. "I know, right? We should have ripped up the boy's shirts. But this will make it easier to run. You better tie up your dress somehow, so it doesn't get caught on all the thorns."

I turned to see Aiden, but when I looked up, I could only see a flash of black. He had climbed up faster than I had expected. No one made a sound. I tried to hear what was happening above, but the soft breeze muffled every sound with the soft swish of the leaves. The only indication that Aiden made it over was the casual steps of the watchmen. I waited fifty more seconds until I dared to go up the ladder.

I wrapped the torn cloth even tighter. My palms were sweaty, and my heart was racing. It was time. My mental timer turned on and the countdown began.

Fifty.

Forty-nine.

I dove into the bush and grabbed the first rung of the ladder. I pulled myself toward it and pushed with my feet. My dress got caught in the oversized thorns but ripped away after a hard tug. My covered hands got a hold of the second rung, and I began to pull myself upward. The largest part of the bush lay below, tugging me down and back into the training center. My hands kept going up.

Forty-two.

Forty-one.

Forty.

I almost reached the top. I couldn't help feeling this was like the night when Skyler made me climb to the top of the roof. My covered hands still felt the occasional pinch of the long thorns.

Thirty.

Twenty-nine.

Twenty-eight.

Twenty-seven.

Once I stood on the wall, I walked to the edge and stared as the ground below. This felt just like the school's roof, but now

I knew what was coming. I knew that this fall would hurt a lot more. I searched for something I could use to lower myself to the ground. Aiden's body wasn't sprawled on the ground beneath me, so there had to be some way to get down safely.

Twenty-three.

Twenty-two.

Twenty-one.

I searched for something to help me down the other side of the wall, but I couldn't see anything. Could it be that there was nothing to help me get down? Would I have to throw myself into the void and wait for Aiden to miraculously catch me? Aiden would have come back if something was wrong. Maybe he got caught. I knew that hesitating now was the worst thing I could do, but it was the only thing I could do.

Fifteen.

Fourteen.

I could feel my time running out. I grabbed a small, loose piece of the wall and pulled it out. I threw the rock straight down below me. The rock fell silently and conspicuously bounced off of the wall. It hadn't hit the wall, but there was something sticking out. I noticed a grey painted ladder. It was so dark out that the ladder was invisible to the naked eye.

Nine.

Eight.

I climbed the small rail that helped the watchmen stay on the wall and not fall. I aimed myself at the same spot where I had thrown the rock. If I had had more time, I would've tried to see how big the ladder was, but now I would have to risk an injury or my life. I threw myself at the vague target.

Zero.

My time ran out just as I grabbed the first rung of the ladder. I banged my elbow against the wall. Pain ran up my arm as I slid downward. My grip loosened, and I slipped down to the next rung as a watchman passed over me. I looked up and pressed my body against the ladder. I was wearing white from head to toe, and my hair, shining silver in the moonlight, acted like a spotlight. The watchman didn't even look down. I exhaled in relief and lowered myself rung by rung. I tried not to look down. I chanted to myself, "Hand, foot, hand, foot..." Skyler's vivid image appeared in my mind. I could feel his arms pushing me away from the ladder and down into the long fall. My feet lost contact with the metal rungs, and I yelped. I hung by my two hands. Looking down made everything harder. I saw the distance between the ground and my feet. I would be dead if I fell.

"No...no...no...no...no," I murmured to myself. I looked down again, scanning the walls for something to hold on to. Underneath me, some feet down, was another rung of the ladder. I cursed under my breath, as I let go without thinking of everything that could go wrong.

I fell in the darkness for longer than I wanted. The longer I fell, the harder I would land. The air around me rushed by and angrily bit my cheeks and lifted the skirt of my dress. I could feel it pull me downward.

The metal rung appeared in a flash. One second I was falling, and a second later, I was hanging from my hands again. My arms ached from the intense jolt. I began climbing down again, one foot after the other. I had almost reached the ground when the metal rung broke underneath my weight. I cried out as my feet hit the ground and my body followed. I banged my left elbow on the dry soil.

"Gosh, Aiden couldn't you have caught me?" I gasped.

"Are you okay?" Aiden rushed to my side and helped me sit up. "We have to crawl to the side fast if you don't want to get crushed by the next person." He helped drag me to the side, and then we sat with our backs to the wall.

In the faint light, I lifted the wrecked skirt of my dress so I could see my bare legs underneath. They were covered with scratches that stung whenever the breeze blew. I quickly dropped the skirt over my legs and sighed. "How was your fall?" I kept my voice low, even though I knew no one could hear us.

Aiden hadn't even checked himself for injuries. "My back had a pretty tough time," he admitted, resting his head against the wall and closing his eyes. I could see him flinch every now and then, but I didn't want to ask.

Seconds stretched into minutes. Where were Ren and Juris? Aiden remained sitting with his eyes closed, and I had my legs tucked beneath my skirt. I stared at the terrain stretched out in front of us. What seemed like miles of grass separated me from the thick, dark and wild forest. The dry earth that was below us was gaining terrain on the grassy field. I didn't know if I could sprint that far. A front of trees stood like soldiers, guarding the training center from the rest of the forest. A few mountains were visible, like cloaked shadows huddled beneath the illuminated sky.

"Where are they?" Aiden asked with a troubled voice. "We should have reached the forest by now."

A scream pierced the night and increased in volume as it got closer to us.

A body crashed to the ground.

I screamed.

The silence of the night was broken by the cry of sirens.

Chapter 19

I covered my eyes, since I didn't want to see who it was. If it was Juris, then there was no way that Ren could have survived whatever was happening above us. Colored dots appeared on the inside of my eyelids as I pressed harder. The limp body kept crashing over the ground, and I could hear the bones cracking. The force with which the head had hit the ground made my body go limp and my blood pressure dive. Suddenly, Aiden wrapped his arms around me and whispered into my ear as he rocked me back and forth. "It was the guard from the walkway, don't worry. We need to run for it."

"What?" I tried to pull him down and stop him from running, but he pulled me up with impressive strength. "Aiden, don't. We have to wait for them."

He froze and looked at weathered ladder. "Don't you hear the sirens? Don't you think all this effort is worth at least saving two? Juris can handle himself, and Ren is smart. They'll do better own their own than with us." I considered. "Besides, who do you think threw the watchman over the rail? They'll be right behind us."

He was right. They wouldn't be so bad off by themselves. Juris knew how to get to the backpacks, so we could wait for them there. "Fine." My legs weren't used to running. It felt good to finally sprint. Aiden was fast. I ran behind him, and every now and then, looked back. Finally, we reached the grassy field. The distance between us the training center slowly got smaller, and the border of the forest crept toward us. I heard someone scream. The scream was closer than the other sounds. I turned around before I heard Aiden warn me not to.

Ren and Juris were running toward us. Juris yelled words of encouragement to Ren, who passed him like a bullet.

The watchmen on the wall saw what was happening and didn't hesitate to take action. They pulled out what looked like guns. They were going to kill us. They began to shoot at the closest targets. Juris and Ren ran faster. There were no more words of encouragement; just the desire to live. The shots fell closer and closer to their targets.

One watchman took careful aim and shot.

Ren fell to the ground.

Juris ran faster to reach her. An arm held me back. How could Aiden hold me back from helping her? Juris picked her up, and she nodded at him. They began sprinting toward us.

Aiden grabbed my hand and spun me around. His breath was heavy and his grip was firm. We ran into the forest. Our feet crunched the dead leaves that were scattered on the ground. I began searching for the markers. Everything looked normal.

Maybe the markers were overgrown. As we ran, I made sure to look as closely as possible. Aiden also searched. We ran straight through the thin trees. They looked young and weak in comparison with the forest that surrounded Ashwick. Maybe we were in the same country, in the same continent.

Aiden slowed down so he was running next to me. We dodged low branches and jumped tall shrubs simultaneously. "Do you think we could have passed the first sign?"

We couldn't have. I began to hesitate. "Stop!" I yanked Aiden backward. "Look." I knelt on the ground and touched the base of a rock. It had fluorescent paint on it, just a bit. When I went to touch the heavy green moss that covered the rock, it fell off.

Aiden grabbed the net of moss. "It's fake. Here." He signaled at the circle painted in black right above the strip of fluorescent paint. "What does that mean?" he looked up at me. Ren and Juris caught up to us. They slowed and gasped for air as they observed the rock.

"A marker?" Ren breathed in heavily between each word. I nodded. She rounded the object and pointed at another marking. "X marks the spot. I guess we have to run in the direction the X is facing."

Juris silenced her with a gesture. "Listen." He whispered. It sounded like a mix of a helicopter and a plane. Beams of light appeared farther away. The forest was not as dense as I had expected, and it gave us no cover. "We have to move, and fast." He took off after covering the rock again with the fake moss. It didn't take long for the rest of us to react and follow him. He searched from the left, Ren searched the right, and I followed behind her. Aiden, who ran last, made sure no one overlooked a signal.

We kept on running, occasionally bumping into marked rocks. All of them had the same strip of fluorescent paint at the base, a black circle that faced the direction in which we were running, and then an X that determined our next move. All we had to do was run straight and bump into them. The spacing between the rocks was irregular. Some rocks were only minutes apart, while others seemed to take forever to find.

Left.

Around a clearing.

Right.

Right.

Left.

The noise of helicopter propellers came and went. The trees got thicker. The ground began disappearing under our feet replaced with short plants. Fallen logs and branches required more and more energy to pass. We had already been running for a long time, but we had to find the supplies.

Ren tripped and fell to the ground. Her hands stopped her from falling on her face, but she stayed there. "Please, no more running." She turned around and lay on her back.

"We have to reach the supplies before we can rest." Juris offered her his hand.

Ren pushed his hand away and kept breathing deeply. "Can we at least wait fifteen minutes?" she pleaded.

Aiden sat down next to her. "She's right, we could use a break. My legs are aching." His wiped the sweat from his forehead and looked around.

Juris planted himself on the ground. "The faster we get to the supplies, the sooner we can rest."

"The more we rest, the faster we can run," Ren defended her point firmly. Her hair, which had been held up in a neat half bun, hung in a tangled mess. I didn't even want to know the state of my appearance. All I wanted was a shower, water, and a mattress.

Juris shook his head and began to jog away.

Ren sighed in frustration. "Gosh, he's so stubborn!" She dragged herself up.

We couldn't run anymore. We all jogged, our legs too tired to hold us up, and we stumbled every now and then. My legs burned. My feet felt like concrete bricks, and my knees creaked with pain every time I took a step forward. I was wet, covered in sweat, and I prayed that whoever was searching for us wouldn't use dogs. Everything was too quiet. It felt as if the searchers weren't putting much effort into the search, as if they we letting us go. But somehow they had known we were going to escape, because the Golden of Water had told me he knew what we were going to do.

The trees got thicker and thicker as we ran deeper into the forest. The pale moonlight filtered through the bare branches like spiderwebs. Suddenly, the dense forest ended, and we hit another clearing. But this one wasn't as clear as the others. There were five weeping willows arranged in an unusual way—

one in the middle and four circling around it. Of course the one in the middle was the largest. Our supplies were there. We all took off, sprinting toward the tree, using the last drops of energy left in our bodies. To my surprise, many of the trees still had their leaves, which helped with coverage. Out in the open, I felt exposed and unprotected. Lights suddenly burst around us. We took shelter at the base of one of the surrounding weeping willows and looked for a way to protect ourselves. Juris and Aiden had dark clothing, so they could hide more easily than Ren and me. But we all knew I was the biggest problem. I was dressed from head to toe with white and glitter. If one spotlight or flashlight caught me, I would show up like a disco ball.

Aiden turned to me and pointed to a low branch. "Climb the tree with Ren. Juris and I will dig, and then we'll come back here to get you guys."

"But won't you need help?"

"Just do it." Aiden offered to let me step on his hands so he could push me upward, but I told him I could climb on my own. I called to Ren in a low whisper and told her what we had to do.

She smiled and quickly climbed the branch. I stared in awe as I watched her swing herself into the air. With one push off of the trunk, she was already sitting elegantly on the branch. "Come on, you slowpoke," she mocked. Wasn't she tired?

I climbed up with much more effort and much less grace and elegance than Ren did. Once I was on the lowest branch, Ren helped me climb up a few more so we had more coverage. I rested my back on the trunk, and Ren, on the same branch, stretched out with one foot hanging down. Her arms were neatly folded on her chest, and her hair cascaded off the branch in a harmonious mass of curls.

"What do you think they'll do to us if we get captured?" She opened her eyes and looked above the green canopy that hid the stars.

I yawned and stretched my arms. I spotted a light near the edge of the clearing. I saw the bright circle through the curtain of leaves. I couldn't help feeling vulnerable. "I have no idea, but I hope we won't have to face that situation." Instinctively, I lowered my voice.

Ren turned her head to look at the light. We both stopped talking in case someone could hear us. One thought flashed through my mind as the bright beam moved toward the trees. Aiden and Juris. They surely were at the base of the tree looking for the supplies, and probably hadn't seen the oncoming danger. I wanted to yell a warning to them, but I was too scared of being discovered. However, Juris and Aiden weren't that stupid. They probably were already hiding in the tree and waiting for the danger to pass.

A large man holding an immense flashlight walked right up to our tree. Ren held her breath and picked up her dress and hair. I gathered what was left of my skirt and pressed myself against the trunk and the branch, hoping that the tree would swallow me up. I dared to look down and catch a small glimpse of what was happening.

The man holding the flashlight wasn't alone. Three people were behind him. They all wore strange black suits. I couldn't see them up close, but I noticed a lot of small pockets. They wore helmets that matched their suits. The helmets had large visors emblazoned with figures in little colorful lights.

"Why are we searching now? It's always more fun when we give them a head start," one of the young men snickered. A head start? Was he so sure that they were going to catch us? I looked over to see Ren's expression. She had also heard. One of her eyebrows was raised.

"Remember what happened last time? Remember what happened to the last bunch of searchers? This is our job, *not* a game," a much older man spoke; he was probably in his forties. His voice was scratchy. Surely, he was the first searcher I had seen, because he spoke with an air of authority over the other three.

He took something out of a pocket; I could hear the rasping of Velcro. "We all know what happened, but that won't happen again, not with the equipment we have now. And what's the harm of having some fun?" a woman with a soprano voice inquired.

A red line of light washed over the whole clearing and turned off with a beep. "Nothing," the young man spoke again. "We might as well move on and gain some more ground. If we missed them, the next group won't. And isn't it always better to secure a perimeter before they get there?"

Ren caught my alarmed appearance. I mouthed Aiden's and Juris's names. After I nodded, her eyes widened and she mouthed another word. I was glad I didn't understand it.

The searchers underneath us remained silent. I didn't know if they were gone or if they had heard. They couldn't have eavesdropped, because we weren't saying anything. Still, the thought of it troubled me.

The leader of the group finally spoke after considering the young man's idea. "We might as well do that. If we find out that any of you are helping them get away, you are going to end up like Zareh. You understand me, right?"

"Yes sir," they replied in unison.

The flashlight flicked from side to side as the team left the clearing. I heard two soft *thumps* nearby. Aiden and Juris had somehow made it past our first obstacle. They didn't speak; neither did Ren and I. There was no need, and we'd have plenty of time to talk later when we were safe.

I couldn't help thinking of Steven. I felt like I was six again, and we were playing hide and seek in our backyard. I always hid in the same tree and on the same branch, hoping he wouldn't guess I was stupid enough to go to the same place twice. It worked the first few times, but then he realized that I wasn't ever going to look for another hiding spot. So, he walked around the yard as if he were trying to find me before rediscovering my spot once more.

I could see him standing underneath my branch and smiling up at me. "It took some time, but I found you." He rolled his eyes and huffed. "But do you know what would make me take even longer?" I shook my head. My short, straight bob swayed around my head. My face always had a curious expression.

"Finding a new place to hide." He turned back to the kitchen door, which was our starting point. "You seek." His annoyance faded away once he told me that I had to find him. He loved hiding.

"Hey, Ary, where did you go?" Ren asked, pulling me out of my memory. She was already a branch below me.

I looked at her, confused.

She sighed and rolled her eyes as she lowered herself until she reached the ground. "Hurry up, we have to clean things up before the next search party comes." And with that, Ren took off toward the supplies.

I climbed down slowly, making sure I didn't slip and fall. I looked at Juris, Aiden, and Ren. Cleaning things up meant covering the hole that Aiden and Juris had dug. I helped cover the wooden doors that concealed a small concrete compartment in the ground. Four backpacks were propped against the tree. "How did you guys dig this up so fast? And without the four searchers noticing?" I asked without slowing down.

Aiden wiped his forehead with his wrist, since his hands were dark paws made of mud. "They didn't see it. They came from that direction and then walked right next to it, but they were on the opposite side of the trunk. I guess it was just luck. And Juris is a super fast digger."

"And how did you guys know this was the eastern side of the tree?"

Aiden stopped shoving dirt back into place and pointed to a bright star that shone between the leaves of the willow tree.

"That's the Southern Cross right there. It points south. That's south and this is east." I was impressed with his knowledge.

We covered the hole quickly, since it wasn't that deep and there were eight hands helping. We patted down the fresh soil and took one backpack each. When I placed the heavy backpack on my shoulders, I swayed backward, taking hold of the tree for balance. Ren and Aiden were doing the same. The only person unaffected by the weight of the backpack was Juris. Typical.

He gave me one quick, cold look and then began marching forward. "Let's get back into the forest until we can find some coverage, and then we can stop to look at the map."

We walked in silence. No one wanted to complain about sore feet, tired backs, growling stomachs, dry throats, or heavy legs in case Juris got fed up and made us run again. He wasn't in charge; it was just important to not leave anyone behind or let anyone stray ahead.

Aiden spoke to me in a low voice. "I saw Skyler in the group. He didn't talk, but he was there." Why was he telling me this? Were they forcing Skyler to search for me? Did he volunteer so it wouldn't seem as if he helped us escape? Did all of the protectors have to search too?

I couldn't tell how much time had passed since we dug up the backpacks or since we began to run. I kept my mind busy so the minutes wouldn't stretch on. Ren told me that about fifteen minutes had passed when I phased out on the branch. It felt like seconds in my mind. I wanted to think of ways I could somehow get back to Ashwick and see my family again. I needed to see them, even if they wouldn't recognize me. I had to check on them, maybe talk to them like a complete stranger. Somehow, each time I was deep in thought, Skyler's name would randomly pop up. I didn't get him, and I never hoped to understand his mind, but something told me that he played the game better than anyone gave him credit for. What game? Lying? Plotting against invisible dangers? Skyler knew a lot of things, that I knew for sure, but what he knew remained a mystery. I sighed in frustration.

Ren walked beside me. "Is it just me, or was Skyler with the searchers?" She kept her voice low. The crunching dried leaves and fallen twigs helped cover our conversation. Juris walked a few feet ahead, and Aiden was right behind him.

"Yeah, he was with them, or so Aiden says." I couldn't keep the tension out of my voice.

She sensed my mood and spoke softly, with sympathy. "Were you guys close?" She stepped quietly and lightly, her movements reflecting her approach to the topic.

I shrugged. "Well, I don't hate him, and we started being sort of friends, I guess."

"No, but were you guys *close*?" I knew she had been insinuating something else from the beginning, but I chose to play it safe. If I had jumped to this conclusion, it would have made her doubt my answer when I said no.

I had felt things for him, but after being killed, I hadn't felt anything positive about Skyler. "No, Skyler and I were never into each other. Plus, if we did like each other, there would be nothing we could do. He would die before we turned nineteen, and it's forbidden." I stared at the back of Aiden's head, as I thought once more of the kiss we shared.

Juris and Aiden dropped their backpacks on the ground and turned to us. Aiden caught my fixed gaze and broke a small smile through the exhaustion. My eyes darted to look somewhere else. Ren giggled next to me. She pushed me softly with her elbow and dropped her bag once we got closer. My face felt hot.

Juris unzipped his backpack and began piling the contents at his feet. He sat silently while he made a list in his head of all the objects that were in his bag. We all followed his lead.

I slumped down against a tree and began pulling one item out at a time: three large water bottles, a strange sleeping bag, a pair of brown leather boots, two different outfits, a folded piece of paper, matches, a flashlight with an extra pair of batteries, a first-aid kit, and a tied-up cloth. I untied the string that held the cloth together and rolled it out. Four knives were strapped inside. I looked around to see my companions' items.

Juris recited his findings. Exactly the same items I had, except for the four knives. He did have much more water, six bottles instead of three. A pistol with extra ammunition made him crack a sinister grin.

Aiden had three bottles of water, but his weapon was a long dagger.

Ren discovered five bottles of water, and what Juris identified as a kukri, a medium blade with an edge that was curved inward. All the rest of the objects were the same. "Do you think we might have trackers in our clothing?" Her voice was tired and lethargic. She held up the oversized moss green t-shirt. "I'm not changing in front of you guys, just so you know."

Juris and Aiden grabbed their clothes and turned around, disappearing into a bush. I could tell that Ren didn't completely trust them, so she slipped on her pants under her dress and put her shirt over her dress before shaking it off. I did the same, noticing that the clothing was meant for a man and was a few sizes too big. I stashed the extra boots in my backpack in case I broke the ones I was wearing. We called the boys back, and they had also changed.

"I say we hang our backpacks in a tree, just in case." Aiden suggested. He was packing all of the items in his bag again, except for the sleeping bag and a bottle of water. He took a small sip and looked around to see our reaction to his suggestion.

Juris nodded, and Ren offered to climb the tree. Juris eyed Aiden and his bottle of water. "I say we should evenly spread out the water. We only drink when we really need to. I don't know how long we'll be out alone."

Aiden exhaled noisily and compiled all the bottles of water. We had a total of seventeen. After dividing everything, we each had four bottles of water, except for Juris, who had five.

After I received my water bottles, I felt as if something was missing. We didn't have all the supplies we needed. "There isn't any food." I grabbed my backpack once more and double-checked that I had grabbed everything. Empty.

Juris turned to me. "We can hunt tomorrow. In the meantime, let's figure out how we're going to set up camp."

Fire boy looked curiously at his sleeping bag. "Why do you think it's a sack with a zipper and six strings?" He played around with the bag, trying to figure out the function of the strings.

I observed my own sleeping bag. When the zipper faced up, the six strings did too. We didn't have tents. Not one of us had gotten a tent. Maybe the sleeping bags were some sort of a tent too, just smaller. The strings were evenly spaced along the sleeping bag, two at the top, two in the middle, and two at the end, almost as if the bag was meant for hanging.

"We have to hang them. Sleep over the ground," I thought out loud. Ren had just jumped back to the ground, and the boys looked at me quickly, catching on to the idea. I walked over to the first tree that I knew I could climb and threw the sleeping bag over the lowest branch. I pulled myself up and ascended two branches. I didn't want to be higher than necessary, just in case I fell. I tied the strings safely to the branch and let the bag drop so it was hanging. The strings looked strong, so I unzipped the bag and got inside. I swayed in the wind, and little holes throughout the whole bag let fresh air come in.

I could hear Juris's voice right underneath me. "It camouflages perfectly once you get in it. It must activate once it feels weight."

I unzipped the closure and climbed out. I sat on the branch, too lazy to get down and climb back up afterward. My legs hung freely beneath me and thanked me for the rest. "Can we go to sleep now?" I whined.

Everyone nodded and climbed different trees to hang their bags. Before I climbed into my own bag, Juris suggested that the first person who woke up in the morning should wake up the rest so we could get moving. We hadn't yet determined the best time to move, but that would surely be the talk of tomorrow. I sunk into the roomy sleeping bag and let the wind cradle me to sleep. All I could hear was some owls every now and then and the rustling of dried leaves.

Part 2

S. Elizabeth Dover

"Why are you calling me?" Nina answered the call. The screen appeared over her coffee table, revealing a very dressed-up man. Not that she wasn't dressed up—Nina wore a long, black, silk gown that hugged her curves elegantly. She leaned back into the couch, as she stared at the Monarch of Water.

He stared back at her as an equal. "I just wanted to tell you that they have escaped." He gave himself the pleasure of smiling.

She took a sip of wine before speaking. "That was part of the plan, wasn't it?"

"Yes."

"Then why are you calling me, Wiley?" She caressed the golden necklace, which , reminded every citizen in Arcane that she represented the element of fire in the government.

Wiley fidgeted in his seat. "Apparently, she has an unknown skill..."

Nina's eyebrow rose. "Who?" Her curiosity was now peaked.

"Aurora, the element of air."

Nina turned her head sharply in the direction of the screen. "Wasn't she the very one who deliberately disobeyed everyone?" Her long, claw-like nails scratched her scalp as she rearranged her short hair.

Wiley looked down for a moment while biting the edge of his lip. "Yes."

"Did you find out before or after she left?" She playfully read Wiley's expression with a smirk.

"After..."

Nina laughed, her shoulders relaxing against the soft, plush material of her couch. "And how do you plan on retrieving her?"

Wiley's golden ring shone in the light as he rearranged his tie. "I will not bring her here; she will come by herself, because she will need me."

Nina sat up straighter. Her slim waist was exposed through large slits in her dress. "You just love it when they need you," she said with a chuckle. "And how do you suppose to get her to need you?"

He pulled out a glass flask filled with a fiery-colored liquid. "Because someone else needs me as well..."

The Golden of Fire turned to the side to see who had entered her room. She grinned at the visitor and turned to the screen one last time. "Happy hunting."

Chapter 20

We all sat in a circle around the two folded papers with our sleeping bags stored in our backpacks. The first paper explained most of the items we received: the hanging sleeping bags and the weapons and their functions. The knives in my backpack were throwing knives. Perfect.

"I can't believe this is what is supposed to guide us!" Juris spat bitterly. We all stared down at the map that lay open between the four of us. I had to admit I also was disappointed. Whoever was helping us had fifty years to prepare, and all they could give us was a piece of paper with four single drawings: the training center, the weeping willow, a river that crossed the paper and an X. One single X that looked just like the ones on the rocks.

Ren tilted her head, examining the map. Her coral-orange curls were tied up in an elaborate braid. If we hadn't been such in a hurry, I could have asked her to teach me. Her blue eyes shone brightly under the confusion of her messed-up makeup. Her loose-fitting brown shirt, rolled up to her wrists, and her oversized pants made her look as if she were the typical farmer's daughter about to start a day filled with manual labor after a wild night out.

"They suck at drawing maps," she commented. "A five-year-old could do better." Her eyeliner was smudged under her eyes, and her eye shadow was smeared.

I couldn't help feeling a bit self-conscious about my own makeup. When I went to wipe my eyeliner, smudged mascara, and faded eye shadow, my shirtsleeve came away stained by a mix of black and shiny grey. I kept on wiping just in case.

Aiden stared at the paper. "There's a compass in the corner there. And we dug on the eastern side here and then left in this direction, so we're heading north now. And that's good, because we just have to keep going straight. The sun rose on that side, that's east, that means that direction is north." He pointed the way.

Juris clapped his hands and rubbed them together. "Let's get moving." He pulled on his backpack and waited for the rest of us to follow. Even after resting, I didn't feel as good as I was expecting. I had remained awake with the fear of being found, and when I finally fell asleep, nightmares invaded the peaceful darkness. My knees still creaked with each step, and my legs were numb.

We weren't as careful as we should have been with keeping the noise down. Our feet stomped their way through the mix of dirt and dried leaves. I shivered. The sun had just risen, so it wasn't providing heat yet. This motivated me to keep on moving, since the more I walked, the warmer I would get. We didn't need to check our campsite for any garbage or tracks. We couldn't throw away anything because we needed it all.

I glanced at Juris. He looked handsome with his dark skin matching the tones of the trees and his eyes mirroring the colors of the leaves. Even though his appearance wasn't bothersome, *he* was, so I quickly turned away to observe my surroundings.

Now that daylight had broken the darkness, the environment looked less menacing. Trees surrounded us, leaning on each other, or upright like soldiers. As I passed them, I tried matching a characteristic to them, like graceful, lazy, eccentric, or twisted. Wild plants and bushes created coverage for a variety of small animals. I wondered if there were any dangerous predators roaming the woods that we should be aware of.

Crack.

We all turned in the direction of the noise.

Crunch. Beep.

Beep?

Juris took hold of Ren in one jump and hid in some dense shrubs. I froze, paralyzed with shock, staring at the Aiden. We're going to get caught, was all I could think. The searchers had lied. There would be no head start. I looked for a place to hide but saw nothing, so I took off toward the north. I could always meet up with the others at the river. My feet enjoyed the small sprint, but they tired quickly. I found a clearing surrounded by thick bushes. I dove into them without caring about the insects that could be living there. I sat down, hugging my knees to my chest, and waited.

What was I waiting for? For Juris, Ren, and Aiden to walk by as if nothing had happened? Or the searchers? At least I knew what I wanted. I wanted to go back home. It would be impossible and, of course, my family and friends wouldn't recognize me. Would they be able to remember? Could I make them remember? My breath was agitated, and my mind ran wild. Now wasn't the best time to get distracted and homesick. Now I didn't even have a home to miss.

A hand touched my shoulder. I fought the urge to scream, but another hand was already on my mouth. "Shhh," Aiden whispered in my ear. He slid past the curtain of green leaves and sat down beside me, pressing his shoulders against mine. "Sorry I crashed your hiding spot; I thought you had kept on running." His voice was a low murmur.

I nodded. I didn't want to talk at all. I couldn't hear any more noises, but I was sure the searchers were nearby. I caught movement out of the side of my eye, but when I turned to see what it was, there were no signs of anyone or anything. I searched in the different shades of greens and reds and oranges around us. I shifted my weight, making branches and twigs snap.

"I'm sorry I moved too fast on you yesterday..." Aiden's voice was too loud for the situation. I looked at him, confused. "I just wanted to do that ever since I saw you. I hope you didn't mind." He held my gaze, searching for any hint of acknowledgment. I knew exactly what he was talking about, but I wanted to see how long he would avoid the word kiss. "Don't you remember the...?" He inched a bit closer, trying to trigger my memory. I stared out to the open, to the forest, searching for movement. "The kiss, Ary."

I smiled. "No, I'm not mad." Despite the tension of the moment, I found a little peace. "I'm glad you did it," I added. Aiden squirmed next to me, a big grin on his face, his cheeks slightly flushed.

"Good to know." He spoke in a monotone, as if he were only mentioning the weather. "Then I hope you don't mind if we repeat that in the future." I couldn't help beaming.

I leaned my head on his shoulder and inhaled, a sudden calmness washing over me. We were hiding in the forest from our captors, and someone was stalking us, and we were here, talking as if nothing had gone wrong in our lives. Aiden smelled like cinnamon. It was strange since we were in the forest and we were dirty, but a strong smell lingered at the base of his neck. I tilted my face a bit to catch the scent better. Aiden lifted his head once more, and as he did, I saw the small vapor that came out of his nose as he exhaled.

He turned to me, concerned. "Are you okay?" He wrapped his arm around me, trying to move as silently as possible, and pulled me closer.

I let him hold me; I didn't mind the extra heat. "Do you think they're doing this on purpose?" My question unsettled me. What if they were planning to freeze us to death?

"Who?"

"The Golden Four, the training center, I don't know. Arcane?" I folded my hands in between my knees and torso. My hair hung freely like curtains for my ears.

He sniffled. "Maybe they want us to light a fire at night to keep warm. That way, they can blame our own stupidity for our capture. Then again, Ary, it's winter—well, autumn. Are you still cold? Because I think I can help with that," he offered.

"And how would you do that?" Something *cracked* farther away. I remained unnaturally calm.

He shrugged. His golden irises danced in the whites of his eyes. He rested his nose against mine, his breath warm on my face. "Just guess."

I shook my head but kept our noses touching. "I'm very bad at guessing games." I knew the answer. He had warmer skin, and it was cold outside. We were like a puzzle with only two pieces. I inched closer to him, our eyes closing. We stopped only millimeters away from each other. I held my breath.

"Oh, get a room!" Ren called from in front of us. She held the branches apart and stared with a mocking face. "Come on, there's no danger. Must have been a deer or something like that," she said as she walked away, leaving Aiden and me to make our way out by ourselves.

I pushed myself out of the bush without minding about the noise I made. I jogged up to Ren and matched her pace as we kept walking. Aiden took the rear once again. "How long until we reach the river?" His attempt to cover the awkward situation was in vain.

Ren's eyes lingered on my face, making me replay the scene in my mind, as if watching it from afar. How long had she been standing there? "I have no idea," she replied, "I hope not too far 'cause then we're going to have to make it to the X, which is much farther. That is, if the drawing is proportional to reality."

"What about food?" I asked, my stomach growling.

"I think we're going to start hunting during our next break." Ren hardly made any noise as she walked. I looked down at her feet. She had taken off her boots and now walked barefoot. Her feet were already stained with dirt. "Oh, and Ary?"

"What?"

"Since when have you two been hooking up?"

I looked behind us. Aiden was walking with his head low, and he was humming some song I didn't recognize. His eyes looked shut, but I couldn't tell for sure because his hair fell into his face. The natural reddish highlights in his brown hair shone bright in the sunlight. "May I know the reason for this intrusion?" I asked.

Ren rolled her eyes, as if it was completely obvious. "I'm just saying you shouldn't fall for the first dude that you like as compensation for your broken-up life."

"I'm not using him, if that's what you think."

Crack.

Juris cursed.

A rabbit dashed right in front of Juris, not caring if he was a predator or not. It was already being chased. The grey rabbit sprinted past in the blink of an eye and disappeared as fast as it had appeared. We heard a few last branches crack as the small animal broke dry sticks underneath its padded paws.

"That almost gave me a heart attack," Juris remarked. He rested one hand on a tree trunk to steady himself. He stared into the spot where the rabbit had appeared. Unquestionably, he was looking to see if the predator would come running out too. Maybe the predator had caused the noise we heard before. But what animal beeped?

Ren joined him to look for any danger. "Man up and let's keep walking before whatever that things is comes after us." She passed him, bouncing on the tips of her toes. I watched her go with confusion muddling me. I could not understand her personality.

Just as Ren and Juris began to walk, Aiden following them, an orange figure appeared in the greenery. It peeked out and locked eyes with me. A fox. That was what must have been chasing the rabbit. Its soft fur looked silky. I wanted to reach out and touch it, but its brown eyes stared at me, making me feel uneasy. I didn't move. I didn't dare. The fox tilted its head. Its pupils suddenly dilated and contracted. That was not normal. Its orange ears perked up, and it looked away, distracted by something else. It turned around and began running in the opposite direction from which it came.

I furrowed my eyebrows, unsure of what had just happened.

Chapter 21

I didn't tell anyone about the fox. I wasn't sure of what I had seen, and I didn't want to freak everyone out over nothing. I continued to look for the fox as we walked. I'd searched for it during the morning and afternoon. We maintained a constant pace, leaving more distance behind us with each step. We agreed that walking for hours would be much better and more efficient that running until we died of exhaustion, taking a long break, and then running again. The small five-minute breaks allowed us to nibble on some small animals we had managed to hunt and sip some water. It was important for us to remain hydrated, so until we reached the river, we were allowed to drink as much water as we pleased within range of four water bottles each. I was down to a bottle and a half of water. My feet were already hosting a few blisters because I was still breaking in the boots. I would have risked a few moments with the boots off, but if I left my feet unprotected, keeping warm would be a difficult task.

Things had been going easy for the first day, a bit too easy for my taste, so I kept my knives close to me and easy to grab in case of emergency.

Ren walked silently next to me. We kept each other company and occasionally carried each other's bags when they got too heavy. She carved a thick stick to keep herself busy while we trekked. I watch her turn the piece of ordinary wood into the rough shape of an animal.

Juris hardly spoke, but when he did, his voice no longer carried a threat or intimidation. He seemed almost nice and happy. When we stopped to rest, he would sit in the soil and close his eyes and meditate. I felt uneasy with him acting too cooperative and thoughtful with us. I was used to him being violent and irrational.

Aiden, on the other hand, spent his time walking behind us. We had shared lunch together, but other than that, he didn't speak. It was as if silence had put a spell over us all. Sometimes, Ren and I thought he was speaking to us, but he denied it. He would mutter to himself and then fall back into the eternal silence, his back slumped and his hands playing with each other, as they had back in the training center.

I picked at the little clear stones stuck onto my nails. The polish had chipped at the corners, but I didn't have anything else to entertain me, so I wanted it off completely. I smiled in satisfaction whenever I peeled off a stone.

Ren touched my arm lightly. "What do you think this is?" She held up a half-carved figure.

"It could be anything with four legs," I sighed. "But I'd have to say maybe a cat since you've already tried dog, horse, and cow."

Ren tilted her head and crinkled her nose. "I don't know."

"You don't know what it's supposed to be?"

"Nope," she answered innocently.

I patted the braid that Ren had given me at midday. "Isn't that great?" I added sarcastically.

Juris turned around with a wide grin on his face. "Do you guys hear that?"

I closed my eyes and listened with all my might. I heard it. Yes. If I wasn't mistaken, it sounded like trickling. Water trickled. That meant a river.

Ren's eyes lit up, and she nudged me to the side. "I am so up for a race right now. The last one there jumps in first," she called as she raced forward.

I took off after her, a new source of hope coursing through me. The river! This meant we were close to the halfway point. My feet found steady places to land. I passed Juris, but I couldn't reach Ren. I breathed heavily as I tried to push my legs faster beneath me.

I stumbled on a rock, falling toward the ground. Juris caught my arm and pulled me upright. "You almost fell there," he said and took off. I stared at him in awe. Had Juris just helped me? I began to run again. I didn't want Aiden to pass me and end up in last place.

The river appeared before us, breaking the forest floor with its roar. I felt like diving in head first, but I stopped. The current was fast. I approached the riverbed, took off my boots, and stuffed them in my backpack. I stuffed the end of my shirt into my pants and prepared myself to tread. Ren looked at and me shook her head. "What?" My feet got cold.

She already had her shoes off and her pants rolled up to knee length. "We don't know how strong this is. I'm going to go in first. I'll leave my backpack here, so I don't have too much weight on me. If the current is too strong, I know how to swim my way out." She had already left her backpack next to Juris. Before I could say anything, she walked into the water. "Holy sh…" She stuffed her fist into her mouth so as not to swear. "It's freezing!" she exclaimed as the skin on her legs began to turn blue. She pulled out her foot. "Who knew? Webbed feet." She took in the new image of herself in a much more friendly way than she had the first time. Aiden watched Ren passively.

She struggled to stand still, so she dove into the water and disappeared from our sight. Twenty seconds went by before she popped out of the water with a grin. "I already got used to the water, but you guys will totally freeze to death." I held back a gasp. Her face was light blue, and her hair fell in dark curls of midnight blue. The only thing I could recognize as her own were her eyes. When she pushed her hair out of the way, a webbed hand with dark blue nails that shone silver poked out of the water.

I gawked. "This cannot be real."

She blushed. "It takes some time to get used to, but I like it. I'm like this exotic naiad thing that I read about at school."

"The sky is getting cloudy," Aiden reported from beside me.

I stared up at the sky. Innocent white clouds moved slowly in the atmosphere. Why had he said that? I decided to play along. "Let's get going then." I tightened the straps of my backpack and walked into the freezing water. Juris tossed Ren her backpack, and she grabbed it without difficulties with her frog-like fingers. I shivered. I stepped into deeper water. I might as well get over it, so I began swimming. The current was strong and pulled me down river. I tried to fight it, but it made me swim in a diagonal line. I tried to rest my foot on the ground, but I sank. Completely covered in ice water, the air I inhaled felt like small needles on the insides of my lungs. My limbs, paralyzed by the sub-zero water, moved slowly. I tried to swim up to the surface. I was rewarded with five seconds to breathe, but once more I was pulled under.

What a way to waste efforts. I felt like just sinking into the flowing liquid. It would have been much easier, and I would be left in peace, but pictures of my family popped into my mind. All of them were sitting on my mother's dresser, untouched and immaculate. I was waiting for my life to flash in front of me, but it didn't. I tried to swim some more, but it was useless. I was waiting in vain. Something hard hit me and stopped me from going with the current. I held on. My lungs cried for oxygen. I climbed up the slippery surface and gulped in air. I rested my face on what looked like a jagged rock. Something stained the water red. Blood? My blood? I didn't care, nor did I feel it. I was so cold, a lot colder than the dark limbo I had walked in as I waited to be reborn.

My fingers slipped from the rock. It was covered in moss, thus making it harder for me to hold on when the current pushed me away. I gulped for air as my nails cracked, ruining my weak attempt to remain on the rock. The current crashed against my body, spraying water into my nose.

"Ary!" I heard someone scream from far away. My grip finally loosened, and I slipped into the dark water once more. I dared to open my eyes, catching a glimpse of the sunlight playing on the shifting water above. The oxygen in my lungs was fully consumed. My throat trembled, forcing me to breath in water. I wanted to stop myself, but my body demanded oxygen.

Someone grabbed me. I was limp in his arms. The pain was the only sign that I was alive. As consciousness slipped from me, the arms tightened their hold on me. I felt like a newborn, so weak and small.

I fell on the muddy bank. My hair stuck to my neck and shoulders like bloodsucking leeches. I convulsed while spitting out water. Unbelievably, it was colder outside of the water than in it. Aiden held up the back of my head, so I didn't choke on the water I was trying to expel from my lungs. The dark sky threatened to rain on us. Juris looked at me from above.

"Don't ever do that again! I can't believe you were so..." He turned away in frustration and didn't waste his breath on finishing the sentence.

I dropped onto my elbows, breathing as much air as I could. "Like I ever want to have another near-death experience. I've already had three, thank you." I sat up, feeling better, still cold and exhausted, but better.

Ren walked by me without offering to help me up. Aiden was with me, though; he helped me up and hugged me. He pulled off his shirt and pressed me up against his chest, so the heat that came from within him warmed me up. If it weren't for his strong hold, I would have fallen back, weary from the dizziness. My head drummed, mimicking the rhythm of the waves.

"That is one nasty wound." He pressed his shirt on my forehead and held it there. When he pulled it back to press again, I saw the red stains.

Juris mumbled as he wrung the water out of his shirt. "You should have waited a bit, and you would have crossed much more safely and without losing your backpack."

"What?" I mumbled, looking incredulously at my sopping companions. I hadn't lost my backpack, had I? But when I went to grab the strap, it wasn't there. I looked at the other side of the river, but no backpack was there either.

Juris heaved a sigh and ran his hand over his short hair, shaking out the water. "I don't care if it's night or day or whatever, but we're all going to get pneumonia if we keep walking like this. We better get dry."

Walking back into the forest was almost as easy as balancing on a tightrope fifty feet above the ground. Dizziness made it hard to concentrate. Juris walked quickly in front along with Ren. I grabbed Aiden's arm as we made slow progress in comparison with the other two.

"Take it easy," he whispered in my ear as he kissed the top of my head. I wanted to fall to the ground and fall asleep in his arms, but I had to push myself forward. Put one foot in front of another.

"Thanks," I said, as he saved me from falling on the ground face first. My wet clothes hung against my body, allowing the soft breeze go through the garments. When Aiden observed this, he offered to help me change into his shirt, which was a bit dryer than mine, but I turned down the offer. I did not want him changing my shirt. Sure, I had hit my head hard but not that hard.

Juris called to us from ahead. "I'll go look for firewood with Ren. Aiden, you can make a small ditch and make sure Ary doesn't do anything stupid while we're gone." He was back to his normal self.

I sat on the ground and watched Aiden get down on his knees and begin to dig with his hands. His wet hair sent drops down his forehead and down the bridge of his nose. It would have looked like sweat if his whole body wasn't in the same state. His reddish-brown hair, tan skin, and strong shoulders made him look like a lion. His golden eyes ran over the area in which he was digging. His muddy hands were dark paws. "If you don't stop staring at me, I'm going to have to put my shirt on," he said from his crouched position without looking up.

I nodded in a silent answer and didn't move my fixed gaze from him. Something was there that hadn't been the night we left, maybe some sort of courage. Or maybe it was hope. Or, perhaps his shirt was off and that was enough to set my mind spinning.

Ren approached carrying some dead twigs and placed them in the shallow hole Aiden had dug. She handed him one of the small boxes of matches from her backpack. "Light these, and then we'll add Juris's branches."

Aiden frowned. "The matches are all wet, but I can try something else." He leaned in on the stack of dead wood. He rubbed his hands swiftly and blew into them. The small orange spark turned into a flame. He stuck his hands underneath the branches and waited patiently. Softly, the flame leaped onto one of the branches. Aiden withdrew his hands and started another small flame in another part of the branches. They caught fire, and the flame spread slowly.

Ren watched in admiration as Juris walked up and added more firewood to the fire. "We need to organize the food and water again because of our unplanned loss." He spoke in a low voice. The crackling of the wood sometimes drowned out his voice. "Ren, you'll share your sleeping bag with Ary. Now about food, how much do we have in total?" He picked up the last pieces of smoked meat. "We'll have to hunt again tomorrow. Now pass me the water." No one objected. "We have five empty bottles and seven and a half that have water." He tossed two full bottles to everyone except for me. I got a bottle and a half.

I looked down at my water. It was the same amount I had before I fell in the river. "I think we should fill the empty bottles with river water," I suggested, hoping to gain some of the provisions I had lost.

"We don't know if that water is okay to drink," Ren extended her hands to the flame, warming her wet skin. She sat with her legs crossed and her eyes fixed.

"We could fill the bottles with water and find some way to boil it," Aiden suggested.

Juris considered silently. "Fine. I'll go fill the bottles in the river, and after we're all dry, we'll keep on making our way to the X. Oh, and get ready for a stroll during the night. We need to make up for the time we're losing."

Ren lay down on the ground and heaved a sigh. "Great," she muttered.

Chapter 22

Who knew how long it had been since sunset? All I knew for sure was that the temperature was dropping even faster than normal. Winter used to be my favorite season of the year, because I loved covering myself with loads of blankets. I loved the warm drinks and food, but now that I had none of that, I didn't like it at all. I couldn't find a way to get warm. Juris and Ren were suffering from the same problem, but Aiden walked steadily, unfazed by the cold temperatures. He had given me his shirt and Ren his second one, so we could be warmer. The sun was setting earlier than before. And that meant that the freezing nights were slowly getting longer. I used most of my concentration now to see what was below my feet. I squinted to get a better view, but it was no use.

"Pass me the load; you've been carrying it long enough." Ren tugged at the backpack on my shoulders. Once we started on our way again, I quickly offered to take it first myself. Guilt consumed me for losing one of the backpacks, so I was trying to make everything easier for the others, even if that meant ending up exhausted at the end of the day. I shook off the backpack. "Are you okay?"

Other than tired, cold, hungry, and thirsty, I was just fine. I didn't want to eat or drink anything until I really needed it. My head had finally stopped bleeding, but we had to take it easy for me not to get dizzy. "I'm feeling kind of sick, though..." After eating meat from the animal Juris had managed to hunt, my stomach wasn't holding up so well. It was possible that I hadn't been able to digest the meat due to the stress of almost drowning.

"Really? Me too. Maybe its Juris's cooking, but food no longer tempts me. Every time I eat meat, I feel like gagging."

I placed a hand over my stomach as I felt the food in me churn. Weird sounds came from my abdomen as my guts twisted inside. I ran my fingers over the smooth surface of the crystal. It hung around my neck, hiding itself in my t-shirt. The cool stone reminded me why I was here, why I had chosen to escape, and what I was headed toward—the truth.

Ren and Juris began to talk to each other. I wasn't paying attention to what they were saying, nor was I interested. Instead, I looked back toward Aiden, who was walking silently with his head hung low.

Something was wrong with Aiden. I needed to figure out what.

I thought about how he had acted at the party, when we met in the halls, and right when I told him that we would escape. Juris had changed for the better out in the wilderness without any tests or competition, while Aiden was withdrawing into himself. My heart wished for it not to be permanent. I walked slower, falling behind, to walk next to him. He gave no signs of recognition. "What's wrong?" I kept my voice lower than Juris's and Ren's, so I wouldn't interrupt their conversation.

"Nothing," he said innocently.

I touched his arm lightly with my fingers. I loved how our body temperatures clashed with each touch. "That's not true. You hardly talk to me anymore. What's up?"

He forced a smile and took my hand. "I guess this whole escape thing is messing me up. Rations, walking without end, hardly any sleep, and always having to keep my guard up...I really didn't think we'd make it out here, and that's why I came. I thought we would get caught and be sent to take the test, so we could take the positions we deserve in the city." He looked up to me. "The clouds look like they're going to bring a storm, don't they?"

I wasn't convinced. "Aiden, don't change the subject." So, he had wanted to stay in Arcane? Didn't he feel scared of what could happen to him if he went to the southern side? There was a fifty percent chance that we would spend our lives being experimented on in the most painful ways.

"I say we might have a day or two if the weather holds, don't you think?" Was he ignoring me, or did he really not hear me? After I asked him if he was all right, he kept on talking about the weather.

He jerked his hand out of mine. "Aiden?" My expression was troubled.

He put his hand to his head and faked a smile once more. "Just a headache. Sorry." But he didn't hold my hand again; instead, he stuffed his hands in his pockets.

Ren screamed.

A shadow in a dark suit took had taken hold of her. A searcher. His hands grabbed her arms and pulled them behind her so she couldn't use them. The searcher's face was stoic, as if he wasn't doing anything wrong and was unshielded by the strange helmets I had seen when we sat on the branches of the weeping willow. Instinct took hold of me, and I grabbed one of the throwing knives. They hadn't been washed away in the river because they were tucked beneath my clothes. I threw the knife, only taking a second to aim. I aimed at the searcher's head, but instead, the knife dug into his shoulder, and he cried out in pain.

The quick reaction took its toll on me and sent a new wave of vertigo. My brain pounded inside my skull, creating pressure over the area I had hit on the rock.

The searcher remained unfazed while immobilizing Ren, but she kicked him in the groin before he could push her against the ground. The man let go of her momentarily, which was long enough for Ren to turn around, pull the knife out of his shoulder, and slip away into the darkness.

I stared at the wound I had inflicted on the searcher. Blood gushed out of him, staining the cloth of his suit with a glossy liquid that shone in the night. How could I have done that? With effort, I was able to take out another knife, but not to kill him, just in case he jumped on me. I promised myself I wouldn't harm anyone unless it was absolutely necessary. Juris ran to the man and punched him in the ribs, going for him with his large dark fists over and over again. I couldn't watch. An action movie was one thing; living it was quite another experience.

Before I could turn away and cower, someone grabbed me by the throat and hauled me away. Stabbing at the fingers around my neck would have been completely reckless. I could have stabbed myself in the process, so I just pulled at the hands. The grip got stronger, blocking my air passage. I panicked. I tried to scream, but a soft, helpless whimper escaped my mouth instead. The searcher who was choking me slammed my head back against a tree. At least the concentration of pain in my head helped me forget about the fingers around my throat that were blocking my windpipe. He looked at my knife and held my wrists against the trunk so I couldn't hurt him. He pressed his body against mine, so I was completely pinned against the tree. "Skyler," I hissed as I kicked my legs out into the air.

He grinned. I couldn't see the different colors of his eyes in the darkness that surrounded us. "Nice to see you, Ary." He banged my hand against the tree so my grip on the knife lessened, and I dropped it.

"Let me go!" I kicked some more, but my efforts were in vain. I tried to hit my head against his like I had seen in so many movies, but the outcome wasn't the same, it just ended up in a weird nod.

He grunted. "What was that?" I asked myself the same question as I tried to clear my headache. He swiftly snuck a piece of paper into my hand as he reached down for the knife I had dropped. I backed into the tree. He was going to stab me again. I had nowhere to run, so I just gawked at him, waiting for his next move. "Good luck." He placed the weapon in my hand and walked backward.

I took hold of his wrist and pulled him closer. With one swish of the blade, I tore his suit at the side of his torso. He gawked at me as the truth slowly dawned on him.

It was like ripping off Band-Aid; it had to be done quickly and without hesitation. If I hesitated, then I would screw it up.

I took a deep breath before striking him again. This time there was no cloth to stop the blade from biting his skin. I didn't want to swipe the blade lightly, only giving him a small tear. No. I thrust my hand forward, digging the knife deep into his side. The sharp metal ripped open his leathery skin. I felt how it cut each layer of tissue. Skyler screamed in pain. He squeezed his eyes shut and grunted as he grabbed my hand and pulled out the knife. Blood rushed from the wound, as I tried to fight back tears.

"You can't go back without a wound. They'll notice," I said quickly. The wound wouldn't kill him. I had learned that in the training center.

He pressed his hands over the puncture and stared at me incredulously. His fingers were stained with his blood, and it kept pouring out, filling the air with its stench. I was about to throw up, but I had to send him off to get the wound cleaned, or he'd get a nasty infection.

"Go. Leave, you idiot!" I pushed him backward, hoping that it would knock him back into his senses.

Skyler staggered backward but still looked at me. "How could..." I didn't answer. Instead, I took hold of the tree in case I would throw up. My stomach contracted and my vision went foggy.

After the wave of nausea passed, I quickly caught on to what he had done. He had pulled me out of the center of the conflict, so I wouldn't get hurt. I had to use that as an advantage to help the others. I quickly wiped the blood off the knife on a nearby leaf and held it in my hand. Juris, back from the attack, found me standing there. "Climb up there and throw your knives." He pointed to the tree Skyler had pushed me against and ran back into the clearing where the fight was taking place.

I climbed for three reasons—so I wouldn't have to fight, so I wouldn't get hurt, and so I could help my companions in case they got injured. I climbed up as fast as I could without letting go of my knife and making sure I didn't stab myself with the other hidden blades. Once I was on the first branch, I climbed out as far as I could without becoming too visible and without falling. I pulled out all the knives I had hidden and held three blades in my left hand and one in my right, ready to aim and throw. Despite the darkness, I could make out five searchers in the clearing. The first one I attacked was unconscious on the ground, surely because of the loss of blood and Juris's pounding. There was one on top of Ren. He began to pull out some sort of square device when she lashed out at him with her kukri. I looked over at Juris. He was pounding his searcher with his fists, when suddenly he remembered his pistol and slammed the butt into the man's head. Aiden was pinned on the ground. The searcher who was overpowering him was small and frail—a girl. She held out his arms and pressed her knees against his ribs. Aiden tried to get free, but she didn't budge. I had to help him. I aimed the knife and threw it.

I missed.

Of course, my foggy eyesight and pounding headache didn't allow me to think clearly. I took a bit more time to aim and prayed for the knife to hit her. I am helping Aiden, I repeated to myself as the knife struck the girl, digging deep into her back. Aiden pushed the girl off, and she landed face up. I closed my eyes, imagining the blade being pushed even deeper. The image of Skyler's skin also popped into my head, which didn't make this any easier. The girl stared at the sky with frozen eyes.

Aiden looked at me and wiped his brow. He picked up his long dagger from the ground. Another searcher jumped out at him, but this time, Aiden looked at his attacker. Right when the man was about to jump on him, he ran right into Aiden's knife. Fire boy looked at his outstretched arm with disgust and let go of the weapon. The man took a step back and brought his hands to the knife in his guts. He looked around and then began to make his way slowly in the direction from which he came. Before he could take his next step, he fell to his knees and looked up at the sky. I stared at him as the life slipped from his features and turned to stone. His body toppled to the side, falling into an eternal sleep.

Two shots sounded through the forest.

I whipped my head around.

Juris stood over three bodies; two searchers with bullet holes in them and Ren, who was sprawled on the ground. He pushed off one of the dead bodies from Ren and propped her up against a rock. Juris checked for her pulse and sighed softly. "She's okay." He pulled out what looked like a dart. "Great. Who knows how long she'll be knocked out?" He checked her neck and shoulders. I jumped down from the tree and went to his side. There was a thin pink line on her right shoulder blade.

I touched the scar. Her skin was slightly lifted over the mark. "What is it?"

Aiden stood next to us, watching.

"Looks like some sort of taser scar. Maybe when they thought it wouldn't work, they shot her with the dart." He rearranged her shirt so it covered her shoulder and turned to survey the scene. Aiden's attacker was pretty; her pixie face held large brown-green eyes, and her long eyelashes almost looked fake. Her lips were already light purple, and her skin was as pale as mine. I shut my eyes momentarily so as not to meet her vacant stare. I had killed her. Actually, Aiden had killed her, but if it hadn't been for my knife...what would have happened?

"I'm going to look around to see if anyone is dead," Aiden said. "You guys check the searchers in this area and keep guard on Ren. Who knows what was in that dart." As he left, a dark figure sprinted past us and knocked him down to the ground.

I reached for the knives, but two hands were already pinning me down to the ground. Many dark figures suddenly appeared like shadows in the night. They moved swiftly as they bound our hands behind our backs and covered out mouths with wet cloths. I turned to see Aiden shutting his eyes, his head lolled as if he were sound asleep. I tried to yell, but the cloth muffled my scream. The sour taste made me grimace.

I felt control over my body slip away. I tried to move my arms, but it was useless. I felt numb all over; the only thing I could do was look straight ahead at the black mask my attacker wore. He didn't move; he just waited for me to fall. My vision doubled as I saw another man appear from behind a tree. The world I heard around me was muffled, mocking me with different sounds I had never heard before. I rocked forward and the ground caught me. The leaves enveloped me in a friendly embrace as they cushioned my fall.

I felt as if my essence were drifting away from my body. The searcher grabbed me and carried me over his shoulder. The swaying movement started to lull me into a soft, dark sleep, but I didn't want to let go of consciousness. I wanted to watch and see what was happening.

Reality swirled in a mix of colors. I got dizzy as the swirl changed direction with each of the searcher's steps. A soft voice called to me from inside of my head. It echoed and made my skull vibrate. "Ary, let it go." The voice was vaguely familiar. I had heard it before too many times, usually when it gave me warnings and advice. My adviser. Yes what was her name? Sarah? No. Eve? Eva? Era? Yes that was the one—Era. Her silver eyes pierced the darkness that had clouded my vision. "Let it go, darling, and enter in," she beckoned.

I entered in. The warm darkness was gone. Now I was filled with the cold hard obscurity I had felt when I had died.

Had I died again? I doubted it. They wanted me alive for the Golden Four. My punishment for escaping would feel far worse than death itself.

* * *

I woke up with a gasp as ice-cold water splashed my face. When I tried to wipe the droplets from my eyes, I found that my hands were bound to the armrests of the chair in which I was seated.

"You have a visitor," a half-element dressed in a dark uniform stated dryly, as he tossed the metal bucket aside. The bucket clanked as it hit the ground and rolled to the side.

The floor swayed and tilted. My breaths were steady as a drop of water ran from my hair, over the bridge of my nose, and fell onto my shirt. I sat in the middle of a dark green tent; metal poles and tensed wires held the cloth above my head and sheltered the tables, which were covered with electronic devices. By the looks of it, I was probably in a campsite the searchers had established in the forest. I could hear the leaves swaying outside, and sunlight rimmed the cloth curtain that separated the interior from the outside. They had set up a floor to cover the dirt. The chair I was sitting on was bolted to the ground, so I couldn't inch my way out.

When the curtain parted, the bright light blinded me. Once the cloth fell back in place, I allowed myself to open my eyes.

"Aurora," the tall man who entered spoke with an air of authority. "You are not intimidated easily, are you?" His movements were calculated yet graceful. He was powerful. I didn't think that because of the circlet of gold that surrounded his head, but because of the way in which everyone seemed flustered around him, bringing him a chair, tucking it beneath him, and pouring him a glass of wine, which rested on a small metallic table.

When he looked up at me, I inhaled sharply. Those turquoise eyes and wavy red hair belonged to the same man who had poisoned me and later danced with me; the same man who sat in front of me as one of the members of the Golden Four—the Golden of Water. His hair was braided along the side of his face and fell onto the shoulders of his carefully crafted green military uniform. He signaled one of the searchers to release me from my bonds. Once the cuffs cracked open, I resisted the urge to rub my wrists.

The Golden of Water crossed his legs in the usual way men did, breathing calmly. His intense stare reminded me of the night of the escape. "My men found this." He pulled a piece of paper from his pocket and held it between two fingers as he extended it in my direction—a silent invitation for me to grab it. "I believe you were carrying this when we caught you. One of the searchers I sent to capture you had this idea of 'helping' you. Now, we both know who this is. He deliberately went against my orders, and that is unacceptable. Do you understand?"

I couldn't answer. My tongue sat still in my mouth like a dead slug. I took the paper out of his hands and unfolded it. It was a map of all the campsites we should avoid while on the run. Skyler had wanted to help me escape, and all I had done for him was injure him and destroy his efforts.

The Golden continued, not waiting for me to respond. "We are in difficult times, Aurora, and we must stay firm to our true mission. His actions have resulted in serious consequences. I, as a chosen leader, must enforce punishment to rectify those who have misbehaved, those who distract the rest from their vocation. Since he is your protector, I do believe that you should be informed of his punishment." He paused in order to let the words sink in, and he could observe my reaction. When I didn't twitch, the corners of his mouth slightly curled upward. I didn't twitch mostly because of the effects of the drugs I had inhaled during the night.

The room spun slowly around me, but the Golden sat still. I didn't even want to know what he thought of as punishment, considering he had already poisoned Skyler and me.

"I have given the order for a public whipping, so his peers may learn from his mistakes. Your actions will be punished as well. You have escaped the training center despite my warning, killed half-elements, and stabbed your own protector. Just the first offense is enough for me to order a death sentence, but we have excused the whole group from punishment. We believe that your underdeveloped minds have been strongly influenced by others. There is no way a group of young elements, such as yourself, could have come up with that plan. I have spoken with my fellow peers, the other monarchs of the city, and we have come up with a solution.

"You will be pardoned if you work for us, *with* us, to find the lost elements of the previous generation. We will return your equipment and supplies so as to not raise suspicion, along with a special tracking device that you will activate when you meet their leader. Do this and you save you and the other elements in your group. Deny this opportunity, and we will kill them, one by one, until you are the last one standing. We will kill them in such a way that you will never be able to forget that you were the cause of their deaths." His proposition sent a shudder down my spine. "And just to give you more motivation..." He signaled to his men.

His men pulled aside the curtain to let in a small, fragile teenage girl. It was Ren. They pushed her down to her knees and pulled her hair back, revealing her pale face, which was twisted with fear and panic. Her eyes darted from the man to me, as if somehow I was allowing him to do this. I wanted to stand up and take the gun from one of the guards, shoot them all down, and then try to make a run for it after finding the boys. Of course, I was outnumbered and wouldn't dare try a stupid move like that.

"Ary? What's happening?" Ren whimpered.

The Golden of Water picked up his glass of wine and took a sip. "I chose her because she falls under my reign, mainly. I am her elemental brother, and as her monarch, I think it would be most suitable for her to be the one. It would also stir less trouble with the other monarchs." The wine danced in the cup as he swirled it lightly. His delicate hands showed no signs of hard labor. "Tie her to the chair again."

Two men closed the cuffs around my wrists once more, as another half-element came out of the shadows dressed in white. He looked like an angel as he hovered toward us, but he most likely would have been sent from hell as he carried out his task. He pulled out a small gun and aimed at the back of Ren's head. "No!" My yell was muffled by the shot. Ren wasn't expecting it, so when he pulled the trigger, her eyes bulged out with shock and surprise.

Droplets of her blood splashed my clothing. I cried out for the life of my friend. I hadn't been close with her, but to watch her die felt like falling into a dark pit—cold, endless, excruciating. The men tossed her body aside and turned to me.

"Will you take me up on my offer?" The Golden of Water stared at me with disgust when he noticed the scarlet spots staining my clothes.

His acts only reaffirmed Zareh's words. They were cruel, and they didn't care for their subjects. He hadn't even blinked when they shot Ren. What would they do to the elements that had escaped before us? They would kill them; I was sure of that. They let us escape, so they could manipulate and blackmail me into searching for their runaway citizens, dragging the others into the deed. He didn't have to kill her.

"Murderer," I whispered, as the pool of blood around Ren's head began to spread. The red halo darkened.

The Golden brought his face closer to mine. "Shall I bring in one of your other friends?" His turquoise eyes were light spotlights.

"No." I answered hastily. "I'll do it as long as you don't touch them." I spoke as fast as I could, but the words fell out of my mouth in slow motion. The world around me slowed down. How was I going to tell Juris and Aiden? I escaped to leave the city before the conflict reached its boiling point, but by doing so, I stuck myself in the middle of it. "Why me?" I asked the question out of helplessness, not curiosity, but I was shocked with the answer I got.

The Golden leaned into my ear with a mischievous smile on his lips. "Because you fascinate me." As he pulled away, he walked toward one of the tables and passed me a small box. "This is for your friend, a reward for obeying us so willingly." He dropped the box on my lap and left.

I opened the box, which held a small flask. "What is this?" I turned the flask around in my fingers. It was filled with an orange-yellow liquid. There wasn't anything special about it except for a small piece of paper, which was tied to its neck. It read:

A sip a day keeps the nightmares away.

The Golden of Water turned before leaving, looking back at me once more. "He'll know." Who will know? He never said whom it was for, but it was too late to ask, since he had already walked out of the tent.

The remaining men unbound me from the chair. They pulled me up and out of the tent. I struggled, making it hard for them to handle me. It was the least I could do. When they killed her, they didn't let me close her eyes. They didn't even let me say good-bye. Not that I would have had much time...As I left the tent, I could see the beginnings of Ren's body turning to water and mixing with her blood. My resistance trickled out of me as I realized what had happened.

Because I made us run, Ren was dead.

I killed Ren.

My body was a hollow log drifting through the camp, as if it were a tranquil river. Finally, I arrived at a second tent full of equipment. On the center table, I found my backpack and all the items scattered over the surface. I noticed some food packs with my name written on the lids.

One of the men who brought me here saw me staring at the packs. "Running doesn't seem like such a good idea when your allies don't give you food, am I right?" I noticed that he felt some pity for me. In the corners of his mouth and in the soft stare of his eyes I saw pity and compassion.

I turned to him and stared him in the eyes. "You killed her, and you dare talk to me like that?" I spat the words in his face before grabbing my things.

He grabbed my arm, his fingers like claws dinging into my skin. I waited for him to say something, anything, but nothing happened. He just gave me a hard look and instead of wasting his time on an adolescent runaway, he pushed me toward the exit and turned away.

I readjusted the weight of the backpack on my shoulder and stood in the middle of the campsite. I stood like an outsider, my clothes sprinkled with blood and my silvery hair arranged in one huge knot. The half-elements walked about with rigidness in their stride and chins held high. They all wore the same dark uniform and the headset with the visor I had seen before.

Green tents stood in the clearing like elephants. Their massiveness almost hid the forest. Each stake that held the cloth down was one large foot, and the tensed strings were their trunks and tails. Out of one of these tents, the boys appeared. Juris and Aiden were lead by four half-elements. Halfway there, the half-elements stopped and released the boys from their bindings. Aiden ran in my direction and crashed into me with an embrace.

I melted in his arms. He had no idea. He must have heard it, but he didn't have the slightest clue of what had happened. I pressed my face up against his chest; his smell surrounded me, and I let some tears escape despite my determination not to cry. There was something about Aiden that didn't allow me to act strong. His nearness tore my guard down and exposed my raw emotions.

"Ary," he whispered my name into my ear. His arms kept pressing me into his body.

Juris approached us slowly. He was staring at the space around us, trying to find something. Someone. "Ary, where is Ren?" When Aiden softened his hold on me, letting me face Juris, I didn't need to say anything. The tears gave away the answer along with the red spots on my clothing. "What happened to her?!" he demanded. A group of searchers stopped and looked.

Aiden wanted to hold me tighter, but I pulled away and grabbed his hand, staring back at the searchers who returned the gaze. "I'll tell you in the woods." Juris nodded, understanding that it wouldn't be wise to talk in front of them. Anything we said could be reported back to the Golden Four.

We didn't run. We had the luxury to take it slow for now, so we took advantage of it. I hated hearing one fewer pair of footsteps, not having Ren's bright bunch of curls next to me as she carved her stick or relying on the small talk we often had. Guilt punched me in the stomach while panic held me upright. I should have gotten to know her better. Sure, we had been through a lot together, but I didn't know her. Nobody knew her well. She died without being remembered by her family, since she had none now; she died without being remembered by true friends, since we didn't have the time or space to get to know each other. That didn't mean that I wouldn't remember her.

I would remember her and use that as leverage against Arcane. They would feel the guilt of killing off an innocent element. I would make sure of that. But the time had to be right. I would wait for that time.

"Ary?" Aiden pressed my hand.

We stopped. The sun had already set, and I hadn't even noticed.

"You need to tell us what happened." Juris's voice was softer than usual. He approached us from ahead and sat down on some rocks.

We would set camp here, I was sure of it. I dropped my backpack and sat on the ground in defeat. This was it. I had to tell them everything. I just let it run out of my mouth, since I didn't want to think about it too much.

"They shot her." Aiden sat down a few feet away from me, as if I were the source of evil that had killed her. "They told me that we would be pardoned for all our crimes if we worked with them, for them, and found the previous group of escaped elements and turned them in. I have a tracking device for when we meet their leader. They shot her so I would cooperate. If I didn't, they would have killed you as well. Both of you. So I said yes, because I knew they would." I glanced at Aiden. "I knew they would kill you."

Aiden came closer, something I found a bit surprising since before this happened, he had been pulling away from all of us. His eyes were closed and his mouth was set to a frown as he processed my words.

Juris's worried expression fell off of his face in a couple of seconds. His eyes began to water and his face reddened. "They, they can't-." he stuttered. "They can't just kill her."

I hugged myself trying to push the flashbacks away. "They did." I should have seen if coming though. I could have avoided it if I had paid attention. We shouldn't have let our guard down after the ambush. We should have fled. Why was it that I couldn't get anything right?

Juris blinked back the tears. "So we have to act innocent in order to get close, and then hand them in?"

"Yeah."

"If they can play that game, then the others can play back, I'm sure of it. How do you think they managed to stay hidden for so long? They must have outsmarted the searchers more than once," Juris thought aloud.

I began to pull different items from my backpack. My hand touched the glass flask. When I pulled it out, I remembered what the Monarch of Water had said. "This is for your friend..." But which one? "The monarch gave this to me. It's for one of you guys." I held up the flask, letting them see it.

Juris looked confused as he stared at the orange-yellow liquid in the flask. Aiden, on the other hand, seemed to know exactly what it was. He stared at it with disbelief. He spoke first. "What does the note say?"

"A sip a day keeps the nightmares away," I read aloud.

Aiden grabbed the flask as fast as he could and opened the lid. I watched him carefully as he smelled the liquid. For all I knew, it could have been poison, but he took a measured sip from the bottle. He stashed it in his pocket and turned away, rubbing his temples.

"What does the note mean?" I asked. My question drifted through the fresh forest air and vanished into silence.

"I've just, um, had really bad flashbacks in my dreams," he replied quickly, "so, uh, it lets me sleep so deep that I don't dream." Aiden sat with his back facing us.

Juris stared, perplexed. "Anyway...what do you think we have to do?" Was he handing me over the leadership? Juris had always been the one who told the rest of us what to do, so why was he consulting with me? Had this whole situation made him rethink how he felt about me? I wondered how close he was with Ren and how much it affected him.

I ran my fingers thought my hair and stared at the Southern Cross, which sparkled in the dark night. All the stars here seemed to explode in the sky, their intense shine usually concealed by man's light pollution. "I guess we just have to keep moving forward, don't we? Get to them and let them help us out of this...situation, if you can even call it that."

Juris grabbed his backpack and tore it open. "Well, since we lost another backpack, we only have half of the supplies. That includes sleeping bags." He let the silence sit between us.

"I'll sleep with Aiden." I could see the relief in his face when I answered. There was no way I was going to share a sleeping bag with him. Ever. "Now, if you don't mind, I'm going to skip dinner and just hit the sack. Let's start early tomorrow. There are some food packs in my bag if you didn't get any."

Before he could ask anything else, I pulled out my sleeping bag, hid my backpack in some bushes, and climbed a tree. I watched Aiden out of the corner of my eye. He was leaning against a tree, playing with his hands as he always did.

I whistled at him, making him look up.

"Seems like we have to share. I'm going to sleep, okay?"

I couldn't tell if it was the shadows or if his mouth was turned upward. "I'll be right up."

I entered the sleeping bag and felt it sway from side to side. It didn't take long for Aiden to join me, laying with his back toward me. We shuffled in the sleeping bag before we were comfortable. The space wasn't tight, but since we were sharing a sleeping bag that was hanging from branches, we both rolled to the middle.

I listened to his breathing. His body warmed me up, and he kept me company as I tried to fight off the horrible flashbacks. Talking to him sounded like a better idea than letting the images of dead people or bloody injuries drift on the backs of my eyelids. "Are you okay?" I whispered.

He turned to look at me. I turned to look at him. Before we were back to back, staring at the bag's black material, but now our faces were only centimeters away.

"After this experience, I don't think I ever will be." He matched the volume of my own voice. His golden eyes were now consumed by his dilated pupils.

I pressed my arms close to my chest and made sure not to breathe in his face. I meditated on his answer. We had killed people. I was seventeen and a murderer. I could only have done it with the help of training. They had trained us to kill, to defend ourselves. But from what? From whom?

He closed his eyes for a second too long and then stared at me with the clarity I could only get from him. "I've been thinking, besides the whole escaping thing, everything that I thought I had figured out is just a mess now." We lay in silence. "I overheard you and Ren talking the other day..."

I looked at him suspiciously. He always walked behind, so it could have been possible that he had heard almost everything we had said. "And what were we talking about?" I asked him, trying to sound as calm as possible.

"About us taking it slow."

I exhaled, letting all the tension escape me. This was one of the moments my stomach enjoyed somersaulting through my body. I didn't try to calm it down, because if I did, I would think of the bloody knives in my backpack and the spots of blood on my shirt. "She's right, you know. We have such a long life ahead of us, why rush anything?"

He folded his hands underneath his head like a pillow. "You know, I really think we could have something worth all these years of nothing. And I'm okay with going slow. I even think we both should wait and see what happens."

I nodded, completely agreeing with him. After everything settled, whenever it settled, maybe my feelings would be more recognizable. Maybe the only reason I liked him was because he was stable. Everything else in my life changed at an incredible speed. I needed some anchor to hold on to.

"But I want to ask you a favor," he added.

Despite what had happened before, he managed to make me laugh nervously. "What?"

He leaned closed to me, resting his nose on mine. "Can we forget about that for five minutes?"

I raised my eyebrows, a bit taken aback by his request. "Oh." I unfolded my hands and set them on his face, tracing his jawline over and over again. I pushed back the hair that fell in front of his face. My body tingled with excitement every time I touched him. "Aiden, I really think it would be best if we..."

He didn't let me finish. His lips were on mine. They had come down more forcefully than last time. He pulled me closer to him and wrapped his arms around me. There was no way I was going to get out of this. "Just..." He went for air then came back for more. "Five..." I ran my fingers through his hair, stopping at the base of his neck. "Minutes..." He wandered from my lips, kissing the corner of my mouth, my cheeks, but always came back.

"Please." I pulled away to breath. This. Was. Insane. He pulled closer to him. I saw the flames again. I welcomed them. He slipped his hands under my two shirts and stayed here. His hands were warm, and his lips ventured to my neck. I tangled my fingers in his hair. The flames licked my skin. I could feel them. The warm pulse of the flames, their graceful dance, led us on.

I felt them.

They burned.

Aiden's lips burned my neck. "Aiden." I called, separating us momentarily. He brought me back into him, too carried away by the moment to hear the anguish in my voice. With each breath, each kiss, the flames became more real, more alive and hotter. "Aiden, stop." I pushed him away. He took his time detaching himself. My skin burned. He kept his hands on my back. I clawed at them. "Let go of me, Aiden." He stared at me, unmoving. "It burns! Your hands!" I screamed at him. I knew it wasn't his fault, but it hurt so much.

He removed his hands quickly once he saw the pain he was causing. "I'm sorry. I'm so so so so sorry, Ary. Is there anything I can do?" He kept his hands to himself, too scared to touch me again. Fear was etched into his face as he searched for damage.

I touched the skin on my neck. It was scorched. I couldn't even press my fingers down for more than five seconds without tears fogging my vision. I touched my back. It wasn't as bad as my neck, but it stung.

"I'm fine," I lied and closed my eyes to hide the surging tears. I wouldn't let him see the burned skin. I wouldn't let him see me cry.

Chapter 23

When I awoke the next morning, the boys had already been up for a while. We sat silently, eating the food that the searchers had given us, but feeling the painful absence of our friend. I experienced everything again while I slept. My dreams were tinted with the blood and death of the searchers and Ren. On top of the horrid nightmares, my neck and back still stung from last night.

Aiden sat next to Juris, as far away from me as possible. This morning, he had already left the sleeping bag, allowing me to have my space. He didn't talk to me; he avoided all contact, but he tried to get a peek at the damage he had done. I hid the burned skin on my neck by letting my hair loose and hanging it on one side.

Juris, on the other hand, seemed oblivious to the tension between Aiden and me. He kept on ranting about how cold it was and how we needed to find the X before we froze to death.

The temperature had dropped at an incredible rate, and I was fully convinced that this was part of the Golden Four's plan.

After packing up everything, we began making our way back through the forest, but this time unafraid of any attacks. I pondered at the events that happened the day before. None of us had gotten hurt during our confrontation with the searchers. We killed them, we hurt them, but all they did was give us some bruises and a sleeping dart. They didn't seem to carry anything lethal. In thinking over the whole episode, it seemed that the searchers never meant any harm.

But they killed Ren and blackmailed us, I reminded myself.

It had been planned, though. The Golden Four sent the first group of searchers as a diversion. After we defeated them, we might have thought it was over and let our guard down. Then the next wave of searchers would be able to carry out their task, unless the first group was a test. If we defeated them, then our training had been a success, and we were valuable. But if we were an easy catch, we weren't the right ones to retrieve the missing generation.

The question that begged an answer was: Why us? If Golden Four had all the resources to find and capture the previous generation, why didn't they just do it and leave us alone and oblivious as ever? Why didn't they kill Zareh and eliminate the risk of us finding out? Who had the bright idea of keeping a prisoner with valuable information in a place where he could access the youngest generation and corrupt them? Why did they need to send inexperienced elements who ran a high risk of turning against the city, especially after they were threatened and one of them was killed?

"What's that around your neck?" Juris signaled toward the crystal with his chin.

I set my palm over the crystal in a protective manner. *I just have an involuntary power that affects your behavior, but no one knows exactly what I can do, and this neutralizes it...* "It's a necklace Era gave me before we escaped. She gave it to me as a farewell gift, since she knows that we probably wouldn't ever see each other again." My lie passed imperceptibly. I was getting the hang of saying things that weren't true.

"None of us got anything from our advisers..." he said suspiciously.

I moved the crystal on the chain, but the silver scraped against my burned skin. I hid the wince and left the crystal alone. I would have to wear it someplace else so it wouldn't hurt me. "I was really close to Era. Were you close to your adviser?" I decided to shift the focus of the conversation to him to play it safe.

He glanced at me with his foliage-green eyes. "Why do you have that crystal around your neck?" His voice wasn't distrustful, but I was getting that feeling from him.

"I already told you. Era gave it to me as a gift before we left."

He rubbed his hands together and blew into them as if he were mimicking Aiden. "No, Ary, I don't think you're getting me...why do you have it?" He emphasized the why as if the crystal were something bad.

"I can't tell you," I said softly, hoping he wouldn't hear me.

Juris hit a tree trunk with one of his hands and then turned to me, pulling out the pistol. He was enraged, and I was terrified. Who knew what he would do to me if he thought that I was double-crossing them? I couldn't reveal my power. Mae had told me not to. But why should I obey her if she was part of the city I was running from?

"Why can't you tell me? If you're not helping the searchers, then break it. Show me that you are not bound to Arcane." His heavy breathing puffed mist into the air.

I grabbed the crystal now, its smooth sides digging into my cold hand. I didn't want to break it. And even if it was a tracking device, I didn't think I could ever break it. No. It was the only way I could live in peace. I didn't want to use my power on Juris, no matter how convenient it would be, or on Aiden. "I can't break it."

"Then give it to me. I'll break it."

"No!"

He chuckled. His eyes burned with the treason he thought I had committed. "You little rat!" He walked closer to me, one fist balled up, while the other raised the gun to my face. I turned to look at Aiden, but he was standing with his head bowed, completely unconcerned about what was happening. Was he teamed up with Juris? Why the hell wasn't he doing anything? "All night I've been wondering why they killed her. Why not me? And why did they choose you to carry their special message? And then I see that around your neck, and you don't want to tell me? How do you think I feel about this, about being manipulated by the Golden Four and having to do their dirty work?!"

I shielded myself with my hands after hiding the crystal deep under my shirt. "Juris, you don't understand. This isn't a tracking device or whatever you think it is...it's a neutralizer." It spilled out with less effort that I thought it would take.

"What the hell is that?"

I shook my head nervously. What? How could he not believe me? "I'm not lying, Juris! I have to wear a neutralizer because of my power." I said the second sentence softer, hoping Aiden wouldn't hear it.

He stared at me incredulously. "What power? You don't have powers."

"I do, but no one ever told you. Aiden doesn't know either. I shouldn't be telling you, but you're so skeptical that I have no other option." I couldn't believe I was actually going to tell him.

"Why would you need a neutralizer for your power? What is your power? Why can't you tell us?" I couldn't tell exactly what was going on in his head. He bombarded me with more questions than I could take in.

I considered each answer before I said it. How could I explain it to him in the least number of words possible? "My power is involuntary, so I can't control it... it just happens," I said, still unconvinced of my own explanation. "And I don't know what it can..."

Juris raised his eyebrows. "The power of what?"

"I don't know. I haven't figured it out yet, but it already began to influence you guys the other day." I lowered my eyes and remembered the day I had started to receive special attention in the cafeteria. "I wasn't allowed to tell you...I didn't know what to tell you. How do you want me to explain a power whose effects even *I* don't understand? Can you please put the damn gun away? I can't think when you are pointing it at me."

"That sounds like a load of shit," Juris said with a know-it-all tone.

I sighed in frustration. He didn't remember? Now my power, which had felt like a burden, seemed like a useful resource. I could use it to get things that I needed, wanted, and the victim wouldn't remember at all. "Well, whether or not you choose to believe me, let me know. But I'm going to keep on walking, because I can't stand this stupid forest!" If I wasn't going to be able to convince him in five minutes, then it wasn't worth the time. I stormed past him, tired of having to give explanations, of being used and not trusted.

I heard him reattach the pistol to his belt and signal Aiden. "Let's keep on moving." His jaw was clenched with irritation. "This matter is not over!" he called to me.

"Bite me," I snapped back.

I just wanted to go home. I missed my family, the human days. Who did the Golden Four think they were to tear me away from the people who loved me and cared for me? I thought of my father just returning home and me not being able to see him. I had waited so long to see him, and I had only had, what, three days?

S. Elizabeth Dover

I hated the forest for three reasons. First, it reminded me of Ashwick and my family and what I lost. Second, the cold temperature seemed to be tearing us apart and cultivating suspicion between our trio. Lastly, Aiden was changing here. Was he really like this or like the element I met in the training center?

We had been walking for a while without one interruption from Aiden. Was he even alive? I looked back just to check. Yes, he was.

Juris stiffened. He wanted to say something, but he held back the words. After a quick glance at Aiden, he decided it was okay to speak. "So, this necklace is a neutralizer? And if you lose it, take it off, or break it, your power, in a way, 'activates' itself?"

I hugged myself and ignored him.

"Oh, so now you're going to act all offended."

I felt something explode in me. My hands gripped his shirt and pushed him backward with all the strength I had. "You asshole! You think you can talk to me like that, expect I'm going to answer you when you point your freaking damn gun at my head?! You think you're the only one suffering with all this crap going on? You never think about anyone else. Selfish bastard. They killed her in front of me. I wear her blood. And you think I'm going to want to cooperate with them? The only reason I said yes was so we could leave, and so they wouldn't kill you."

When Juris regained his composure, I went at him again. I pushed him once more and then started hitting him. I had to vent all the anger that was bubbling inside of me. I felt no pity toward Juris. He deserved every single strike.

But soon enough, Juris grabbed me and pushed me aside. He raised his hand to return the punches, but Aiden stood next to him, his hands on fire.

"I dare you to touch her," Aiden growled between clenched teeth.

When Juris backed down, Aiden didn't come near me. He was still afraid of burning me. I covered my neck instinctively and began to weep. I was breaking. This forest would be the end of me. I was going insane.

"Ary..." Juris called softly, but Aiden just shot him a warning glance. Since when did Juris pity me? And why did I long for Aiden's touch yet shudder at the thought of it?

Aiden cleared his throat and looked at the sky. "Come on."

Juris nodded. He extended a hand toward me as a sign of peace. "If you promise that it's not a tracking device, we better take good care of it." He gave a half smile, but it disappeared as fast as it came.

I walked past him without acknowledging his efforts to reconcile.

Chapter 24

Juris, Aiden, and I sat down around the fire. We didn't care if this would call attention to us. It didn't matter anyway. All we wanted was a bit of warmth before we went to sleep. My socks were curled up in tiny balls inside my boots. I wiggled my toes in front of the fire. Juris sat to my right with his stare fixed on the dancing flames. His brown skin looked golden, and his eyes were sad.

Aiden, who was sitting in front of me, looked down at the ground and played with the dirt. His shirt was off, and he was sweating. He hadn't even looked at me after the conflict with Juris that morning, and I was beginning to question where my relationship with him was headed. He looked around at the dark forest as if he were searching for someone. His eyes were squinted, creating creases in between his eyebrows and the ends of his eyes. "Someone is following us."

Juris put his hands up to the fire. "It's possible. Anything is possible."

Tired by the monotonous sour feeling that settled between us, I decided to go to sleep, or at least hide for a while in the sleeping bag until Aiden interrupted my isolation. Having him next to me wouldn't be any more different than sitting next to a rock.

I slipped into the bag and created a wonderful world of silence in the darkness around me. I imagined that I had gone camping with my father and brother. I was human, and my hair was still brown. Violet was still my best friend, and everything was predictable and safe.

The zipper opened.

I inhaled quickly, startled by Aiden's sudden appearance. "Sorry," he said softly as he lay down next to me. He turned his back to me. He was too afraid to look at me, thinking that his gaze would scorch the skin off of my face and melt my muscles.

"Don't be," I answered back.

He stiffened. Then shifted. "I really am. I wish I hadn't kissed you. I regret touching you," he said. His voice cracked as if he were about to cry. He wasn't sad, no, he was angry at himself. I couldn't imagine burning someone. It must have been terrible. He must have thought that he was a monster. Maybe he just didn't know that I too wanted to kiss him.

I touched the side of the sleeping back to steady myself as it rocked in the wind. "I don't." How could I be mad at him? Even if the kiss did burn me, I couldn't say that I hadn't liked it. "It happened once, Aiden, and I don't think it will happen again."

"I'm afraid that next time, I'll just lose myself completely. Who knows what will happen if I can't stop?" He paused for a moment, deliberating whether to tell me or not. "You should have heard how you screamed." He mumbled the last part in a low voice, barely audible.

"Are you okay?" This was about the fifteenth time I had asked him the same question. Maybe he didn't notice, but he always gave me a different answer. Which one was the real one?

"I've never been okay, Ary."

"What is that supposed to mean?" I turned around just to stare at his back. What was his facial expression? What was he talking about? I remembered the night we escaped. He was about to tell me why he couldn't leave. He had looked so scared right then, as if leaving would kill us all. Maybe it would. Maybe it has. "Aiden, talk to me. I need to know the truth. Why do you keep hiding things from me?" I sounded like Juris. I guess we all had secrets, and it was just a matter of time before we started to slowly discover them, unwinding them like a thread from a spool.

Aiden remained silent. Had he already fallen asleep? He never fell asleep before I did. He usually stirred and spoke to himself low enough for me not to make out what he was saying, except for my name; he always let me hear that.

Don't push it. I knew it would be no good trying to get him to give me the answer I needed. It would probably offend him and leave us on bad terms. I felt as if we were fighting, but I didn't quite know what we were fighting about without knowing I would never be able to win the fight or surrender. I let myself float into sleep. The wind cradled me into Aiden. My neck hurt because of my posture, and I wasn't treating it as I should. Resources were limited, so the burn wasn't high on my list. I tried to ignore the pain and slowly drifted off.

I stood on one side of a large, dark room. The posts in the middle were still standing in dried pools of blood. That was Zareh's blood, I pondered as I looked around. Skyler stood across the room with a row of people kneeling at his feet. I knew them all: my mother, my father, Steven, Violet, Era, Zareh, and Ren. Mae stood beside him. She was the person in the training center who let you know whether what was about to happen to you was good or bad. This, I supposed, was going to be bad.

Mae shifted her head to the side and stared at me. Her eyes pierced my skin and saw everything inside of me. I shuddered. "You are always causing us trouble, aren't you?" She held Ren's kukri tightly.

I looked over at Skyler to read his expression. His face was neutral, but I could tell by his posture that he wasn't on my side. He kept a gun aimed at my friends and family just in case they made a false move.

"What are you talking about?" My voice swayed as my mother, I realized, looked up at me in horror. Her own little baby girl had turned into a monster. Her lips trembled and her eyes were glossy. I couldn't quite read her expression. Fear? What could I do to get them out of this situation? Maybe the Golden Four could erase their minds again. Now I understood

why half-elements did what they did. I knew it was selfish, but it would be better for them if they didn't know. "Why do you have them here like this?"

Mae snickered. "What do you mean why? You know why! You ran away. You made your own kind look weak and irresponsible. The first time, the Golden Four blamed the security; we half-elements weren't doing our jobs. But this time, elements are blaming our own monarchs. Since I obey them, and they are not happy with you, I have to make sure you mend the damage," she hissed through a clenched jaw.

"We didn't do anything," I protested. "Well, yeah, we escaped, but it's not like we ran into a town or city screaming that we were elements and showing them our powers. It couldn't have been that bad. Just tell me what to do, and I promise I'll fix it. Just leave the humans alone." *I hated referring to my friends and family as "humans."* "And why do you have Era and Ren? They don't have anything to do with this. I made Ren escape. I forced her on the night of the party."

"You have to tell us where the other six are hiding, and we'll spare your friends. Even the human ones."

The other six? We were only four. "What?"

Mae rolled her eyes as if the answer was completely obvious. "Your two element companions and the other four that escaped fifty years earlier."

I panicked. *I had no idea where they were. I didn't even know how I got here. I knew I was in the underground cells, only because I had been here before and the dried blood on the floor had freaked me out. I tried to think where I was last. The forest...but then I couldn't remember anything else.*

"I didn't even get to the meeting spot myself," I replied.

Maybe the monarchy had tracked us using my necklace. What if Era had made me escape so they could track us with my necklace once we got to a certain area where we would be "safe." I touched my neck to feel the cold crystal. It wasn't there. I looked at my wrists, but the silver chain wasn't there either. In its place I saw small fragments of broken crystal dug halfway into my skin. I stared with revulsion. How could they do this to me? I looked around helplessly. There was nothing I could do. I had been fooled, and now I was paying the price for being so trusting.

"Not saying anything? Maybe this will encourage you." Mae stepped behind my father and put a knife to his throat. She dug her knees into his back, and with one strong, sure movement, she slit his throat. Blood from his wound gushed over the floor, coating the stone with a new layer of blood. "Every hour that passes without us finding the other elements, we'll kill one of them."

I gasped, and my mother cried. She covered her face with her hands and screamed. Skyler aimed the gun and shot her in the middle of her forehead. She fell facedown against the ground. The rest of the hostages bit their cheeks and lips, so they wouldn't make a sound. One sound, one deadly bullet. Their faces were pale, and Era looked as if she were about to throw up. I ran toward my dead parents right when a bullet hit my heart. All I could feel was the splintering crystal of the replacement.

"Ary. Ary, it's okay, calm down."

I opened my eyes to see the side of the sleeping bag. Aiden's arms were wrapped around me. I could feel the weight of his arms and the pull toward his body. My face was wet, probably with tears. I tried to slow my agitated breath.

"They're going to kill everyone."

I couldn't tell if this was the dream. Aiden was hugging me and talking to me. I touched my wrists. No crystals. That meant my parents weren't dead. But what if this had actually happening while we slept?

"Ary?" Aiden was concerned. My heart melted. After all these days of coldness, he finally was talking to me. Would this end after he realized that I was okay?

I wiped my face. "It was just a nightmare, nothing else." I was expecting him to release me from his grip, but he didn't. He just pulled me closer to him. I couldn't wrap my mind around Aiden. Freaked out as I was, I didn't have the energy. But I didn't want to go asleep and emerge back into the dream, continuing where I had left off. I thought I knew him, but I had no clue about who he was. The sweet boy I liked was now gone, absorbed by an isolated version who feared to look at me in case I suddenly burst into flames. If only I had the power to read minds, I could enter into his and listen to what he didn't say. He spent so much time without speaking. I let Aiden hold me and emptied my mind. I knew that I would regret staying up tomorrow.

Chapter 25

I tried to swallow the food I was given in the campsite. Its bland flavor was repulsive now. I hated it and suspected that soon enough, the mere sight of it would make my stomach churn in disgust. Juris watched me, trying not to smile. I couldn't even imagine how he was putting up with it. Aiden hardly ate it anymore, only when he was driven by hunger. Usually, he just sat and waited for us to finish our meals. I thought that maybe walking while eating would help me not to think too much about the flavor, but who was I kidding?

I put the food away and straightened my backpack. This morning, I had found some of Ren's carvings deep at the bottom of the pockets. I had tossed them into the forest, because I didn't want to be reminded that she was gone. And who cared if it left a trail? They weren't following us anyway.

Juris looked over his shoulder at the boy who trailed behind. "Do you know what's wrong with him?" He asked the same question I had been asking myself for days. He was trying to act nicer with me to compensate for the whole gun situation, but I still held onto the grudge. The fact that he held up the gun to me reminded me of Ren, just moments before she died.

I shrugged and tried to appear indifferent. "No." The image of my father being killed and the bullet penetrating my mother's skull appeared in my mind. I shivered. I tried to push the memory away, but it lingered in the back of my mind. I wanted to drink water, but my supplies were already down to two bottles. I didn't really care about the food. Any moment, I was going to start eating tree bark.

Juris looked around at our monotonous surroundings: trees, dirt, and plants that went on and on forever. I knew it bothered him that I didn't continue the conversation, but I didn't want to talk anymore. My throat was dry, and all the liquid had been drain out of my body from crying at night. I wonder if I'd stop needing to go to the bathroom at some point, or in my case, the bushes, if I continued not to drink.

Something in the corner of my eyes moved too quickly. I tensed. I turned to look, but nothing was there. I heard a small crackle in front of me. My head whirled in the direction of the sound.

Juris stared, confused. He took out his gun.

Right in front of us was the fox. It stared at me with its brown eyes. What if it was just a plain simple fox? No, something was odd about it; the pupils couldn't expand and contract that quickly. Juris stopped in his tracks next to me. Aiden kept on walking slowly behind and did not know what was happening until he reached us. I searched for my knives. I got a grip on one that I had tucked into my pants pocket in its homemade sheath. I pulled it out slowly, hoping that the fox wouldn't predict my actions and move. I threw it quickly, surprising the boys. The fox stayed still until the knife flew over its head and struck a tree. It stood peacefully and then trotted away.

"Get it, Juris," I told him, while I rushed to the tree to pull out my knife.

Juris stared at me with even more confusion. "But what...?"

"Just do it!" I exclaimed. I ran after the fox. It was swift. It leapt over branches and some rocks and turned with ease right next to the trunk of a tree without even crashing into it. Juris ran next to me. His breathing was heavy, and I could hear him count in a low voice. Why was he counting? He ran past me with his gun in his hand.

I tired easily but decided to push myself anyway. I hadn't slept well, and I was about to fall to the ground. Sprinting was too much for me. I dropped onto the ground. Juris had disappeared, still in pursuit. Aiden walked up to me and then sat down. He looked up at the sky.

"That's a big storm coming," Aiden commented and then looked back down. He pulled the flask from his pants and took a sip of the liquid. I still didn't know what was in that flask, and Aiden hadn't told us anything about it.

I looked up at the sky. The dull grey weaved together in uneven waves. Who knew how long we had before the rain came down? The breeze was chilling me to the bone, but that didn't mean anything. My head pounded and my mouth had a metallic flavor, almost like blood.

I could hear a shot in the distance. It echoed in the open space. Had Juris shot the fox? We heard another shot. He better have good aim, or we were going to lose one of our most useful weapons because of a stupid animal.

A short time passed before Juris reappeared with the fox in his arms. Its head was pounded in and its side was punctured with two bullet holes. He probably slowed down the fox with the bullets and then finished it off with a rock. He dropped the fox's limp body onto the ground in front of my feet and pointed at it with the stone.

"Explain why it doesn't bleed and why it survived when I shot it twice." His face was dotted with sweat.

Juris probably thought I had known since the beginning, which was slightly true.

"I saw it some days ago and thought it was strange that it didn't run away from us." He still wasn't satisfied, so I decided to go along with my gut feeling. "So, I considered the idea that it was some sort of invention that the searchers could be using to follow us." The explanation sounded so much better in my head.

"No, you knew more than that. You can't just decide to hunt a fox with an 'it may be...' You knew something and you hid it from us. Why? All the signs you're giving, all of the information you're hiding makes me believe that you are with the searchers and that you want us to end up in Arcane." He dropped his weapons in frustration and glared at me.

Aiden still had his head bowed, as he watched himself play with his hands. If he had been staring at me with the same lack of trust as Juris, I would have probably broken down. I couldn't help feel that everything that could go wrong was going wrong. I ran my fingers through my grimy hair, but made sure it still covered up my throbbing neck burn.

"The first time I saw it, there was something off with its eyes and the way the pupils dilated and contracted," I said.

"This could have been any fox. And you somehow just knew it was the fox you had seen the first time? Either you have too much luck or you're on to some plan," Juris accused.

I shook my head helplessly. I how could I make him understand? Why couldn't his tiny little earth brain understand that I was on his side.

"I just guessed it was the same one because it paused to stare at us. And when I threw the knife, the fox didn't even budge until after the knife struck the tree. A normal fox would have run off and disappeared in seconds." Yes, yes, that was good enough.

Juris kneeled next to the dead animal-robot and dug my knife into its side. The metal blade sunk in until it hit something hard. Juris dug the knife into the same place once more, with a little more strength. *Clank*. He stared up at me for a split second in shock and then began skinning the animal. The realistic fur fell off in chunks with fake meat, or what I supposed was fake meat. Juris took off enough skin to leave the fox with his left rib cage completely exposed, but it had no ribs. Instead, it had a smooth metallic surface. There were no buttons or bolts, and since there was no blood, Juris kept skinning. I couldn't figure out why he kept skinning it. The fox was dead. We were safe. Done. We had to keep moving. And it was completely unnecessary to find out what the fox was made of. Or, maybe Juris was onto something...

Soon, the entire fox was bare and stripped from its coat, except for the head. The robot was a beautiful creation. It was sleek and realistic. It could have fooled anyone if it hadn't been for the lens-like eyes. Juris prodded at the hard shell that kept the whole mechanism intact. There was no way of getting into it, except for the two bullet holes that had pierced the metal and turned it inward. We decided to open the fox through these holes. Juris and I took separate holes and stuck our knives into them, hoping we could crack it open. Aiden just sat there leaning against a tree and watched us work, occasionally mumbling incomprehensible words. I pitied him for his loneliness, but he had us. He had me. The burned skin couldn't be the only reason. I already told him that I forgave him.

"Here, look," Juris exclaimed as the part of the fox he was working on suddenly opened. I shuddered as gears and layers of chips were revealed. There were two boxes—a yellow one that was attached to the head with a cable, and black one that was attached to the yellow one. Juris ran his hand over the yellow box and searched for buttons. He pressed the first one he found. The box opened, revealing a rack of CDs. We both stared at each individual CD in awe. Juris moved on to the black box and searched for buttons. As he swiped his fingers over the front, a screen activated, showing a series of dates, one CD per day.

There was a lot of space on each puny disc. He selected some random day with his large fingers, and the recording began to play. We both watched silently as we saw and heard ourselves on the screen—four wet elements climbing out of the river, along with the entire conversation that followed.

I didn't know what to say. Now I understood why the searchers had attacked us that night. They knew that we were going to keep on walking, and they knew that our morale as well as our supplies were running low. Perhaps they thought that the intervention would save us.

Juris sucked in a breath and let it go slowly. He stood up and kicked the fox, its light body rolled over the ground and smacked into a tree. He tore the CDs out and broke them before sprinkling the ground with the remains. He continued kicking the fox's head, hoping it would detach from the body. I had never seen him act so violently since he tried to choke me in the hallway.

"Juris, stop." I pleaded, hoping he would quit. He didn't.

"It's going to rain," Aiden repeated once more.

Juris paused and stared up at the sky. Suddenly, the anger vanished from his face, replaced with determination. His hands, however, remained curled up in strong fists. "Let's make a shelter before it rains."

We walked a few yards away from the fox, just in case someone came to reclaim the mechanical wonder—not that we cared much. We began brainstorming how to build a shelter. The shelter had to be waterproof, or everything that we had would get soaked in a matter of seconds. There weren't any large leaves or big chunks of broken tree bark that could help us.

"We might as well just walk in the rain and get drenched. There's no way we can build a waterproof roof," I stated the obvious.

"That's not a choice. We would leave footprints in the mud. We have to appear to be running away, just in case they find us. Besides, we would probably get sick," Juris countered. He opened his water bottle and took a small sip, licking his lips with satisfaction.

I thought of other alternatives, but there were none. "Are the sleeping bags waterproof?" I asked him suddenly.

"Probably."

"We can make a roof with the sleeping bags. We could hold them up with some sticks and sit under them," I said, proud of my idea. It wasn't much, but in this kind of situation, it was a pretty big deal. I pulled out the sleeping bag I shared with Aiden and tried hanging it from the low branches of a nearby tree. The branches were too high. We would all have to stand.

Juris pitched in by grabbing some sturdy branches and propping them up so they wouldn't fall. Together, we made a poor-looking tent with two big problems: we didn't all fit, and once you got inside, it would cave in on us. We discarded that idea and kept trying different ways to hold up the sleeping bags.

Juris asked me to hold up a stick. I did, and he tied one of the sleeping bag strings to it. "That will do," he said as he backed up. He stuck one end of each stick in the ground and the tied other end to the sleeping bag. The other two strings stretched out to some low-hanging tree branches. The sleeping bag was open and inclined diagonally so the water that was caught dripped down to the lowest side where Juris placed our bottles. Not only would we stay dry, but also our empty bottles would be filled with rainwater.

Juris sat under the sleeping-bag roof, admiring his own construction. I felt as if I had been dragged back to the old days where I would build magnificent tents with the dining room chairs and mother's most colorful blankets. Of course, Steven would either take over or destroy them. I sat next to him, enjoying the moment.

Thirst crept up on me, so I took a sip from one of my water bottles. I closed my eyes and counted the sips that I drank: one, two, three. That was it. If I drank more, then the bottle would empty too quickly. I put the bottle back in the backpack and lay down on the dirt. I closed my eyes and listened to the first raindrops fall on the makeshift roof. So it has begun, I said to myself. I grinned at the idea of resting for a while. I didn't mind. But the part of my brain that had already adapted to the idea of being an element, and the fact that we had run away, urged me to stay alert.

I sighed. I couldn't possibly relax, not with all the flashbacks coming to mind whenever I let down my guard. My blood froze when I thought of my whole family being slaughtered just because I dared to disobey. I opened my eyes to see Juris resting next to me with his eyes shut. He breathed heavily, and his arms were folded over his chest. I didn't allow myself to stare. I drew my attention away from him and observed the pattern the drops created on the surface of the sleeping bags. Little dents appeared and disappeared in different sizes, depending on how big the raindrop was or how hard it fell. I turned to look at Aiden next to me, but there was no one there.

I sat up and watched him sitting in the rain, playing with his hands and his fire. The small flames were extinguished immediately, leaving a fine white line of smoke.

"Aiden, come over here!" I called him, pulling him out of his world and into the real one. His eyes, filled with the reflection of the small flames, were now an opaque gold. He stood up and sat next to me silently and obediently. Once he was comfortable, he began rubbing his hands together again until they created a flicker. This flame stayed in his palm as if waiting for instructions. Its body flickered from orange to yellow, but the base always remained the same light blue. I straightened myself and looked forward with a slight pout. I could see Juris staring at me with one of his eyebrows raised, but I ignored him.

I decided to spend my time watching the sky, not that I had anything else to do. The clouds moved slowly, but I pushed myself to observe each change in the darkening shades. Because we couldn't see the sun, it was impossible to know the time. Was it evening? Late at night? I jumped as the sky flashed. The clouds went from a dark blue to a light purple and then back to dark blue. Different silhouettes of the same clouds shaded the trees as more and more lightning appeared. This was going to be a huge storm. Lately, we had been lucky with the weather and now the winter storms were coming at us. I shivered. We could die out here. I usually joked about it in my head, but now the possibility felt more realistic.

A massive lightning bolt crossed the sky, spreading out over the clouds and creating a layer of hot white branches. It faded away, but the streaks were marked on my vision, and I could see the figure of the lightning in bright green. I rubbed my eyes, and a mix of browns and oranges appeared on my eyelids. I sighed as another bolt flashed ahead, followed by another and then another. Juris sat up next to me, very still, staring up in awe. What if we got electrocuted? It would be a shocking ending. My inner voice giggled at its own cynical remark.

The trees creaked as the growing breeze stretched and shook their limbs. Leaves fluttered around soared high into the air in flocks before diving to the ground, pinned by transparent bullets. Besides the roar of the increasing storm, the forest was silent. I hadn't realized the amount of wildlife that surrounded us until now. No birds were chirping their joyful songs, and I couldn't hear the muffled cracks of dry twigs under the paws or hoofs of careful animals. The soil's color darkened, and various puddles began to form. I wished for a tree trunk to rest my back against. I was holding myself upright by wrapping my arms around my knees. I shivered in the cold breeze, but suddenly I wasn't so cold.

"Aiden, turn it out!" Juris yelled from my left. His eyes glowed with fear and shock, and his face was illuminated by firelight. Fire...

I turned to my right to see the source of the heat. Aiden's hands and forearms were consumed with bright flames. They waved in the air and licked at the makeshift roof. *No!* I couldn't tell if I had yelled it or if the shout echoed in my mind. The fire spread slowly over the sleeping bag, savoring each thread. One at a time, the threads disappeared in smoke and ash. The smell was intoxicating, and adrenaline coursed through me. I jumped quickly from under the makeshift tent while grabbing my backpack. I looked back at the raging fire in panic. Aiden was hypnotized by his blazing arms. Juris called to him from my side. How did he get here so fast? He tore off his shirt and ran to Aiden, covering his arms and patting them forcefully. The shirt caught fire too.

"No!" This time I could feel the shout burst out of me. Was Juris stupid? Now he would definitely freeze. But that wasn't the most important concern right now. We had to turn off Aiden's flames.

The first string of the sleeping bag snapped and the whole thing fell down to the ground still hanging by the threads attached to the tree. It waved over Aiden's head, threatening to fall on and cover him. Juris grabbed Aiden's feet and dragged him out. Aiden waved his arms in protest. The waving and the raindrops extinguished the fire, exposing unharmed flesh. The sleeping bag still hung from the branch, waving in defeat. Half of it had already been consumed before the rain could stop it. Why didn't the rain extinguish the fire? It only stopped when Aiden's arms went back to normal.

I tried to slow my racing heart as the raindrops pounded into me like stones. Many of the trees were bare and unable to slow their fall. I was already drenched and freezing. There would be no fire afterward to get dry and regain the body heat that we had lost. And we couldn't all go to sleep, because we had lost both sleeping bags. I wanted to sit down, but the damp earth would get my clothes even dirtier than they already were.

"You idiot! Do you know what you have just done? Are you crazy?" dark-skinned, green-eyed Juris yelled at Aiden. A vein on his forehead throbbed, and his hands were once more curled into fists. At this rate, he would kill someone. He was getting angry too frequently. "Now where will you sleep? Learn to control your stupid damn power before you get us killed." He turned to me. Raindrops fell over his face, making his short hair stick closer to his head. He could have looked like a wet puppy with his softened expression. "Are you all right?"

I nodded, looking past him. I was fine, but Aiden wasn't. His stare was filled with guilt, and his eyes were watery. He stood up and excused himself, saying that he needed some time alone. He disappeared into a silver sheet of rain and into the darkness, which frequently glowed with lightning. His shady figure was there and then suddenly gone.

Juris began gathering long sticks. "I'm going to see if I can make a roof...*again*," he said bitterly before I could ask.

I rested my backpack next to his and stood drenched in the rain. There wasn't much for me to do or much to keep me dry. "I'm going to go look for him."

Juris began to protest, but I shot him a cold look. "He didn't mean to burn it, and we can't let him wander off. You probably would have wanted me to do the same thing if it had been you."

I turned my back to him and wandered off in the same direction as Aiden. I watched my step and tried not to make too much noise just in case he hadn't run off. If he was nearby, I would just turn around and not bother him. The rain was coming down fast, and the earth was getting muddy. I moved forward, holding onto trees and branches and stepping on roots so I wouldn't slip.

Thunder began to crack now. It shook me from the inside and brought me back to the human days when I was scared of it. Terrified, actually. I would run down the hall and open the door of my parents' bedroom. Only mother would be there, and she would call me into her bed once she saw me at her door. I would snuggle close to her and let her hug me to sleep. But now I was alone, wet, and scared. I kept on walking until I heard Aiden's voice. I walked closer to him, but I stayed behind a tree so he couldn't see me.

I peeked over the side of the trunk and saw him leaning against a tree. He faced the tree and rested on his forearms while he held his head. Aiden's hair was matted down with water, and his clothes were stuck to his body.

"You never should have left," he said to himself. Over the pounding rain, I could have sworn that I had heard him sniffle. Was he crying?

"I'm not going to tell," he said in a lower voice. "I will not hurt," he added, and then he paused as if talking with someone or thinking of the right words to speak aloud. "If I could just shut them up..." Aiden brought his hand down on the tree and yelled, "Why doesn't it work?!"

He pulled out the flask of liquid and took more than a sip.

I clutched the tree to hold me up. I wanted to help him. I was scared, not only for myself but also for him. Why wasn't he talking to us? I began walking back to Juris when, halfway there, I heard Aiden yell again. The horrible cry made goose bumps spread all over my skin.

Chapter 26

Aiden had asked for time alone, but how long did he need? We waited for him to come back, but he never did.

"Where the hell is he?" Juris demanded from under a poorly-made roof of sticks. He wiped his eyes and looked around, hoping Aiden would pop out of nowhere. His hands were curled into fists again.

I pushed my hair out of my eyes and sneezed. I was getting pretty cold; everything was wet. "I can't stand this. Let's go after him. What if he's hurt?"

I tried to push the thought that he could be burning himself to death or hurt by animals. Juris stood up and didn't even help me to my feet. I lead him to where Aiden had been. I retraced my steps, moving silently and cautiously, while Juris stomped and broke every possible twig. My heart leapt into my chest just to plummet to the ground.

"He's not here."

"Aiden!" Juris called at the top of his lungs. Anger shook his voice, and the sky turned pale with a flashing light. Juris trembled. I took a step away from him. His green eyes seemed to vanish into a black hole; his pupils were fully dilated. His dark hands called the earth from underneath and shot it up toward the sky. A huge spike of earth, sharp and jagged, shot out of the ground. He jerked even more. The ground moaned at his orders, and another point appeared with great force. The second one came out near where I was standing and threw me against a tree.

My shoulder took the first impact and then the rest of my body followed. Pain sparked around me and chewed softly on my insides. I couldn't tell what hurt more. The ground shook almost with the force of an earthquake, and branches snapped. I could hear the roll of thunder overlap the sound of the ripping crust and mud. Some birds took flight, loudly flapping their wings, hopefully dodging the sharp ends while they rose. Forcing myself to an upright position nearly killed me from all the tremors, but what I saw amazed me so much that I forgot about the pain. Spikes were everywhere. Long, fat, prickly, dangerous masses of earth formed a high, uneven ring around Juris, the earth boy.

I walked slowly, curiously, toward the center. It wasn't easy, because there was hardly any space between each spike, and I was still in pain. My clothes got caught on some of the uneven edges, but I finally made it to the center. I found Juris in a surprising state. He was lying down on the ground, face in the mud, silent. This isn't a good idea. You should probably leave. I walked over to him. He looked up at me with his green eyes back to normal.

"I'm sorry, I didn't mean to. I just…" He exhaled and a single tear dropped out of his eye. "I was so angry that I lost it, and then…" He stared at me vacantly. I didn't really know what to do, so I offered my sleeve to wipe the mud off of his face. I should've been angry with him, but I was too weak. The cold, the rain, and the loneliness was draining my energy. I almost didn't care that he lost control…that he almost killed me…that Aiden was gone. I just wanted home—Mom, Dad, Steven, Violet, the awkward conversations with Emma; I missed it all so much.

In a panic, I checked the crystal underneath my clothes. The cold stone met my touch, and relief washed over me. I offered my hand to Juris to help him up.

"We need to keep on moving. I want to get this over with," I sighed.

Juris took my hand and slowly stood up as if all his energy had been drained by his power—it probably had been—and steadied himself on a nearby rock.

"How do you think we can hide this?" I bit my lip as I tried not to scream. My neck was so hot. It felt as if Aiden was burning me again. Juris raised his hands and then, with his eyes closed, he lowered his hands pushing the spikes back into the ground. It seemed as if he finally got a handle on his power. Of course, some things could not be corrected; some fallen branches, a crooked tree, and some bushes were transported to new places, and the earth was scarred where the spikes had emerged. Cracks and small mounds of mud and dirt had appeared.

"I need to rest," Juris protested.

I made sure that my hair covered my neck and turned to him. "Fine, you can do that while I explore..."

"No." Guessing what I was going to say, he cut me off. "We have to stay together. What if they take me or get you while you're gone? I don't mind, I'll walk," he said and strode passed me, faking renewed energy.

I let him hold up his act for the first few minutes. I raised my head and called his name. "You're exhausted; let me lead. I can walk in a straight line," I told him as he rubbed his eyes. There was a slight pink tone to the whites of his eye.

He thought and then finally gave in. "Sure, why not?"

I thought of a conversation topic to bring up. I couldn't think of any that wouldn't make him mad, uncomfortable, or end up in an awkward silence. We were broken and low on spirits. What could I possibly say that would lift the mood? *Maybe you shouldn't try talking to him.* Why was it that my two male companions lacked the desire to socialize? *Maybe they're on their periods.* I giggled in my head and prayed that I hadn't said it out loud. I probably would have a better conversation with myself than Aiden or Juris. *You could always try.* I would go insane, I answered back. I couldn't believe that I had just answered myself.

Our pace was slowing down because of Juris's lack of energy. Several times, I tried to convince him to sit down and rest, but he pushed himself to continue, until he finally gave in. I offered to take guard while he slept on a branch.

"I promise I won't leave," I told him as he closed his eyes slowly. He rested on the branch like a sleeping feline. His dark chest was covered in tight muscles that contracted and relaxed as he breathed. I didn't stare, quickly engaging myself with observing the rainfall. Juris quickly fell asleep.

I wondered what Era was doing. I knew that Skyler was out in the campsite after being whipped, and Zareh was probably still locked up in the underground dungeon. Era was probably now in Arcane, in dark room as her illusions danced around in the space entertaining the hidden audience. What did elements dress like in Arcane? Did they have wacky futuristic outfits, or did they dress in plain ecological clothing?

I let my mind wander, forgetting the cold weather and my soaking skin, until I heard voices. Voices? I felt the urge to run toward them since they could be our saviors, the elements in charge of helping us. I kept my calm and took a few steps toward the noise. I was still afraid of what could be approaching us, so I didn't stray.

"Hello?" I called out. When no one answered, a chill ran down my spine. Who could be out there? I remembered the conversation I had with Zach and Mae in the training center, when they had explained everything, and I immediately discarded the option of it being human. I was in a different dimension, or *realm*, as they called it; no human knew how to get in. This left three options: weird talking animals or parrots, the searchers, or the elements we were looking for.

The last option was the most probable. "Juris, wake up!" I called.

He stirred on the branch. "What is it?"

"Listen."

We heard the murmur again.

Juris jumped down from the branch. "What the heck?"

"Is it me, or does it sound like a whisper?" I mumbled to him. The voices were soft, but they seemed to be much closer than we thought.

Aiden suddenly burst out of the trees, running toward us. His eyes were filled with fear, and his voice seemed to be caught in his throat.

A nearby shot almost left me deaf.

Aiden fell to the ground with a small dart sticking out of his chest.

"Aiden!" I yelled, running toward him. I managed to reach him before two more shots rang out.

I felt a needle sink into my back and instantly fog my senses. "Juris....run." My voice lowered from a warning to a whisper.

Four men walked out from behind the trees and started peeling us off of the ground. A firm pair of hands grabbed me and pulled me over his shoulders. The world I heard around me was muffled, mocking me with sounds I had never heard before. The group began to walk away, each man with an element over his shoulders, except for the guide. The swaying movement started to lull me into a soft, dark sleep.

Chapter 27

The floor swayed as I sat up in the bed. A bed... where was I? I tried to remember the last thing that had happened to me, when I recalled the sharp dart in my back. The blankets that had been laid over me while I slept were thin and smelled of mothballs. The strong odor pierced the nausea that crept up my throat. The room I was in was quite small. There were two beds opposite each other; one was neatly made, while mine was messed up from restless sleeping. The wooden frames were dark and matched a single cabinet in the stone wall.

I held my head as it throbbed. I touched the back of my neck with the other hand. The skin was covered in bandages, and a sharp burst of pain erupted in my shoulder. I rested back against the pillow and suddenly smelled the faintest hint of shampoo on my hair. I smiled, happy that I was bathed. But...if was bathed, that meant that someone bathed me...I shuddered in horror. My old clothes were replaced with striped pajama bottoms and a loose, long-sleeved shirt obviously meant for a tall and muscular man.

I tried to slip silently out of the bed and steadied myself, but my legs were too unstable. I crashed onto the floor, crying out in pain as my shoulder hit the side of the bed frame. My skin felt as if it were ripping, so I decided to lower my arm and cradle it.

Where was I? Where were Juris and Aiden?

The door suddenly opened, and a large teenage boy hurried to my aid. His skin was dark, not as dark as Juris's, but it made his pale green eyes pop. I stared at him incredulously. Could it be? He crouched down next to me and smiled.

"Hi, I didn't know that you were already up." He put one of his hands on my back and the other underneath my arm to get a sturdy grip on me and help me up. When he saw me wince in pain and the color drain from my face, he opened the cabinet took out scissors, along with some alcohol and cotton.

"You must have pulled a stitch," he told me. "That's why it hurts so much. Now, I'm going to have to ask you to remain really calm while I fix it, okay?"

"Who are you?"

He looked up briefly, carrying the items to the bed. "My name is Demetrio."

"Where am I, and where are the others?"

"I can answer that in just a few minutes; but first, let me help you. Okay?" He arranged the items on the bed. "I need to take off your shirt. Don't try to struggle, because your shoulder will hurt even more. I promise not to look."

This was it. We had been rescued. If we were in Arcane, Demetrio wouldn't even have asked if he could help me, and probably a half-element would have been the nurse. I would have felt more relieved if embarrassment weren't turning my cheeks pink. Thankfully, I gave him my back.

Demetrio carefully removed my shirt and passed it to me so I could cover myself with it. Out of the corner of my eye, I could see him open the bottle of alcohol and soak the cotton with it. He ran the cotton over the scissors' blades. When he removed the bandage, he set it next to me so I could see the blood-stained cloth.

Why did I need stitches? I never cut myself. What were they doing to me? "Stop!" I inched forward, suddenly filled with doubt.

"What's wrong?" His voice was soft and kind. It made me want to trust him, but the image of them shooting us with tranquilizers popped into my mind. Why would they need to tranquilize us? Why didn't they just walk up to us and say, "Hey, we're here to save you!"

My stomached churned, and my throat contracted. "What's happening?" The room turned cold, and my body began to shiver. My shoulder protested against the involuntary shaking, and my stomach threatened to empty itself.

Demetrio stood up and pulled a bucket from underneath the bed. He handed it to me while checking my forehead for any signs of fever. "Have you eaten any food in the past week?" I barely managed to nod as I began to gag. "Try to stay as still as possible for a few seconds,," he said, as he ripped of the bandage from my neck and lower back. I managed to suppress the trembling when I felt the scissors run across my skin and cut of the stitches. "Two more."

I could feel the bile creeping up my throat, the acid burning the tissue.

Snip.

One more left, but I couldn't hold it back any longer. I leaned forward into the bucket.

Snip.

Demetrio set his large hands against my back and began to whisper unrecognizable words. This strange source of energy seeped from his hands into my body and spread slowly over me, branching toward my head, shoulders, and arms. I could sense the green tone of his power on the backs of my eyelids as I relaxed. The acid burn in my throat and mouth was now gone, and my stomach calmed. I could feel the remains of the burns Aiden had left slowly healing and the cut over my shoulder blade beginning to seal.

I sighed with relief. I felt much more like myself: strong, healthy, and renewed with energy. The shakiness was now gone, and my thoughts no longer flashed. The power that enveloped me in a strange net of vines slowly withdrew itself back into Demetrio. He removed his hands and collected the used bandages, while I collected myself.

"What did you do to me?" I asked after I put my shirt back on.

Demetrio threw everything into a small trashcan in the corner and stared up at me. His face had a serene expression on it. "My power allows me to physically heal living organisms. The reason why I wasn't able to do so before is because I can't heal all the time, only in the proportion of my own health and energy." He walked back to the bed and sat on the end, giving me enough personal space yet not appearing too distant.

"Why did you tranquilize us? Why did I have stitches? Why didn't you send us any food? Why did..."

"One question at a time, please." He raised his hand, cutting me off before I could finish. His back was slightly slouched as if he were relaxing. His hair fell into his eyes. "The reason why we had to tranquilize you was because of your friend Aiden. Our intention was to meet you in the forest and then walk back together while having this conversation. But your fire companion did not make it easy on us. I don't know why he fought so much, but we couldn't control him. When he ran away and found you, we didn't know if we were going to be able to manage the situation."

"So you shot us."

Demetrio was upfront and willing to answer all my questions; a change I wasn't used to. I looked down at my hands, since I couldn't hold his gaze. My mind wandered to Aiden and how he had screamed before disappearing. The way in which he had spoken to himself made me wonder if he was insane or just under a lot of stress.

He chuckled. "You could say it that way. But it wasn't our intention to start off like that. Anyway, we took advantage of the situation and decided to take the chips from your shoulders. Luckily, I had to..."

"Wait, what chips?" I interrupted.

"They didn't tell you? Not even Zareh?" I couldn't remember. "Well, in the training center while you're still living as a human, they insert a chip into your left shoulder blade. This chip allows them to monitor your body's conditions, like temperature and heartbeat, but it also allows them to keep track of where you are. This last function only works if you are standing over or under what we like to call 'the grid.' This is basically an enclosed territory where the chips work. If you step out of the grid, for example, when you escaped, the signal is lost, and they can't receive any information from it. The thing is, while you were running away, the searchers had established some campsites where they were setting up a limit for a grid, so they would be able to find you easier. We had to take out your chips so they couldn't find you, and we could leave a false signal for the searchers. How did we do this? Easy—we just put the chips on some wildlife, and presto!

"Now for your other question. We didn't send you any food because you didn't need it." I opened my mouth to speak, but he raised his eyebrows and shot me a look, which made me close it again. "Thank you. The Golden Four are basically control freaks. I bet you already figured that out, but what you may not know is that in order to control elements and avoid uprisings and chaos, they lie to them constantly. One of the things they do to keep everyone in check is to weaken them. And yes, before you ask, food weakens elements. We aren't made to eat; we are not like humans who need mineral ions to work. We are elements. All we need to survive is constant exposure to our element."

The dark-skinned element looked at me expectantly, waiting for me to say something. But when he realized that I was too confused to formulate a question, he explained himself. "Let's see. We can eat food, we have teeth, a stomach, and intestines, but that doesn't mean we need to eat. The reason our bodies are capable of digesting food is because we needed to appear human; it was a protection mechanism to fight suspicion when we lived with humans. Eating a bit of food now and then is okay, but eating too much makes our bodies use up most of their energy trying to digest the food. So, instead of eating, for you it might be best to get some fresh air and exposure to some wind. For me, it's best to have constant contact with the earth and surround myself with rocks and nature. Water elements have it best near bodies of water or humid and damp areas. Fire elements are a lot stronger in warm and dry areas, out beneath the sun and near fire. Now do you understand?"

I was about to ask him a question, when someone knocked loudly on the door. "Demetrio, I need to speak with you and the girl," a strong voice called from the other side of the door.

The earth element turned to me, a bit surprise by the sudden request. "Okay, I guess it's time for you to meet Al. I'll answer all your questions later." He opened the door, signaling for me to follow him.

I stood slowly and cautiously followed him out of the room. My legs trembled beneath me, but I couldn't figure out if it was because I was still weary or because I was anxious and slightly nervous.

We walked down a narrow hallway covered in sleek stone. The ground was made of earth, which made me wonder if we were in a cave. The small corridor opened into a wide central area where many other tunnels broke off into the ground. We took the second opening to the left and entered a room furnished with a table and some benches to sit on.

Juris was already seated. His eyes lit up when he recognized me. His hands were curled into fists yet again, but they soon relaxed when I came near.

"Hi," he said, as he watched Demetrio sit down across from us. I could tell by the way he tensed his jaw that he didn't start on the right foot.

"Hey. Did you wake up a long time ago?" I sat next to him on the bench.

Juris was about to answer when a male air element marched in and tossed our backpacks onto the table. Our equipment crashed onto the wood and flew out of the backpacks.

"What the hell is this?" the air element demanded, picking up a plastic container of food. His large hands dented the cover, and his eyebrows were raised. We hadn't even greeted us, and he was already yelling. Juris and I remained silent. "We did not give you this. This does not grow on plants." The air element flung the food aside and grabbed what seemed to really anger him. Now I understood the dilemma. I hadn't even checked the bags for it, but there it was—a small silver bracelet with the insignia of the Golden Four carved in the front. The air element held it with extreme care so as not to set it off, but with enough force to make the veins of his hands pop out. "Whose side are you on?" He stared directly at me. It was almost as if he knew what had happened; that I had agreed to cooperate with the Golden Four.

Suddenly, I realized that Aiden wasn't here with us. I felt guilty for not having noticed before. I needed to talk to him, to hold his hand, to look into his eyes and feel confident in what I was doing.

"I can explain..."

"If you were with us, you would have ditched this in the middle of the forest. You would have gotten rid of it, or at least tried." The air element's golden hair shone in the dim light of the torches like waves of grain. His grey eyes were a storm of frustration. "I know you don't have a lot of answers, and I know you may be confused, but if you ran away to be with us, you wouldn't have brought this or the rest of these supplies." His shoulders slouched as he seated himself in front of us. "If you confess to be working with the Golden Four, we will leave you at the foot of the mountain with your tracking device and disappear."

I looked over at Demetrio. Hurt was etched all over his face as he put the pieces together. He had healed us and helped us break free from the restrains of Arcane. He answered all my questions kindly and asked for permission before taking action. The betrayal on his face made me wonder if they would believe the truth.

Juris spoke first, making sure that the silence wasn't an affirmation of their suspicion. "We had to bring all these things here. We had to because they..."

Al, or so Demetrio called him, threw our backpacks onto the floor. He stood up once more and stared down at the younger earth element. "Don't try to make up some stupid excuses to cover for you!"

"They killed Ren!" Juris slammed his fist on the table and matched Al's stance. Both men looked at each other, eye to eye. "The bastards killed Ren in front of her to manipulate us." He pointed at me. "They play with us to do their fucking work, and the last thing we need is for you to doubt us. You even know how hard it was to walk here? Your stupid map is poorly drawn and you didn't give us any explanation on why we were starving to death." The vein that ran along his neck and in his forehead was bulging. "We have been through hell these last few days, and on top of that, you keep Aiden away from me when he is breaking down!" My head shot up as I heard Aiden's name. Why were they keeping him away from us?

Demetrio stood and tried to break the tension that grew between the earth and air elements. "Well, we weren't quite sure what had happened to the water element, but you must understand what we might think when we find your backpacks full of items we didn't give you." He looked back and forth between the angry teenagers. "Al, why don't you go and get some fresh air while I talk to... sorry, I don't know your name." He looked at me and gave me an awkward smile.

"Aurora. But you can call me Ary." I added quickly

Al glanced at Demetrio. "I'm not five years old."

"Then stop acting as if you were, Aeolos," Demetrio replied.

Aeolos refused to leave but stood against the wall and stared at me. His body was tensed, revealing strong muscles. His blonde hair fell to right above his shoulders. He had a similar complexion to the Achilles everyone imagined: fit, blond, graceful, and handsome. If it weren't for his pale-ish skin, he would have looked like the boy who inspired Homer to write the legendary character. When he caught my gaze, I turned away.

"Ary, do you want to explain your situation?" Demetrio said gently.

I wiped my hands on my pajama bottoms. "Juris mentioned the most important parts. They caught us and then killed Ren in front of me. They told me that I had to help them capture you guys by activating the tracking device when I met your leader. And if I didn't, they'd kill Juris and Aiden and who knows who else. I was forced to agree, and then we thought it would be best to see what to do once we found you. But apparently, that didn't work out." I glanced back at Al for a second to see if he believed me, but a hard expression was still displayed on his face.

Demetrio laced his fingers in front of him. "So, you want to cooperate with us."

"We wouldn't have even risked escaping if we didn't."

Once Demetrio nodded and gave no other signal of doubt, I took advantage of the opportunity to make my own demand. "I want to see Aiden."

Al looked at Demetrio and uncrossed his arms. The elder earth element looked down at the table. "About him. When we brought you..."

Juris coughed, interrupting him mid-sentence and eyed me.

Demetrio paused and followed his gaze. He licked his lips before resuming. "We believe that the tranquilizers have released some sort of secondary effect on him. It won't take long before the effects wear off, but there is a possibility that they might remain permanent. We doubt that this will happen, but I think it's your right to have all the information."

I kept my eyes fixed on Demetrio's face. There was something off about his expression. It didn't reflect the words he was saying or his previous behavior while healing me.

"Thank you for telling me that. Now, I would appreciate it if you would take me to him." There was a certain edge to my voice, which made Demetrio nervous.

"Al, why don't you take Ary to Aiden's room?"

Chapter 28

We walked back to the central hall where all the tunnels connected and continued down a different branch. Walking behind Aeolos, I realized how good looking he and his friend actually were. There was something about them, like an inhuman glow that emanated from their bodies. Juris, Aiden, and I, on the other hand, lacked the air that they carried and looked more human.

Aeolos slowed as we reached a series of doorframes covered by floor-length cloth doors. When he turned to me, I could see that all the irritation and violence I had seen in him before were gone. Instead, I saw a dark glow of pity. I didn't want to know the reason why, so I strode into through the doorframe he motioned toward.

The curtain fell behind me, shutting Aeolos out and allowing me to have as much privacy as a piece of cloth could provide. The room was dimly lit by some torches, which were hung on the far corner of the room. They created long, dark shadows on the rocky surface, which crept from the ceiling to the floor. Their elongated fingers threatened to take me into the darkness.

Aiden stood up from a cot that was built into the wall and stared at me. "Ary." His voice was just a whisper. He looked at me as if I were a hallucination and couldn't quite believe I was standing there.

I walked over to him and hugged him. At first he didn't know how to react, or perhaps he was afraid of touching me again, but his hands moved to my back and pulled me close. I smiled as I recognized the faint smell of cinnamon on his skin.

"I thought you would never want to touch me again." I kept my voice low so Al couldn't eavesdrop on our conversation. I wanted this moment to be just between us.

Aiden kissed my forehead and broke the embrace. His eyes scanned my features and read my thoughts. "I long for your touch. I crave your attention. But we need to stop this, Ary. I don't want to hurt you anymore." The shadows on his face disfigured him.

What?

"I don't understand," I muttered, taking a step back.

Aiden ran a hand through his messy hair. His bright gold eyes were still dimmed. "No matter what I do, I will always hurt you. If I touch you, I scorch your skin, and if I keep my distance, I can see the pain in your eyes. I really like you, but I can't keep on putting you through this." He exhaled slowly.

I tried to figure out what to say. My tongue was tied and my heart drowned out the sound of silence. After all we had been through, I genuinely thought that we would be able to get to know each other better, that we would be able to discover if our relationship would grow once we were rescued. There was no point in hiding our attraction to each other, but why would he dismiss it so easily? The times that he had hurt me were involuntary. I knew he hadn't burned me intentionally.

"If you don't want to hurt me, don't shut me out. Be honest to me. I need to know what is happening to you so I can help you, but you keep putting this barricade between us."

Aiden brought up his hands to his head. Wincing in pain, he turned around and fetched the flask. It had only been a couple of days since the Monarch of Water had given it to me, but it was almost empty. Aiden swallowed the last drops and fell to his knees.

"Aiden, what's wrong?" I took a step forward, unsure of what I should do.

He waved me away. "Just leave. Leave me alone." I would have turned away and left if he hadn't been panting in pain. "Shut up!" he screamed at no one.

I ran to him and rested my hand on his back. "Please, tell me how to help," I begged.

Aiden sharply turned toward me and grabbed my hand. He pressed down forcefully on my skin and tore my arm away. "Stay away from me." When he spoke to me, he almost seemed possessed. But when he realized that he had bruised my wrist, he stared down at himself and then at me. "I told you." His worry was quickly replaced with anger. "You bastard! If only you could contain yourself!" he yelled at himself.

I took that as my signal to leave. When I turned, Al was already holding the curtain aside. I ran past him and down the hall, trying to escape Aiden's screams, but I could still hear them. I heard not only one, but nineteen more, since his cries echoed off the walls and down into the other tunnels.

"Ary!" Al jogged up to me and grabbed my elbow.

"What do you want?" I spat at him, as I tried to escape Aiden's voice. Al's skin was cool against mine, like mine must feel to him, and sent shivers down my spine.

He let go of me. "Why don't I take you outside? Some fresh air may be good for both of us."

I immediately regretted speaking so harshly. All he wanted to do was help. And I bet he had overheard most of my conversation with Aiden. "Sure."

Al guided me down the halls, but my mind strayed. If only I could go back in time and avoid getting killed by Skyler. I was on the brink of tears, but I kept them back. I couldn't keep on regretting what happened. If life gave you lemons, you made lemonade. But you needed sugar, and all the sweet moments were obscured by a dominant bitterness.

I held onto my crystal. I could take it off and discover what my power really was. I could try to fix this. There was a reason why I had the crystal, though. I didn't know what I could do. I remembered how both Juris and Aiden had lost control of their powers before getting a grip on them. Not only could I not control my powers, but it would be almost impossible to stop me if it got out of hand. If Skyler were here, I know he would help me.

The thought of Skyler vanished as soon as I saw light around the bend. Al's figure was surrounded by a golden halo as he stepped onto the mountainside. I remembered the mountains I had seen when we had originally escaped, but they hadn't come to mind while we were on the run. I hadn't even noticed the soft incline until now.

A small balcony protruded from the side of the mountain, overlooking the forest. I could see the river gleaming silver in the distance, a ribbon that smoothly slid through the trees. And not so far beyond, a large building shot up from the wilderness like a tombstone. The grey walls that surrounded the training center clashed against the shining roof. If it weren't for its dull color, the training center would have looked like a gem.

Al saw me staring at the construction. "It's covered in solar panels. That's why it shines so much during the day." He walked over to some rocks and climbed them. He seated himself at the top, his golden hair glowing like fire under the sun and blowing in the soft breeze, His lips were sturdily set into a thin line, giving him an air of authority, almost like the ruler of this land.

I stared at the wilderness with awe. Never in my wildest dreams had I ever thought that I would become an element and live in this alternate realm where nature was found in its purest form. I could feel the breeze lift my own spirits and strengthen me, which made me think of Demetrio's explanation.

"Your friend told me that food weakens us and that the Golden Four use it to control their citizens. But I don't understand how digesting food takes up energy and weakens us. Why do they keep feeding us if food makes us sick?" I asked.

Al never looked down at me while he answered. He kept his eyes on the horizon and breathed in the pine-scented air as if he were meditating. "They stick drugs in the food, which makes you crave it. Food prevents you from developing your elemental senses. These senses are, for example, a danger sense with your brothers and sisters. When I say brothers and sisters, I do not mean it in a biological way but in the elemental bond. We are brother and sister of the air children. Soon enough, you'll be able to tell if I am in danger. The strength of your power is noticeably reduced if you are continuously eating mundane food. Also, your physical strength is directly linked to the state of your element. If we were to go to a highly contaminated atmosphere, then your strength would be decreased. But as it can decrease, it also can increase. Here we are always exposed to fresh, unpolluted air, so we are always stronger. So, you see it is much easier for the Golden Four to control everyone if they are twice as strong and everyone else is twice as weak."

I was amazed with the intricate relationship elements shared with their surrounding environment. And now that I thought of it, with global contamination and the accelerated greenhouse effects, the only elements that would be at an advantage were the fire elements.

"So, the elemental realm is like a safety net for elements? We at least have one place that will never be contaminated," I ventured.

"Yes and no. Yes, we should not feel ill here since there is nothing that affects us. But the more humans pollute and contaminate the environment, the smaller the realms get. Many areas have disappeared or have been consumed by contamination. Our role as elements is to preserve the earth and make sure that everything is in balance. Occasionally, we have to unleash disasters to keep humans in line, show them who's boss, and that they do not own the planet.

"This is the Golden Four's strategy to keep humans in line. Have you noticed how North America continuously suffers from every single possible natural disaster? You name it, and they have experienced it. The Golden Four believe that the human race was a mistake, that humans should be eliminated to allow the planet to thrive with its original splendor. That is one of the reasons that motivated us to escape."

He slowly scooted over on the rock and invited me to sit down next to him. I gripped the rocks and climbed with ease.

"What are the other factors?" I asked. "How did you guys come to be here?" Once I sat down next to him, I got an even more breathtaking view of the realm. I could see the slope of the mountain and the small trail that had led them up here. I wondered if these elements had created the caves or if the caves were a natural formation. I saw how the river we crossed actually turned up into the mountains and then curved far into the forest.

Al's voice was pleasant to hear. And his openness to answering questions and sharing information made me believe that I made the right choice in running away, that despite the deaths, the violence, and Aiden's current situation, we would be okay. All we had to do now was solve the tracking device problem.

"Many of the factors that influenced you to leave were the same one we had," Al continued. "Things were different when we woke up, though. Instead of just one child of each element waking up, all of the element children were reborn and judged. Then only two would be able to live in the northern side of the city, while the rest had to serve the Golden Four in the southern side. I suppose, with what I've heard, they didn't let you know the destiny of the other children." He stared at me in hopes that I could contradict his suspicion, that more than just half of the elements born would suffer a life of experimentation.

I had been told a different story. "They told me that only four of us were selected to keep on living our lives as elements, while the others would keep on living as humans, unaware of their true nature, and later die when their scientifically prepared body degenerated—something like Alzheimers. But I doubt that what they told me is true, not nearly half of it was."

"They are very smart and always find a convincing way to lie to you. Deceit and manipulation are some of their strongest assets. So, back to when we were in the training center, my protector, Zareh, had managed to find many truths that altered his vision about Arcane and the government. He warned me what would happen, and I thought it was best to escape along with some other friends. At that moment, my closest group was Demetrio, three other boys and two girls. I told them about Zareh's discovery and how I managed to leave, but hardly anyone believed me. I managed to convince Demetrio, who later helped convince everyone else, except one male companion. When we ran for it, both girls died in the process. After that, we knew that what we had discovered was true.

"We managed to run up to these mountains and conceal ourselves. The caves were part of the mountain, and we took advantage of the hiding spot. They are well hidden unless one manages to see it at a certain angle. We stayed here for almost three whole months until a resistance group from South America found us. Apparently, the story of six runaway elements leaked out of Arcane and managed to cross the borders. The South American elements heard of our story and thought it would be wise to retrieve us. A small group of seven infiltrated the borders of the realm and sought us out.

Before escaping, though, we promised Zareh that we would come back to fetch you if you escaped. We knew that this time, the Golden Four would be better prepared to track you, so we made sure we were one step ahead of them." He let the story sink in before I asked another question.

So, there were more elements around the world? We weren't the only ones? And why would the South American elements want to rescue them? It all seemed too complex for me to understand. "So, there are other elements in the world."

Aeolos nodded. "Millions...They all have different traditions, different forms of government, and they are located in different realms."

"And why would it be wise for the elements of a different realm rescue you? It makes no sense for them to intervene in the affairs of a different realm," I puzzled.

"Let's just say that they are aware of the abuses of the Golden Four and know of their plans to eliminate the human race. They want to stop them before it's too late. In order to do that, they needed fresh information." He spoke proudly of his role in defending humanity. But then he remembered I was there and probably assumed my thoughts. "You don't have to belong to the resistance, though. We just came here to give you freedom. By forcing you into this, we would be acting a lot like the Golden Four." Indirectly, he was sticking me in the middle of this, forcing me to choose his side in this oddly mundane conflict.

What would he do to me if I decided to stay impartial? Would I just be dropped off in the human world where I would have to adapt and live a life of a nomad, swatting off suspicions that I was a vampire because of my slow aging? Or would I be able to choose where to live, in whichever realm suited me best for my lifestyle? It almost felt as if these realms were different continents in the same world, just one world inside the other. I rubbed my head and tried to make sense of my thoughts, but they flew wildly in my head without letting me grasp one.

"You'll have to let me think about it first, Al."

"Of course."

While I considered whether I wanted to get directly involved with what seemed like a war, I saw two figures slowly climbing the trail toward us. I couldn't quite make out who they were or see their clothing, but I was sure that one of them had bright coral orange hair. "No..." My voice trailed off as I remembered who had bright red hair.

I prepared myself to jump off of the rocks, but I wanted to make sure that my suspicion was correct. Al noticed my sudden awareness and put a hand on my shoulder, laughing. How could he laugh? If only he knew that the very man who had murdered Ren had bright coral orange hair.

"Relax, it's only Leith." Aeolos slipped past me down the rock and extended his hand to help me down. He guided my fall.

Together, we walked back into the cave in search of Demetrio. We found the earth element leaning over a pile of wood in the middle of the main hall, trying to start a bonfire. This fire would produce enough heat to warm most of the small tunnels. I hadn't even noticed the cold.

"I see the fresh air renewed you, Ary," Demetrio smiled. "I'm sorry for what happened with Aiden. I honestly didn't think that he would react to you like that. From what Juris told me, I thought that you actually would bring out the best in him."

I bit the inside of my cheek to keep myself from hearing him. Aiden didn't want me. He felt the same way I did, but he didn't want to hurt me. Of course, I would have felt touched if he hadn't kicked me out of his room in such a violent way or if he would stop concealing the truth from me. Should I just move on? What if all I had with Aiden was attraction but nothing else?

"Anyway, I do hope that he gets over it soon, because if not..." Demetrio began.

Al saw the mortification on my face and decided to quickly change the subject. "Kenneth and Leith are here. I suppose they're going to arrive in about half an hour. Why don't you give Ary some clothes while I get the fire started?"

Demetrio saw Al's signal and led me to my new room. He showed me the room I was supposed to share with Ren and the pile of clothing they had brought from the human world. He gave me some privacy to change.

"I'll wait by the fire. You come when you're finished, okay?" he said as he unhooked the curtain from the wall and let it slip into place, dividing the rest of the caves from my room.

I stared at the torch in my room and watched the flames dance. Every single room had a fire or a torch. Everything reminded me of Aiden, and when I tried to think of something else, my mind kept coming back to the empty bed intended for Ren. Water and fire, two elements that one would consider opposite but somehow found perfect harmony when it came to torturing my essence. I had killed one, and the other had killed me.

I didn't change my clothes until I heard greetings and a clamor of voices. I had been staring into the darkness at the fire, somehow wishing to be swallowed by it whole, kept in secret where time could not pass because it could not be measured.

Chapter 29

When I finally had enough courage to leave the room, I blew out the torch and hooked the curtain back to the wall. I could hear Aeolos laughing in the distance with someone else. As the mouth of the tunnel opened, and I walked into what could have been called the common area, I could feel all eyes fall on me and the conversation stop. Thankfully, I was able to change my extra-large pajamas into some jeans and a t-shirt. The shirt was one size too large, but I was thankful for the bagginess when they all turned to me. I knew that the other two elements would be male, but now that I was actually with them, and Ren was not here. I felt a bit too...observed.

"Leith, Kenneth, this is Ary." Demetrio stood up and introduced me.

Kenneth was a lanky teenager with dark chocolate hair and tan skin. His skinny body looked even smaller under his oversized shirt. I had been expecting his eyes to be a lot more shocking, but they were brown with a hint of orange in them. He sat with his legs crossed and a bag tossed next to him. His hair was a mess, and a subtle pink tone flushed his cheeks.

Leith, on the other hand, looked a lot older in spite of the fact that he and Kenneth were the same age. His hair was a soft red, and the stubble that shaded his jaw was what made him look older. His shoulders were broader than Kenneth's, giving him a larger frame. He had dark-blue irises, which looked more similar to Ren's than to the Monarch of Water. His eyes weren't on my face, unlike Kenneth's; instead, he stared at my necklace.

I covered it quickly and realized it was the first time I had left it outside of my shirt. Leith noticed my reaction but didn't seem to care.

"What's your power?" he asked, without the need for more introductions. He didn't seem to fear me or act suspicious in any way. Perhaps he knew what I was wearing and what it meant.

I made myself comfortable next to Juris, since he was the only piece of sanity I could find at the moment. Somehow, I had grown used to his presence despite what I had thought of him previously in the training center. It didn't seem very important now that we were far away with no intentions of going back. "I'm not one hundred percent sure of what I can do," I said truthfully.

Leith's friends looked at him, wondering why he had asked. No one else had seen the necklace.

"Then why are you wearing a neutralizer? You'll never discover it that way..." He stood against the cavern wall with his arms crossed and a tranquil expression on his face. His high cheekbones and strong angles played in his favor.

My voice was weak when I spoke. "I...um...don't think it would be a good idea."

He smiled at me, maybe encouraging me to take it off. "I bet it's not that bad. We've dealt with many cases in South America...unless your power can't be controlled. Something involuntary, maybe, but those cases are rare."

I tensed, knowing I would have to tell them about my power. I was hoping this could wait a bit further into the future, but hiding the information could make them suspicious, which I didn't want if my freedom depended on them.

"She can influence people, but we don't know in what way," Juris spoke for me, knowing that it would be much easier for me to hear it than to speak it. "And she is one of those cases."

Now, all eyes were on me, and they weren't going to turn away so easily. I could hear Al whistle and Kenneth laugh. Demetrio sucked in his cheeks and his eyes bulged, but I only watched Leith's reaction. He smiled.

"How stupid they are to let you go. We could use your power with much benefit."

"Hold on, we won't be using her power. It's her decision, and she hasn't even decided what she's going to do when we leave here," Al jumped up.

Juris turned to me with a frown. "You mean you aren't going to join the resistance?"

"I don't know."

"She hasn't decided."

Al and I spoke at the same time. Demetrio and Kenneth seemed to respect that, but Leith didn't agree. And apparently, neither did Juris.

The youngest earth element stared at me with bewilderment. "Why wouldn't you? They killed Ren, and look at Aiden."

"What about Aiden?" I raised an eyebrow, suddenly feeling that Juris wasn't sharing information.

Kenneth nodded, finally understanding why there was a missing person. He hadn't asked about Aiden. Had they already told him?

"So, that's what happened to the water chick."

Aeolos retrieved something from his pocket that made everyone become silent. It was the tracking device.

"We can discuss what's going to happen with Aurora later, but first we have to decide what to do with this." Kenneth began to open his mouth, but Aeolos spoke over him. "Yes, this is a tracking device. Yes, they brought it." Once Kenneth settled down and everyone was listening, he continued. "Now that we're all here, I think it should be our priority to figure out how we're going to continue with the plan with this small inconvenience."

Juris stretched out his feet and slouched against the rocky wall. He avoided the suspicious looks from the newly arrived elements. "Can't we just follow your original plan and dump the tracking device? They'll never know where we went. Heck, I don't even know why they let us go with such a weak plan." He spoke without really paying attention to his words. And now that he said it, I felt a bit wary too.

Why would the Monarch of Water kill Ren and send me here with just a tracking device that I could choose not to turn on? I knew that the threat was motivation. He had definitely scared me, and I wanted to protect my friends' lives, but nothing could stop me from joining them and ditching the tracking device. Something was missing in this plan... the threat implied that they had direct contact with my friends, so they could kill them. However, they didn't know where we were, so we could just run away to the human world and evade the whole threat.

Everyone was silent while we thought, so silent that we could hear the echoes of Aiden's screams. I pulled up my legs and covered my ears. I could feel goose bumps crawling over my arms and legs.

"What is that?" Kenneth stood up. He inched his body closer to the tunnel.

Demetrio, Al, and Juris looked at each other. Finally, Demetrio spoke, "Kenneth, I think you should meet their third party member, Aiden. Oh, and let me talk to you about the supplies..." He dragged Kenneth out of the central area. I watched as their figures faded into the darkness and finally disappeared. Kenneth was a lot taller than Demetrio and, because of his lankiness, it looked like he had been stretched.

Al and Juris kept on staring at each other. If I wasn't mistaken, it almost looked as if they were silently communicating between themselves. It amazed me how quickly Juris had adapted and changed. Perhaps his dominant tendencies had been softened in the forest while we ran. Or when Ren died, perhaps his rebellious part died as well. It seemed to me that the main reason why he had been so eager to join them was because we had a common enemy. Had they not been against the Golden Four, would Juris have resisted?

I could feel Leith looking curiously from the other side of the room. A gleam in his eyes brightened when he discovered I was one of those "rare cases."

I remained in my balled-up position and thought about something else, something that would distract me. I started humming the songs I knew from my human life and remembered the moments when I listened to them—riding my bike around town, trying to draw a proportional face, reading in my room, hiding in the corners of the public library, cooking with mom, and dancing around my room when I knew no one was home. I couldn't help thinking of the life I had before this transformation, and I couldn't help feeling the desire to go back and relive it all one more time, observing everything and absorbing the memories so I would be prepared to leave it all behind.

But would it be the same if I had known I would die? What would have happened if I had been raised knowing I was different from everyone else in a way no one would understand? I would have probably isolated myself, fearing that if I got too attached to something, then it would hurt. Instead, I felt everything a human did. I picked at my nails as I pondered. Perhaps the knowledge of a human experience helped elements relate to humans and understand their ways. Knowledge got lost if you didn't refresh it, though. The elders in Arcane must have carried a point of view that ignored human reasoning and thought; whereas, the younger ones probably had the memories fresh in their minds.

I tried to imagine what it would have been like to live in Arcane instead of running away, but I just couldn't. Instead of elegant gowns and an organized city, all I could think of was the wilderness and these caves. I remembered the view from the mountainside and smiled. If I hadn't escaped, I would never have seen that breathtaking view. I would never have learned about how the Golden Four controlled the power of their subjects.

I looked around at the caves. The cold, rocky surface and the winter air didn't bother me anymore. The fire crackling a few feet away from me felt pleasant but unnecessary. I turned to the boys. Al had left, vanishing into one of the tunnels that broke off deeper into the mountain, but Juris sat next to Leith and showed him his power. He concentrated and managed to crack the ground at his feet and then close the gap.

Leith spoke in a soft voice and, with what I could hear, was teaching him how to control his power and make every move more efficient.

"See? Now that you feel the earth through your feet, you don't have to do much to make it crack. We don't have independent powers; we work in harmony with the nature around us. You have to feel the element of earth in your surroundings and channel its power through yours."

Leith pulled out a water bottle from his satchel and opened the cap. He dumped all of the contents onto the dirt and watched it puddle. "Whenever I want to make my power stronger, I work with my element." He closed his eyes for a couple of seconds. When he opened them, something was different; a soft shine glowed in his dark blue eyes.

I stared at the puddle that had begun to disappear, sucked up by the dry dirt. Leith's hands moved slightly and, with little difficulty, the water began to flow back up and spiral toward the ceiling. When Leith's movements changed, the water fell to the ground and disappeared.

He ran his hand against his forehead and caught me staring. I diverted my gaze and kept on watching from the corner of my eye.

"My main power is not controlling water, but I can control it to some extent just by being born a water element. You can cause massive movements in the earth, Juris, because your power and natural ability are one."

"And how did you manage to suppress it?" Juris inquired. I remembered how he lost control in the forest. It would be best if he learned how to hold back to prevent it from happening again. I didn't even want to think of what could happen if he lost control in the caves.

"Well, remember how I told you to direct the earth's energy through yours? You just have to do the opposite," Leith replied. "Give the earth your energy and breathe slowly. This also can help you give power to someone else that belongs to the same element."

"She's not going to want him." I heard a group of voices make its way toward us. "He's marked."

"Shut up, Kenneth. We don't know that."

"Yeah, right. You know how she..."

"That's enough." The last voice I recognized as its echo boomed—Aeolos.

When they reached us, Demetrio was carrying handfuls of bottled water. He handed them out, while Al spoke. "I think we've had a pretty intense day, at least for some of us, so why don't we all go to sleep before the sun sets so we can extinguish the torches?"

Chapter 30

I waited until I was sure that everyone was asleep. I slipped out of my bed and felt my way to the doorway. I silently moved the curtain aside, as I sneaked into the hallway and stopped to listen. I could hear several snores from where I was standing, loud enough to cover any unexpected sounds. Despite my advantage of not being heard, I moved cautiously and silently, feeling my way against the walls.

When I reached my destination, I pulled aside the curtain and slipped into the room. I was careful with each and every step. Any wrong movement or sound could wake him up, and if he woke, the chances of me being able to stay with him would quickly vanish. The torches were extinguished. Hardly anything furnishing adorned the room, but it was still difficult to find the cot in the darkness. Not that I didn't know where it was; I didn't want to crash into it and wake him with the jolt.

I reached the covers and instantly felt the body underneath. His warmth radiated from under the sheets. I welcomed the warmth as I settled next to Aiden, just as I had done in the sleeping bag when he was my only source of heat in the middle of the punishing winter air.

I forbade myself to breathe, while he rearranged his position and muttered under his breath. His words were unrecognizable; I had given up trying to decipher them a long time ago. Once he became still, I settled down next to his him and took his hand into mine.

"You'll be fine in a little bit; the secondary effect will fade away. You'll be as good as new," I whispered, trying to raise my own hopes. How long could he stay like this?

My fingers roamed freely over his. His skin was smoother than I ever thought. He felt like a flame as it danced over a wick, swiftly dodging contact and burning you if you came too close. I had already played with fire and got burned. The secret was not to approach his fire when it was fully kindled, but when it was dormant and unaware of its surroundings.

In the darkness, I worked my way up from his hand to his arm, which was completely exposed. Our breathing was the only sound I could hear as my fingers swirled, drawing on him, as I went up. He didn't flinch. He didn't make a sound.

"I still miss home," I confessed in the loneliness of his company. "I don't know about you or the others..." I wanted to be closer to him. Whether it was the homesickness or a side effect of my constant feelings toward him, I wished for him to be fully conscious and hold me. *It's okay to want to feel wanted.*

That is what we all want to feel: loved. My mother had told me this once. Sure, so it was okay to feel this way; however, I didn't know how to act on those feelings. I snuck into the room of a boy while he slept. I wanted to lie next to him now, because if he were awake, he wouldn't let me be near him. Were my actions incorrect or inappropriate? I would never know. I needed guidance from someone older and wiser.

Despite the tangle of emotions I felt, I kept stroking his arm gently. Memorizing his shape, my hands moved up to his neck and quickly crept to his face. The straight, firm angles of his features welcomed my cool fingers. Suddenly, I felt self-conscious, as if my touching his face meant exposing myself to him. My heart pounded in my ears, and my breathing became more jagged. Too scared of what would happen if I continued, I removed my hand and tucked it safely over my chest.

"I miss home too," he muttered. I sucked in my breath. He was still half asleep; I could hear that much in his voice. But that also meant that he was half awake. "Ary?" He turned around and put his arms around me, pulling me closer to his body and trapping me in his firm embrace.

My heart was about to jump out of my chest. I woke him up, damn it. "Aiden..." My voice was only a whisper, but I felt as if I were yelling.

He entwined our legs and placed his head between my shoulder and chin. "Stay." His plea tore me in half. I could stay here in his warm embrace until dawn, as I had done in the sleeping bag, but I ran the risk of getting hurt when he woke up.

Or I could leave him and perhaps make him suffer one of his "episodes."

I closed my eyes and thought of each part of me that touched him. There was no way I could escape his grasp, so I wrapped my arms around him and caressed his hair. Could it be that he was finally reemerging? That the sleep helped wear off the side effects? I thought of the flask the Golden Four had given him. Why would they want to help him?

But those thoughts could not linger in my head for long. Not when I was burning with such intensity. We were one tight knot that would not come undone easily.

"I'm right here."

"I'm sorry," he spoke slowly.

"For what?"

His steady breaths were hot on my neck. I could feel his mouth come closer to my skin, but he contained himself. He didn't want to, or maybe he couldn't get himself to do it. I stopped caressing his hair and suddenly became aware of the situation. I felt the muscles underneath his skin tense and his body stiffen. One of my hands roamed down his arm, while the other gave him a gentle push.

Aiden brushed his lips against my skin. I swore I could have melted and evaporated into the atmosphere. My spine shuddered with the strong effect of the smallest act of love. I slammed the breaks on my thoughts.

Whoa. Had I just thought that?

Love.

It was just a simple four-letter word, but it carried so much emotion, so much depth when it was said properly. Did I love Aiden? And if I did, why?

Why?

He made me feel normal, nervous, and anxious, I pondered. And not only that: I wanted to be with him; I needed to be with him. I loved when he stared at me, and it felt like a collision between two opposite forces that couldn't help but attract each other. How, with every touch and kiss, he consumed me.

...he consumed me...

...he consumed me...

...he consumed me...

During this whole mess, he was the one thing that felt one hundred percent right and normal. Everything else had been upside-down lately, but not him. Well, he used to be right-side-up.

So, did I love him? Or did I just like him intensely?

I tried to come up with the answer, but I couldn't think straight with so much of him touching so much of me. I could already feel him falling back into a dreamless slumber. His limbs were limp, and his face was completely relaxed.

I gave myself five more minutes next to him, before I left to try to organize my thoughts.

Chapter 31

After waking up, I thought that the previous night had been a dream. But as the morning dragged on and the memory only got clearer and clearer, I knew that it had actually happened.

I smiled to myself as I helped with the daily chores. First, I had to hand out the water bottles, while the boys lit the torches once more. Then, I had to pick up the empty bottles and place them in a small crate near the exit of the cave. My third task was to gather blankets from all the rooms, fold them, and then take them to the central area.

Apparently, we had to move to a smaller cave nearer to the forest, since we needed to meet one more member of the resistance before actually passing to the human realm. While I was doing the chores, Juris insisted on making up my mind for me about joining them, but the conversation I had heard the day before while Kenneth, Demetrio, and Al were walking down the hall haunted me. Who was marked, and why wouldn't they accept him? My mind jumped to the possibility that the "him" they referred to was Aiden. But if it was, how was he marked?

"Hi Ary." Leith walked next to me, while I carried a large pile of blankets. I looked down at his hands and saw a medium-sized crate.

I grunted as I tried to see ahead of me. "Leith," I couldn't' manage to say much more because of the strain the blankets placed on my arms.

He swung the light crate as if he were mocking me. "So, you probably were told about the move."

"Yeah."

"Then you know we're going to go back to the human realm."

When I felt that my arms were about to pop right out of my sockets, I stopped and leaned against the hard, sharp wall. "Where are you going with this?" I heaved and looked once more at his crate before rolling my eyes. I knew where this conversation was going. Juris surely had told Leith that he hadn't been successful with me, so he had to send someone else to try to convince me to join them. Honestly, the sound of going back to Ashwick and trying to spy on my family sounded like a great idea. I missed them so much, and I couldn't tolerate thinking that I was putting political affairs over their needs.

Leith looked nervously at the crate in his hands and then back to me. "Well, since we aren't sure about your choice after we leave here, we need to make sure you look more...how could I say this....human-like?" He lifted the lid of the crate, revealing a whole set of contact lenses with different iris colors, boxes of hair dye, and makeup products.

"You want to give me a makeover?" I raised an eyebrow as I looked at the contents of the crate. They had to be kidding...

Leith cleared his throat. "I don't want to give you a makeover; I have to give you a makeover. That is...unless you join us."

I shook my head in disbelief. So, that's how they would try to convince me. Join us or we'll screw up your appearance and leave you alone to figure out everything. There was a bit of logic to it, but if we were all headed to the same place, why would I need a makeover if I chose to make my own way?

"Here, let me see that." I handed him the blankets and grabbed the crate. I made sure we still walked in the same direction, while I rummaged through the items. I saw some plastic bowls and bags that would be used in case I dyed my hair.

When I picked up a pair of scissors, Leith didn't hesitate in responding to my questioning look. "We'd also have to give you a new haircut. The Golden Four would expect us to dye your hair."

"Can I ask you something?"

"Anything!" he responded, struggling with the new load.

I made sure that my voice didn't change, nor did my posture as I asked my question. "What is wrong with Aiden?" While I was sleeping, a thought had occurred to me. If the Golden Four had given him an antidote or something of the sort to help him sleep well, it probably meant that the problem Demetrio claimed he had originated before the darts, not after.

I could hear Leith fumble with his stride and fall one step behind. He was hesitating...or just delaying the answer. "I think it's something to do with the sleeping dart..." His voice was stiff, as if his words were rehearsed.

I snapped the crate shut and placed it on top of the blankets he was carrying. "I am not going to join you, and I will not get a makeover either." I glared at him and marched off.

"Ary, wait! Come on, let's talk about this," he called from behind.

I didn't want to talk. I hadn't intended for my reaction to come off so stubborn, but I needed to know what was happening here. I needed to know what was going on with Aiden. He couldn't live like this, and neither could I. I almost felt as if I were back in the training center with studied answers and silent glares. And Juris.... Juris of all people should have been helping me instead of jumping into the rebellion.

I soared through the halls and found myself stopping at the exit to the cave. Demetrio, Al, and Juris were piling up bags of supplies that we would carry. Aiden was sitting on a rock, breathing the fresh air. With the sun beating down on all of their faces and immersing them in a golden light, I could have sworn everything was normal. But the scowl on Aiden's face when he saw me and turned away reminded me why I was here.

The three other boys stopped what they were doing and looked up. I stood in the mouth of the cave, speechless. What was I going to say? "I want you to answer my questions." I kept my tone firm and steady.

Juris set down the knife he was using to cut rope and approached me. He looked over his shoulders at the others and then back at me. His tongue ran over his bottom lip as he assessed the situation.

"Why don't we go talk inside?" he asked quietly. I could see the muscles in his arms flex as he began to herd me back into the darkness. My feet were planted on the solid rock.

"No. I want answers here, and I want them now!" As my voice rose, Aiden turned to watch. His eyebrows were drawn over his eyes and his jaw clenched. His frustration seemed so different from the relaxed hands I had held last night.

The winter breeze carried the scent of the mountain and the forest below. That would have been enough to calm me if I was a human, but as an element, it stirred strength in me that could not be contained if not for the necklace. The cool stone that was pressed against my skin grounded me. It reminded me why I was here and what I had to do.

Al noticed the dangerous look in my eyes and signaled Demetrio. "Why don't you take Aiden inside?"

"No," I protested. Demetrio and Al ignored me. They carried Aiden away from the light and back into the darkness of the cave. Aiden struggled, but he didn't have enough strength to stop them. His wiggling and kicking would delay them, but together they had the upper hand. I couldn't let them drag him back in, not after he had spent so much time in the dark. I grabbed Al's shoulder and pulled.

I didn't expected to achieve much with my attempt, but when I saw Al fall to the ground and Demetrio release Aiden, I froze.

I was so surprised I had managed to do something that I hadn't seen it coming.

"Stop it!" Aiden's voice boomed as his hand slapped my face. He was so strong that even after he removed his hand, I could feel pressure on my cheek. It burned so bad. Tears began to cloud my vision. He had actually slapped me!

I could feel my heart beat on the left side of my face. Juris's mouth hung open, his eyes wide with astonishment. Everyone was shocked. No one expected Aiden to act like this.

Aiden took one look around and clearly saw what he had done. I pressed my lips together to keep from crying in front of him. He took a step back.

"It's your fault!" he growled to no one in particular. "It's all your fault!" He grabbed the knife that Juris had set down and held it over the artery that ran through his neck. I could see the skin above it jump a little with each pump of blood, bumping momentarily into the sharp blade.

Aeolos, reacting quickly, managed to remove the knife in the blink of an eye. He tackled Aiden to the floor and pinned him there. I couldn't utter a single word. I smothered by shame and fear. What was going on?

Aiden made his move. Realizing that there was no way he would be able to get out from under Al's brute strength, his arms abruptly ignited.

"Shit!" Al jumped back, unprepared for the flames.

Demetrio disappeared into a large cave, as Aiden stood up, the fire running from his hands up to his elbows. It began to creep further. He knocked down some of the bags and kicked them. Everything he touched began to burn. The small area where we stood got warmer and warmer, and smoke curled up toward the sky.

He was about to attack something else when white foam rained down on his party. He screamed as if it actually hurt him. The chilling sound made my tears overflow. Demetrio and Kenneth had come back with a fire extinguisher. I crumpled on the inside, kneeling on the floor, holding myself. Instead of showing my emotions, I stared with a vacant expression, hoping that someone would realize what was happening. Like an answer to my silent plea, Juris wrapped his arms around me, turning me around so I didn't have to watch as Demetrio and Kenneth dragged Aiden off in a wrestling hold.

"I'm sorry." It was barely a murmur, but I heard it. I heard his meaning, his intention.

I inhaled sharply.

"You knew," I accused Juris. Only after reading his posture and Al's did I realize what was actually going on. "You all knew."

"Ary..."

"You all knew!"

Kenneth came back with an empty needle in his hand. "No! "I'm sorry..."

"You all knew! Don't touch me!" I fumed when Juris approached me to calm me down. I shoved him away. How dare he? When I turned to Juris, his head hung low, avoiding eye contact. Of course, he had been one of the first to know. Demetrio would have told him. How sick was that? All this time they kept it away from me, smiling at me and reassuring me that everything was going to be okay. But at the end of the day, they all knew they were lying to me.

"I expected better from you." Juris reacted as if I just spat on his face. I didn't want to be with them. I just...I just wanted to be alone.

I ran past Juris, but he caught my arm and turned me around. How could he touch me? I couldn't insult him; I didn't have the energy, but I voiced my thoughts with my fists as they rained down against him. The tears that ran down my cheeks blurred the world around me, but I kept swinging my arms.

"Enough!" Juris tried to grab my shirt but instead, his hand curled around a fine strand of silver. The chain snapped and fell to the floor. I went to grab it, but the crystal rolled away from my hand and toward Juris's large feet.

Crack.

No.

Snap. Crack. Crunch. Scrape.

No. No. No. Why was this happening? I managed to push Juris out of the way and stared blankly at the floor. There it was, the crystal was no longer in one piece—millions of little shards of glass-like stone sparkled on the ground. It was beautiful. It was mocking me. Suddenly, it hit me. I got down on my knees and began to put the pieces together. There were so many.

"No!" I cried out, my hands trembling, while I fumbled to gather the pieces. I looked up. "Why did you step on it?"

"I didn't mean to." Juris lowered his hand to help me up. I could see the pity in his eyes, and I could see my reflection tinted in green. Betrayal. That was the only word one could use to describe my expression.

I slapped away his hand, sending all the little shards flying into the air. "Why!?"

He grabbed my shoulders and shook me. "It's just a damn necklace!"

Shocked, I relaxed in his grip, wishing that he were right. It was just a necklace. Who was I kidding? Soon they would start changing their behavior, and that didn't mean they would change for the best. Juris's expression changed when he realized what type of necklace it was.

At that moment, I broke. Something in me just cracked. I raised my hand and slapped him across the face, imitating the offense Aiden had inflicted on me.

"Don't touch me ever again." I hissed the words before running down the mountain trail.

Chapter 32

Careless, irrational, stupid...all of these words and more could describe my behavior, but I didn't care. I didn't care about anything right now. I ran down the mountainside, as the air surrounded me in a frigid embrace. I didn't know where to go. I could easily slip and fall off the trail, but I ignored the thought. Juris...how could he have kept this from me?

I ran. Not sure where I would end up, I just ran with the hope of getting as far from the other elements as possible, far from my new life. As I ran, I could hear all the hints Aiden had dropped along the way.

"Ary, there's a problem...I don't think it would be good for me to run away with you tonight...But it would be dangerous...I'm not talking about that, Ary. What I mean is, I can't leave; there's something that's..." All this had happened before we escaped.

In the sleeping bag, Aiden's voice had trembled when he said, "I've never been okay, Ary."

"I've never been okay."

He seemed to be yelling in my head. I stopped, leaning against a tree for support, and gave in to my despair. My cheek burned even more as the tears poured over the red mark Aiden hand had left behind. I had no idea how I arrived at this tree or how long I had been running. All I could hear was Aiden's voice and the warnings that had gone unheard. How could I not have noticed it? He tried to tell me, but all I did was worry about myself and blame his behavior on the rest of our group.

"It would be dangerous."

"Ary, there's a problem."

"I'm not normal."

I hit the tree trunk with my fist. It hurt more than I thought it would, but I could tolerate the physical pain more than the tornado inside me. I struck the bark again until I shed blood. I put Aiden through this by forcing him to escape. I allowed the Golden Four to taunt me with the flask they gave him. And now, there was nothing I could do because my powers would be unleashed; powers that I could not contain.

I continued along the trail at a slower pace, searching for a hiding spot. I knew that one of the boys would try to console me and lure me back into the cave, so I wanted to concealed myself before they could try any of that crap on me.

My heart raced and my insides bubbled. I loathed Juris. I thought he had changed, but he was the same deceitful piece of garbage he had always been. He kept the secret from me—a secret I never would have kept if it regarded someone he loved.

The trail was steep, and I could see plenty of crevasses and nooks to hide in. Soon enough, I found a small gap hidden by a pair of prominent rocks and a bush. I fit myself into the tight gap and then felt every emotion slip from my fingertips and leave me empty. I was pressed into a ball with my head between my knees and my arms wrapped around my legs in a tight hug. I could feel the rhythmic flow of blood through my head in the silence of my hiding place.

My eyes were pressed closed, but water still managed to leek from them. Things had been going too smoothly, and now the whole world seemed to crumble in the blink of an eye. The silence tormented me, finally allowing me to hear my thoughts. My clothes began to turn red from the blood that trickled from my knuckles.

"Ary!" I didn't want to know who it was. I wished for whoever came to fetch me to leave, to walk back up the trail and forget about my existence until I could figure something out. "Ary, come back! I'm sorry. Can we please talk?"

It was Juris.

I pressed my body into an even smaller ball and let time pass and his voice faded into whispers. By the red glow of the rocks near my hideout, I could tell that it was sunset. The day was dying, staining everything red. The moon would rise soon enough at the price of the dead star. I closed my eyes so as not to stare at the gory rocks, but even then the insides of my eyelids were tinted with the blood of the innocent water element. Ren. What would she have done in this situation? Would she have told me?

My mind drifted into a vacant state in which I lost all sense of reality. At one point, I could have sworn I heard the boys walking down the trail. But when I tried to break free from my illusions, all I could hear was the wind whispering through the needles of the pine trees.

When I tried to move out of my small nook, I needed to use more energy to change my position than I thought I would. I could feel my joints creak and crack as I struggled to remove myself from the gap, but it was impossible. I was too weak to carry out the task. I slumped back into position, fully aware that I was more visible now.

I could used a bit more solitude.

* * *

When I opened my eyes a second time, I heard a voice right next to me. "Come here." A pair of arms found me and gripped me tightly. I couldn't help him pull me out of the nook, because I would have squished his arm against the rock. Instead, I allowed him to pull me out and carry me. I felt too weak to walk, so I was grateful to rest against his chest. It was Aeolos.

"How did you find me?" I whispered, still feeling a little groggy.

The stars danced around the moon, as he cradled me in his arms. I could feel his cold skin beneath his shirt.

"Well, I watched you run down the path and then saw where you disappeared into the rocks. There aren't many crevasses large enough to hide a teenage girl." He spoke softly in my ear, probably to avoid ticking me off again.

I was still angry, but I hadn't drunk anything in a while, and I still felt light headed from the long nap I had taken. With my energy low, I could barely think. I had run off, pissed at the world because my necklace was broken and because Aiden was sick. But I still didn't know what was wrong with him. I started to cry again. It felt as if I had no control over my feelings anymore; I manifested them before I felt them. I wiped my tears with the back of my hand.

"What's wrong with him? What did you do?" I pleaded.

"We didn't do anything to him." I hated how he was so calm, how his stride didn't falter under the pressure of my questions or my weight.

"What does he have?"

"Do you want to know?" Al's gaze was heavy on me. He took in the tears, the messy hair, and the broken girl without looking away. Of course I wanted to know. The time passed silently, giving away Al's inner debate about whether he should tell me or not. He gave in. Al wrapped his arms around me even tighter, bringing me closer to his body in a lame attempt to protect me from the truth. "He has strong hallucinations and voices in his head. He also runs the risk of suicide attempts. If he were human we could give him antipsychotics, but they don't work on elements."

I pictured Aiden with the knife to his throat. Only millimeters from death, his hand had been so steady. It wasn't fair. Why him?

"What do you mean, if he were human?" I asked, not sure I really wanted to know the answer.

Al pressed his lips into a small line and kept his eyes glued to the ground ahead of us. He probably couldn't see much in the dim moonlight, but his footing was steady. "As elements, we can't suffer from human illnesses. Human medicine doesn't work on us. We have a different constitution. This means that human medicine is useless and whatever Aiden has is not natural. " He paused to see if I understood. "Someone caused this alteration in his brain."

"You're lying!" My voice cracked, as I realized the truth in his words. They matched Aiden's behavior.

"I wish I was," Al replied.

What was supposed to I do now? I just discovered that my companion in this adventure, my crush, my friend, had had his mind toyed with. Aiden couldn't be cured. He would never be normal again. He would never know peace. If what they had done to his brain couldn't be cured, it meant that it would last throughout his lifetime until death, or maybe even causing it. I cried more fervently now, because that's what one does when you find out something like this—you cry. Al didn't budge, as I pressed my face into his shirt, crumpling it under my fists, and drenching him with salty water.

"Why him?"

Al cleared his throat and pulled my hair back from my face. "I'm sorry."

"It's not your fault."

"No, but I know how you feel about him. Juris told us." He shifted his weight. Was he uncomfortable? My weeping subsided. "This must be very hard for you."

I placed my hands against my chest, removing them from his shirt, and curled them beneath my chin. Whenever the recent scene replayed in my head, I squeezed my eyes shut, hoping that it would stop.

"Will you do me a favor?" I asked.

The night air blew around us. I needed to feel the crystal on my chest, digging into my skin, but I was well aware of its absence. I wanted to hold on to the cloth of the dark blue shirt Al was wearing. I wanted to disappear in the shadow of the trees. I wanted to go back in time. If I had known that this would happen when we escaped, then I wouldn't have wanted to leave.

Al loosened his grip on me and lowered me to the ground. He wrapped his arm around my waist to make sure I wouldn't topple over. He slipped his free hand into mine.

"Whatever you want."

"Don't let him kill himself."

I felt the calluses in his hand and on his fingers. Someone had caused this; someone had messed with Aiden's brain. They wanted him sick. They knew what would happen if he escaped. They gave him a limited amount of medicine. They knew that his would happen. The Golden Four had planned all of this.

"Of course I can do that, but you have to grant me one favor in return."

I wasn't in the mood for joking around. "What should I do?"

"Nothing yet...I'm going to keep my favor for later. I think you should get some sleep."

We entered a smaller cave that ran straight into the mountain side. No secondary tunnels or gaps could have been used as rooms. Demetrio, Kenneth, Leith, and Juris were sitting on the ground in a circle. Their faces were long, and their heads were bowed. It looked as if everyone was in the same cloudy mood I was in. When they saw me, Demetrio looked as if he was about to stand up, Juris sank in even deeper into the rock wall he was leaning against, Leith held his head, and Kenneth turned to look at me.

Suddenly, Kenneth looked a lot like Aiden.

"He wants to talk to you," Kenneth said.

I didn't have to think it through. I walked into the cave until I met a male figure sitting next to a lantern. The lantern cast all types of shadows over the rocky wall, a nightmare for anyone who suffered hallucinations. Aiden was looking down at his hands as they played their usual game with each other. The natural crimson highlights in his hair shone under the light. Only when I sat down next to him did he acknowledge my presence. My weight sank into the thin pile of blankets they had placed beneath him in a weak attempt at a mattress.

"I tried to tell you."

"I know."

He fixed his gaze on me, searching for something. Did he expect me to stop liking him? To be horrified that a nightmare was living inside his head?

"You don't get it."

I wrapped both of my hands around his, so I could feel the warmth that came from him. On many occasions, I had longed for his warmth, a symbol of comfort. I wondered if sometimes he wished for the touch of my fingers. "Help me understand."

I thought he would hold back like he usually did, but he didn't. He withdrew his hands from my grip and grabbed the sides of his head.

"The voices never shut up. They talk constantly, never letting me sleep, not letting me think. They say horrible things, and they speak so loud." He paused to calm himself. "I don't know what thoughts are mine and what thoughts are theirs. They've told me to kill you. How can I be at peace when my inner voices tell me to hurt the person I care for the most? To take your life away...And the worst part is that sometimes I feel that I really want to kill you, that I would enjoy it."

Aiden took a deep breath. I could see the sweat gather on his forehead. I couldn't even imagine how much effort he was putting in this.

"I didn't want to hit you. I never would have hit you." He looked into my eyes, allowing me for the first time in a long while, to see into him. His golden irises that were once were foggy shone with a renewed brightness. His pupils relaxed, widening a bit more. I could imagine the voices speaking in the darkness of his mind, tricking him to perceive reality in a different way than it actually was.

"I knew that I had this in the training center. I was walking back from the doctor when I first met you. They told me that I was sick, and that I would be able to receive treatment to be cured. But until then, I had to take medicine daily. I thought I would be cured. That's why I didn't tell you earlier. I thought that if I told you, you..." His voice cracked. I tried to finish the sentence in my head, but there were so many ways he could finish it. "If I told you, you wouldn't want to..."

Aiden lost control over himself. It was his turn to cry. Of course, when I thought I didn't have any more tears, they magically appeared. I hugged him, or he hugged me. I didn't know who was consoling whom anymore. He forced himself to speak, as I rubbed my palms over his back.

"Then you told me you wanted to leave, that we had to escape," he continued. "I had no other option but to leave...It started in the forest. I thought I could keep it under control, but I couldn't. At first, they started talking to me. They're always there. Always. I couldn't sleep. I didn't want to tell anyone. That's when they started to persuade me to hurt you. Then I saw it for the first time—my shadow, my darkest side revealed. I can see it everywhere I go. There is no place to keep it at bay."

Every word he was saying was making him suffer even more. I shouldn't have made him tell me so much. If I let him continue, it would be the end of us both. I didn't want to cry anymore. I didn't want to see him cry either. So I took his face in my hands and kissed him.

I had wanted to do this for so long that at first, I savored the kiss. His hands rested on my back as I kissed his cheeks first, so I could distract him, shut him up. Then I kissed the tears that marked his cheeks. The salty flavor covered my lips so when our mouths finally met, we both tasted grief. We were desperate for getting back what we thought was lost. My fingers ran over the warm, smooth skin of his jaw. He tangled my hair at the base of my neck.

We parted momentarily to catch our breaths but then came together again. Even though my eyes were closed, I could still see him through the thin skin of my eyelids. My hands mimicked his as they ran through his hair and pushed him closer to me. His lips moved slowly on mine, without any urge to push things further. We were both content with the lazy motion and the strong beats of our hearts as they fought to match the other's rhythm.

Deciding it would be prudent to hold back before it got too out of hand, I pulled back. Aiden tried to pull me back against him, but I resisted, raising my fingers to my mouth. They sizzled; the sound that came when something cool met with something scorching hot. A tingling feeling inside of me began to spread all over. My insides swirled, and my head spun with giddiness. A strange emotion bloomed inside me, the perfect blend of heartbreak and bliss.

Chapter 33

After the kiss, I didn't want to leave him. Knowing what Aiden was going through, I couldn't possibly leave him alone in the dark. We lay together and turned off the lantern. Even though we were deep into the cave, we feared that leaving the light on would attract unnecessary attention. I had fallen asleep in his arms, my head tucked beneath his chin and our legs intertwined.

Aiden held onto me for a while before the demons corrupted his thoughts. I woke several times during the night and saw him pull away from me to a far corner, where he would mumble and argue with himself. I knew there was nothing I could do when he screamed. The rest of the group had decided to sleep near the mouth of the cave to give us as much privacy as they could, but they probably heard Aiden's accusations of attempted murder and how he was fighting off the idea of suicide.

The sun had just risen when I woke up and found Aiden curled up in a ball beside me. His hands were pressed into tight fists, exposing the bruises and cuts on his knuckles. I looked down at my own hands and saw the same cuts on my own skin. Noticing the calm expression on his face, I stood up and left him, so he could enjoy the peace of mind sleep brought.

I walked slowly to the mouth of the cave, making sure I didn't step on any of the relaxed limbs of the sleeping elements. I sat down on a flat rock that looked out to the forest below. We were only a couple of feet above the treetops, minimizing the view I had had before but allowing me to see nature without the training center mocking me in the distance. Freedom was so close. All we had to do was meet their leader, and then we would make our way out of the Golden Four's realm. But what would I do once I was out? My power was released and couldn't be contained, and there was a large probability that the Golden Four would keep searching for us.

Did I want to join the rebellion? Leith said that he could work with me and help me understand what I was capable of. But what about Aiden? The medicine the Golden Four had given him to taunt me had run dry, and Demetrio and his group didn't know what to do with him. Antipsychotics couldn't be the answer, since human medicine didn't work on elements. They would have to alter his brain, but they didn't know how.

Now, more than ever, I had reasons to fight against the Golden Four. They burned Aiden, poisoned Skyler and I, killed Ren, and then blackmailed me to finish their job. They whipped Skyler and messed with Aiden's brain. What was stopping me from fighting against them, from using my power to help the resistance? Why couldn't I say yes as easily as Juris?

I put my head in my hands and tried to clear my mind, hoping that once the muddled thoughts were gone, the answer would appear out of the haze. When I looked up again, I could see grey clouds slowly inching over the forest, pulsing with life, threatening to rain down on it. I stared into the washed-out waves that rolled above. "It's going to rain." I could hear Aiden's voice in my head, a memory from before we crossed the river.

"I'm sorry I didn't tell you," Juris apologized weakly, as he sat on the ground next to me. That was something typical of Juris, quick to hurt others, but he could barely gather enough courage to ask for forgiveness. "I guess that if that would've happened to me, I would have preferred you to tell me something."

I turned to him, but he was staring at the dirt to avoid my gaze. If I hadn't slept so well, I would have probably been a lot angrier. But I knew that there was nothing we could do now but wait. "You knew I was going to find out anyway, so why did you decide to postpone it? Don't you know that finding out later, rather than sooner, is always worse? I felt deceived. I thought that we were in this together."

"Seriously, how did you expect me to react?" His arms tensed as he spoke.

I played with my hair, looking into the cave for a moment to see if anyone had woken up. "I want you to tell me everything. I don't want secrets anymore, because the only people I have now are you and the rest of them. If something stands between us, we will never make it." I kept my voice low so that our conversation would stay only between us.

His dark skin and green shirt made him look like a tree. His hair was longer now, and it lightly brushed his forehead. "What are you thinking about?"

"What do you mean?"

"Well, you sound as if you are planning something, and that was the intro."

The only thing I had been thinking about was Aiden. He was sick. He kissed me. I wanted to find a cure for him. He kissed me. He had to get better. But how?

"I want to save him."

Our eyes met. Juris felt sad for me; I could see it with so much clarity, and it made me sick.

"We all do," he offered.

"But you're not doing anything about it." I could feel my words digging deep into him. Yes, at times like this I would use his guilt in my favor.

He turned quickly to silence me. "Don't do it, Ary. I know you are hurt, but don't act like I do. Please." The intensity in his stare kept me from saying anything.

"You'd never understand," I began to say when I thought I was about to plummet back into the darkness that lived in me. Aiden would never be cured. Before, it was a statement, a thought, but now it turned into a reality. I could see it each time I saw him. Only now did I comprehend the meaning of Aiden's words: "You don't get it."

Juris snorted. "I've been through everything you have. Try me."

I grabbed a small pebbled that rested next to my foot; its surface was full of edges and irregularities. I threw it as hard as I could and watched it tumble down the mountainside.

"Stop being an ass and admit you have no freaking idea about how it feels. You'll never know."

"You think I don't care. But let me ask you one thing: Who do you think he asked, no, begged for this whole issue to be kept a secret? He threatened me to keep it a secret. He didn't want you to know, because he didn't want you to worry. I never saw him so afraid of himself. He. Burned. You. You call me stuck up, that may or may not be true, but don't act like the center of the world or a stupid know-it-all."

Once the words were out and rearranged themselves in the right order in my head, I understood what he was saying. Aiden told Juris that he had burned me. Why? To convince Juris to hide the truth? I began to stand up, when Juris pulled me back down.

"I'm sorry."

"Why did you say that?" It was all that I could manage to utter.

He held my arm, afraid that if he let go, I would leave before he even had the chance to explain. "For the same reason you called me an ass."

"How did we come to this? How is it that our lives have changed so much in so little time?" I closed my eyes and felt the need to give up. But what would I sacrifice? What part of me would I have to cut loose?

Juris rubbed his chin and exhaled softly. "I always think that breaking down is a blessing. We get to improve ourselves as we put the pieces back together again."

I took in Juris's words and found myself surprised that they came out of his mouth. If I put myself back together differently, I had to change; I had to improve myself. But I wasn't ready for so much change. I couldn't leave Nicole. Even though I was her, she did not belong to me, not anymore. Her family, friends, habits, and traditions were all in the past and had no place in my life now.

I sucked in my cheeks, as I realized what I had to let go. Who I had to let go...Nicole.

I closed my eyes, as I stored her in the deepest corner of my mind. She fit perfectly and didn't struggle as I closed the door. There was a vast emptiness where she once stood. Everything related to her, her worries and hopes, had once occupied this space. But in the new space, I could see my own hopes and worries bloom. Aiden—his name was etched onto so many petals.

"How do I do it by myself? I can't take so much pain." I turned away from my own thoughts and reemerged in reality.

Juris put a hand on my knee, his large fingers touching me for the first time. "That's why you have friends." He sensed my discomfort and removed his hand. "I tried to do it alone, at the training center, but you can't do it alone and succeed."

I stood and walked to the edge of the cave, staring at the rolling clouds. I could see how they were full of humidity, pregnant with rain. Their bellies were tinted a darker shade of grey.

"I think I'm going to join you," I finally said.

He stood up. "What?" I didn't even need to turn around to sense his confusion.

"I am willing to join the rebellion. I can't stay indifferent after all they've done." I tried to reassure myself that I was making the right choice. But what if I was making the wrong one? There was no way to know for certain unless I chose.

The boys woke up as if summoned by my statement. Juris proudly announced that I would join them, and I was suddenly looked upon with approval. The boys chatted about how important it was that I agreed. If I learned how to use my power correctly, I could be quite useful for the rebellion. But as they spoke about my power, I wondered if it was my power convincing them that I was such a good idea. Since I had no control over it and I didn't know what I was capable of, I observed them closely.

I didn't notice anything strange, as we placed all the blankets at the very end of the cave, along with the water bottles and lanterns. Aiden woke up last and didn't interact much with us, but at least he forced a smile for me every now and then to let me know that he was fighting and still alive.

Walking down the mountainside and back into the forest refreshed many unpleasant memories. My shirt was still stained with the blood I had shed after punching the stupid tree, but walking through the woods made me question if it was my blood or Ren's. Her name echoed in the forest—the cry of a ghost hidden in the songs of the birds and the moaning of the trees. It sent a shiver down my spine.

"I think we should start gathering large branches we find on the ground. If there aren't very many, we can always break off the dead ones from sick trees," Al called from ahead, as he scanned the ground.

I turned to Kenneth to ask him why, but he already sensed the question coming. "We need to make an arch, something like a doorway that we can use as our passage into the human world." Kenneth and I watched as the boys walked off into the forest. Aiden was left sitting on the ground next to a pair of backpacks.

"Want to fetch branches with me?" Kenneth asked.

I turned away from Aiden and smiled politely. "Sure." We made our own trail by shifting rocks and placing broken twigs in certain patterns so we would be able to return to the exact place. I thought it would be easier to find broken branches in winter, but there seemed to be a scarcity of injured trees.

"What are we going to do once we enter the human world?" I asked, placing my weight on a weak branch.

Kenneth and I had decided to break one off since we weren't going to find many scattered on the ground. He pulled the branch toward the ground, bending the wood and testing its resistance.

"Well, since all of you are going to come with us, we're going to go to our meeting spot where a couple of other elements will pick us up in cars and drive us to the nearest dock. We already have a small cargo boat that will be waiting for us, and that'll take us to Mexico. Once we're there and out of the Golden Four's territory, we can take a plane to one of the biggest realms on earth—the Amazon. Of course, it's getting smaller because of humans' contaminating activities, but it's still pretty big. The second biggest is the Sahara Desert."

The branch cracked and protested against the aggression, but we only needed one branch from the tree, so we kept at it. I helped Kenneth pull down on the branch and finally snap it.

"Are there many elements in the resistance?" I asked.

"You mean in South America? Yeah, tons. We don't kill off elements to ensure power," he managed to say before the branch fell on top of him. As he hit the ground, thunder rumbled through the air. I jumped, startled by the unexpected sound. "Sorry," he chuckled, as he wiped the dirt off of his pants.

"Why did you say sorry?" I furrowed my eyebrows while dragging the branch back in the direction we came.

Kenneth's face became serious for a moment and then recomposed itself into a wicked grin. "I made that sound." Noticing my confusion, he offered, "Just let me show you." He pulled his shirt over his head.

"Wow, hold your horses." I covered my eyes just in case he was taking something else off as well. Why was he taking off his clothes? "Kenneth, put it back on."

He laughed. "It's just my shirt."

When I opened my eyes, I was staring at Kenneth's lanky body. He looked a bit too skinny for his height, but it gave him a geeky charm. It didn't take long for me to realize that whenever his heart beat under his chest, it had the faintest sound of thunder. Why hadn't I heard it before?

"My body does this every time a storm is coming. The closer and stronger the storm gets, the louder the noise. Come closer."

He invited me to gape freely at his chest. I moved closer and placed my hand over the spot where the noise was coming from. I could feel the vibrations beneath his skin. My hand pulled away when small sparks, trapped beneath his flesh, flew out of his heart and disappeared into his veins. With each beat, the thunder followed the lighting that had shot out of his heart just moments ago.

Too afraid to touch him again, I wondered if he could electrocute me. "So what exactly do you do?"

He flicked his finger at the sky and a terrible, deep sound echoed from the clouds above us. When my skeleton shook, I couldn't help laughing as well. Kenneth seemed to blush a bit, as he picked up his shirt from the ground. "Thanks. It's not really useful, but I can control lightning too."

"Not useful?" I gaped.

"Compared to the others. I can't bring someone back from the dead or heal anyone..."

I raised my hand in the air, stopping him midsentence. "Leith can resurrect people?"

"Yup."

And here I thought that having an involuntary power was pretty powerful, but I couldn't save anyone, control a storm, heal, or do whatever Al did. What did he do?

"And what about Al?"

Kenneth grinned, as he grabbed the tree branch. "Maybe you should ask him. But it's not half as interesting as mine." He winked and continued to pull at the tree's broken limb.

It didn't take long to drag the branch back to where Aiden sat. We met a small pile of twigs and medium-sized pieces of wood. Aiden seemed relaxed with his head tilted to the sky and his eyes closed. I thought it would be prudent to let him enjoy himself, while Kenneth and I started building the arch.

We chose a small, clear area where we would build the frame of the doorway. One of the backpacks was full of tools that would help us build. We dug two small, deep holes into the ground and slipped the longest branches into them. We made sure that the branches were perfectly straight before we filled in the holes. Aiden offered to help us support the branches with smaller ones. We tied these together with wire.

As the other boys brought more branches, some stayed to help us build. Soon, only Al was searching for the more branches. At first, the process was slow and required a lot of patience, as we placed and removed different sticks. Demetrio insisted that it had to be constructed just right or the rock would not be able to create the passage to the human realm.

I remembered what Era had told me about the passageways to the human world. There were two different ways to pass through realms: natural doorways that contacted both realms and doorways that could be created with talismans.

Over the arch, Leith and Demetrio made a ring out of twigs where the talisman would be placed. They used several roots to create a net that would hold it above the doorway. When Al returned with his last branch, he found a completed arch. It had taken us half a day to build, so I wondered where Al had been this whole time.

When I asked, Leith answered for him. "He does things in his own time."

I eyed the air element as I retrieved a water bottle. Building the frame left me parched and anxious to drink.

"Ready to open the doorway?" Demetrio inquired while pulling out a small box from the second backpack. It wasn't very elegant; simple would have been the best word to describe it. The box was made out of metal with no decoration. It reminded me of the PF2 and the training center. But as his dark fingers curled around the lid and peeled it off, all my thoughts withered away. The talisman looked like a very large emerald. It was roughly the size of my fist, and it looked heavy. I doubted the arch's ability to hold the rock in the mesh made of roots, but when Demetrio placed the glittering stone into the net, it stayed in place and began to glow.

"I hope you're prepared to meet Beth," Aeolos spoke from beside me.

Chapter 34

As soon as the talisman began to glow, small vines shot out from the ground and began curling around the arch. They grew up and around the arch, stretching toward the middle where they met and knotted together. Once every inch of space was occupied with vines, the vines began to glow as well. The light that came from the stone and the doorway began to get brighter. I could feel my retinas burning in the backs on my eyes, so I shut them. Aiden began to yell and Juris cursed.

Then, everything went silent.

I dared myself to open my eyes and search the silence of the small clearing. The doorway no longer glowed. The vines were gone, and the only thing left was the rickety group of branches tethered together with silver wire and a stone stuck on what looked like a dream catcher. Where was the portal, the passage to another realm? I couldn't help feeling disappointed.

"Did it work?" Juris inquired, as he uncovered his eyes.

Everyone remained silent. I looked at the faces of the elder elements. Confusion? No. Al's jaw was set, but a faint smile played on his lips. It worked. But if the passage was open, then why wasn't anything happening? Shouldn't this Beth stride out into the clearing from the human realm and take us to Mexico?

"Guys, I honestly don't think that this..."

"Shh!" Al cut me off by raising a finger in my direction. "Wait for it."

I could hear the birds singing in the distance and saw a large animal walking near us. Nothing was happening. With a broken neutralizer and a mentally tortured fire element, I could not afford patience.

"Aeolos, nothing is happening." I glared at him.

"What's not happening?" A strange voice spoke from in front of me.

"You missed it," Al mumbled, as I turned to meet Beth. She stood in front of the doorway with a satchel hanging over her shoulder.

She dropped it onto the ground and looked at us. "Where's the water child?" Her black hair was streaked with white, and her round eyes were noticeably brown. Nothing about her looked like us, nothing at all.

She didn't belong to any element. She wasn't a half-element either.

Demetrio answered first. "She was killed."

"What are you?" My thoughts somehow left my mouth as words. My brain couldn't process the fact that there was a human standing in the element realm.

Beth glanced at me and narrowed her eyes as they scanned my body. I could see how they stopped when they saw the blood on my shirt.

"And who killed her?" she asked while walking forward. Her knee high brown boots crushed the broken twigs we had peeled from a few branches. Jeans were snug, showing her fit legs, and an army green coat, one size too big, hung over her body. It had been forever since I had seen an outfit so human-looking. I couldn't help gawking.

I instinctively longed to take a step back and keep my distance from the stranger, but if Beth was in charge of the rebellion, I did not want to look like a coward. I stood my ground, as she walked in my direction.

"The Monarch of Water," I stated, making sure that my voice didn't give away my emotions.

"Monarch," She spat the word from her mouth as if it were venom. "You must mean tyrant." When she was close enough, she gripped my shirt and exposed the stains to everyone. "Then whose blood is this?" I could feel her growing suspicious, and I doubted that she wouldn't be skeptical when I told her why.

"Mine."

Everyone remained silent. Out of the corner of my eye, I could see Kenneth, Demetrio, and Leith looking at her with respect and keeping their postures straight. Al was watching, but he didn't seem as interested in what was happening. Juris looked as afraid as I was. By the expression on his face, he also must have wondered how a human could be standing in front of us. I noticed that Aiden was standing and watching the scene, but his gaze was half gone. He seemed to be staring off into another dimension. At least his face was flat and showed no emotion rather than being disfigured by the voices in his head.

"Doing what?" Now that Beth was up close, I could see the wrinkles that were carved into her skin. They made her expression a continuous frown. She could have been near my mother's age.

I raised my hands from my sides and turned them in front of me. "I punched a tree."

"Once?"

"No."

One of her eyebrows rose, and the corner of her mouth turned upward. "And why would you punch a tree?"

I hid my cracked knuckles behind my back and glanced over at Aiden. He came back to the present and began playing with his hands like he used to do all the time. Aiden was uneasy with Beth's presence.

Demetrio, knowing that I wouldn't want to explain myself to this stranger, told her the truth they had hidden from me.

"Aiden's brain has been altered, so he suffers from hallucinations and paranoia."

As I heard the facts once more, I couldn't help but want to crumble to the ground. He said it so calmly and easily, without knowing what he actually meant.

"So the tyrants modified his brain activity?" Beth inquired, looking over at the Aiden.

Demetrio paused and met my gaze before answering. "Yes."

"Why did you even keep him?" Beth wrinkled her nose. "He's marked. Useless."

"What?" I roared. Beth hardly jumped at my growl. "He's sick."

She pushed a fallen strand of hair behind her ear and stood straighter. "He is not sick. He has been played with by the Golden Four, and I want nothing of theirs prancing along with me. I take runaways with me, not experiments."

"I want to go back to the caves. She's going to shoot me," Aiden declared.

My hands balled up into fists. How could she say that in front of him, especially after everything he had been through, everything we had been through? "He is not an experiment. You can cure him; reverse what they did."

Beth chuckled. "You must think me mad to open someone's skull and poke around in his brain without any plan. I have no idea what they did to him or how they did it. I will definitely not take some element that is of no use to the rebellion."

I took a deep breath and gave myself a moment to control my impulses. "Then you will not be taking me. I go where he goes." The thought was clear in my head. I would stick by Aiden, use the tracking device, and let the Golden Four pick us up. He would have done the same if I were in his place.

Beth turned around and grabbed her backpack. "I'm fine with that. I'll be taking the boys and your fellow earth element. What's your name?"

"Juris." He wasn't looking at her anymore; instead, his eyes were glued on me. His mouth hung open and his eyes bulged. I didn't expect him to understand why I needed to stay.

"Beth, I think your opinion would be different once you..." Leith began.

"Once I what, Leith?" Beth growled menacingly, as she opened her satchel. She must not have imagined that things would go this way. Did she think that all four of us would be here, and that she could take us to her rebellion with the others and use us?

Leith took a brave step forward and cleared his throat. "Beth, you don't know everything we've discovered..." His voice trailed off into silence, letting her take the initiative to keep the conversation going.

She crouched down as she rummaged through the contents of her satchel. "What do I need to know?" When she stood, she held a thin metal object and some matches in one hand and a gun in the other.

I instinctively took a step back while Leith spoke. "They have been threatened by the Golden Four to hand us in, so they carry a tracking device. Also, we..."

"They have a tracking device here with them?" Beth raised the gun, and I ran over to Aiden.

He trembled in my arms and whispered, "She's going to shoot me."

"What the hell, Leith!" Beth exclaimed. "You let them bring a tracking device, and you bring me a faulty element?" Her frustration was evident as it marked her pale forehead. She placed a finger over the trigger and aimed it at Aiden and me.

I turned Aiden around and hugged him. He didn't like the idea of turning his back to the gun, but at least he didn't have to see it. I stared into his eyes and whispered softly to him that everything was under control, and no one was going to shoot him.

I could hear Leith trying reason with Beth. "She has an involuntary power. Do you know what it would be like to use an involuntary power against the Golden Four? How much more powerful would we become? And imagine stealing it from the Golden Four!"

It. I wasn't Ary to them, I was an involuntary power; a weapon they could use. It was funny how they wanted me so badly without actually knowing anything about my power.

"What can she do?" Beth's voice suddenly became a lot calmer and even a bit interested.

Al's voice came from further away. "We aren't sure, but whatever it is, it's useful."

Beth sighed, and I could hear the gun click again. I peered over Aiden's shoulder and saw her sit down on the ground and play with the weapon.

"So, what do you want me to do?" she asked. "I can't take him, but she won't come unless he does."

I let Aiden go, but he didn't want to let me go. He held me close, and his eyes were shut. The creases on his forehead and his furrowed brow were my only clues that his mind was fooling him once more. I let him hold me.

So, now Beth wanted me. Knowing that she could use me, I suddenly became valuable. I still wanted to fight against the Golden Four. I had every reason to want to join the rebellion, but I couldn't leave without Aiden. It was almost as if the Golden Four had done this, so I couldn't turn against them.

"No," I gasped, as I realized what was happening. There had always been a larger plan behind this, something much bigger. Of course, the Golden Four wouldn't just let us walk away with no guarantee of coming back. That's why they played with Aiden's brain. They knew. But how? How could they know that I would fall for Aiden and refuse to leave him behind? They had killed Ren, and they also would kill my family...Nicole's family.

I felt the air get thin and my lungs unable of retaining it. I could hear the faint voice of worry, but I couldn't concentrate over the roar of my thoughts. They played you. You fell for it. You let them do this.

"Ary, Ary, what's wrong?" I recognized the voice, but I couldn't identify the person it belonged to.

The Golden Four gave Aiden the flask to let me know that they could cure him. They knew I couldn't leave him behind. They gave me the tracking device so I could return. But they were letting Juris go. Was that why they killed Ren? So she couldn't leave as well? So, all they wanted was Aiden and I back in the city. All of this was probably to get information. I knew where the rebels were, and I knew how to get there. I knew what their goal was. And the resistance wouldn't be able to kill me, because they wanted my power.

"They knew!" My voice sounded hoarse.

Juris grabbed my face and tried to look into my eyes, but I closed them. How foolish could I have been to accept escaping? "Ary, what is going on?" His large hands lacked Aiden's temperature.

When I looked up at Beth and saw her concerned gaze, I knew I was right.

"They used us," I whispered to him.

Juris stretched his arms and forced me to meet his gaze. "Who used us?"

His irises danced around his pupils in a green haze. They looked like the talisman. "The Golden Four knew that this would happen all along. They knew Beth wouldn't accept Aiden, and that I wouldn't leave him. That's why we have a tracking device. So they can find me once I made my decision." He let go of me.

Leith's head popped up from behind Juris. "But we won't let you return. The probability of finding another element like you is very low."

Beth kept on staring at me without muttering a word, while the others tried to come up with a solution. Al didn't even bother to persuade me; he saw my determination in the way I held Aiden's hand. I wouldn't let go. Ever.

When Beth decided to speak, everyone let her pass until she faced me. "I will not let you go, not with your power. But I can't force you to come either. What I can do is make an agreement." Aiden tightened his grip on my hand. "You become part of the rebellion and work for us from Arcane. You have to try to fit in and learn as many things as possible. This way, you can work with us and be with him, but I cannot promise to claim Aiden when the time comes." Her voice was low and steady. I could feel her approaching the topic cautiously so as not to frighten me away.

We both knew, though, that I had full control over the agreement. There was nothing that she wouldn't do to ensure that I was on her side in the rebellion.

"You include Aiden as well, or I will not agree," I stated.

"But he is of no use to me."

"But I am."

She sucked in her cheeks and stared at our joined hands. "Fine, but you must give Aeolos a full report each week of the activity in the city. I will make sure that the rebellion inside will contact you so you are not alone, and so they can keep an eye on you. If I don't find your information useful, or if I find out that you are going behind our backs, we are cutting Aiden from the deal. Am I clear?"

She raised the long metal rod with the sharp edge. There was a series of buttons on the side that made me question the purpose of the object. She promised me security and that Aiden would be included. But I had to report to Al...was he coming?

"How do I report to Al?"

Al spoke from behind the mass of elements that had gathered in front of Aiden and me. His grey eyes never wavered as he explained. "I'm a drifter. I have the natural ability of passing through realms: the element realm, the human realm, and the dream realm."

My mouth dropped open. "There is a realm of dreams?" Just when I thought I had begun to understand everything.

"The spheres created it to help guide the humans. They wouldn't allow elements to communicate directly with them, but they allowed us to use dreams to grant visions or provide guidance." His voice was nonchalant, matching his casual posture. "But we use it to pass messages between elements and to steal information from the Golden Four."

This was the second time I had heard of the spheres, and I still didn't understand who or what they were. Before I could ask, as if Beth were reading my mind, she signaled to the boys.

"Enough talking," she ordered.

Kenneth and Demetrio grabbed Juris and pulled down the neck of his shirt, while Beth struck him with the long metal device. Juris howled as the strange piece of equipment marked the skin on his back.

Al grabbed me and gave me an apologetic look while holding a damp cloth up to my face. He must have grabbed it from Beth's satchel when I was negotiating with her. Leith did the same with Aiden. I didn't pass out, but I could feel my awareness dim and my brain go foggy.

Everything around me moved slowly, but I couldn't grasp what was happening. I could feel the hot sting of something on my back and then being placed on the ground, leaning on something warm. Someone circled me, holding something thin and long that eventually ran out. I closed my eyes and tried to concentrate. All the sounds around me blurred into a confusing symphony; it made me dizzy and forced me to open my eyes. I saw a bright green glow drench everything in its light and then quickly vanish.

The only image my brain could retain was the symbol I had seen on Juris's back—a circle with a leaf in the middle. *That's the rebellion's symbol*, my brain cleared out the doubt.

You belong to the rebellion now.

Chapter 35

When I recovered from the substance I had inhaled, I realized that an object was sitting in my lap. The tracking device was lit and beeping—a blue light on the surface flashed with every signal it sent. I could feel Aiden's heat, since our backs were pressed together and we were tied to each other.

"Why are you going back if I'm the one who's sick?" His voice sounded just like it did when he woke up. He stirred, probably realizing that he was tied.

I leaned my head against his back. "You may be sick, but that doesn't mean that I would let you go on your own. Remember the night we escaped? We have to stay in pairs..." Aiden had been present when I made the agreement with Beth, but I questioned how much he actually took in.

"Are you sick?" He struggled with more strength.

"No," I replied.

I didn't have the patience or strength to wait. I needed to get back so the Golden Four could cure him. There wasn't much I could do, though. The tracking device had already been turned on, and the others had left through the portal. The only thing they left behind was the threshold. I wondered if the searchers would believe me when I told them that when I tried to turn on the tracking device, it had been too late and the rebels escaped.

I wouldn't believe that poor excuse, but it was all I had at the moment. I couldn't tell the searchers that I belonged to the rebellion, but perhaps they would find out when the saw the brand on my back.

Time was hard to tell, since I didn't know how long I had been in this semi-conscious state. The evening light was already disappearing, and the long shadows cast by the sunset took over the forest. If the searchers didn't find us soon, Aiden wouldn't have an easy time keeping the shadows and voices at bay. I could hear him fighting his fears and mumbling to himself.

"Aiden, are you okay?" I kept my voice soft and sweet, so he could pick out my voice from those in his head. Since I still had my head on his back, I could feel the pull of his muscles when he turned his head to the side.

"Can you talk to me, please?" he begged, his breath agitated. His back was sweaty.

I sat up straighter and tried to meet his eyes. "What do you want me to talk about?"

"Anything, something pleasant."

His body was getting warmer and warmer, and I feared that he would erupt into flames, so I tried to think of something I could tell him. But at times like this, the pressure didn't help. Coming up with a pleasant thought was hard, so I decided to tell him random information that might distract him.

"As a human, my favorite possession was a stupid postcard. My father had sent it to me when he was away. He was a soldier then and was constantly deployed. If you saw it now, you wouldn't think much of it. It's just a postcard that he sent for my fourteenth birthday. When I received it, it made me the happiest girl alive. It represented the two most important things..." I paused as I imagined the faded postcard on my night table. It probably didn't even exist anymore, since it was evidence of Nicole and all of that was forgotten, but I kept it hidden in my memory and flipped over the card. Nicole's father's handwriting was impressively neat. Occasionally, it was hard to read since he squished the letters together, but it was very pretty to look at. "...that he thought of me and that he was alive," I finished.

I could hear Aiden's breathing become deeper and slower, more rhythmic. I didn't know if what I said helped or if it was just my voice, so I kept on talking. I told him about the fondest memory I had of Nicole's childhood: spending hours in the library with her mother and then going to have ice cream in the afternoon. I told him about Violet and about Nicole's childhood games. He sat and listened.

It was already night, and I was tired of speaking. I found it strange that no one had come to claim us yet. The Golden Four were supposed to act quickly as soon as I turned on the device, so they could catch the other elements.

The wind picked up, and even I felt cold. I knew that as an element of air I would adapt to the cold easily, and I also had Aiden to warm me. But the breeze bit my cheeks and nose. I could sense the air moving through the trees and its purest state. As I sensed the movement of the wind, I sensed interruption. It wasn't a tree or something that belonged to the forest that contributed to the constant flow, but something foreign.

I inhaled sharply as I realized that the interruption in the flow of air was approaching us, and quickly. In a matter of seconds, I could hear the hard footsteps of imminent company. I imagined the Monarch of Water gliding into the clearing with a wide smile of satisfaction.

But he didn't show up. How could I have thought that a monarch would bother to fetch two runaway elements? Mae marched in front of a dozen of searchers. Two groups of six each carried two large boxes. All of them carried guns and all sorts of darts attached to their chest straps. They wore tight black suits and odd-looking headsets. Their faces were covered, but I could still see the copper-colored hair that sprouted out from their heads.

When Mae raised a hand, they stopped advancing and four searchers approached us. Mae's expression was hard and callous, as she watched them untie us and hold our arms behind our backs. I allowed them to untie us, but when they held me with a strong grip and their fingers dug into my skin, I cried out.

"Mae!" When I called her name, she whipped her head around and glared at me. "They found out. I tried to hold them, but you took so long, they found out and left."

The covered faces kept staring at us when the arms that held me began dragging me toward one of the boxes. I kicked wildly and tried to release myself. Aiden, on the other hands, let them lead him.

"Let me go! I did everything he asked. I did my part!" I protested.

Mae stared at me with ire. "Don't you dare speak of them." She punched me in the stomach, causing me to double over. There was a bit of satisfaction on her part when she saw the pain etched on my face. This wasn't the welcome party I had been expecting.

"Load him into Box 2," she demanded. "I'll take care of her in Box 1." What? They were going to separate us?

"No, he stays with me! Aiden!" I yelled.

Aiden met my eyes, as he walked calmly into the one of the boxes. He was seated in a built-in chair and buckled in with straps that wrapped tightly around his body and didn't allow any movement.

"No!" I jerked even harder against the searchers' strong hold on me. Their nails dug into my skin and they kicked my feet, hoping I would fall over. When my knees made contact with the ground, hot, white pain shot up my legs.

Something cold pressed into the side of my face. A gun. They were going to shoot me. No. No. No. What had I done? No, wrong question. In the whole mess that I had made, what was the trigger for pressing a gun to the side of my face?

"Stay put Aurora, or I will kill you," Mae spat in my face. So, this is how they treated those who controlled the elements of the earth? I was dying to know what Arcane would be like.

"Don't separate us," I pleaded while trying to stay as still as possible.

Mae returned the gun to a clip on her leg. Her fingers pushed my chin skyward. "I guess Wiley was right. Who knows what he sees in you..."

Before I could protest or even move, they tossed me into the small box and strapped me in, as they had done with Aiden. The box was tight, dark, and silent. Being restrained and swaying in the tiny box made me dizzy. My head throbbed as the air inside got thick and heavy. I felt myself becoming tired and weary. I couldn't help but wonder if I had made the right choice. They had only come with two boxes, so they knew it was just Aiden and me. Had I made the wrong choice for us both? Had I sacrificed my freedom in vain? I knew that I wouldn't mind giving up my freedom in exchange for Aiden's health, but by the way they received us, I doubted they would even treat him. My train of thought derailed as the darkness lulled me to sleep.

Part 3

Nina knocked on the door quickly and rearranged her hair before grabbing the golden tray. A small teacup filled with boiling water clattered over the tray as it bumped against the sugar bowl and milk jug. She had never taken tea to someone else, ever, but this was a special occasion, and she wanted to be the one who delivered the drink.

"Come in," the old man answered from behind the large set of double doors.

Nina rarely came to the wing of the Golden Hall that belonged to the Monarch of Air, so she felt a bit uneasy with the colorless walls and mirrored floors. When the doors opened, she strode in with the tray in her hands and tried to act as calm as she could. She hadn't felt so giddy and excited in a long time.

"Good afternoon, Guthrie."

She set the tray on his desk, ignoring the envelope he stuck in the drawer. Guthrie's pen rested in an awkward position over a stack of papers, and the golden wax he used to seal documents was still a warm pool of glimmering honey. He set down his glasses and leaned back in his chair. His continuous state of calmness irritated Nina.

"What brings you around here?" His voice revealed no obvious stress, but some deeper knowledge was laced with the words. Nina couldn't tell if she was just acting paranoid. She turned to his maids and doormen.

"I wish to speak with him in private."

The servants nodded and quickly left the room, glad that they had been liberated from Nina's presence. Once everyone was gone, Nina fixed her gaze on the old man.

"I have some news to give you." Her small hands pushed the tray forward.

His shaky grasp moved slowly and carefully, making sure that he did not even spill the smallest grain of sugar. Nina's patience was running thin, wanting to persuade him to drink his tea, but she held back the urge. It only would make her look more suspicious.

"So you brought me tea."

Nina nodded and took seat in front of him, giving her a front-row view of the show.

"How kind of you."

His gray eyes followed the movements of his hands, as he set the tea bag in the water and added precise amounts of sugar and milk. He stirred the beverage, occasionally bumping the silver spoon against the delicate porcelain.

Clink.

Clink.

Clink.

"Aurora has come back with Aiden and only Aiden." *Nina raised her chin and straightened her back. "So, as you see, the mission was unsuccessful."*

The old man raised the cup to his lips and smelled the steam that rose from the hot tea.

"I wouldn't call it unsuccessful that you got her back. She was the only one you all cared about; the rest are dead to you."

Finally, he took the sip and Nina exhaled. She smiled as he watched him set down the cup.

"You're right."

"Nina, I have learned in my life that my purpose is not to lead the elements to their doom or to their salvation, but to pave the road for those who shall follow me." The old man raised his hands to his head and removed the crown. He set it down next to the tea tray. "You kill me so you can get what you want, but you cannot kill everyone."

He sat still and kept his eyes open as his body stiffened and then slowly turned into a silver dust. A faint breeze born from inside the Golden of Air blew his remains into the wind and out the window where they would roam the atmosphere freely forever.

Chapter 36

I woke up in a small room. It hardly had enough space for the bed and for the door to open comfortably. I was strapped into the bed with six belts; one on each leg, one on each arm, one over my forehead, and one broad strap over my torso. They were treating me as if I were being transported to a mental ward. I tried to test how much I could move in my restraints, when they began unfastening and retracting into little slits built into the bed. Of course, the bed wasn't a typical bed with a mattress, sheets, and pillows. This was more of an uncomfortable metal table. It had a bit of cushioning, but they definitely weren't making an effort to make me comfortable.

The areas of my body that had been under the black straps were red with irritation. Had I fought against being put in here? Was this a truck? There was hardly any shaking or jerking or any sound that indicated I was in a truck. Actually, no vibration was coming from the walls, the floor, or the ceiling. I couldn't feel anything. I wasn't in a car, truck, or train. I thought

I could be in a boat or plane, but I eliminated the thought of a boat because I couldn't feel a rocking motion.

I decided to try my luck by attempting to open the door. It didn't budge. There were no windows or even cracks in the walls. Taking a second glance around the room, I realized it looked like a cell. What if I wasn't in transport but already in Arcane? Were they really going to lock me up? Hadn't I done what the Golden of Water had told me to do?

The door slid open, a thin membrane that slipped into the wall, and revealed a small corridor leading to another door. I took it as a sign to leave the room. When I took a step outside of my tiny living space, the membrane went back into its original position, but I could see through it. Anyone could have been standing outside of my room watching me while I was looking around. The thin door was a wonderful invention, but it was a bit creepy as I imagined a stranger watching me sleep.

The door in front of me opened into a small living room. The floor was white marble with little golden designs. Against the wall was one white couch, which shimmered gold when the light hit it at specific angles, and a dark wooden coffee table with four abstract sculptures on it. Each sculpture represented a different element. The lights were hidden in folds of the ceiling, making the room glow.

"We will be arriving in ten minutes," a voice said. It was a male voice, so at least I knew it wasn't Mae.

No one entered the room, contrary to my expectations, so I gave myself the liberty of sitting on the couch as I pleased. I kicked up my feet and looked around the room for clues about where I was. The coffee table had a small drawer, so I opened it carefully. I was scared that if I jerked it open, one of the sculptures would fall over and shatter.

In the drawer, I discovered a little white square. I didn't know what it was, but it was the size of a small remote control. On it was a clear circle. I tried pressing it, but nothing happened. I ran my finger over the circle, hoping that some idea would pop into my mind, when the wall in front of me began to vanish. I finished tracing the circle as quickly as I could. The wall was no longer there, allowing me to see what was on the other side.

I pressed my face against the transparent wall, as I stared in awe down at a huge plantation. It seemed to go on forever, full of different types of crops. The crops were separated into different sections, and by the looks of it, probably by different climates. But that wasn't the main source of my awe. The fact that all of this was underground really blew my mind away. Whatever I was in was slowing down. Half elements were everywhere, tending the plants and doing their jobs. A few of them, wearing long brown lab coats, walked around holding different items in their hands, stopping here and there. Another group of half elements, wearing grey lab coats, was checking boxes on supports that held up a rocky ceiling. The workers wore different-colored clothing, depending on the sector they were working in.

When I thought this was the only thing I would see, a large, low, white building came into view. It sat in the middle of the plantation. There was an entrance that looked like a garage door; it seemed to be the only way to enter. I tried to think of what could be in the building, when it all vanished behind a smooth metal wall. A large tunnel guided me in the darkness. I grabbed the controller, traced the circle backward, and placed it back where I found it.

I waited silently for a few moments, and then the wall that had turned to glass slid to one side. A pristine platform awaited me. It looked a lot like a high-end subway station. This one, though, had a line of women in dark navy uniforms standing on it. Mae and another woman, who had a card around her neck, stood at the end of the platform.

The woman looked a lot like Mae, but her clothes weren't navy, they were a deep shade purple. She wore thin glasses, which seemed invisible. Only the two lenses were noticeable, the extremely thin wires were hard to see. The card around her neck was black with a gold seal on it, the same seal that was on the marble floors of the room I was in.

"Come forward," she commanded with authority. Her voice and her posture warned me not to mess around.

I obediently began to move in their direction. Walking onto the platform gave me a chilling sensation. I was in Arcane. I was in Arcane. There definitely was no turning back now. I couldn't screw up for Aiden's sake and for my own.

"Stop." Her voice echoed in the empty room. She turned me around and bound my hands with some sort of modern handcuff that fastened around my wrists, giving me little mobility.

While she did this, I looked at the vehicle in which I had been transported. It had a sleek, black, aerodynamic front. The rest of the dark body had slanted and curved sides, nothing like what I had expected from the inside. The whole device was hanging below a metal rail—not hanging, exactly—it seemed to be floating just beneath it. If wheels and straps were attached, then they were invisible. I couldn't imagine how it could possibly be suspended.

I was quickly guided to one of two sets of doors. One pair was tall and silver, while the other was polarized glass. I was headed toward the glass doors. Two security women unlocked and pushed open the doors, and I found myself in a small room with a table and two chairs. I would have thought this a regular room if I hadn't checked out the controller on the monorail device. They didn't need a mirror here; they could just make the wall look transparent from the other side, and I would never find out.

Four escorts stood in each corner of the room; and Mae stood in front of me. The other woman, who had unlocked the door with her card, stood outside, waiting for us. I figured the interrogation would be swift.

"How dare you come back like this?" Mae accused. "You had a task, a mission to carry out; but you have failed the Monarchs and your city. You will have to face the consequences of your choices, and I will not have you whining." Mae slammed her fists against the table, losing her cool.

She straightened up and glared at me. Her hair, which had come loose from her ponytail, looked like little horns had appeared on her head. She obviously hadn't slept well. There were dark shadows under her eyes, and she could barely hold herself up due to exhaustion.

"You have been accused of leaving the city—a serious crime in Arcane—convincing your companions to leave with you, killing searchers, and injuring your protector. Basically, you broke not one but three major rules. You should be dead."

But I wasn't, I was about to say. I kept it to myself. "The Golden of Water knew the risks by sending me to carry out his mission. I tried my hardest, my best, but the rebels found out." I didn't crumple under her stare. I used the truth and altered some facts.

"You don't get it, do you?"

"I do, and I brought information back, so you can capture them and get what you need, not just a couple of teenagers who don't have the slightest clue on what's going on. Everything is not what it seems. I am willing to tell you everything I know. Everything." I spoke my words without guilt, since I knew that the rebellion wouldn't mind. I wouldn't tell Mae the specifics, such as that the rebels were in the Amazon, though they might already know that, or that they were leaving by boat to Mexico.

Mae looked a bit entertained by my outburst. "Go ahead, tell me everything."

The guards, who stood in each corner, sent each other silent messages through their glances. I wished they would just leave, so I could speak to Mae alone, or at least think I was alone, since there was probably someone behind one of the walls.

"They grabbed Juris and said that they would take him out of the Golden Four's realm. They are headed to South America..." I began.

"And you don't think I know that? That they live in the Amazon? Demetrio has the power to heal, and Leith can revive people from the dead. Do you think that we don't know what they have been up to?"

"How do you know?"

Her flattened palms left small halos of haze on the surface of the glass. "Because even though we know the information, we cannot capture them or punish them for their crimes when they are not in our realm!" After speaking, she immediately shut her mouth and looked down at herself, as if she didn't understand how she could have told me so much. "Who do you think you are to even consider that you could deserve so much information?"

I could only think of one reason. "Because I am an element."

"Yes, you are...and you're making your first mistake. I may work for your race, but I do not work for you. I work for them!" She pulled out a card and flipped it over. The emblem appeared once more in front of me—a thick golden line over a white background. The Golden Four. "That's right, and you have to explain some things and try to save your sinking ass from the shipwreck you just caused."

Could she actually speak to me like this? I didn't have to go through this. I wanted to see Aiden. "Why do I have to tell you anything? You probably know everything you need to know already, right?"

"You come back just to use us, and you think we don't know it. I will tell you something, Aurora; there is a reason why we are still a secret to humanity. Do not underestimate us, and don't overestimate yourself. Tell me the reason you let the others escape before we could capture them." She finally sat down and stared at me at eye level. This was much more intimidating than when she was standing up.

Should I tell her? Perhaps they were doing this to Aiden as well, and he had already told them everything. Besides, she said she already knew everything, so lying would just make it worse.

"Look, I was threatened into doing this. The life of my peers and my loved ones were all on the line. Why wouldn't I want to obey the monarchy if I would be responsible for a death if I didn't? I tried my best. I turned on the tracking device when Beth showed up, but Aiden's fragile condition did not help at all. They didn't want to believe us; they said that he was marked, whatever that means." Who said I couldn't mix both the truth and my lies?

"You still are a poor liar," Mae replied. "I admire how forgiving the Golden Four are. They are an example for the rest of us. I would have killed you on the spot but, oh well, an element born can't be killed like that. The city is willing to accept you as a citizen, so you will be given a home now. Let me ask you one more question before you leave. Do you know the purpose of the rebellion?" She was testing me. Mae knew more, I was sure of it, so I couldn't lie.

Right when I thought I was getting better at concealing the truth, I said, "I'm not entirely sure."

She began stood once more and walked slowly toward the door. Her steps emphasized each word. "Don't blame yourself; you're just naturally naïve, ignorant, and stupid. But we can fix that with a little time. Before you leave, here."

She extended her hand toward me. When I saw what she had, my hand trembled. The crystal swinging from the silver chain was hard and smooth. It was attached to the chain with a swirling silver designed hook that ran over its back and sides.

The door opened, and she left. The four escorts closed in on me. I slid the necklace on before two women grabbed my arms carelessly and pulled me out of the chair. I had to walk quickly to keep up with their pace, unless I wanted to be dragged. No. Being dragged would look like defeat; I wanted to come out walking with my head held high. Not surprisingly, the second door was an elevator. The glass walls allowed us to see the ancient stones surrounding the elevator shaft. In just a few moments, the doors opened. I was about to take in my surroundings when someone tied a cloth around my eyes.

"What? Why are you doing this?" Confused, I began to twist and cock my head. My escorts didn't answer; they just pulled me along. We took so many turns I felt like I was spinning. I didn't get dizzy easily, but this was making me queasy.

When one of the guards removed my blindfold, I was outside. When did we leave the building? I hadn't felt any change of temperature or even a slight breeze. There was one main street. It wasn't even a street but a wide sidewalk. I didn't see any cars or bikes or scooters. It seemed as if the elements were so ecological that they only accepted walking by foot. The sidewalk went on for quite a distance. The houses lining the pedestrian street were modern but small. One or two elements could fit comfortably, three would be okay, but perhaps four would be too much. We made our way through the deserted walkways, passing the glass and white stone houses. Their structure was very studied and artistic. Each house was made to represent something; from the materials and the shapes, I could guess I was in the sector of air elements. The trees had silvery leaves, which shone in the sunlight, and pale bark. Colorful flowers filled the flowerbeds, which surprised me, since elements took color very seriously. I thought that if this part of the neighborhood was dedicated to air elements, then everything would be white, silver, or transparent.

We turned onto a sidewalk made from light grey stone, which led up to a house with large marble double doors. In front of the house, the guards removed my handcuffs.

"Go in," one of the guards ordered.

There was no handle or doorknob, so I just pushed the door open. The slab slid smoothly on its hinges, and I entered a spacious living room. The windows were huge, and the division between the dining room and the kitchen consisted of a wall of suspended stones. They hovered above the floor without bumping into each other, leaving just enough space between them that it was obvious they weren't glued to anything but close enough to hide the other room. I was admiring the soft, fluffy sofas, which felt like clouds, when someone turned me around and pressed me to his chest.

"Thank God they didn't do anything to you." The voice, the smell, and the size only belonged to one person: Skyler. His arms wrapped tightly around me, so tight I couldn't breathe against his grey shirt.

I pushed him backward. "You scared the hell out of me!"

He wore a goofy smile, even though I was yelling at him. Skyler hugged me again, pushing my face into his shirt so my shouting sounded muffled while I choked on the cloth.

"Forget everything that happened out there."

Once I squirmed out of his arms, I glared at him menacingly. Forget everything that happened? I wish. How could I forget that I had almost drowned, that there were animals with cameras in their eyes, that I had kissed Aiden the way I'd always wanted to after he told me he was sick, that Aiden had burned me, and that he had haunting recurring nightmares even during the day? Was he demented, or was he just putting on an act?

"Show me the scar," I demanded.

Skyler didn't hesitate to pull up his shirt and show the thick, pink, and puffy line that had sealed the nasty gash I had given him. I sighed with relief. They had taken care of him, of course, since he was injured while trying to capture me. My mind was overwhelmed with thoughts, and it kept racing on a full speed until I got a headache. My body, suddenly weak and filled with overpowering emotions, plopped down on one of the cloud-like sofas. It would have felt like heaven if I hadn't had hell inside me.

"Skyler..." My voice was small and distant.

"What?" He sat down beside me with concern, his movements slow and soft.

I leaned on my knees and stared at the smooth, polished floor.

"I'm scared."

When I admitted it, I finally felt the weight of the emotion. It was as if my brain registered what was happening, but I didn't want to acknowledge it. Skyler laid his hand on my shoulder. The weight was comforting, so I didn't shrug it off, as I would have done under different circumstances. I was on the brink of tears, but I held back. This was the new life I had accepted; this was my choice, and I had promised myself not to mope around and cry. I had to be strong or at least look it. Nicole was dead.

I couldn't see him since my eyes were closed, but I felt him move closer. His fingers moved lightly in circles on my back. He didn't push me to say anything or to give him an explanation.

"I know."

"They separated Aiden from me. I don't know what they're doing to him or where he is. I just thought that coming back would be the best option, that it would be good for us, for him."

I touched the crystal. It was a habit I acquired out in the forest; it always made me feel more secure. Skyler pulled back his hand, and I looked up at him.

"I'll find out what's going on if you want," he offered. "It might take some time, so you'll have to be patient."

He tried to smile to make me feel better, but all he could come up with was a weird contortion on his face. He opened his mouth to say something else, when a speaker crackled and a voice began to speak.

"All elements in Arcane must report to the front gates of the Golden Hall where a public announcement will take place. The event will start in ten minutes. After the announcement, everyone must return to his or her assigned task immediately. Thank you."

I was still trying to find the speaker when the brief message concluded. "Don't even try. Those things are hidden well, so you can't take them out." He made me return to reality. "I guess you better get going."

"Where?"

The phone rang. I had a phone? Skyler picked up a curved piece of metal and answered. "Good evening, madam. Yes, I understand completely. Thank you. Yes, madam. Yes, madam. Don't worry; I will take care of everything. Of course. Good-bye."

He set down the phone on the coffee table and stared at it for a while. My eyes bounced from the phone to Skyler and then back to the phone several times. Who could have been on the other end of that phone? And what could they have said?

"You are in so much trouble."

Those six words took the air out of my lungs. How could I possibly feel that something good was going to happen here when Skyler, my protector and the boy who always tried to be positive, told me I was in in trouble.

"They asked me to make sure you don't go to the public announcement. You obviously are going to be mentioned there, and who knows what they're going to say? Just go take a bath and we'll talk afterward."

He began to pace, grabbing the back of his head with both hands. I didn't even know where the bathroom was, but taking a bath sounded like a good idea. I made my way past the dining room and the small kitchen to a glass set of stairs. I walked close to the edge until I reached the top, afraid that the glass would crack under my weight. There were only two doors, and each had a silver nameplate. One read Skyler and the other one had my name written on it in fancy handwriting. Skyler was going to live with me? That was...awkward.

My room was incredible. Two whole walls were completely made out of glass. They had a circular control on the wall next to them, so I could close off the walls whenever I wanted. I had a view of a wall of silvery trees, so no one could see me and I couldn't see anyone else. At least I had privacy. My bed was large with white sheets and lots of pillows piled up against the headboard. A network of lights was arranged in an intricate pattern on the ceiling. A large mirror and three wardrobes stood next to the open bathroom. It had a large, wide bathtub with jet streams and a showerhead above.

I turned back into the room to fetch some clean clothes from the closet, when I noticed a letter on my bed. It hadn't been there before, or perhaps I hadn't noticed it. The letter had no envelope; it was just a thick piece of white paper with typewritten text on it.

Aurora

Tomorrow morning at eight o'clock, you must present yourself in the medical wing for some obligatory tests and checkups.

Skyler knocked on my door.

"Come in," I invited.

He stood in the doorway with his hands in his pockets. His eyes were glued to the floor, and his shoulders where hunched.

"Guthrie is dead."

Chapter 37

Who was Guthrie?

That was the first thing I asked when Skyler told me about the public announcement. Guthrie was one of the Golden Four, and he was dead. Actually, the air element who represented us in the monarchy had been killed. Technically, they didn't say that to the whole community, but Skyler explained that an unexpected death here only meant an accident or a murder, and it wasn't a coincidence that he had been killed on the same day I arrived. Not everyone knew that. He also mentioned that elements believed in signs. So technically, Guthrie's death made my arrival take on a negative connotation. Usually, when elements turned eighty-one, they were "sent away to the next stage of their life," when the next four elements were reborn. A death on the day of our arrival made both Aiden and I look like grim reapers.

I tried to avoid glances from the elements who were walking down the street. Skyler walked a few paces behind me, since he was tired and I was eager to get away from all of them.

Hopefully, I would be alone with the doctor or nurse. Those who roamed the streets looked like different variations of each other and myself. Two elements who walked a few feet ahead of me had completely different hair color, since that was all I could see from behind. The female element's hair had a strong gold tone, while the male's was grey, almost like ash. I wondered if their clothing was so different because of their jobs or their own personal taste. "Goldilocks" wore a tight pair of pants under a large coat, all the same shade of light blue, while the boy wore baggy cargo pants and a tank top.

When we arrived in the central area of the city, I could see different branches of the same race blend. Four main sidewalks ended at common buildings. From each walkway, a current of earth elements dressed in bright tropical colors, greens, and browns mixed with the million shades of blues of the water elements. The fire elements' black, red, orange, and yellow were a stark contrast to the pristine and clean grays, whites, and light blues of the air elements.

The buildings, which were located in the middle of a well-kept garden and wide green spaces, were two stories tall. They all had some architectural references of each element; waterfalls, log walls, stone details, and large windows. Signs on the main sidewalks displayed arrows pointing to each building. I looked for the medical wing, but all I could find was a hospital. I headed in the direction the arrow indicated and found myself standing in front of two doors displaying a pair of hands cupped over some swirled lines, which must represent healing powers.

I opened the door and stepped inside. I had been expecting white and metal as the interior, but instead, I found myself in what looked the middle of a forest. Whatever they had used to make the room look infinite was definitely working. The main desk was a rough rock that protruded from the ground. The floor was a walkway of white tiles that led to the front desk, which was surrounded by masses of flowers and trees. Two separate doors appeared to be floating in the forest.

A plump half element wearing a brown dress looked up at us. Her bright smile disappeared when she saw me. After composing herself once more, she clicked the pen against the desk and set it down. She moved to one of the two doors and opened it.

"Aurora, please come with me," the woman commanded.

I followed her through the door and into a small room with an examination table in the middle.

"Take a seat."

While I sat, the woman walked over to a tree and pulled down on a piece of fungi, or a handle that looked like fungi. A series of drawers popped out of the tree. She rummaged through the drawers' contents and began asking me some questions.

"Have you been drinking any unknown substances or medicine?"

She handed me a small plate with a pill on it and a cup of water. I bit my lip. I hated pills.

"Here, have this. I suppose you haven't had any intimacy with an element, am I right?" Her eyebrow was raised.

"Yes."

I put the medicine in my mouth and took a sip of water. I couldn't swallow with her watching me, so I forced it down, feeling it fall the whole way.

"Open," she directed.

I did. She shut my mouth with her hand. Had she just checked to see if I swallowed?

"Very well, I need to take some blood and a strand of hair."

She pulled a large needle from her pocket and removed the cap. Not only did I hate pills, but I also despised needles. She pushed up the sleeve of my shirt rubbed a humid cotton ball against my skin. She pressed her fingers to the inside of my elbow, and once she found the pulse and tracked my vein, she stuck the needle into my forearm. I gasped as the needle began to fill with red liquid. I began to feel lightheaded when she removed the needle and then stored a vial of my blood in a box. With a pair of tweezers, she yanked out one hair from my head and placed it in a plastic bag.

I gripped my head and rubbed the spot where she plucked the strand. It hurt much more than I expected. I rolled my sleeve back down and was about to get off the table, when she stopped me.

"I need to check one more thing."

She pulled up my shirt without my permission and checked my shoulder. I froze momentarily wondering how she would react when she saw the insignia burnt into my skin but after a heart beat I realized it was on the other shoulder. I tried to conceal my relief.

"Of course, you'll be given a new chip since you are a permanent resident in Arcane. Now you may leave. Remember that if you are feeling sick or strange, you can come here anytime."

She wiped her hands on her dress and dismissed me, while she shut the box with my blood and my hair and placed them inside a black envelope. I was wondering what they were going to do with my blood and hair, when I found Mae waiting for me outside. The streets were a bit busier than before but just as calm. I stopped in my tracks and stared at her. I had been expecting Skyler to walk me back home.

She cocked her head in the direction we were headed. "You shall be spending the day with your adviser, Era, while Skyler works. He'll pick you up at Era's home once he finishes his task." And with that, she led me back the way I came.

I didn't pay attention to my surroundings as we walked, as I didn't want to meet the suspicious glances and the glares from other elements. When I heard Era's voice, I jumped.

"Aurora!" Era grabbed my shoulder; her distinct cold touch was a trait passed on through our element.

We hugged each other with the joy of meeting each other again but with the sorrow of knowing the danger I was in. When we took a step back, a radiant smile played on her lips.

"I've been given the honor of hosting you today," she told me.

When we arrived at Era's house, she pulled the door wide open and let me in. She hesitated briefly, as she shut the door in Mae's face, leaving her outside.

"How's Ellil?" I asked, knowing that she would appreciate the question.

I thought that each house was going to be exactly alike, with slight variations, but I was wrong. Her living room had white 18th century chairs and a metal table designed to match the style. An encased chimney with glass walls was the centerpiece of the living room. Curtains that draped the windows were coiled like snakes, hugging the bar that held them up before cascading to the floor.

"Ellil is upstairs, but I think we have to talk about some other things now," Era said. "Ary, I don't think you are aware of what's going on around you. I don't want to worry you, but don't take things for granted. After the announcement they made and what you've done, I think you should be more aware. Things aren't always sugar and rainbows here, even though they tell you that."

I sat down on the couch and felt the smooth the fabric while she spoke. I knew that I wasn't everybody's favorite person at the moment, but I didn't realize that I was in so much danger. I kept quiet. I had no idea how to answer to that.

"I didn't mean to scare you or anything, but I'm just worried."

I nodded. "I get it, thanks."

Era sat next to me, reminding me of the conversations we had had in my room in the training center. "I think you might like to know that Aiden is fine."

I raised my head quickly. "He is? Do you know anything else?"

"I don't know what's going on with him, but I know that he has been admitted to the hospital. He's being treated, don't worry, and our doctors are the best."

My fingers had been curled around the edges of the armrest, but now they hung freely in relief. He was being treated; that was great. I couldn't find any words to say, but Era understood so she filled in the silence.

"I've been worried about you on the outside and wondering if the other elements ever found and rescued you in the woods. Ellil told me these stories about the searchers. When he told me that you stabbed Skyler, I just couldn't believe it. You didn't really stab him, did you?"

"Yes."

The warm light of the living room cast small shadows on the ground, almost like dark puddles on the cream-colored floor. Her smile vanished, as she imagined me stabbing someone.

"I honestly didn't think you had the personality to do such a thing...Well, my partner also mentioned that your chip had been removed. I never really understood the purpose of those things, and he won't tell me what they are for. He says it's for my own protection."

That sounded a lot like me. I had wanted to know so many things at first, and I never got any answers. I still didn't have them. At least I knew what the chips were for.

"You have to get used to the secretiveness of our race," Era continued. "I know I did. Elements have been kept hidden from humankind for so long, not just because of the technology we have or the assistance of the half-elements, but also because we have a certain way of being. We are secretive; we don't express ourselves to each other the way humans do. Tell me, ever since you have been reborn, have you had the desire to let everyone know what's going on with you, so they can comment or give advice?" I shook my head. "Exactly. Look, I wouldn't even be telling you so much if I weren't your adviser. Usually, we're only open with one other element and, in our case, he is usually your partner or best friend."

Era stood up suddenly and led me to the kitchen. "Are you hungry? Ellil and I love having early lunches. He'll be down in a moment."

The kitchen had a lot of electronic devices and appliances used for cooking, probably more appropriate for a better chef. I hardly knew how to boil pasta, and that's why my kitchen delivered the food steaming hot through a metal chute in the wall. I watched as Era pulled on her apron and finished cooking lunch.

"I'm very glad you could come over, not only because we get the day off, but also because I have been desperately longing for your conversation. You are so different from most of the young elements here."

"How are things here?" I asked. "How do the different element groups interact? What are their jobs?"

I helped bring three plates from the table to the counter where Era served steaks and mashed potatoes. She grabbed a smaller bowl with sauce and poured it over each steak in a swirling design. The design was just for fun, since the liquid quickly dispersed once it touched the meat.

Era carried the plates to the table and set them down on the glass mats.

"Ellil, come down!" she called.

I grabbed a jar of water and filled the wine glasses. Ellil stomped down the stairs and kissed Era on the cheek before sitting down.

"Good evening, Aurora." He nodded in acknowledgement.

Era began explaining, while her partner and I stared at the food. I knew that I shouldn't eat it because it was poisonous to my body. But I couldn't not eat anything without arousing suspicion.

"Air elements study a lot," she began. "This gives us a bond with the water elements. We're very similar in some aspects, but usually air elements dedicate themselves to the performing arts—acting, singing, illusions, some sports, art, composing, a few know how to play instruments, and others are dedicated to architecture. Similarly, water elements tend to dedicate themselves to crafts such as weaving. Weaving is for retired water elements, though. The eldest of their branch is an expert and has designed some astonishing creations. Another common hobby of theirs is embroidery, studying, sculpting, and anything involving the use of their hands. They are very dedicated elements and do everything with love and care. Most are extremely patient and introverted. Wind elements tend to be a bit more emotional than the rest of the elements, except fire elements, who are pretty intense."

"So, you're saying that each element has a characteristic temper?" I took one bite of the food and played with the rest.

Era took a sip of water, while she thought of the answer. Her delicate fingers seemed hardly to be holding the cup.

"We have stereotypical classifications inside Arcane. Air elements are considered to be extremely aware of their image and love to be the center of attention, while fire elements are known to have wild tempters and exhibit inappropriate behaviors when it comes to interacting with the opposite sex. Water elements are known to be the source of most reliable gossip, but I believe that the rest think this because their whispers sound like running water. And the earth elements believe that they are natural warriors and the main reason for our survival. They are usually strong-headed."

The meat was tender and juicy. I had never eaten such good meat. My efforts in holding back were going down the drain. I knew that it was just the drugs in the food that made us dependent, but I never thought that they would act so quickly. I took a sip of water, hoping it would wash away the craving.

Ellil wiped his hands on his napkin and joined our conversation. "We are very different from what others perceive. The fire elements are not always 'slutty.'" The word sounded very strange when he said it. "They just follow the example of their monarch, who likes to underdress very often."

"What do you mean?"

Era giggled and patted his hand. "What he's trying to say is that they like to wear clothes that expose a lot of skin. Since they are very active elements, they are usually in their prime physical state, so they can wear just about anything. They like showing off their bodies. This habit is relatively new, since the Golden of Fire was selected. Her name is Nina. At the moment, she is the beauty icon of many."

Just when I thought I had escaped the whole beauty obsession of female humans, I had fallen in the same pit again. Most elements thought they were superior to humans, but they had a lot of things in common, including bad habits and attitudes.

"So, now that I know about the abilities of water and air elements, but what about the other two?" I asked.

"Well," Ellil started, "fire elements are also good at crafting, but they are much more dedicated to the metals and precious stones. Our best jewelers are fire elements; they created the original four crowns for the Golden Four. Also, as we mentioned before, they are very good at physical activities. Not many have enough patience for sitting down and studying, so they'd rather spend their time moving around or inventing. Besides creating beautiful jewels, they build the weapons for our army and transport and all sorts of useful devices.

"Earth elements are much more dedicated to the planet. They are usually generous, kind, and steady. They defend those who cannot defend themselves. I think that it is a characteristic they acquired by protecting animals and plants. As Era said before, they are natural warriors, which is a characteristic that they share with those from fire. Many of the earth elements are exceptionally loyal. Usually when they retire, they dedicate their time to landscaping, gardening, creating new breeds of animals, researching the planet's condition and figuring out how to help. They are our environmentalists."

I took in all the information I could, knowing that it would be very useful in the near and far future while I lived here. "But all these separations and labels make each branch sound very separated, as if they don't really relate with each other."

Era brought a basket of bread to the table. She grabbed a piece and bathed it in the leftover sauce that remained on her plate.

"Well, I don't know as much about the youth as I did before," she replied. "Many things change once you settle down with your partner, but usually we are sociable with one another. On free days, we all meet up in the leisure centers where we can share sports, games, dinners, and even intellectual information in the library. You also will have a job that allows you to meet plenty of elements. The community isn't that large. You'll attend parties with the same group for many years, if it isn't a general one. Soon, men will be interested in you, because they want to look for a partner before they are assigned one."

"Wait, you can be assigned a partner?" I asked, shocked. What year were we in? This was the modern world—no assigned marriages or partnerships.

Ellil readjusted the metal wristband on his arm. Why didn't I have one yet? "Yes. Usually when you are assigned a partner, it is not a life bond, just a breeding agreement. Once elements find someone to spend the rest of their life with, they can ask the Golden Four to cancel the breeding partnership and give them a new bond. This breeding partnership doesn't force the two elements to live together. The only obligations are that during breeding time, they have to...you know..." He coughed, obviously uncomfortable. It was almost as if he were trying to explain the birds and the bees.

I flushed a bit. "I understand."

Beep, beep, beep.

Ellil excused himself from the table and moved to the living room. When he came back, he was holding a thin tablet. The tablet reminded me of the PF2. I pondered, Would I ever get another one? I remembered when I had looked for Violet, Steven, and my father. I recalled talking to Aiden about our parents and siblings, and he had suggested that humans weren't really our biological families. And then, Ellil spoke about breeding...

"Who are my biological parents?" I asked.

Era, who was carrying the plates back to the sink, set them down with a loud clatter. She apologized in a low voice and turned around. The color in her face, the little color she had, was flushed.

"What did I tell you about that topic?" she asked. Ellil shut off his tablet and enclosed her in his arms.

"I'm sorry, I didn't mean to upset you; I just want to know," I continued lamely. I had to know, and she had to understand.

"Aurora, why don't you give us a minute." Ellil suggested I go into the living room, so I did.

I knew that I belonged to the city, and that's why I couldn't know who my real parents were. But it would be nice to know. I needed to know. I couldn't belong to a city; it wasn't natural. I needed to know who had given me life. Perhaps if I still had adoptive parents, I wouldn't be so curious because they would love me so much it wouldn't matter. But I didn't even have adoptive parents; my parents were human and didn't even remember me. I needed to find out who I was. I wondered why the city didn't allow us to hold attachments to our bloodline.

I sat down on the couch and stared at the picture the couple had placed in the center of the coffee table. It had been taken when they were younger, in their early twenties, at their partnership ceremony. They were both wearing white, which made them look like a ghostly fairytale couple. Ellil had a much softer expression than usual, as if the picture had been taken with only Era and the photographer in the room. Era, on the other hand, looked as if she were radiating happiness, typical in wedding pictures, but her face still looked immature. At what age had she accepted partnership? Her eyes were light blue but darkened to a clear grey near the pupil, and her silver blonde hair, much longer than it was today, reminded me of someone. Everyone here had different shades of the same colors.

Era and I had the same colors....exactly the same colors.

Irritation and anger stirred inside me. Era had insinuated this, but she wasn't straightforward. She acted just like the rest of the elements contained between these walls. I could hear Era and Ellil talking behind me, arguing or debating on a topic they disagreed on. All those moments when she acted as though I were her child...

I stood up and headed toward the front door. When I opened it, I saw Skyler standing there, looking confused.

"Ary, hi. What's wrong?" he asked.

"Nothing. Let's go."

Without saying good-bye, I walked past Skyler. He caught up with me and stopped me in my tracks.

"Ary, calm down." I clenched my jaw. "Just breathe. I came to fetch you, because you have been summoned to trial."

His words hit me like as hard as the ground when Skyler pushed me off the school roof. Trial?

"Is it bad?"

"I wouldn't call it bad, but you might find the experience, umm...unpleasant."

Chapter 38

Unpleasant.

That word played itself over and over again in my head, as I walked down the endless hallway. Skyler had guided me to one of the buildings in the main park, but once we entered the double doors, I knew that this was no ordinary place. The corridor had the whitest floor I had ever seen; it seemed to give off its own light. Large arches held up the ceiling and rounded it off.. It gave the illusion of walking through a partially clouded sky. Clearly, we weren't floating in the sky, since I had entered a building that was relatively large. How did this hallway fit in it? I hadn't taken a single turn since we entered. By "we," I meant the two guides dressed in a teal suits and Skyler trailing behind. I felt more like a prisoner than a guest.

We had been walking for so long that when we reached a room filled with half elements, I felt that we crossed into a different dimension. The new room was large, but I couldn't figure out if it was actually large, or if the endless sky effect made it look bigger. The half-elements who bustled around also wore teal clothing. A middle-aged woman, hair pulled back in a slick bun, guided our group of four to the nearest door.

"Please enter. You must wait out here."

She put her hand against Skyler's chest and kept him from following me. The door closed right before the discussion began. I wanted to open the door and let him in, but one of my escorts, sensing my thoughts, pushed me forward.

I walked into a large round room with a circular table that bordered the room. Large, dark- paneled walls reached up to a high ceiling where a series of lights illuminated the room. The circular table allowed seven elements to have different views on whatever was taking place in the middle of the room. One of my escorts pushed me into the center. The seven elements sitting around me had different expressions, but they looked almost the same.

"As expected, you have arrived late, Aurora," one of the women spoke, as she uncapped her pen and placed it in between her index and middle finger.

"I am very sorry, but I didn't know that I had to be here. I wasn't told about this gathering." I decided to keep my language a bit more formal because I was dealing with the Circle of Seven. I gulped.

One of the men to my right spoke now. He appeared to be one of the eldest at the table with his wrinkled skin and drooping eyelids. It must be horrible to be frozen at the age of seventy for fifty years. Aging took longer to catch up here, but it also stuck around.

"You did not know of this, because we did not want you to know. Your protector was assigned to that duty. We will commence with some questions, and you will answer them. Do not speak unless we allow you to. Do you understand?"

What did he think I was, stupid? "Yes, sir." I nodded to add a bit more respect to the answer.

"We will begin with a series of easy questions to test your honesty. We will not tell you when these series of questions end, because we expect you to be consistently honest. If we find your answers are deceptive, we will not hesitate to hook you up to the polygraph."

It seemed as if they already had everything memorized and were waiting for their signal to talk. I counted the total of men and women, while they continued with their speech. There were three women and four men. Their ages varied, and so did their appearance. One of the women looked much softer than the other two; she had soft strawberry blonde waves that spilled over her shoulders. Her irises contained such intense silver that they reflected a bit of her surroundings like small mirrors.

"How did you escape from the party the night before your test?"

I doubted that this question was about honesty. It was probably more about curiosity, and they used the polygraph as an excuse to scare the truth out of me.

"We broke the window of my room and used the ladder in the garden," I responded. "We timed each escape with the rounds of the guards on the walls. After climbing over to the other side, it was pretty easy; we ran in a straight line."

I met their eyes and tried to control my fidgeting, so I didn't look like I was trying to hide anything. I had seen on a crime show that if a suspect touched his ear or picked at the cuticles on his nails, he was almost always hiding something.

"Did you stab your protector?"

I stopped keeping track of who was asking what. Instead, I merged their different voices into one and concentrated on the questions.

I nodded. "Yes."

"With what weapon did you harm him?"

"A throwing knife, Sir."

"Why did you harm him?"

Skyler probably gave them an explanation when he arrived at the camp with a bleeding side. How was I going to know what he said?

"I stabbed his side to keep him safe. My companions were shooting to kill. Your searchers ambushed us with only sleeping darts to defend themselves. We, on the other hand, had ammunition and knives. I knew that if I injured him, my companions would let him go because they would think he would die before he got anywhere." I crossed my fingers in my mind, hoping that the circle of seven would believe my story.

"Who gave you weapons?"

"The four elements which escaped before us had buried bags filled with supplies that would be useful for our survival until we reached the meeting point."

"Where was the meeting point?"

"I'm not sure. We met up in the woods with no specific landmark."

"Did you ever reveal your power to them?"

"They saw my necklace." The questions made my head spin. I had to answer quickly and confidently. This was the hardest ping-pong game I had ever played. The worst part was that they had the upper hand. I was playing ping-pong against seven separate players, seven different opinions and judgments. Convincing them all was wishing for the impossible; however, I could try to convince the majority.

"Did you go to the medical wing and ingest the pills, extract a blood sample, and get a hair removed?" a woman asked, finally raising her gaze to me.

She had a long pointy nose shaped like a hook at the end. I hadn't noticed before that nameplates were encrusted into the table, facing the center. Her silver nametag read Serafina. I checked the other names to see if any were familiar. The eldest man, who was probably in his seventies, was called Bavol. The governor with the hoarse voice was Camdene, and the other two were called Favonius and Makan. The women's names were much simpler and less exotic than the mens'. The woman with the strawberry blonde waves was called Briseas, and she sat opposite Kareela.

"Yes, I went to the medical wing," I responded.

Kareela noticed me staring at her and raised her chin a little higher. "And do you have your chip?" she asked.

"No."

"Who removed it?" She leaned forward to study me more closely.

"I'm not sure; I was unconscious when they removed it."

"Then let us put it back in." One of the corners of her mouth tugged up in a malicious smirk. "Bring in the table," she ordered one of my escorts.

I hadn't noticed before, but the lights above me swiveled around a painting on the ceiling. It was the face of an old man whose hair was snowy white, but it was so thin that it almost looked invisible. His wrinkles ran deep in his light skin, and his eyelids drooped over nickel-colored eyes, which showed wisdom beyond compare. He looked like an old philosopher from ancient Greece. A strangely shaped golden crown ran from behind his head up to his temples. Its swirling design, expertly jointed, was made out of thin threads of gold. The painting was probably a portrait of Guthrie. But now that he was dead, would they have to change it to the face of the new Monarch of Air, whoever it might be.

A pair of half-elements and a doctor walked in carrying a cushioned table. The Circle of Seven commanded me to lie down on the table. I left my back exposed to the doctor, so he could place the chip underneath my skin. The table was designed so that I couldn't move my body, and my face fit snugly into a gap in the headrest. The cushioning was made out of foam that took on my body shape when I lay down to provide comfort.

I thought that they were going to cut my shirt, but this time they weren't going to place it back in my shoulder. It would have been too easy to extract again if I ever wanted to take it out.

The doctor stuck a needle into my lower back and pressed the fluid into me. My lower back began to tingle before I lost feeling. To make sure that the anesthetics were working, he hit me with a special hammer, but I didn't budge.

"We will keep on asking you questions while the doctor implants a new chip. We will be gluing the chip to your spine, so in the future you cannot remove it again." My interrogators kept on throwing their questions at me.

I could hear the doctor and his assistants rattle the scalpel and other objects they would need to use on me. A shiver went down my spine, but I could only feel it go halfway down.

"Did Zareh introduce you to the idea of escaping?" Somebody asked from my right.

I could feel the tickle of the blade opening my skin. Was there a special reason for keeping me awake? Why did they tell me they were going to glue that damn chip to me before they did it? Now I was paying extra attention to their movements.

"Yes." My voice trembled, as fingers separated my skin and made their way downward. Whatever they gave me didn't allow me to feel pain, but I could feel pressure as they touched me. I could feel what they pushed aside, and I could feel the pressure on my tissue.

"We need to have a clearer answer. You are saying that without Zareh you probably wouldn't have escaped?" A male voice asked this question, probably Makan, since I hadn't heard him until now.

"Yes."

There was a moment of silence, which ended when someone walked out the door. Once the lock clicked into place, they continued.

"There have been reports of you searching for your biological mother. Is this true?"

"Yes," I answered again, glad that they could not see my face. Being able to feel someone moving my insides to reach my spine was just wrong. The reason why pain was useful in these cases, I believed, was that you couldn't concentrate on what someone was doing because it hurt so much. I bit the inside of my cheek to hold back a scream.

"Have you found any results?"

Everyone waited expectantly for my answer. Even the doctor stopped prodding for a moment. I let out a sigh and felt the sweat trickle down my forehead to the tip of my nose and splash onto the ground. I was already trembling a bit because of the shock. That's when the doctor pulled out another needle and injected the liquid into my neck. I suddenly felt much more relaxed, sinking deeper into the foam.

"No," I lied, hoping they wouldn't catch the deception in my voice.

The doctor opened a small box and uncapped something.

"Do you have anything else that you want to tell us?"

"No."

One of the assistants sprayed something against my back and wiped a cloth over the sealed skin. The doctor helped me off the strange table and left me standing in the middle of the room.

I looked up blankly at the fourteen eyes that stared at me as if I were an insignificant lab rat.

"Your honesty is much appreciated, now please exit the room."

I walked out alone, gaining a bit more sensitivity on my back with each step. Skyler had been waiting outside for me the entire time. He quickly stood up and led me out of the building.

"I don't know what you said, but we're about to find out," he told me.

The anesthesia wasn't that strong, so its effects were beginning to wear off, diluting itself in my bloodstream. But I still felt uneasy when I was outside and didn't quite understand how we could have left so quickly when walking in had taken so long.

Outside was a different world. Yes, the sky looked similar to the walls inside, with lazy clouds drifting above and the sun high in the sky, but everyone moved in the same direction.

"The public announcement begins in five minutes. Anyone who has not presented themselves at the arch must do so immediately," a female voice warned from the speakers.

Skyler led me to a steel arch, where a mixed made me walk through it and place my finger over a scanner once I walked through it. The woman checked something on a tablet she was carrying and ushered me along, so as not to stop the flow of the line. I followed the air elements in front of me to the front gates of the Golden Hall. All five sectors had been called to this public announcement. Four sectors had a limited amount of space in front of the stage and continued backward. These sectors were

S. Elizabeth Dover

filled with the four different elements. The fifth sector, filled with half-elements, was located behind the other four sectors.

The stage was covered in a red carpet accentuated the gold emblems. Three tall thrones sat on a taller platform in the back, and another chair sat front and center; this one was much simpler and made from metal. Bleachers were set up on both sides for a larger but also important crowd. A small podium stood not too far from the metal chair.

Elements around me spoke in hushed voices and looked at each other with confusion; some even looked scared. The last time a public announcement had taken place, one of the Golden Four had died. That couldn't be the case this time, because there were three thrones; but no one could imagine what would come next.

Everyone fell silent as a half-element wearing a burgundy robe made his way toward the platform. He cleared his throat and grabbed the microphone, bringing it close to his mouth. His fingers wrapped around the sides of the podium in front of him. There was a small golden box next to one of his hands.

"Good afternoon. I would like to ask you to remain silent during the entire announcement, and then head to your assigned tasks afterward."

He stepped off the podium and stood by the metal chair while an anthem played from the surrounding speakers. Rows of elements from each branch took their rightful places on the bleachers. Twenty-eight of them, seven from each element, were taking their seats. That meant that these were the Circles of Seven.

"This isn't right," Skyler whispered into my ear. "Usually the Circles of Seven don't come onstage unless..."

I glanced at him quickly. Skyler was messing up his hair and rubbing his hands on his pants. He was nervous. This only made it worse.

Once the twenty-eight elements were seated, three came out wearing long black capes. The Golden Three wore dark clothing and sat on their thrones. The Golden of Earth, Lur, had his short groomed hair. He wore a black tuxedo with a black shirt and a wine-colored tie. His crown looked exactly the same as the one I had seen on Guthrie's portrait. The other three wore the same crowns and colored outfits, but with slight variations. The fire element, Nina, didn't wear her crown over her short hair; instead, she wore it around her neck. Her dress was the same color as Lur's tie, but it was more revealing and had amazing black details on it. The water element, Wiley, wore a burgundy shirt under is black tuxedo, with no tie. He stared at me. I thought that he was looking at someone else, but when I turned back to meet his turquoise gaze, he smiled slightly.

When the anthem finished, Nina made her way to the microphone. Everyone was inching forward with anticipation. I tried to read her expression, but she kept it neutral and solid.

"Thank you for gathering here with us," she began. "I know that there is a certain question that is going through all of your minds right now: Why did they call for a public announcement? Our answer is that, after over forty-five years of trial and punishment, we have tolerated the presence of a disloyal citizen."

From the back, two security men dragged in Zareh. I had never seen him in such a bad state or in daylight. His skin was so pale he could have looked like he was a member of the air elements. The little hair he had had been shaved off, and his skin was marked with fresh scars. His right leg hung at an odd angle, moving like a broken wheel, as they carried him forward.

"Zareh, the former protector of Aeolos, a child of the air, has finally exhausted our patience. We have given him the option of telling us the location of the lost members of our city, so we could bring them back to safety and raise them properly. But he denied the privilege and accepted punishment and suffering for what he did wrong. We do admit that he has brought us wonderful innovations, but this year, he once again helped our four youngest and most innocent brothers and sisters to escape. They are not to be blamed, since he manipulated them. The last testament we have recently received has confirmed his wrongdoing and we have condemned Zareh to his rightful death penalty." Nina's voice was soft as she spoke to the crowd, but there was an unmistakable coldness in it that suggested she liked sentencing Zareh to his doom.

The crowed reacted in many different ways. Some smiled and cheered, while others covered their mouths and gasped. I believed that no matter how bad someone's crime, he or she should not be sentenced to death. The Golden Four weren't the creators of his life; they had no right to choose how or when he should die.

The two guards forced Zareh into the metal chair and strapped him in. Metal cuffs grabbed his wrists, ankles, and forehead. He was wide awake while they did all of this. From a distance, I couldn't really tell if he was crying, but his eyes were watery. He didn't protest, he just acted like a rag doll and let them move him around and strap him in place. There was the possibility that he was drugged, but it was very unlikely. Basing on the way Mae and Era had spoken to me about the city, the Golden Four wanted us to feel and see what he did wrong so we would learn the lesson. What killed me was that I had done this to him. I just came out from an interrogation with the Circle of Seven, where I declared Zareh guilty of telling me to escape.

I sent him to the chair.

"We will inject venom into his bloodstream for a quick but painful death."

Nina stepped back from the microphone and handed the golden box to the man who was standing behind her. While she was speaking, the man had adjusted a chinstrap to keep Zareh's mouth shut and strapped a device onto his finger. The wire ran from the tip of his finger to a small screen. The man then accepted the box from Nina and pulled out a syringe. One of the guards unbuttoned Zareh's shirt and exposed his chest. The man plunged the needle into Zareh's chest near his heart and pushed the golden liquid slowly into his body. It was like they were injecting honey into his veins and watching him die.

Nina took her place on her throne, and the men who had prepared Zareh took a step back so everyone could view the show. At first, nothing happened. The screen he was hooked up to flashed with every heartbeat. The flashes went off quickly because he was both nervous and scared. I could only imagine how my heart would be racing if I were in his situation. My hand instinctively placed itself on the left side of my chest where I could feel my own blood pumping through the muscle.

The first effect took place. Zareh's hands clenched and unclenched, and his chest rose and fell in agony. His eyes were pressed closed, but something was forcing him to keep them open. His breathing became more agitated, and his body jerked to one side. The cuffs were irritating his skin, turning it a bright red. I grabbed Skyler's arm and dug my fingers into his flesh. Skyler stared at Zareh without moving. The flickers on the monitor were going off like sparks. They flashed one after another with an incredible speed, making the venom travel faster through Zareh's veins. He went still for a second before slamming to the other side of the chair with so much strength, I was sure he would break the chair. His head was trembling, and his eyes rolled back, exposing full whites, and foam poured from his mouth as if he were possessed.

I hid myself behind my protector, hoping he could keep me from watching this. But just when I thought I would be able to shut it out, the screen began to beep with each flash. The beeps got faster and faster, until they finally slowed down and stopped. I decided it was safe to look since I knew Zareh was dead, but it was worse than I thought. Part of the foam he had expulsed from his mouth was red and, in some other parts, pink. His pale skin had turned grey, and his eyes remained turned back and open. The guards unlocked him from the chair and pulled a black sack over his head. Zareh's body was so small that it easily swung around while they dragged him off the stage.

Wiley, the Golden of Water, took the microphone. He had been watching me the whole time, but now his attention was on the rest of the elements. His long cape made him look ominous, so different from what I had seen when I first met him.

"Before you all leave, we have one more surprise. We found her because she began to speak about us to humans. Somehow, when our sweepers erased everyone's memory in the human realm and took everything away that could trigger them, they forgot about one minor object. This human retriggered her memory and began to search for a missing person, an element. We could not permit a human to know about our existence, since it could ruin the efforts of our ancestors to keep us a secret. I am afraid to say that the only measure we can possibly take is to eliminate her, since she does not belong in Arcane or in the human world with all the knowledge she has acquired."

The same guards who had carried away Zareh's corpse were now guiding a female figure toward the center of the stage. She wasn't being guided to the chair, though. I almost didn't recognize her because she was such a mess. Her hair was grimy, and she looked anorexic, as if she hadn't eaten in a long time. Skyler tensed next to me, his eyes bulging outward and his face turning red with anger.

I was about to call her name and yell for them to stop, but my voice was stuck in my throat. Just when I thought all of this was over, that I had finally accepted who I was, this had to happen to me, to her. She looked frightened and didn't know where she was due to the cloth wrapped over her eyes. How could I have missed the details that gave her identity away? No one else recognized her, naturally, since they had never seen her before.

"Violet!" I managed to scream. Heads whipped around and eyes stared at me with the sharpness of a dagger. Lur didn't show any expression at all, but Nina was smirking with her eyes. Wiley avoided my gaze all together.

I ran toward the stage, but half-elements dressed in dark security uniforms stopped me and carried me away from the crowd.

"Don't kill her!" I lashed out at the men who were pulling me away, but they didn't budge.

Skyler didn't follow me; instead, he lunged toward the stage and began yelling at the Golden Three. He waved his arms around and pointed at Nina. I couldn't see much more, because the men who were manhandling me turned me around.

Just when I had forgotten my past life, when I had accepted who I was...I thought that Violet was safe and that the rest of my adoptive family was as well, because their minds had been erased. It would have been so much easier that way.

The men pushed me into my house and slammed the door behind me. I crumpled to the floor.

Chapter 39

I slammed my necklace onto the floor. I didn't care if the crystal controlled my power. I didn't want anything that came from the Golden Four. The crystal cracked when it hit the ground but didn't shatter. I stomped on it repeatedly, releasing all the anger from my body. I needed to break something. I grabbed the first thing I saw.

"Ary, what are you doing?" Skyler took the glass vase from my hands before I could smash it against the floor. I had been holding it above my head for a while now, deliberating on whether to throw it or not.

I was fuming and frustrated, a lethal combination since I couldn't suppress it. My eyes were dry, and I couldn't seem to cry even though there was a growing knot at the base of my throat. Skyler lowered my arms and hugged me with extreme care, as if I were about to shatter any moment.

I tried to hug him back, but my arms were drained from holding the stupid vase for so long. "Why are they doing this to me? To her?"

He stroked my hair and rested his head on mine. If I felt like my usual self, I would have told him that I didn't like it when he hugged me. But now, the only two people I really trusted were Skyler and Aiden.

"It wasn't supposed to happen like this…" he mumbled to himself.

I shoved him away. "You knew?"

I felt my spirit crack a bit more. How could he have not told me about this? In my head, I took back my thought about trusting him; I couldn't trust him at all. Whenever I thought I knew him, he always pulled some sort of trick to make me think otherwise.

"Well, yes, I kind of brought her here."

"What!?"

"I'm really sorry this happened and that I didn't tell you, but I had no other option…"

I slapped him hard across the face. He hadn't even tried to dodge it, so I guess he knew he deserved it.

"You brought her into this city, the city everyone told me to run away from. Are you stupid?" I avoided the word *insane* since, in the woods and in the caves, I had experienced the true meaning of it. "What were you thinking when you brought a human into a city infested with two-faced, dishonest, human-hating elements? And on top of that, she's my best friend!" Despite of my efforts, I couldn't manage to yell at him for too long.

Skyler grabbed my forearm and dragged me toward the couch with so much force that I was left rubbing the red marks off of my skin when he dropped me on the cushions. I stared up as Skyler, completely startled that he would treat me like this. He *did* kill me...

"Can you just listen to me? Do you seriously think that I would have brought her here if I had an alternative? Stop acting like everyone here is trying to attack you!" His arms were tensed, the veins near his wrists popped out in blue threads. "They were going to kill her. Would you rather have that? Because just a few moments ago, when I saw you screaming for your friend, I thought I had done the right thing." He walked around the room in frustration before plopping down on the sofa next to me.

"What triggered her memory?"

Skyler ran a hand over the shadow of the growing beard on his chin. He had probably been so stressed that he had forgotten to shave. "It was the journals you both had hidden under the alstroemerias. Violet's parents were thinking of digging up a pool and found them. Once Violet began to read the journals, she figured out that you had disappeared and that you weren't part of her imagination. She began to make noise around the town, and people thought she was crazy. My only option was to eliminate her, but I convinced the Golden Four that bringing her here would be a much better strategy."

"Strategy for what?"

"It doesn't matter now."

I brought up my knees in my usual couch-sitting position and looked over them onto the wall. "I don't think I will be able to sleep again after what we just saw. The worst part is that no one said anything."

I could still see Zarah's eyes rolling back, exposing the whites, and the foam pouring from his mouth. A shiver ran through me, causing the hair on my skin to rise and goose bumps to spread over my limbs.

"Zareh knew this would happen to him sooner or later," Skyler replied. "It's what he wanted, to die happy, knowing that he helped elements break free from the chains you bear once you're in Arcane. Besides, what would they have said? You protested, and the guards pulled you away."

Together, Skyler and I watched a few of the elements returning to their assignments through the front windows. I wondered if they were staring back, criticizing me with their narrow minds, unable to think out of the box that the Golden Four had inserted in them.

I pleaded to the voice in my head not to let me turn into them in the future. Perhaps this is what I had been escaping from in the first place. "How long has she been here?"

We watched Ellil and Era walk up to the house, parting from the crowd.

"A week."

They pushed aside the door, and Era ran over to me. I wished there was a lock I could turn to shut them out. I didn't want to talk to Era.

"Ary, how are you? This is awful...I just don't understand...How could you behave like that? You just always act so..." She grunted when she couldn't find the right words to say.

My mouth dropped. She was telling me that I should act like everyone else, bite my tongue, when it had been her idea for me to escape. If I hadn't obeyed her, I wouldn't even be in this situation. I backed away from her.

"You are such a hypocrite," I accused, crossing my arms in front of my chest, so I didn't wave them all over the place while I spoke.

Ellil stood behind his partner and grabbed her shoulders in a soothing manner. "What she means is that you have acted in a very irresponsible way, and it may have grave consequences. Sometimes, you must think before taking action, especially in public." His tone was serious and fatherly.

"We just want what's best for you," Era added with a weak smile.

My hands flew up in the air to shield myself from those words and my face twisted. "Stop saying those kinds of things!"

She had just sounded like my adoptive mother when I made a bad choice. She used to sit me down at the kitchen table with the rose centerpiece, with the curtains half-drawn to let in the afternoon sun without heating up the whole kitchen...The memory vanished in seconds, as if it were just a scene in a movie, something that didn't belong to me anymore.

"I beg your pardon?" Ellil arched his eyebrows. "You do not speak to your..."

"My what? My adviser? I don't think that was what you were about to say."

He looked baffled at my words; he was smart enough to guess what was coming next. Skyler, on the other hand, didn't have a clue what was going on. He hugged the backrest of the couch and stared at me and Ellil as we confronted each other.

"Why couldn't you have just told me that you were my parents instead of lying to me?" I spat out the words like poison.

Era covered her mouth and leaned against her partner's chest. A tear streamed down her face for every time she insinuated that I was her child, for every time she wanted to tell me but held back because of the city's rules.

"You can't know," she breathed.

I knew things that I shouldn't and that always got me in trouble, but this was her fault. "The picture on the table in your living room. We look exactly the same, you can't deny that."

Ellil swayed on the spot. Yes, that also meant that he was my father, even though I hardly looked anything like him.

"Well, now that you know, you cannot tell anyone," he commanded.

He was cold; no hug or expression of feelings. This surprised me, because Era was the type of person who loved affection. Not that I would have accepted a hug from him now; he too was guilty in some way.

Skyler leaned back in admiration. "This is the weirdest family reunion I have ever seen."

"You haven't been in any." I rolled my eyes. I didn't realize that I had been tensing my shoulders this entire time, so when I relaxed my stiff muscles ached.

Era moved toward me with open arms. "I'm sorry I didn't tell you, but I could have been punished. Can you forgive me?"

No matter what happened, the punishment excuse fit every occasion. Did the Circles of Seven plant microphones on people here? Were there hidden cameras?

"Era, Ellil, and Skyler, please arrive at the Seven Winds Edifice in fewer than ten minutes." The loudspeaker inside my house turned off after the brief message.

Era turned away without waiting for my answer, and the two men followed after her. They left the door open when they exited, so I moved to close it.

"I hope you don't mind the company," Mae said, leaning on the doorframe and looking down at a letter in her hands. I saw two large men standing on the sidewalk behind her. Their backs were turned toward the street, shielding Mae and I from any passersby.

"What do you want?"

I couldn't close the door in her face, since she was blocking the way. My fingers curled over the door's edge as I tried to contain the frustration and anger bubbling inside of me.

Mae pushed the door to the side and walked into my house. "I have to give you this," she raised the letter and set it down on the coffee table.

I shut the door behind me and stood next to the wall of floating stones. From here, I could put as much distance between us as possible without making it too obvious that I hated her presence and wanted her gone. This gave me enough comfort to continue the conversation without feeling the need to flee and hide.

"Your job really does suck." I thought that distracting her from the conversation she had probably heard would help her forget the tiny detail that had caused so much conflict.

"Tell me about it; I have to go after you all the time. I have to admit, it was much more entertaining when you were on the run, and I had the opportunity to chase you and keep track of you. But this? Bringing you mail and escorting you is not what I signed up for."

Mae ran a hand through her loose hair. I had never really seen it loose before. I was used to seeing the impossibly small and tight bun, so this was rather shocking. She looked more feminine with her brown hair curling around her face.

"Then why do you still do it?"

"Because it is my duty to serve those who gave birth to my race. Do you think I am the only one who doesn't like what I do all the time? We just don't complain, unlike you. You are so selfish and self-centered; everything has to go your way. If you can't get your way, you get in trouble just to be noticed, so they can change it. I still don't understand why they keep you alive."

She sat on the couch, kicked up her feet, and made herself comfortable as if she were planning to stay for a while. I sat on the seat in front of her, intrigued with the letter resting on the table just inches from my reach.

"At least I don't watch passively as innocent people die for no reason," I snapped.

She snorted. "No reason? That man lost six of our eight youngest citizens, and your friend wanted to trigger the memories of everyone in Ashwick."

"She wouldn't have found the journals if your team of sweepers wouldn't have left them behind, and Zareh only gave me an option. I chose to leave just like those who escaped before us."

"If you think you are so brave, then why didn't I see you take your place on the chair? I don't need to listen to garbage come out of your mouth, so why don't you just read the letter and get on with it?"

Mae kicked the letter, so it slid over the smooth surface to the edge. Before it fell, I grabbed it and stared at the blank surface. When I turned it over, I saw the gold wax seal with the Golden Four's emblem pressed into it.

I could feel Mae staring at me while I opened the letter. She probably had no idea what was in there, but I was sure it had come from the Golden Hall, since it had to be guarded. The seal broke off easily. I dropped the envelope and pulled a sheet of paper. The letter was written in very neat handwriting.

Dear Aurora,

After the first reading, you must follow the instructions given. All contents communicated in this letter must remain a secret.

Ever since the death of Guthrie, Monarch of the Air Elements, we have been on an exhaustive search for his replacement. We have set aside some priorities for our city and its inhabitants, for it is not right that we leave an empty chair on the throne, leaving one-fourth of the community without representation in our government. This search usually takes at least three months, because we must be confident that the candidate chosen is prepared for the responsibilities that come with such an honorable title. Not everyone may qualify to be a member of the Golden Four. This time, amongst the candidates, your name has been presented.

Just in case you are not aware of the rules, there is an age limit for the assumption of the throne. You are the youngest candidate ever presented, the only one under the age limit and the least experienced of all. We have already inquired the Circle of Seven of the Air Elements for the reason of your appearance amongst the candidates. Their statement was full of truth, but how do you suppose we chose you over other elements who have numerous graces and whose wisdom is greater than your own? They have known the city, the elements who inhabit it, and the way we run the government for more than one hundred years, yet they lack your determination and power.

Aurora, if you were merely a candidate, we would not have mentioned any of this information to you, unless you had the possibility of being selected. We believe your escape has shown promising abilities, and once educated properly, could be used for a good cause. Despite our choice, you still must decide whether you are willing to join the monarchy. We would never force this decision upon any candidate.

Before you make your decision, we must communicate what must be carried out regardless your choice. Mae brought a pen she will lend you to write your response on the back of this paper. You must place your signature at the end of your answer and on the front of the envelope. Once that has been completed, seal it once more and hand it to the half-element who is supervising you. She will bring it back to the Golden Hall without delay.

If your response is positive, you shall be submitted to training and preparation so when you are crowned, you shall possess enough knowledge to begin working. Of course, you also will receive guidance from the rest of us for the first few weeks.

The fate of your human friend, Violet, rests in our hands and depends on our judgment. If you deny the position, communicating why, we will make sure that the human receives a similar punishment to Zareh.

If you agree to assume the throne, all your crimes shall be pardoned, and you may take your place at your friend's trial.

This, however, should not define your choice but make it easier for you to come to a decision. We prefer to receive your answer today. But if you wish to have more time, Mae must stay with you and you may not receive any visitors or speak to anyone else until you have given your answer.

We advise you to choose wisely,

The Monarchs of Water, Fire, and Earth

About the Author

S. Elizabeth Dover was born in Puerto Rico but has lived in various countries the first ten years of her life granting her a profound love for different cultures. As a teenager, she turned to the bookshelf to seek these wonderful worlds and began creating her own. Sophia currently lives in Argentina and is working on the second book of The Elements series.

Contact me at unwindingsecrets@gmail.com
Or through instagram, pinterest, facebook and twitter

www.ingramcontent.com/pod-product-compliance
Lightning Source LLC
Chambersburg PA
CBHW030841030726
47495CB00005B/1323